THE SWEETEST DESIRE

Devon bowed. "May I have the honor of escorting you home?"

Cassie giggled. "I would be delighted, Monsieur le Marquis. But how are we to escape with so many enemies between us and the front door?"

"Quite easily," he said, offering his arm. "We will use the garden gate."

She accepted his arm and walked with him down the steps into the torch-lit gardens.

As if it were a lovely spring day, they strolled through the night. The paths of the garden wandered past plants trimmed and banked for winter. Indeed, now that Devon was away from the house, he could feel the chill in the air. She rubbed a hand up the lace sleeve of her gown, as if she felt the cold, too. Unbuttoning his coat, he slipped it over her shoulders.

"I'm all right," she protested, stopping as if to remove it.

He caught her hands on the jacket. "Even the faerie queen can take a chill. Please, leave it on. When I take it back, it will have your scent."

She swallowed, eyes huge. "If that is your desire."

He smiled at her. "If you grant me my desire, *cherie*, you will not go home tonight."

OTHER WORKS BY REGINA SCOTT

The Unflappable Miss Fairchild

The Twelve Days of Christmas

"Sweeter Than Candy" in
A Match for Mother

The Bluestocking on His Knee

"A Place by the Fire" in
Mistletoe Kittens

Catch of the Season

A Dangerous Dalliance

The Marquis' Kiss

"The June Bride Conspiracy" in
His Blushing Bride

The Incomparable Miss Compton

The Irredeemable Miss Renfield

Lord Borin's Secret Love

Utterly Devoted

Perfection
(Coming in September 2003)

STARSTRUCK

Regina Scott

ZEBRA BOOKS
Kensington Publishing Corp.
http://www.kensingtonbooks.com

ZEBRA BOOKS are published by

Kensington Publishing Corp.
850 Third Avenue
New York, NY 10022

Copyright © 2003 by Regina Lundgren

All rights reserved. No part of this book may be reproduced in any form or by any means without the prior written consent of the Publisher, excepting brief quotes used in reviews.

If you purchased this book without a cover you should be aware that this book is stolen property. It was reported as "unsold and destroyed" to the Publisher and neither the Author nor the Publisher has received any payment for this "stripped book."

All Kensington titles, imprints and distributed lines are available at special quantity discounts for bulk purchases for sales promotion, premiums, fund-raising, educational or institutional use.

Special book excerpts or customized printings can also be created to fit specific needs. For details, write or phone the office of the Kensington Special Sales Manager: Kensington Publishing Corp., 850 Third Avenue, New York, NY 10022. Attn. Special Sales Department. Phone: 1-800-221-2647.

Zebra and the Z logo Reg. U.S. Pat. & TM Off.

First Printing: June 2003
10 9 8 7 6 5 4 3 2 1

Printed in the United States of America

*To Roger, Walt, Roy, and my beloved Larry
for encouragement, sound advice, and solid research
in helping me dream beyond myself*

And to Amy and Hilary, for being willing to take chances

Prologue

September 1811

"So you refuse to let me view your father's effects," the duke said.

Reginald Ames, his private secretary of many years, nervously smoothed down his brown frock coat. The duke of Devonlee never spoke above a conversational tone. When one controlled half of England, one didn't need to raise one's voice. It was when the duke lowered his voice, as he had now, that Ames knew fear.

The young woman across from them did not seem so affected. Perched serenely on an armchair, she regarded the duke with light-gray eyes, head slightly cocked so that the haphazard knot of white-blond hair on the top of her head threatened to fall into her angular face. "I am sorry, Your Grace. I refused my father's colleagues in the Royal Society. I see no reason to grant permission to a lay person, however titled and powerful."

Ames risked a glance at his employer. By the way the duke's lips compressed in his lean face, he held his temper under tight control. His posture in the immaculate black coat and trousers was just as rigid.

"More tea, Your Grace?" the dark-haired girl at her elbow piped up, lifting a dented silver pot. The pretty young lady, who had been introduced earlier as Miss Bentbrooke's ward, Elise Kearney, obviously hoped to salvage the situation with pleasantries. Unlike himself, Ames thought, she could have no idea of the stakes. Money, not respect, kept the Devonlees in power, and thirty years of lavish living was taking its toll. Only he knew how tight the purse strings had become, and how quickly they would snap if the Sebastien treasure was not soon found.

The duke ignored the girl, who slowly lowered the teapot. "Perhaps you do not understand what I can offer," he said to her guardian. "Your father was an astronomer of some note. I could see his work given its proper credit."

"As my father has been dead for three years," she replied, "I hardly think he will care."

The duke relaxed against the back of the sofa on which he sat, and sunlight from the windows of the sitting room reflected off his raven hair, highlighting the gray that had wormed its way into the dark. Ames was perplexed by the signs of aging. He had somehow thought that even time obeyed the duke.

"Then perhaps you would like compensation for having to gather up the material for me," His Grace allowed. "I have instructed my man to offer you a handsome stipend."

Ames obligingly opened the satchel on his narrow lap. He drew out a bank draft with an impressive number of zeroes on it. Miss Kearney's green eyes widened. Miss Bentbrooke's narrowed.

"You are too kind," she said. "But the answer is still no."

Ames glanced back at his employer. The duke smiled, and Ames clenched his elbows to his rib cage to still his trembling. No one ever refused the duke. Indeed, it was only the repeated failures of his underlings to get the correct response from Miss Bentbrooke that prompted His Grace here today.

"I admire your convictions, Miss Bentbrooke," the duke replied, though Ames was sure he lied. "However, I cannot help but wonder why you would refuse my offer." Ames watched as the duke let his cold blue gaze roam about the sparsely furnished room, to come to rest on the out-moded black dresses both women wore. The duke's gaze met Miss Bentbrooke's. "I could see you richly rewarded."

"Money means nothing," she said. "I know you cannot understand, Your Grace, but I am using the materials."

"Miss Bentbrooke is an astronomer as well," Miss Kearney offered with a worshipful gaze at her guardian. The other woman sat a bit straighter as if she expected censure for such a ridiculous statement. His Grace merely deepened his smile.

"In that case," he purred, "perhaps I might see *you* awarded entry to the Royal Society—as an honorary member, of course."

Her face tightened. "If I am awarded a place among the King's scientists, my lord, it will be because I earned it. This interview is at an end. Allow me to show you to the door."

The duke's eyes flashed as color flared in his cheeks. "That will not be necessary," he said, rising. "Come, Ames."

Ames stuffed the bank draft back into his bag and scrambled to his feet to follow his employer to the door. He caught a quick glimpse of Elise Kearney staring at him, face ashen. Miss Bentbrooke stood regally. As no servant appeared, Ames ducked in front of the duke and flung open the door to let His Grace storm down to the waiting carriage. The duke's face was composed by the time the horses set off for his estate on the edge of town.

"Impossible woman," he murmured. "I would simply arrange a robbery, but we have no idea what we are looking for, so we can hardly take possession while she is out."

"If she ever goes out," Ames muttered.

The duke shook his head. "I refuse to admit defeat. I have been kept from the prize ever since Jean-Luc Sebastien disappeared twenty years ago. No more. Keep watch on the house, Ames. If my cousin does not arrive forthwith to confront the woman, send word."

"You expect Captain Sebastien?" Ames frowned,

fumbling in the satchel for his paper and pencil to make a note of this new task. "Why would he come here?"

"Because he received a note from the Astronomer Royal just as I did. Why do you think I insisted on coming today? My cousin is at our heels. The insufferable puppy claims he wishes to find his uncle Jean-Luc. What he wishes to find is the treasure."

Here was a wrinkle. By fair means and foul, the duke had managed to keep the heir to the treasure, his cousin Devon Sebastien, away from the hunt. "How much does he know?" Ames fretted, licking his lips as he made a note on the paper.

"Enough to be dangerous. We will follow him until he finds the treasure and take it from him."

"Will he not protest, Your Grace?"

The duke turned his gaze to the passing landscape in obvious dismissal. "Most likely, but I see no need for concern. He is powerless to stop me, even if he aligns himself with a starstruck spinster. If he gets in the way, he may disappear as thoroughly as his uncle."

One

"Impossible man," Cassie murmured as she closed the door on the duke and his trembling lackey. She glanced at her ward, but Liza only looked perplexed. "Why would they want our father's materials?"

As Cassie passed the eighteen-year-old to return to the sitting room, Liza shook her dark head. "I don't know. Do you think it has anything to do with that man watching the house?"

Cassie grimaced as she started to gather up the tea service. "There is no man watching the house."

"You may claim ignorance, but I've seen him from the sewing room window. He hides under the trees across the street."

"Let's be logical about this," Cassie tried. She liked logic; it was neat, clean, and precise. If more people applied it, she would be spared confrontations like the one she'd just ended with the duke. "We do not live in a particularly fashionable neighborhood," she told her ward, "so this fellow cannot expect favors. We do not own anything he might want to steal."

"Unless you count your father's astronomy equipment."

"Doubtful, despite the duke's interest. And we aren't engaged in any criminal or immoral activities, so he cannot wish to blackmail us. In fact, we are probably two of the most boring creatures in London. Such intrigue does not seem likely, worse luck."

"He must be after the treasure," Liza said.

Cassie calmly picked up a cup. "And wouldn't that be interesting?" she asked as she pointed Liza toward the pot. "Unfortunately, we really don't know there is a treasure."

"My father said there was a treasure," Liza replied doggedly with a shake of her black curls. "Of course, he wasn't in the best of spirits when he told me."

"He was dying," Cassie supplied, setting the last of the cups on the tarnished tray. "And we did look afterward, if you recall. In fact, we have looked repeatedly over the last nine years and found nothing resembling a treasure."

"Then why is there a man watching the house?"

Cassie shook her head. At least the girl hadn't brought up some sordid reason why a man would watch the house of two lone women. "Liza, sometimes I think you create these stories just to keep me from going mad."

Liza scowled, setting the pot on the tray so firmly, she nearly spilled the liquid on her thin black mourning dress. "It isn't a story, Cassie! He may not be after the treasure, but we may have something of value! What if your brother doesn't arrive to inherit? You will be rich."

"I will never be rich," Cassie corrected her, "regardless of whether my brother chooses to claim his inheritance this Friday. You remember what it was like when my mother and father were alive, Liza. We were never rich."

"You were wealthy enough to keep my father as an assistant to yours and my mother as your governess," Liza argued. "Now we can't even afford a cook!"

A cook isn't the only thing we can't afford, Cassie thought. The duke's money had been harder to resist than he could know. They were approaching beggary. All the less reason for someone to care enough to watch their house.

She had to prove Liza wrong, for both their sakes. Going to the sitting room window, she drew back the curtains and trained her gaze on the small park that graced the center of their little square. Bright leaves fell from the trees; a nanny held her charges' hands on an autumn walk. It was as bucolic a scene as one would wish for. She turned to her ward. "I see no one, Liza."

"Perhaps if you trained your telescope on the park instead of the sky," Liza replied with a sniff, "you'd believe me."

"I cannot change my mount," Cassie scolded. "The Great Comet is just coming back into range. I must keep up my observations. I promised Mr. Pond."

Liza sighed dramatically. "Well, I suppose one must keep a promise to the Astronomer Royal. I just wish he'd pay you."

"If I prove my worth, he may yet approach the regent for a salary for me." Cassie started at the yearning in her voice. The duke might have scored there as well, if her pride hadn't gotten in the way. She tried another tact. "I'm sorry I was up so late again. Thank you for calling me when the duke arrived. I suppose you've been awake for hours."

"Several," Liza admitted. "I cleaned the kitchen and dusted the library. I tire of reading. Could we go to the market?"

Cassie didn't have the heart to tell her they had already spent their allowance for the month. "Not today, love. I have to document my observations for Mr. Pond."

Liza groaned. "Must your work always come first? Could we at least go for a walk?"

The sunshine was tempting, but her notes from the night before were even more so. She had sighted the Great Comet for the first time in weeks. Just wait until she compiled her observations. She might even be able to calculate an orbit. "You are welcome to go," she offered her ward, "but just around the park."

As the girl wandered dejectedly from the room to fetch her pelisse, Cassie felt a twinge of guilt. Liza needed a normal life. She had long ago accepted the idea that she herself was an oddity. By four years of age she had been able to outreason her French governess, and by six she had already shown a marked preference for her father's astronomy equipment over the dolls her mother provided. Her mother, Lady Bentbrooke, had given up on her shortly thereafter, claiming that Cassie had surely been switched by faeries at birth, as no daughter of hers could be so lacking in the feminine graces. At times, Cassie thought the explanation made a great deal of sense.

For one thing, she did not resemble anyone in her family. Her mother had been a striking redhead, and her father and brother had wavy, golden hair and eyes of the deepest azure. Her pale hair and gray eyes were like faded copies of the original. To make matters worse, she had a feeling that she did not act like the women of her generation. Not that she'd seen very many. Few women visited the house on St. Mary's Circle when she was growing up. Her father had felt that entertaining interrupted his scientific pursuits.

Cassie was fairly certain, however, that a woman of nearly seven and twenty had usually been married for some time. They were busy mothering children of their own, not watching over an eighteen-year-old girl who had been the ward of the family. If they entertained callers, it was a select group of friends, not an occasional member of the Royal Society or dowdy little Herbert Montague, an old colleague of her father's who lived a few houses down on the square. If they did not rise until afternoon, as she did, it was because they had been up all night at balls or parties and not because they had spent the night making astronomical observations. Yes, she was certain that, whatever way one looked at it, she was an oddity.

But did that mean Liza had to be one? There was no money for her to enter society, but surely she deserved better than to consider a trip to the market a festive event. Of course, when Cassie was younger, she had seldom left the house except to go to church or take a constitutional in the park under the watchful eyes of her governess. After her parents had died and she had been forced to let the servants go, she had quickly learned that proper young ladies did not wander about London unattended. To do so seemed to invite pitying glances at best, and often far more suggestive looks that set her cheeks to blazing. Odd was one thing; wanton was another. Yet she refused to remain inside at all times, like some fungus shut away from the light.

The answer came to her the first time one of her more affluent neighbors mistook her for a servant in her mourning black. A lady's maid could generally pass through London unremarked. All she needed to fit the part was a cap over her pale hair and a humble look on her plain, narrow face. Only the last was any kind of challenge. She had gone about her necessary business for a year that way until Liza was old enough to accompany her. Now they went together to the lending library or market. If no one could tell which was mistress and which servant, so much the better. She preferred the anonymity of her disguise.

But Liza deserved better. If Cassie could prove herself to be an adept astronomer, she could earn enough money to help her ward. For that, she needed her father's equipment and journals. The duke and any interested scientists would have to wait. She had a greater need.

When Liza returned, Cassie saw her out the door, then went to the writing desk in the corner of the sitting room to open the journal in which she recorded her observations. The numbers marched neatly down the page, as precise as the logic she loved. But try as she might, she couldn't seem to focus on the notations below her. She kept seeing the duke's determined glare and Liza's wide-eyed face. What if her ward was right? What if someone was watching their house? The idea seemed to have taken hold of her mind. Annoyed, she rose and opened the curtains again. Liza was nowhere in sight. In fact, the street was empty.

Someone moved across from the house.

Cassie flinched. Then she shook her head. It was merely a gentleman leading a horse among the shadows of the trees. He stepped suddenly into the light. He was tall and well built, in a navy riding jacket. The sun glinted off dark hair escaping from his top hat. As she watched, safe behind her reflecting window, he smiled a warm, approachable, promising smile that somehow made her smile back, even though she knew he could not possibly see her.

Now, there was a man. Her mother had attempted to introduce her to two different gentlemen, but Cassie had been so nervous, she could do no more than stare at her feet. Neither of the men had been so handsome or smiled so beautifully. If her mother had presented this gentleman, things would have turned out differently. Of course, such magnificent specimens were likely reserved for women with fortunes, faces, and families far greater than hers.

However, nothing said she could not admire him from a distance. She continued to watch as he led the horse up to the front of the house. To her surprise, he tethered the chestnut to the metal post at the curb and took the stairs in a single bound. The door knocker sounded before she could convince herself that he really meant to call on them.

Why today? she thought. With Liza gone, she could hardly let a strange man into the house. But oh, what an opportunity! The knocker sounded again, more sharply this time. Cassie hurried for the entry hall.

"He's only misdirected," she told herself, digging through the hall table drawer for the cap she knew it contained. "He couldn't possibly want to see us. It will only be for a moment. No one need know." She crammed her hair into the wrinkled cap. Strands of pale gold still hung loose, tickling her cheek, but she decided she looked as if she had been working hard. The knocker sounded for the third time; he was losing patience. She pinched her cheeks and bit her lips for color, then threw open the door.

Cassie caught her breath. He was even finer up close. He had an aquiline nose, gray eyes flecked with green, and a mobile mouth that was curling now as if in annoyance. His face was weathered and tanned; lines etched his eyes. It was a masculine face, she decided, although the shape of his jaw, more pointed than square, saved him from looking too arrogant. That he took her for a servant was obvious by his appropriately courteous nod. He said in a voice that was deep and not a little rough-edged, "Good afternoon. Is Miss Cassiopeia Bentbrooke at home?"

Her? Why would he want to see her? She fought to keep the surprise off her face as she lowered her gaze and bobbed a curtsy, mind whirling. She could not possibly receive him, though all of her ached to do so. Even if she could have received him alone, she could hardly whip off the cap and proclaim herself the mistress of the house. She would have to send him away. And if he ever returned, she'd have to hope he didn't recognize her.

"I'm right sorry," she said with true regret, "but Miss Bentbrooke is out. Might I tell 'er 'oo called?"

She could only hope she had put in the right amount of accent. They'd had an upstairs maid who talked like that some time ago—Bess, hadn't it been?

She peeked up at him from under her lashes. The tightening of his mouth told her he found her answer less than pleasing, but he kept his smile polite. "I was told she never goes out."

Now who was spreading gossip? His description made her sound like a wizened old spinster. "Oh, la, sir, 'oo ever was telling you such tales? Why, we can't keep straight Miss Bentbrooke's whereabouts most days—that popular she is."

"Indeed." Now the quirk of his mouth told her he was amused. "I have it on good authority that she is rather eccentric, refusing to see callers, hiding in her room for days on end."

"Why, I never!" The words exploded out of her before she could stop them, and she clapped her hands over her mouth in dismay. His eyes narrowed, and he leaned forward. She was caught. Whoever had called her eccentric before would surely revise the opinion once it was known she had masqueraded as her own maid. They would surely think her mad!

He leaned against the doorjamb, mouth twitching into a smile. "Come now, my girl. You know you have given yourself away."

Cassie straightened, meeting his gaze, daring him to call her out. He blinked as if surprised by her show of bravado. Then his smile widened.

"Your mistress is home," he said, "and you are shielding her."

Cassie grinned at him in relief. "Lord love you, sir, but you've guessed it right and tight. Please don't say nothing to the mistress. Faith, but she'd beat me if she knew I let on she was 'ome."

"Very well, my girl, but you'll have to do me a favor as well." He leaned closer. *Oh, please don't let him be one of those who pinch serving girls under the stairs*, Cassie prayed, unable to take her eyes off the approaching face. His hand came up, and she flinched, but it only held a calling card. "Make sure she gets this, will you?"

"Devon Sebastien, Marquis de Renard," she read aloud. She looked up in time to see his eyes widen in surprise. Now what had she done to give away the game? "I'll see she gets this right off," she promised, hand going to close the door. "Good day to you, Monsieur le Marquis."

He started, then offered her a gracious bow, sweeping his top hat off his head. His hair was thick and rich, ranging from ebony at the crown to a deep brown along the edges. He grinned at her as he straightened. "Good day to you as well, Mademoiselle Maid. May we meet again soon."

Cassie nodded, shutting the door firmly and leaning against it, heart pounding wildly. Why would such a magnificent person want to see her? He couldn't be an astronomer; none of her father's colleagues was the least bit robust. He couldn't be a salesperson. One look at the peeling paint on the trim of the house would tell him that there was no money to be spared at the Bentbrookes'. She ran back to the sitting room window and yanked open the curtain, watching him untether his horse from the post. He glanced back at the house and smiled.

What was she going to do if he called again?

His horse shied suddenly as Liza dashed past. He caught at the bridle, frowning. The front door burst open as Cassie let go of the curtains and ran back into the entry hall.

"Murderers, cutthroats, thieves!" Liza cried as she slammed the door and braced herself against it. "Send for the Bow Street Runners or we're done for!"

Two

Devon Sebastien watched as the front door of the Bentbrooke town house slammed shut. So ended his first attempt to contact the elusive Miss Cassiopeia Bentbrooke. Not an auspicious beginning. Shaking his head, he swung up into the saddle and directed the horse toward the park across the street. The animal moved haltingly, unused to his touch as he was unused to a saddle. Five years aboard ship had changed much in his life. The one thing that remained the same was his determination to find the treasure.

He rode into the shadows of the fall trees, scanning for movement. Leaves of gold wafted down, littering the paths and dotting the shrubs. Somewhere far to his left a bird called. When he was sure none of the English was frequenting the area, he pulled up short. "Well?"

His first mate, Henri Richard, moved out from behind a tree. Devon smiled at the sight. At a little over six feet tall and well over three hundred pounds, Henri should not be able to disappear into the shadows; he should be causing them. To make matters worse, the giant sailor had tried to blend in since their arrival from the Bristol docks, where they had left their ship, the *Lady Elise*. Devon did not have the heart to tell Henri that the purple-and-green plaid coat he had found to wear was obnoxious in any country.

"One visitor," his first mate reported in a voice that always surprised people by being so light in one so heavy.

"And you will not like who it is, I think. Your devil cousin was here."

Devon frowned. "The duke descended from on high?"

"*Mais oui.*" Henri's tanned face was puckered. "Does he know about the treasure?"

Devon shook his head. "No, thank God. All he knows is that I want to find my uncle. The Astronomer Royal must have sent him a note as well; I did take His Grace's name in vain to get the information. It may be that the duke thought to do me a favor by contacting the Bentbrookes."

"He will expect you to pay," Henri predicted. "He always does."

Devon could not argue there. He'd been repaying the duke for one favor or another most of his life. He supposed he should be grateful his mother's cousin had been willing to take him in, educate him, loan him the outfitted ship, put him on the path toward making his fortune. He was more grateful that his cunning cousin seemed ignorant of the treasure in jewels his uncle had carried. He was also grateful that some of the Frenchmen who should have inherited those jewels were willing to believe he could find them.

"The only other person I see is the little man with the bald dome," Henri continued. "Thomas says he is one of the stargazers."

Devon made a mental note to check with his second mate, Thomas Spence, who had been spelling the French giant at his post. Of all his men, Thomas seemed to epitomize what the English had to offer. He was tall, slender, and tough; nothing seemed to deter his good nature. Best of all, his mind was sharp, his heart was loyal, and he knew how to remain hidden.

"Were you seen?" Devon asked Henri, trying to keep the suspicion out of his voice.

His man must have heard it nonetheless, for he flinched, bowing his head until all Devon could see was an unkempt mass of black curls. "I think I frightened the little one."

Devon swore under his breath. No wonder the child had dashed past him as if the hounds of hell were at her heels. "I told you to be careful."

"*Mille pardon, mon Capitaine.* This neighborhood is not safe for the *petite m'amselle*. Often when she walks in the park, men follow her. I thought I should watch over her. She perhaps saw me."

"She no doubt saw you. From now on, watch the house, as I told you. The young lady will have to fend for herself." Devon eyed him, wondering how badly they had blundered. He could not change his course. The note he had received from the Astronomer Royal had been specific. He had found awaiting him in London a copy of a scientific paper coauthored by Jean-Luc Sebastien and a noted British astronomer, Alfred Bentbrooke. Locating Bentbrooke's daughter had been easy. Trusting her was impossible. She was English, and there was simply too much at stake.

His man sucked his cheeks thoughtfully. "You think they have found the treasure, yes?"

Remembering the state of the house, Devon shook his head. "If they have, they've been remarkably restrained about using it. But there's something wrong about the place; I can feel it." He thought of the maid he had just met. She spoke with a dialect that was a curious mixture of the English he heard among his crew. Yet, unlike them, she knew how to read, and she could speak at least a few words in French. With a mystery like that, it was just as well he had decided to move carefully since their arrival in London a week ago.

Of course, he was used to being careful. That he had learned from his uncle.

"But I am a Renard," Devon remembered protesting. "Do you tell me to pretend to be cold like my English cousin?" At eleven, he had considered himself a man. Crossing the Channel with his uncle to escape the Terror had been an adventure. Only later had he realized the cost.

"It is no shame to pretend," his uncle had replied with a smile, ruffling Devon's hair with a large, capable hand. "Above all else, a Renard survives; he overcomes. If Madam Fortune frowns, *mon coeur,* you may have to pretend you're someone else."

He'd remembered that advice when his uncle had disappeared. To survive in England, no more was he the son and heir of the marquis de Renard. He was Devon Sebastien, proper young Englishman. The role shielded him from the sarcasm of the duke of Devonlee as his cousin taught Devon what it meant to be the poor relation. It blocked the taunts of his schoolmates, who found his French father beneath contempt. It buffered him from the accusations of his fellow émigrés, who felt his family had failed in their duty to return the treasure to its rightful owners.

That didn't mean he liked pretending to be thoroughly English. In fact, he loathed it with a hatred as deep as his French ancestry. The role was confining. It stifled the spirit. It bound him to a world he despised—a world of icy calculation and dispassionate logic. But soon, that role would end.

He and his men had learned much this past week. The Bentbrookes did indeed seem oblivious to the fact that they could hold the key to a fantastic treasure in jewels. Miss Bentbrooke was supposed to be a penniless spinster, living alone with only her servants and her father's books for company. Like her father, she seemed to fancy herself an astronomer. Those who scoffed said she used her studies to fill an empty life. Those few who admired her claimed she would one day rise to the level of Caroline Herschel, who had been paid by the king for her astronomical work.

There was no doubt, however, that she had no family to watch over her, which should make it easier to approach her. Her brother, Benjamin Bentbrooke, seemed to have disappeared in the Peninsular War. Henri's observations confirmed that her only visitors were her late father's colleagues, and those rarely. The only other people seen entering or exiting the house were two rather aristocratic-looking maids, one still nearly a girl, the other the educated blonde he had met at the door.

It was possible, he supposed, with the other eccentricities ascribed to Miss Bentbrooke, that she had taken in two fallen women to serve her, which would explain the bearing and education of the woman he had met. He certainly wouldn't have minded taking the blonde in hand himself. She would never be called beautiful with her plain features, but the white-gold hair and silver eyes certainly made her striking. The ugly black dress had done nothing to hide her slender curves, either. No, she was not the average maid. It was a mystery he looked forward to solving almost as much as the whereabouts of the treasure.

"What will you do?" Henri demanded.

"Tired of waiting?" Devon commiserated.

Henri shrugged. "*Mais oui*. I am a man of action. Laying about is for cowards and drunkards. Thanks to you, I am neither. Do you remember?"

Devon smiled. "I remember. And I agree you are no longer the man I found addicted to the bottle in St. George's Fields."

"That slum," Henri muttered with a scowl. "Too many French rot there. I am glad you came for me."

His smile faded. "You and Bertrand were like family. When I learned you had escaped France, I had to find you."

"You are a Renard," his first mate said, and in his tone, the name held the reverence it had once held in France. "The Renards take care of their own. My father served yours, and Jesu willing, my son will serve yours."

"The way we're going, my friend," Devon informed him, "neither of us will have sons."

Henri crossed himself. "Do not say so! When I have my share of the treasure, I will settle down, find a nice girl, perhaps as pretty as the young mademoiselle."

"Just remember that," Devon cautioned. "The treasure first, the mademoiselle second. We must go carefully."

"But why?" Henri persisted. "What more do you need to know? Your uncle kept a fortune in jewels, given him by the Renards as well as the families in their care. He trusted no one. He was last seen in London, and he wrote some science lesson with Mademoiselle Bentbrooke's father. Go, ask her. Make her tell you what she knows. That should not be hard for you."

"What, would you have me seduce a harmless spinster?" Devon shook his head. "Such is not the way of an English gentleman."

Henri spat eloquently into the bushes.

Devon chuckled. "Very well. I am no English gentleman. But I will not follow in the footsteps of those we despise. Miss Bentbrooke is most likely innocent of my uncle's blood; therefore, she has nothing to fear from me."

"Not like your cousin?" Henri pressed.

Devon shook his head. Henri and Bertrand Travallier, his purser, were the only two who understood his feelings for his English cousin. "My cousin has his uses. He led us here. Now the only person who could tell me more is Cassiopeia Bentbrooke. I will have to gain her trust. But rest assured that if she will not let me in the front door, I will get in another way."

Henri grinned at him. "The house is not so tall as the mast, *non*?"

He grinned back. "Not nearly so tall. But I have a feeling this is not a job for a second-story burglar. The Bentbrookes require the soft glove. Either Miss Bentbrooke will entertain the dashing marquis in her parlor, or her maid will entertain him in the back of the house." He grinned at Henri again. "I find the thought of the second alternative much more enjoyable."

"Fah." Henri grimaced. "She is all arms and legs and cold coloring, that one, a typical *Anglaise*. You could do far better in Cannes."

"To each his own, my friend." He glanced back at the house, just visible through the trees.

Henri, following his gaze, froze. "Someone comes."

Devon leaped off the horse and pulled both the animal and Henri deeper into the shadows. A young man of military bearing had strode up to the Bentbrooke house. He stood staring at the brick façade for a few moments, and Devon wondered what he was studying. It looked little different from any other house along the dusty street, save that it was taller—four stories of brick, and a central door with double windows on either side and on the floors above. All the houses along the circle had seen better days. Even the park was ill kept, affording his men ample cover.

"He is well dressed," Henri observed in a whisper. "Better than the others that called. That cane he carries looks like ebony, the tip gold."

Devon nodded. "The proper London gentleman. A suitor, perhaps?"

"I do not care," Henri growled, "as long as he does not find the treasure."

Three

Inside the house, Liza stood shaking against the front door.

"Elise Yvette Kearney!" Cassie exploded. "Explain yourself this minute."

Liza wrapped her arms about herself. "There was a man waiting for me in the park. It was the same fellow who watches the house; I know it."

Cassie shook her head. "Is that all? He was probably just out for a stroll. Really, Liza . . ."

"No, Cassie! He paused when I paused, walked when I walked. He was large and imposing, and he had very sneaky eyes."

A sharp rap sounded on the door. Liza gasped. Cassie froze. *Not the marquis, not now.* If she saw him again, she wanted to be dressed in something other than a maid's cap. For some odd reason, a gauzy night-shift like the ones her mother had worn came to mind. She blinked away the thought. In any event, this latest visitor probably wasn't the marquis. More likely, it was Herbert Montague. He habitually took tea with them on Thursdays. Yet, if she remembered correctly, it was only Tuesday.

The rapping sounded again, and Liza jumped. "He's come for us. We must escape, Cassie, out the kitchen door."

"Liza," Cassie replied firmly, "this is sheer nonsense. I

will not be driven from my home by a fat phantom with sneaky eyes." She reached for the door, but Liza ran for the sitting room.

"I'll get the poker!"

Shaking her head, Cassie opened the door.

There was indeed a man standing there, and not Herbert Montague or the marquis. This gentleman had golden-blond hair curling from under the brim of his top hat and eyes of the deepest azure. He stood tall and composed, dressed in a bottle-green cutaway coat and fawn trousers tucked in gleaming boots.

The day could not have gotten any odder.

"Benjamin," Cassie breathed.

The man on the front step frowned. "Major Benjamin Bentbrooke, my girl. Now, if you would be so kind as to . . . oh, my God, Cassie!"

She felt herself blushing as she stepped aside to let her brother in. She had not had time to remove the cap. She considered taking it off now and tucking it away, but that would hardly answer the questions she saw in his eyes.

"What on earth have you done to yourself?" he demanded, striding into the entry hall.

Cassie bit her lip, trying to think of a way to explain the situation. At that moment, Liza leaped from the sitting room, brandishing the bronze fireplace poker.

"Step away from her, I warn you, or I'll . . ." She trailed off as she saw Benjamin for the first time. The poker fell with a clatter. "Pardon me, to be sure!" She turned and bolted up the stairs. Benjamin stared after her for a moment before returning his gaze to Cassie.

"I see," he quipped. "The maid's mad. That would explain why you play the servant."

Pulling off the cap, she tossed it into the corner. "She isn't a maid," she replied, leading him into the sitting room. "I had to dismiss the servants. Liza and I do all the work ourselves." With any luck, he would connect the two statements and assume she wore the cap because she'd been working. If he was incensed seeing her at the door in her disguise, he would have apoplexy if he knew of her masquerade about the city.

Benjamin sank onto the sofa. "Dismiss the servants? What happened?"

She sighed. "I have so much to tell you. You knew Mother and Father died?"

He nodded. "The letters reached me, too late to return for the funerals. I assumed someone would take care of you."

"Everyone seemed to assume that," she replied, trying not to sound frustrated. "But Mother's inheritance was a patrimony—when she died, it went to a younger cousin. Father's will left everything to you, with a small allowance for me to keep the house. It is less than a fifth of what they lived on, Benjamin. I could only do so much."

"Couldn't you even try to keep up appearances?"

She felt herself blushing, remembering her game of playing maid. "I did, in my own way. But I could not protect the Bentbrooke name with nothing in the bank. Have you seen Father's solicitor?"

"I just came from there. You need not fear; you will be cared for." The look on his handsome face bespoke concern. Could it be that he cared?

"You've changed," she said.

He glanced at her before looking away again. "Life in the military will do that."

"Father had hoped it would make a man of you," she replied, remembering. "Mother was so proud when you enlisted."

Her brother smiled. "She never could understand Father's absorption with the stars. Then she lost you to them as well. It's only natural that she would have higher hopes for me."

Cassie did not answer. Her junior by nearly two years,

Benjamin had always been her mother's favorite. Lady Bentbrooke had pampered him as some society matrons pampered a pet pug. What Benjamin wanted, he generally got. On the rare occasion he did not get it immediately, his explosive temper guaranteed capitulation. His tantrums had only served to confuse her father and annoy Cassie.

"She purchased me the lieutenant's commission," he continued. "What a shame she never knew I made major."

"She might have known, if you had written."

He shrugged. "We moved about too much for correspondence."

"Did you ever think they might need you? I might need you?"

"Frankly, no." His lighthearted tone obviously bothered her more than it did him. "Father had his stars, and Mother had her own interests. I had no reason to return, until now."

"Until you were old enough to claim the inheritance," she reasoned.

"Precisely. I have no idea what possessed Father to put it in trust until I was twenty-five, but as of Friday, it will be mine at last."

"He thought you needed time to mature," Cassie told him.

"He thought I needed a good spanking," he corrected. "But that does not matter. I am home."

She gazed at him thoughtfully. His azure eyes gleamed, but the light could have just as easily been from greed than pleasure at returning home. Of course, seven years in the military could have made a man of him. He had risen to the rank of major. He would be used to shouldering responsibilities, making decisions for someone besides himself, putting the good of his troops and the nation before his own. Perhaps he would help shoulder her burden.

His next words would have confirmed her hopes if they had not been said with an overbright smile.

"Yes, sister, now that I am home, things will change. You will not have to die a pauper."

"It hasn't been that bad," she told him cautiously. "Liza and I had each other for company, and I had my observations."

"Observations?" he asked with a frown.

"Father's work," she explained, trying not to bristle as she waited for the condemnation.

He did not disappoint her. "Good God, Cassie, you didn't keep doing that after he died, did you? I can understand why you humored him while he lived. We all danced to his tune in those days. But I thought you would be glad to be freed of the burden. Isn't one lunatic in the family enough?"

"I shall pardon your horrid pun," she replied coldly. He blinked, and she realized he did not even know he had made one. "A lunatic is one who is made mad from gazing too long at the moon, Benjamin. If Father was mad, it was because he was gazing too long at the stars. And I assure you, I am not mad."

She knew some people would argue that point, but her brother waved it aside. "Good. I need those wits of yours. I have work for you."

She frowned. "Work? What are you talking about?"

"I'm talking about our return to society, of course. You may be happy locking yourself away from the world, but I assure you I am not. We have much to do if we are to succeed. And the first thing we change is you."

Liza chose that moment to rattle through the door with a rickety tea cart Cassie had not known they owned. The girl had put on her best silk gown. It had been pink once, with Florentine lace across the bodice and along the flounced hem. Like everything else they owned, it had been dyed black and let out as Liza grew. As a result, it hugged the curves of her figure and made her look several years older than she was.

"Welcome home, Benjamin," she said, with a deep

curtsy. "I thought you might like some tea." She beamed at both of them. Catching Cassie's scowl, she bit her full lower lip. "Or perhaps not. I'll come back later." She left the cart and scampered from the room.

Benjamin raised a quizzing glass. "Who *is* that?"

"It's only Liza." When he frowned at her, she tried to explain. "Elise Kearney, Benjamin. The daughter of Stephen Kearney, Father's assistant years ago? Her mother was our governess. She died when Liza was born."

He waved her explanation aside. "I remember Liza. She was about eleven when I left, a little thing with huge eyes who used to hang after us. Believed every fabulous story I invented, and made up a few of her own. Since when did she look like a French courtesan?"

"Benjamin!"

"Do not bridle. Naturally I assumed you had put her out to work somewhere. She is an orphan, is she not?"

"What has that to do with anything?" Cassie demanded.

"I simply asked," he explained patiently, "because I need to know whether we are feeding her. I need to know how many I'm supporting, don't I?"

He was being logical and kind, two things she had never known him to be. Perhaps that was why she could not trust his intentions. "Very well," she managed. "Then yes, you are supporting her, or rather I am. You remember when Stephen Kearney was killed in a carriage accident."

He shuddered. "Nasty thing, that. Still, does it make us responsible for her?"

"Father and Mother agreed to raise Liza as their own," Cassie reminded him. "When they died of the influenza, she became my responsibility."

"And now mine," her brother murmured thoughtfully.

The idea should have been comforting, but somehow it only made her more alarmed. The way her brother looked at Liza, she would sooner have set a wolf to watch the sheepfold. Very likely most orphans had male guardians, but no one had questioned her right to keep the girl when

Cassie's parents had died. She didn't intend to relinquish that right now. "We need not trouble you. Liza and I rub on quite nicely. She is usually cheerful, and she has the most delightful imagination."

"What a charitable way to put it," he drawled. "Are you absolutely sure she's safe?"

Cassie surged to her feet. "That is enough, Benjamin. Liza is like a sister to me, more than you've ever been a brother. I will not have you disparage her."

He leaned back on the sofa. The light in his eyes told her she amused him. She itched to do something far less amusing, like slap his smug face.

"Are you always this loyal?" he asked.

"Stop playing with me, Benjamin," she commanded. "You said you had work for me. I want to know what."

"Very well." He rose, walked to the door, and shut it decisively. Cassie tensed, bracing herself for what was to come.

"I am in love, sister. I need your help to win the girl of my dreams."

She stared at him, laughter bubbling up at the sheer absurdity of the request. Yet the tension in him forced her to keep a sober tone. "I see. But I thought you'd only just returned from the Peninsula. When did you have time to meet this young lady?"

He avoided her gaze, striding about the room. "Actually, I have been in town several weeks. But how much time does one need to fall in love? She is beautiful, talented, charming; what more could any man ask for?"

"Does this paragon have a name?" She fought to keep the amusement out of her voice. It shouldn't be amusing. Benjamin had ever whined, bullied, and cajoled until he got his own way. Pity the poor girl if she did not reciprocate his feelings.

"Miss Barbara Compton. You'll have heard of her?" When she shook her head, he shrugged. "Well, I suppose that comes from living like a cloistered nun. Miss Compton made her debut this season and immediately became its reigning belle."

"Nothing less for a Bentbrooke," Cassie quipped.

Benjamin stopped long enough to eye her, then apparently thinking over the matter, he continued pacing. "Precisely. And I will not rest until she is mine."

"And what exactly do you expect me to do about this?"

"I shall need a chaperon, of course. Someone who will go with us when we ride in the park, when I take her to the theater. That's what I meant when I said you would have to change. No more stargazing for you, my girl. From now on, you will be far too busy."

"I shall help you if I can," she allowed carefully, "but I cannot give up my observations just now. I am helping the Astronomer Royal track a comet. It is just coming back into range. I expect to be busy for the next few months."

"Months?" Her brother frowned. "I cannot wait months, Cassie. Miss Compton is an Incomparable. If I do not woo her now, someone else will. In fact, she already has half of London hanging after her. I'm lucky she didn't go haring off to the country like most of the beau monde. I have a fairly open field until Christmas. Her father wants to parlay her considerable charms into a title, but I intend to show him I'm a much better catch."

"Of course," Cassie replied, unable to hide her smile. "Who could say no to you?"

"Who, indeed?" her brother asked, smiling back. The amusement did not quite reach his eyes. She felt a chill run up her. His next words drove all other thoughts from her mind.

"There may be others more charming, or with greater influence in society," he gloated, "but the Comptons will not find another so well heeled. Father was a miser, Cassie. He must have hoarded his funds."

"That's impossible," she protested, but he shook his head.

"When I saw the solicitor, I learned that we are wealthy. Wherever the money came from, we have more than we could possibly know what to do with. And I intend to enjoy it."

Four

Henri reported that night that the military man had not left the house. Instead, by evening a host of servants, including a butler, had arrived and were busily setting the house to rights. A casual conversation between Thomas and a willing maid had revealed that Major Bentbrooke had returned from the war and was preparing to help his family reenter society.

From Devon's point of view, more people meant more activity to watch. He didn't think the treasure was actually hidden in the house, but if it was, more activity might also uncover it. He wished he could be more certain about his assumptions, but he still lacked too much information—about the layout of the house, its contents, and its occupants. One factor worked in his favor: tonight the servants would be tired from moving in. Therefore, tonight they would receive a late-night caller.

It was after two in the morning when he slipped through the back gate from the alley that ran along the mews. Every light in the house had long been extinguished. Nothing rustled in the tangled garden. He slid silently to the back door and pressed down on the handle. The door was locked; the butler was obviously conscientious. Backing away, he eyed the windows facing him. Moonlight glinted on each pane. The windows were shut. Thomas had already checked the front. He would have to try the roof.

Whoever had built the Bentbrookes' terrace of town houses had thoughtfully provided a pattern of brickwork where each house joined the next. The outcroppings were easier to climb than the ratlines of his ship. His leather gloves, a shadowy brown like his high-necked coat and trousers, gripped the stones as easily as his soft-soled shoes. The only challenge lay in the extra lip ornament that ran between the first and second floors. It took him a few minutes to lever himself up and over it.

Five minutes later he heaved himself over the last ledge and dropped lightly onto the flat slab of the roof. Immediately he heard a voice. Too late to escape, he dashed the short distance to the chimney cap and flattened his back against it.

"Where are you?" a female voice demanded.

He sucked in a breath. A woman, on the roof, at two in the morning? He kept himself still in the shadows made by the moon and listened over the pounding of his pulse. Where was she? Was she moving toward him? Most important, did she have company?

"Don't try to tell me it's on the horizon, William Herschel," she fumed, "for I have been scanning what I can see of the horizon for over six hours and I tell you it isn't there!"

He narrowed his eyes, waiting for this William fellow to reply, but he heard nothing. Just as he bent to pull the dagger from his boot, he heard a grinding noise. The roof beneath him trembled. Freezing once more, he frowned. What was she doing?

Curiosity got the better of him. Leaving the dagger sheathed, he slid to the edge of the chimney and peered around it. Directly across from him sat a strange contraption, made visible by the hooded lantern set at its base. It was a round dais perhaps ten feet in diameter with a sturdy metal tripod in the center. Perched atop the tripod was a tube about four feet long, one end pointing toward the southern horizon. A woman bent over the lowered end. The lantern illuminated the black of her skirt, but the tube hid her face. Beyond her lay a yawning hole, door propped open by a stick, leading down to the house.

Devon pulled back into the shadows, his frown deepening. It was true, then: like her father, Cassiopeia Bentbrooke watched the stars. As if in confirmation, he heard her continue.

"Where are you? Oh, you are a difficult fellow. And where is your tail, hmmm? I thought perhaps I had you last night, but you like to hide in this moonlight, don't you? You will not escape. I'm going to find your tail first, so you can forget about showing yourself to Mr. Pond or Mr. Herschel."

Pond, he knew, was the Astronomer Royal. Herschel he did not know, but he had little doubt that the man was another prominent English astronomer, one she was bent on impressing. It was an unusual desire for a woman, but if she followed in her father's footsteps he supposed it wasn't too surprising. Still, he realized, he could hardly investigate the house with someone alert most of the night. He would have to find another way in.

He risked a last glance at her. She had stopped gazing through the tube and sat on the dais, a large leather-bound volume spread open beside her. Her hand moved across the page, pausing every so often to dip a quill in a bottle of ink. As she bent lower, intent on her work, moonlight set her face in sharp relief. The glow outlined her soft lips, her high cheekbones, her pale brows. It caught the rise and fall of her breast. Desire ran through him, as sharp as the thrust of a lance, and nearly as difficult to ignore. Miss Cassiopeia Bentbrooke was obviously a creature best viewed by moonlight.

And, he reflected as he slid back to his makeshift stairway, she bore a striking resemblance to her delectable maid.

* * *

Cassie saw a movement out of the corner of her eye and raised her head. She could dimly make out the squat shapes of the chimney tops in the far corner. It must have been a bat that had roused her. Not much else moved this high so early in the morning. She'd been ignoring the bats for years. But tonight it didn't take much to distract her.

Small wonder, she thought as she attempted to refocus on her work. The day had been strange enough, with people supposedly watching her house, the duke demanding her father's materials, the marquis calling, and her brother's surprising return. The four events were surely related, yet she couldn't see how. If she was as wealthy as her brother intimated, they might indeed be watched by a thief. Yet how would anyone know of the inheritance when Benjamin had only just learned about it this morning?

And how could a thief be connected with the determined duke or the dashing marquis? Just thinking about Devon Sebastien made her puff out a wistful sigh, nearly fogging her glass. She hastily polished the eyepiece, feeling silly. There had to be some mistake. Handsome, charming gentlemen like the marquis de Renard did not call on renowned spinsters. He would probably realize his mistake by morning, and she would never see him again. That thought was even more depressing than her inability to spot the comet.

Surely the marquis' visit had nothing to do with their newfound wealth And could they really be so wealthy? Her father had been focused on his work, so she supposed it was possible that he had simply put all his funds away for another time. Yet the idea that she could do what she wanted, purchase anything she desired, was difficult to believe.

Liza had found it equally amazing when Cassie and Benjamin explained the situation that night at dinner. And what a dinner. Cassie closed her eyes in ecstasy remembering. The past three years of privation disappeared with each savory mouthful. Both she and Liza had stuffed themselves while Benjamin watched, amused. She was so warm and full that she could not scold him for choosing their entire household staff without consulting her. Only when he started telling her how to dress did she find her tongue.

He insisted that she needed a new wardrobe. She started to refuse, then caught Liza watching her, lips compressed. The light in the girl's eyes told her how much she wanted to go shopping. Cassie smiled. "Perhaps we could use a few dresses."

Liza beamed.

Benjamin had obviously caught the exchange. "Of course, we might want to wait on dresses for Liza."

As the girl paled, Cassie frowned at him. "Why? If we are this rich, we can afford them."

"Of course," Benjamin said congenially. "I merely thought that she might want to wait until she could choose her wardrobe for her season next spring."

Liza squealed and leaped from her seat to throw her arms about a startled Benjamin. His surprise quickly gave way to amusement, and something else flickered across his face, causing Cassie another chill.

Remembering, she felt the cold creep into her again. She bent hurriedly to note the locations of the various stars she'd observed tonight. The moon was still too full to sight the comet easily, and she hadn't been at her post early enough in the evening. Yet the heavens lay open before her, and she could lose herself in the milky glow of the stars. Any troubles quickly vanished under her fascination. Benjamin's dictates, Liza's worries, her own loneliness were swallowed in the vastness.

If the face of a certain marquis insisted on inserting itself between her and the stars, she wisely chose not to dwell on it.

* * *

Devon was as easily distracted. Though he knew the wisest course was to meet Major Bentbrooke and inveigle an invitation to call, he found himself more intrigued with the major's sister. The memory of her, etched in moonlight, lingered long after his return to the house he had rented nearby. He chose not to question the fact. Such analysis was for the English. It was enough to know that he desired her. Time would tell whether he would have the opportunity to act on that desire and how she would respond if he did. Mademoiselle Bentbrooke would have to be the one starstruck. For the moment, he must focus on the treasure.

He was still considering his course of action when Thomas brought the news the next morning. Major Bentbrooke had left the house and been followed to White's. The London men's club was already talking about Bentbrooke's return when Devon arrived. It was said that Wellington had wept when he heard he was to lose the valiant major. It was said Bentbrooke had returned to nurse his sister back to health. It was said that his father had been fabulously wealthy, hoarding everything, so that the lucky fellow had been shocked to find he was quite well-to-do. It was said Bentbrooke was a congenial fellow, warm, witty, and well liked by the ladies. Devon should have been quite impressed.

Instead, he found himself more than a little annoyed. Major Bentbrooke stood near the window as if he were on some kind of display, accepting with nauseating humility the praises offered him. When the joking grew too intense, he humbly fiddled with the gold pocket watch hanging from his tastefully embroidered waistcoat. True, he had a ready quip for every comment, but nothing he said had any substance that Devon could hear. Much as he knew he must make the major's acquaintance, he couldn't find the desire to approach him.

"Why so glum?" the marquis of Hastings asked as Devon leaned against the opposite wall, watching the antics. "I would say this whole affair is cause for celebration."

Devon eyed the man. Of all the British aristocracy, Hastings had impressed him as a man of worth. Like Bentbrooke, Hastings affected a congenial demeanor, but when confronted, his opinions were sound, his facts well grounded. A trim older gentleman with gray hair, deep brown eyes like an elderly spaniel, and a walrus mustache, Hastings was one of the few who saw Devon's French ancestry as an asset. In fact, Hastings had intimated that Devon could make a tidy living working for the War Office. The fact that he had offered to make him a spy didn't keep Devon from enjoying his company.

"You like our young major?" he asked, curious.

"And you do not?" Hastings winked. "Come now, Renard. You had your share of attention when you brought down those pirates last spring. Let another lad get some of the glory."

"I am always willing to applaud good work," Devon replied, "when it is earned."

Hastings chuckled. "Too good to be true, isn't he? Peacocks always sound the loudest when they are mating." He nodded to where a portly gentleman in puce trousers was listening intently to everything said to Bentbrooke. "Have you met Compton's daughter?"

"I don't believe I've had the pleasure."

"Lovely girl. Worth thirty thousand pounds per annum. Compton was holding out for a title; he'd like something better than an 'honorable' for a grandson. But the young major appears to have captured his attention. Look for the betting book to be opened this afternoon." Hastings chuckled. "Of course, as you have a title and are on your way to making a fortune in prize money, you might make a good candidate as well, eh?"

Devon shrugged. "No doubt the Comptons prefer untainted blood."

Hastings shook his head. "Then the loss is theirs. Come, my boy, and join the party. Let me introduce you."

Devon didn't resist as the older man caught his arm and drew him to the window. Elbowing his way to the front, Hastings grinned at the golden-haired major.

"Bentbrooke, my lad, I thought you should meet another hero of the war. Devon Sebastien, Marquis de Renard, may I present Major Benjamin Bentbrooke."

The major's hand stopped in midextension. "Frenchman?"

Devon did not flinch. "My father was French."

"Oh, not to worry, my lad." Hastings chuckled jovially. "Did you think I would confront you with the enemy? Renard fights for England, same as you do."

The man Hastings had identified as Compton peered closer. "Is he not related to the duke of Devonlee?" he muttered to Hastings.

The tone was curious, but Devon ignored the question. He preferred to stand on his own reputation. He watched as Bentbrooke frowned ever so slightly, as if concerned that the center of attention had shifted away from him. The major withdrew his hand.

"Lord Renard," he acknowledged with a bow. "A privateer, didn't someone tell me? I wish you the best of luck in your work. Now, if you will excuse me, Mr. Compton and I were about to share a bottle. Sir?"

Blinking as if in confusion, the portly gentleman allowed himself to be led away by the dapper major.

Hastings shook his head. "Impertinent upstart. Ah, well, he'll soon learn some manners. Join me for cards, my boy?"

Devon shook his head, watching the two men depart. "Thank you, my lord, but I have a pressing engagement elsewhere."

"Have you settled on a lady, then?" Hastings asked with

a smile. "About time you did the pretty. You let your career take precedence, which can be a dangerous thing, as I well know. If you have made up your mind to court at last, I have no doubt she will be delighted with you."

"Perhaps," Devon replied. "Time will tell."

Five

Ames was out of breath by the time he answered the duke's summons to his private study at his estate.

"Well?" his employer asked, flicking a speck of dust off his otherwise spotless dove gray morning coat. "What did you learn about this Benjamin Bentbrooke fellow?"

"He appears to be honest, intelligent, and trustworthy," Ames lamented. "His record as an officer is commendable—valor under fire, heroic leadership, that sort of thing. He apparently intends to spend his inheritance helping his sister and ward reenter society. The ton is taking him to its bosom. In short, I could find no possible reason why he would want to help us."

The duke exhaled. "Regrettable. But you did place an agent in the house?"

Ames nodded. "Yes, Your Grace. And we continue to watch your cousin's men."

"And how fares the puppy?" His Grace stretched out his hand to smooth the documents on the walnut desk before him.

"He is understandably cautious. He attempted to make the lady's acquaintance, but was unsuccessful."

"Give him time," the duke advised with a small smile. "The Sebastiens have seduced marchionesses and milkmaids alike. Though my cousin has not made a career of such exploits, I am certain he will acquit himself well. I imagine Miss Bentbrooke will just take a while longer."

Ames bowed. "Of course, Your Grace. May I return to my post, then?"

The ruby ring glinted as the duke clenched his long fingers. "A moment. I had a most regrettable conversation while you were in London. A tradesman had the temerity to confront me with a bill."

Ames's eyes widened at the sacrilege. "I shall take care of it, Your Grace. I am stunned that he would dare approach you."

"It will only get worse if we do not find the treasure," the duke assured him. "Now, go and let me know the minute you have news."

By the time Cassie got up that afternoon, the house was in chaos. Painters swabbed down the dining room, upholsterers argued in the sitting room, and a butler taught two maids, two footmen, and a cook and his assistant their duties. Liza skipped about the mess, singing and helpfully getting in everyone's way. After ensuring that her father's equipment and journals were safe from the dust and strangers, Cassie took Liza to visit a dressmaker her brother had recommended, just to escape the bedlam.

She had not shopped for clothes in ages. Liza was forever suggesting it, and Cassie was forever refusing. She simply could not see the attraction, even if she had money. She would not even have been sure where to go, but their new coachman took them straight to the city, where she met "Madam Tulane."

The rather large woman would have been pleasant if it hadn't been for the calculating gleam in her dark eyes. She had Cassie measured, clucking as an assistant noted the numbers. Liza she merely eyed and muttered over. Then she promptly sent them home, promising to deliver everything just as Major Bentbrooke had ordered. Cassie wasn't sure what to think, but just looking at the bright silks and soft muslins made her spirits rise. She could hardly wait to see what the woman designed for her.

"I feel as if we fell into one of those children's stories Mama left me," Liza exclaimed as they rode home in the carriage. "We go to sleep paupers and awake princesses."

Cassie smiled. "It is a bit unreal. Shall I pinch you and see whether you're awake?"

"No, thank you," Liza replied with a grin. "I want to enjoy this dream as long as I can."

Cassie agreed with her, but reality was as close as their town house. As the carriage drew to a stop and she alighted on her new footman's arm, she found one of her father's colleagues waiting for her.

Her father had never had much use for their neighbor Herbert Montague, calling him a middling scientist. Stephen Kearney, Liza's father, had called him a mole. True, his nose was rather long and pointed, and he had the almost comical habit of leaning forward and twitching it when he was about to contradict her on some point. His dark-brown eyes were close together, and, when he squinted through his thick spectacles, they appeared large and almost sightless. His short-cropped gray hair ringed a bald dome and was constantly mussed. However, she had to own that he had been a devoted visitor in the years since their parents' deaths. For that devotion alone, she was generally able to overlook his many faults.

"Such a to-do, such a to-do," he scolded when she greeted him at the foot of the stairs. "Whatever are you doing to your home, Miss Bentbrooke?"

"My brother has returned from the war and claimed his inheritance," she explained. "He is having the house repaired and refurbished."

Mr. Montague shook his head, threatening to dislodge his top hat. "This is unacceptable. Such dust and vibration will surely damage your father's equipment and his journals. I entreat you once again to allow me to care for them as they deserve."

Cassie managed to keep her smile polite. "You are always so conscientious, sir. But I cannot give you my father's materials. I must keep them handy; I use them, you see."

He had been squinting at the painters, who were starting to work on the exterior trim, as if by his scowl he could stop their work. "Use them? Oh, yes, of course. Your father's work lives on, indeed it does. Countless other astronomers scour the night sky even as we speak, in search of your father's comet."

As it was still early afternoon, Cassie somehow doubted many telescopes were at work at the moment, even if they had been powerful enough to locate a comet headed away from earth on a nearly two-thousand-year orbit. "That is very kind of you to say, Mr. Montague. I would ask you in, but as you can see, we are at sixes and sevens at the moment. In fact, we should probably cancel tea tomorrow. Next week, perhaps?"

The little man dragged off his top hat and began to turn it in circles by the brim. "Sorry to intrude," he muttered. "But I must have a word with you, Miss Bentbrooke. Today."

She and Liza exchanged glances. The girl was clearly as puzzled as she was. "Very well, then," Cassie allowed, stepping aside so that he could proceed her up the stairs. Her new footman whisked open the door for her and stared at Mr. Montague so fixedly that the older man stumbled.

"Has my brother returned?" she asked the tall, imposing fellow.

"No, mum," he replied, still eyeing the astronomer, who sidled around him.

"If he does, please let him know that we have a visitor." Cassie turned from the footman and motioned Mr. Montague to follow her into the sitting room. Liza shrugged out of her pelisse and followed as well.

Mr. Montague blinked at the sight of her, and Cassie wondered if the brim would tear as he kept turning it. "I must speak to Miss Bentbrooke alone."

"Why?" Cassie and Liza chorused. The frown on Liza's face surely matched her own.

He apparently realized he was ruining his hat, for he set it firmly down on the table near the sofa. "I have something of a rather personal nature to discuss."

"Well, then," Liza sang, "I shall busy myself in the hall. Within easy shouting distance—should anyone wish to shout."

Cassie scowled at her, but she didn't stop her. Montague perched on the sofa.

"If you would sit down, Miss Bentbrooke?" he ventured. "It is difficult enough looking up at you when we meet at the door. It is impossible when sitting."

"I cannot help my height, Mr. Montague," she reminded him sternly, but she suffered herself to sit in the chair across from him. His nose twitched, and, after a moment's hesitation, he threw himself to his knees before her. Cassie recoiled, but he managed to capture her hand.

"Miss Bentbrooke, will you do me the honor of marrying me?"

She stared at him. Why him? Her mind presented her with a far more pleasing image—Devon Sebastien, down on one knee, the green in his eyes deepening with desire as he begged for her hand. She blinked, and the image dissolved into a short older man with a twitching nose.

"Mr. Montague, I cannot believe you would even ask. You are old enough to be my father."

"Nonsense," he averred. "I was a colleague of your father's, certainly, but there were many years between us. Please allow me to care for you as he would have done."

She managed to wrest her hand from his fevered grip. "My brother is home; I have no need for protection. I appreciate what you must see as a kindness, sir, but I will not marry you."

"But you must," he replied firmly. "Your brother will no doubt marry. His wife will not wish to share this house with you. You need someone of your own. I will make you a marvelous husband."

The very idea made her shudder. "Mr. Montague," she said firmly, "I am certain you believe what you say, but I would make you a horrible wife. I care for nothing but the stars."

"Nonsense," he replied. "That would change once you had a home of your own. And it is possible you might be of some rudimentary use in my work."

"You honor me." She couldn't keep the sarcasm from her voice. "But I prefer to do my own work. Now, excuse me."

"I will not take no for an answer," Montague maintained. He stood up, towering over her where she sat in the chair, as if to intimidate her. She rose as well, to correct the imbalance. He blinked, but he did not retreat.

"Don't do it, Cassie!" Liza cried, rushing through the door and throwing herself between Cassie and a startled Montague. "Do not make such a sacrifice."

"I am not asking her to make a sacrifice," Montague cried. "I'm asking her to marry me. I'm a very good catch!"

"Then go get yourself caught!" Liza cried.

Cassie took her ward's arm and drew her back from the bristling little astronomer. "Liza, that's quite enough. Mr. Montague has done me the honor of requesting my hand in marriage. It is an honor I must refuse, but it is an honor nonetheless." She turned to Montague, who was regarding her fixedly through his thick-lensed spectacles. "Mr. Montague, I must ask you to leave. As you can see, my ward is quite upset."

He eyed Liza as if he would like to upset her further. "Yes, I'll go. But this is not the end of it, I promise you."

Cassie shook her head at his obstinacy, but she escorted him to the entry and made sure the footman saw him out. Then she returned to her ward. "Whatever could have gotten into him?" she asked. "Has everyone gone mad?"

"He heard you are wealthy," Liza replied with a sniff. "He is after your inheritance."

Cassie snorted. "Benjamin is the one who is rich. We are here on his sufferance." The thought was not a pleasant one, but before she could consider it fully, another thought intruded. Was that why the marquis de Renard had visited yesterday? Had he met Benjamin previously and somehow learned Cassie might be an heiress? She could not picture him as a fortune hunter any more than she could so picture Herbert Montague. Surely a man like Devon Sebastien would never bow for money.

"Major Bentbrooke will certainly provide you with an ample dowry," Liza was insisting. "I simply would never have credited Mr. Montague as a fortune hunter. Do you think he will linger on the porch?" Cassie shook her head, but Liza scooted to the window and peered out. Then she gasped.

"Oh, what now?" Cassie demanded, joining her.

"Look," she whispered, nodding wide-eyed toward the park. "He's watching the house again!"

Cassie stared, feeling goose flesh pimple her arms, but she saw nothing save the empty street and the gently waving branches in the park.

"Where, Liza?" Her voice came out sharply in her disappointment.

Liza stamped her foot. "He was there! Right near the entrance to the walking path! If you hadn't come up to the window so quickly, you wouldn't have scared him away."

"Somehow I doubt any man who watches other people's houses is that easily frightened," Cassie countered. "Besides, I thought Benjamin was the one you saw in the park yesterday."

Liza laughed. "Who could be frightened by Major Bentbrooke? I promise you, if he was following me, I'd let him catch me."

"Liza!" Cassie scolded. The girl had always looked up to Benjamin. It shouldn't surprise her that she continued to do so. Yet somehow it seemed wrong. Benjamin was years older and, in all but blood, her brother. Besides, from the looks he gave the girl, marriage was the last thing on his mind.

Liza blushed. "Forgive me. That was impertinent, especially when he loves another. But I tell you, Cassie, there was a man. You must believe me."

Cassie sighed. "I want to, love, but you do have a way of seeing goblins and ghosties when it's only a sheet-covered sofa."

"Well, I like that." Liza sniffed, striding past her. "As if I'd make up a story about anything so important."

Cassie shook her head and turned to follow her ward. She cast one last look at the park and felt her blood run cold. For one second, she swore she saw a man standing in the shadows of the trees. He was large and would have appeared menacing if he hadn't been wearing the most atrocious plaid jacket she had ever seen. She blinked and saw only shadows.

"Curse Liza and her imagination," she muttered, stomping up the stairs to take off her own pelisse.

Devon sat outside the Bentbrooke house, jaw set. Henri darted back into the shadows and winced when he looked up into his face.

"But it is as I said, is it not, *Capitaine*? The wagons and workmen go in and out. Bertrand says it is the same at the back. They spend money at an impossible pace. They must have found the treasure, *non*?"

"It cannot be," Devon gritted out. "I will not let it be." He could not have come so far only to lose. His breath caught in his chest as if he had taken a cannonball in the side. "The fine major must be spending his inheritance. Yet you are right that it should not be large enough for all this."

"So what do we do now? Will you still charm the maid into opening the door?"

Devon shook his head, remembering his discovery the

night before. It was not the maid but her mistress he must charm. "No, Henri. I have tried to reach Miss Bentbrooke in every way I know except one. She seems to have a penchant for astronomers. I find I have a sudden burning desire to study the stars."

Six

Cassie went to the breakfast table the following afternoon fully intending to ask her brother about the man in the park. It had occurred to her while she was making her nightly observations that Benjamin might have placed the fellow there to guard his home. True, Liza had claimed to see the man before Benjamin had arrived, but perhaps her brother had had some inkling of his fortune during the weeks he said he had been in London. Benjamin, however, had risen almost as late as she had and was just finishing as she entered.

"I left a list for you on the table," he said, passing her. "We must keep busy if we are to be ready for the dinner party on Saturday."

"Saturday!" Cassie cried. "This Saturday? But that's only two days away!"

Benjamin grinned, obviously enjoying her discomposure. "Precisely. Get to work, sister." He was down the corridor before she could call more questions.

She went to the table and picked up the list. It included discussions with wine sellers, caterers, and a number of other merchants to see about details for a dinner party. It also included the names of people her brother had apparently invited. None of them meant anything to her, except the three names at the top: Alexander and Elena Compton and their daughter Barbara. He was evidently following through on his plan to win her hand.

She had never organized a dinner party. Her mother had taken care of the few parties at the Bentbrooke house. Cassie had never been trusted to so much as pick a napkin color. As she recalled, the events had been quiet affairs with her father's colleagues, and never more than a dozen people. The names on the list numbered at least thirty. She found her fingers trembling and sank onto one of the dining room chairs. Miraculously, a cup of steaming tea appeared before her. She looked up into the impassive face of her new butler. He stood tall and regal in his black coat and breeches. His gray eyes never moved closer than six inches from meeting her gaze. He had a smooth face, with jowls hanging on either side of a thin mouth that had probably never smiled outside his own chamber.

"Pierson, isn't it?" she asked.

"Yes, madam," he replied, returning the pot of tea to its cradle on the sideboard nearby.

"Have you ever organized a dinner party?"

"Certainly, madam. I have organized any number of parties for my previous employers. How might I assist you?"

A quick conversation was all it took to transfer the responsibility to his capable hands. She had more important things to do, things to which she was far better suited. If Benjamin thought she would rearrange her life for him, he had better think again.

She did not have long to congratulate herself, however. No sooner had she left the dining room then the footman informed her that she had a visitor.

A tremor of expectation ran through her. "The marquis de Renard?" she asked.

"A Mr. Darien, madam," the man explained as she started down the stairs. "He says he is an astronomer. He insisted on waiting. I put him in the sitting room."

Her spirits plummeted, but she shook herself. She had already decided that the marquis was not going to call again. She should be pleased that she did not have to play the society matron, but she could not quell the disappointment. He had wanted something from her. Had one look at her, in her maid's disguise, deterred him? She shook her head. She should be pleased that she had another visitor, an astronomer no less.

"Could you ask Miss Kearney to join us?" she asked the footman as she neared the door to the room.

"Miss Kearney is out on a constitutional," he replied. "Shall I send someone to fetch her?"

"No," Cassie answered. "But stay near the door while I meet this fellow, will you?"

His eyes gleamed. "With pleasure, madam."

Remembering his territorial response to Herbert Montague the day before, she couldn't help thinking that her new footman took a great deal of delight in his role as protector. She glanced closer at him, noting the broad shoulders, the crooked nose that spoke of fights long past, the determined dark brown eyes. Which should concern her more, she wondered, her footman who looked like a misplaced pugilist, or the stranger waiting in her sitting room? Pasting on a polite smile, she entered the room.

Her visitor had been sitting on the sofa. Now he stood and bowed. His hair was as dark as the marquis's, she noted, but he had glasses as thick as Herbert Montague's and a trim black mustache and beard. He was dressed as well as her brother, however, in a crisp black coat and trousers. That in itself seemed a little odd for the impoverished astronomers she knew. Still, she curtsied to his bow and sat so that he could sit across from her.

"Mr. Darien, how may I help you?"

He was staring at her, and despite herself, she felt her color rise. Had she forgotten to comb her hair this morning? She fought a desire to smooth it down. It couldn't be her dress, could it? The black gown was no more rumpled than usual, and not nearly as elegant as the emerald green waistcoat she could see peeking out from under his jacket. She sat a little straighter and met his look straight on. There was something familiar in that gray-green gaze.

"Have we met?" she asked defensively.

"I believe once," he said in a voice deeply accented by French. "You do not remember?"

She peered closer. His face was tanned—another odd feature, for most astronomers slept the day away as she did so they could be up at night. She thought he might be handsome, if the glasses had not distorted his eyes so, but then, who knew what the beard hid? "I fear I do not remember, sir," she admitted.

"Did not your father introduce us at a meeting of the Royal Society?" he pressed.

She blinked. "Certainly not. I was never privileged to attend a society meeting with my father. You must be mistaken."

"I would never mistake meeting so beautiful a woman," he replied. "Especially not a fellow astronomer."

The last remark saved him. The first had had her ready to show him the door. She despised false praise. "Why did you come today?" she asked, knowing she still sounded a bit terse.

He must have heard the tone as well, for he flinched. "*Mon dieu*, but I am doing this badly. I do not mean to offend, Mademoiselle Bentbrooke. I have traveled here at great risk during a time of war between our nations. I am a student of the stars, like your famous father. I had heard you continued his work. I thought perhaps we could trade information."

"I am always happy to discuss the stars, sir," she allowed. "What is your area of specialty?"

"I have heard it is the same as yours."

"Comet hunting?" She could not help leaning forward eagerly. "Have you been following the Great Comet?"

He spread his hands. "What else? It is a marvelous sight, *non*?"

"It is indeed," she agreed with a smile. "I heard it was first sighted in your country, by Monsieur Flaugergues. Have you had the privilege of meeting him?"

"He taught me everything I know," he confessed.

"Oh, how marvelous!" She was so excited that she reached out and clasped his gloved hands. They were strong and firm in hers. "Tell me, what was he using when he first sighted it—a refractor or a reflector? William Herschel is using a fourteen-foot-focal-length reflector, but I think the refractor is more powerful, if one could compensate for the color distortion. What have you found?"

He blinked, and she thought for a moment he had no idea what she was talking about. However, he quickly recovered. "The refractor is superior for comet hunting, certainly."

"I knew it." She released his hands and rose to pace. "Oh, I wish I had something better than Father's old reflector. And what I wouldn't give for a clear horizon. You may have noticed we are the tallest house on the square. Father chose it on purpose. Unfortunately, I still can't see beyond some of our landmarks here in London. Do you have the same problem in—where do you come from?"

He was smiling at her as if she amused him, and for a moment she was reminded of her brother. But he answered before she could take umbrage. "Cannes."

"Cannes?" She frowned. "But Monsieur Flaugergues is in Viviers. That must be hundreds of miles apart. How do you collaborate?"

"I moved to Cannes recently. We felt another observer was needed there."

She nodded. "Yes, very wise. I have been in correspondence with Mr. Herschel at Slough and of course Mr. Pond, at Greenwich. Have you been able to detect a tail?"

"Regretfully, I have been at sea the last few weeks," he replied. "I have not had an opportunity to observe it recently."

"You didn't try from the ship?" She could not imagine passing up such an opportunity. While the horizon might have been rolling, the view should have been limitless.

He spread his hands again. "I am not the best sailor. I was ill most of the time."

She shook her head. "How unfortunate. Will you set up near London, then?"

"I was hoping perhaps I might prevail upon you to use your equipment."

A warning sounded in her head. Why would an astronomer need to borrow equipment? Particularly her equipment? "I'm sorry, Monsieur Darien," she replied. "My telescope belonged to my father; I am certain you will understand why I never loan it."

He was immediately conciliatory. "Ah, but of course. Forgive me for asking."

"Certainly," she agreed, but she could not shake the feeling that something was wrong. She peered at him again, trying to determine what it was about him that troubled her. He caught her looking and actually winked. She recoiled.

"But perhaps we should also discuss this comet of your father's," he continued. "I understand he kept a record of his observations."

"Yes, as most of us do," she allowed. "I continue that work as well. What do you want to know?"

"Everything," he replied with a wide smile.

She had to chuckle. "Come now, Monsieur Darien. My father did not write a great deal, but the notes are meticulous, across a number of topics. If you could narrow your field of inquiry, I think we might have a better chance of finding something of interest."

"Perhaps if I could view these notes you speak of," he returned.

"Impossible. I may be able to extract something for you, but today would not be a good day. My brother is refurbishing the house, and the journals have been put away for safekeeping. Will you be in London long?"

"A day or two, perhaps a week," he replied, and she could sense he was hedging. "I do not know when I may have an opportunity to call again. Would it not be possible to see the books?"

She met his gaze straight on. Those gray-green eyes looked so familiar. Where had she seen them? She was certain she had never met him in connection with her father's work, despite his protestations. Outside astronomy circles and the two men her mother had brought around, she had never met any other men.

Except the marquis de Renard.

She almost gasped aloud but managed to stop herself in time. Still, her surprise must have shown on her face, for he stood suddenly.

"Mademoiselle Bentbrooke, is something wrong? You are so pale."

"Am I?" she managed. "Perhaps it is the thought of disturbing my father's work. I shall consider your proposal, Monsieur Darien. I know your time must be precious, but could you call tomorrow, about this hour?"

He bowed. "I am yours to command, mademoiselle. Until tomorrow."

As he rose, he reached for her hand and brought it to his lips. The kiss should have been chaste, but somehow she felt the warm pressure all the way up her arm. He lingered over the caress, gaze rising to her face. There was a fire burning in those mesmerizing eyes, even behind the glasses. She could feel the heat of it answered inside her. Her heart started beating faster. She snatched her hand away. "Yes, until tomorrow. Good day, sir."

He bowed again and turned to go. She could not move from the spot, watching out of the corner of her eye as the footman saw him out.

So, the marquis de Renard had come calling after all, in disguise. What could be so fascinating in her father's journals that he would take so much trouble? And why did he feel he had to keep his identity a secret, when he had come in person the first time?

Something was going on.

She was determined to find out what.

Even if that meant letting him in her home again.

Seven

Devon made it down the stairs by holding to the rail then pulled off the cumbersome glasses. Something was going on. He could feel it. Why else would Miss Bentbrooke masquerade as her own maid? The only difference in her appearance today was the absence of the white cap. But he was amazed he had ever thought her plain. When she discussed her stars, the passion blazed from her as brightly as the comet. Like a moth, he was drawn to the light of her excitement.

A fascinating woman, that one. He had seen the answering fire in her eyes when he had kissed her hand. Her emotions ran deep, like his. But like gold hidden in the mass of a rock, her passion was all the more precious for its rare appearances. He would enjoy spending time with her. She was not only lovelier than he had first realized, she was also sharper. He blamed himself for not being better prepared. He had assumed she played at her science, like so many of the aristocrats played at one pastime or another. He had never considered that she might be proficient. She knew her subject well; he had had to hedge more times than he liked. For a moment, he had been sure she saw through his disguise. But she had invited him to return. That was all that mattered. These journals she spoke of might hold a clue to his uncle's fate, and that of the jewels.

Before tomorrow, however, he was going to learn more about this astronomy business.

***

Cassie spent the remaining time before dinner entertaining Liza. She was thankful the girl had been out when the marquis had called. Twice she had the chance to glance out the window at the park, but neither time did she catch a glimpse of anyone watching the house. Perhaps, she told herself, Liza's imagination had gotten the best of them after all.

During their time together, she told her ward about her brother's party Saturday. Liza, of course, was overjoyed at the prospect, even though her name did not grace Benjamin's list. She clearly could not understand Cassie's reluctance.

"I attended only a few of Mother's parties," Cassie tried to explain, "and I do not remember a single pleasant moment. The conversation is boring, the food is uninspiring, and the room is overheated with so many bodies. If Benjamin wasn't certain this is the only way to win his love, I would lock myself in my room."

Liza shook her head. "It will be better this time, you'll see. You will be the hostess; therefore, the conversation will be scintillating, the food will be delicious, and you can open a window if you wish."

"No, I can't," Cassie said with a reluctant smile. "For if I do, I will be tempted to look out at the stars and avoid my guests entirely!"

She thought about it again that night, when Benjamin was at some ball and Liza was safely abed. She was bent over her father's telescope, her hands in gloves and her body bundled in a heavy wool cloak to keep out the chill that had crept into the air. Yet the cloak seemed to be woefully inadequate. Each time she thought of her brother's party, she felt cold all over.

She would make a horrid hostess, she was certain. All the comparisons she had made between her life and that of the average society lady would just as easily be made by everyone else in attendance. She could see the curious stares, hear the titters of laughter quickly hushed as she glanced that way. Oh, if only she could appear normal just this once! If only she could go to the dinner in a beautiful gown and speak confidently, as her mother had done, about topics that interested other people. If only the gentlemen would look at her with admiration. The marquis de Renard came instantly to mind, looking as suave as he had the first time she had seen him. He would stand at the foot of the stairs and smile at her in that warm, inviting way.

And she would probably trip over the hem of her gown and fall right into his arms. She smiled, imagining the scene. Even a catastrophe like that had its compensation with a man like the marquis around.

She shook her head and forced herself to concentrate. Across her sight glowed a ball of white fire. The comet! She quickly noted the location, but she could not sight the tail. That was the critical piece of information Mr. Pond still lacked. If she could be the one to find it, she could show she had talent. But her luck had fled as quickly as it had come; try as she might, all she could see was a round, glowing ball. She followed it for a while, then shuttered the scope, climbed down the stairs, and fell into bed.

But sleep was harder to locate than the tail of the comet. She kept thinking of the marquis. Why was he in disguise, and what was she to do about it? She could confront him, but it didn't seem sporting. She would have appreciated more panache from anyone discovering her own disguise. Perhaps if she continued to question him about astronomy, he would be forced to concede. She finally fell asleep constructing her arguments.

She was ready by the time he was announced the next afternoon. He was dressed in shades of blue this time, as crisp and clean as she felt dark and dowdy. Still, she was glad she had sent Liza out shopping so she could meet him alone.

"Monsieur Darien," she greeted him with a smile, ready to do battle. "Did you make your observations last night?"

"I did," he replied, bowing overly long over her hand. The seductive pressure of his lips was nearly her undoing again, and when he released her, she rubbed her hand to still the shivers that traveled up her arm.

"Would you say that the comet was in Leo Minor or Aquarius?" she asked, determined to stick to her plan.

"Leo Minor, certainly," he said, sitting across from her on the sofa. As she blinked in surprise at his correct answer, he leaned back and crossed one booted leg over the other. "Though I would have thought it might have moved beyond by now. Clearly the elliptical orbit calculated by Johann Burckhardt was in error."

She stared at him. Burckhardt's observations had been sent to Mr. Pond, who had passed them on to her. She could not imagine how the marquis could have known. "Clearly."

"Is something amiss, mademoiselle?" he asked calmly. "Did you not see the comet last night?"

"Well, of course *I* saw it. I'm just a little surprised that you could provide so many details. What instrument did you use?"

"A ten-inch reflector. A poor instrument, to be sure, but one does the best one can under hardship conditions."

Cassie looked closer. Could she have been mistaken? Did she so want to see the marquis de Renard again that she conjured his image into another man who slightly resembled him? The gray-green eyes stared back at her, bulbous behind the lenses.

"Take off your glasses," she demanded.

Now *he* blinked. "*Pardon,* mademoiselle?"

"You heard me. Take off your glasses this instant, or I shall call my footman and have him throw you out."

"Very well," he agreed, sliding the lenses from his face. Even with the beard, she was certain. She leaned back triumphantly.

"Why are you in disguise, Monsieur le Marquis?"

Devon sighed. "I was afraid of that," he said, French accent disappearing. "How long have you known?"

"I was fairly certain when you left yesterday."

He shook his head. "All that study for nothing."

She raised an eyebrow. "Did you really stay up last night to watch for the comet?"

"I did indeed. It is a splendid sight. I begin to see why it so fascinates you."

"Where did you get a ten-inch reflector?" she demanded.

He gave her a half smile. "That was an exaggeration. I used my scope from the ship."

"And Burckhardt's work? That could not have been a guess."

"Even a French astronomer can find friends in high places."

She shook her head. "But why? Why go to all this trouble?"

"You wouldn't let me in the first time. Or rather, your maid, who bears a strong resemblance to you, would not."

Remembering, she felt herself blushing. "Yes, well, I had my reasons."

"Being in disguise has its advantages," he agreed with a smile. She could feel her blush deepening. "Does your brother know you wander about London dressed as a maid?"

"Who told you I wander about London that way?"

"Do you deny it?"

She wanted to, but she couldn't seem to lie to him after catching him doing so. "It was necessary," she told him defensively. "We couldn't afford a maid, and my ward Liza and I certainly didn't want to remain in the house our entire lives."

"Completely understandable. I'm sure any young lady faced with the same choice would have done the same."

She was just as sure they would sooner have been caught naked in Hyde Park, and she suspected he knew that as well. He was playing with her again. "Nevertheless, it does not excuse your attempt to fool me," she scolded him. "If you wanted to call on me, you had only to do so again, as the marquis."

"You would have let me in?" His disbelief was patent.

"Of course," she assured him with a frown. "My brother has hired servants. I have no reason to hide anymore. And you still have not told me what you wanted to see me about. It must be important or you would not have gone to all this trouble."

"It is important, to me," he told her. She waited for him to continue, but just then Benjamin sauntered into the room.

"Cassie, Pierson tells me we have a caller."

Devon rose, hastily shoving the glasses onto his nose, and Cassie rose with him. Before she could say a word, he put out his hand. "Major Bentbrooke, I am honored." If he had sounded French before, now his voice dripped with a cultured London accent. "Flavius Darien, sir, at your service."

Cassie frowned, but she caught his eye. The look on his face all but begged her not to give him away.

"Mr. Darien," Benjamin greeted, shaking his hand. "An astronomer, I believe."

"Yes, though not as successful as your famous father. I was telling your sister how much I enjoyed reading his articles."

Benjamin's smile was bored. "Yes, well, the old fellow could spin a tale, couldn't he? Cassie, might I speak with you alone?" He caught her arm as if to draw her into the entryway. Devon caught her other arm.

"I hope we might continue our conversation afterward, Miss Bentbrooke," he entreated with a gentle squeeze.

Cassie glanced at each of them. Benjamin clearly had no idea the fellow beside her was an impostor, yet the marquis felt compelled to keep his identity a secret. Did he fear Benjamin's reaction? No, not fear. She doubted the marquis feared much of anything. Why not admit his true name?

"Yes, of course," she murmured, drawing her arm away from him. "Excuse me."

He bowed, and she let Benjamin lead her into the entry.

"We have things to do," he scolded her. "Why do you let this fellow monopolize your time?"

"Pierson is planning your tedious little dinner party," Cassie informed him. "And two visits should hardly be called a monopoly. Don't tell me you get to win your love, but I can't even have a male visitor?"

He took a deep breath. "I didn't mean it that way." The words should have been conciliatory, but she could hear the edge in them. "You may entertain callers. I merely do not wish you to tire yourself. You have your observations to make, remember?"

"I'm not the one who usually forgets," she replied with a frown. "Now, if you'll excuse me, I'll finish my discussion with our guest."

He nodded absently, turning away. Cassie put out a hand to stop him. "By the way, do you know a man named Devon Sebastien?"

He froze. "The marquis de Renard? Do not receive him. Dirty Frenchman."

She blinked at his vehemence. "There are any number of émigrés in London, Benjamin. Do you hate them all, or just the marquis de Renard in particular?"

"I've been fighting Frenchmen for seven years," he told her. "That has hardly endeared the race to me. And I have heard stories of Renard specifically."

Cassie felt a chill. "Stories?"

"Nothing one would repeat to a sister," he assured her.

"I see," she said, although she did not see at all. "Then you would not be amenable to inviting him to our party tomorrow."

"Not in the slightest," he snapped. "I don't intend to hand Compton a title on a silver platter. Now, finish with your guest. I have work for you."

"Very well," Cassie agreed, mind turning. "Give me a

few minutes. But what you ask had better be important, Benjamin. You hired any number of servants. I am not one of them."

Devon rose as she returned. He had tried to listen to their conversation but had been unable to hear more than a few words. Her head was high, her jaw set, as if she were determined.

"What have you done to anger my brother?" she demanded.

He blinked. Used to those who dealt in innuendo, he found it hard to move with her sudden bursts of honesty. "Your brother?" he hedged.

"Yes," she replied, crossing to face him. "Oh, I didn't give you away. But I did ask him whether I should allow the marquis de Renard to call again. His answer was an emphatic no."

"Now do you see why I came in disguise?"

She frowned. "You knew Benjamin despised you? But why?"

He could hear the bitterness in his voice. "Why do the English despise anything French unless it is a servant?"

"How silly," she replied, waving away years of hostility with one swipe of her hand. "A man should be judged on his character and accomplishments, not birthright."

"An amazingly liberal view," he returned, "for the daughter of the English nobility."

She wrinkled her nose. "I am an oddity there as well, I suppose. You are right that many Englishmen feel as my brother does. I cannot apologize for them, but I do apologize for him. I understand your need to come in costume. Now, please, tell me what you want."

Devon eyed her. She was so endlessly forthright. Would she really tell him what he wanted to know, just like that? Given her brother's dislike of him, he could hardly tell her all the truth. He had little doubt that if

Benjamin Bentbrooke discovered he had a clue to a treasure beneath his roof, he would hardly go looking for the rightful owners.

"I am a student of the stars," he replied. "I really do want to see your father's journals."

Her face, so open, closed. "That is impossible. No one handles my father's journals except me. I would be happy to tutor you in the science of astronomy, but I cannot let you touch the books."

Eight

Cassie sat silently at dinner that night, only half listening to the conversation. All she could see was the determination in the marquis's eyes as she had told him that he could not handle the journals. He had tried to persuade her otherwise, his charm thickening until she could scarcely catch her breath. Some part of her she didn't recognize begged her to give in to him but she had turned him down, just as she had every other person who had tried to see her father's work. By the look on his handsome face, he would no more understand than the others. The journals were everything she had been and everything she hoped to be.

From age seven, she had been her father's scribe many nights. When Stephen Kearney had been killed, she had taken on a greater role. Now she used the journals in her own studies. But more than figures on a page, the journals were her last link to her father. Alfred Brentbrooke had never been affectionate; the one place his love had shown was in his work. She couldn't share that love with someone else, particularly someone who wanted to dissect it, analyze it, criticize it. She had taken the journals to her room for safekeeping while the house was being refurbished. Once things had been set to rights, they would return to the library, behind the glass of the bookshelves, where she could get them when she needed them.

She gradually became aware of the fact that Liza could

not seem to contain herself about the upcoming dinner party. She waited for Benjamin to stop her coldly in mid-description, but to her surprise, Liza's enthusiasm seemed to amuse him. He asked her advice on activities, seeming to take the effusive and somewhat contradictory answers to heart. Only when he asked her which of his coats she preferred did Cassie change the subject.

She had hoped that the marquis would try again the next day, but she soon found she had no time to be concerned when he did not. Benjamin kept her busy, much as she tried to resist. She barely had time to return her father's journals to their rightful place in the library.

She was surprised to find that according to Pierson, who proved to be a font of information, her brother had evidently inveigled his way into the very center of the haut ton. She knew the season had ended in August, yet enough of the fashionable remained in London for him to make a name for himself. His classic looks and heroic stories made him an instant sensation. Reluctantly, Cassie had to admit that the list of his conquests would make Napoleon stand in awe, which intimidated her more than a little. She would be dining with the socially elite. She feared she would never live up to their standards.

Only Liza knew how nervous she felt. Her ward followed her from the nuncheon table up to her room, where she flounced upon the bed and proclaimed herself ready to advise Cassie on how to dress her hair. They had barely started when there was a tap on the door. Liza hopped off the bed, squealing as she saw the footman carrying boxes from the seamstress. She seized the largest box, nearly oversetting the poor man, and carried it triumphantly to the bed. The footman set the other packages down where Cassie indicated and withdrew. Cassie approached the bed with trepidation.

"This will be the evening gown," Liza proclaimed, struggling with the lid. "Oh, what do you think it will look like?"

"I couldn't care less," Cassie proclaimed, feeling her own excitement rising. "As long as it isn't black. I've worn mourning clothes for so long, I've forgotten what other colors look like."

Liza hugged herself. "Oh, my hands are shaking so. I want to prolong the excitement."

"Well, I don't." Cassie laughed and flung off the lid.

The dress was black.

Liza gasped, wrenching the lid from Cassie's frozen grasp. "It's a mistake."

Cassie felt the tears coming and forcefully held them back. She stalked to the other boxes, throwing off lid after lid. Each article of clothing, from the walking dress to the morning dress to the day dresses, was a solid black. She shoved them aside and closed her eyes.

"Oh, Cassie, I'm so sorry," Liza cried. "What will you do?"

She should have known it was too good to be true. Cassiopeia Bentbrooke didn't need colorful dresses or admiring glances like other women. She was the spinster, the recluse, the eccentric. Certainly the seamstress had not seen fit to argue. Now that she thought about it, she realized that the woman had not even cared enough to ask her for fittings. Cassie had been so occupied with the mystery of the marquis that the need had never crossed her mind.

"Do?" she replied. "There's nothing to be done. Even if I demanded another dress, it would never be ready for this evening. I shall have to wear the horrid thing."

Liza sniffed back a tear. "Oh, Cassie, how noble! Refusing to spoil your brother's party."

Cassie nodded, forcing back her disappointment. Liza was right. It would not do to spoil the party. Her brother had worked to make it a success. Someone might as well enjoy it.

"We can pull it off," Liza chattered. "With some jewelry and your hair done up, you'll be beautiful."

"No, I won't," Cassie replied realistically. "But I am the

esteemed Major Bentbrooke's sister. Someone can be made to sit with me, no matter what I look like."

They spent the rest of the afternoon experimenting. It amused Liza far more than it did Cassie, but it kept her ward busy, and it kept Cassie from going to Benjamin and telling him exactly what she thought of his excellent taste in clothing. After she had resigned herself to the color, she had to admit that the dress was beautifully made. It was watered silk, which whispered as she walked. The neckline rose to her collarbone, ending with a delicate ruff of stiffened silk edged in lace. The long sleeves were lace as well, showing her skin through a pattern of roses. The dress was by no means a perfect fit, but the thick black satin bow emphasized the high waist and made her look long and graceful, as did the triple lace flounce at the hem.

Liza chose to arrange her hair in a knot at the nape of her neck, letting a long piece swing free along her back. With her mother's pearl drops on her ears, Cassie felt she looked passable.

Benjamin was waiting in the front entry to receive their guests and looking so perfect in his black evening clothes that she felt dowdy all over again.

"There you are," he said impatiently as she came down the stairs. "I see the dress arrived. Somehow I thought you would look better in it."

"If you wanted me to sparkle," Cassie snapped, "you should have ordered a different color."

"You are in mourning," Benjamin replied, taking her arm and drawing her to his side. "Undue haste to return to the brighter colors would be unseemly for a spinster."

"It's been three years! The only reason I still wear black is because I haven't been able to afford new clothes!"

There was a rap at the door. Pierson materialized from behind her and hastened to do his duty.

"We can discuss this another time," Benjamin hissed as the butler threw open the door. "For tonight, smile, and do everything I tell you."

Cassie grimaced. "But of course, *dear* brother."

Their first guests were an elderly couple who beamed at Benjamin as if he were their long-lost son. Their reason became apparent when their gangly daughter simpered in. More guests arrived. Cassie smiled and bobbed, had her hand kissed, had her cheek kissed, and had her shoulder patted. She counted sixteen times that she had to comment on the weather, twenty that she had to concur what a fine fellow her brother was.

Finally, Miss Compton appeared before her. The young woman had thick auburn hair with tendrils escaping from the knot at the top of her head. Her face was a perfect oval, her eyes a deep, warm brown, shaded by thick lashes that needed no blacking. Her curvaceous figure was enhanced by the exquisite cut of her expensive lavender watered silk gown. She was about Liza's size, coming only to Cassie's collarbone. Benjamin greeted her so warmly, a pink appeared in the girl's cheeks. Cassie didn't know whether to laugh or sigh in envy at her utter perfection.

She found herself more in charity with Miss Compton's parents. Alexander and Elena Compton were both plain people: brown-haired, brown-eyed, plumply respectable. She could easily imagine Mr. Compton playing the country squire and riding to hounds, Mrs. Compton presiding over whist parties and sewing for the poor. They looked solidly comfortable in their well-made but not-too-stylish evening clothes.

She was far less comfortable with the woman who came with the Comptons. A mountain of womanhood, Matilda Smythe-Bellows stood eye to eye with Cassie's six-foot-tall brother, but she must have outweighed him by nearly a hundred pounds. Red-faced and titian-haired, she regarded Cassie with narrowed amber eyes, raising a quizzing glass and peering through it. She dropped it suddenly and crushed Cassie against her purple silk gown.

"You poor child," Cassie thought she heard her rumble, though her ears were rather effectively plugged by the more than ample bosom. "I was overcome by the deaths of your parents." She released Cassie as quickly as she had seized her.

"Did you know them well?" Cassie managed, knowing her voice betrayed her surprise that the woman had known them at all.

"Never met them," Matilda declared, opening a fan and applying it vigorously. "But any man's death is a tragedy for England."

"How . . . very philosophical of you," Cassie murmured.

"You see?" Benjamin smiled, signaling Pierson to close the doors since the last guests had arrived. "I knew you two would get on. Cassie, if you would be so good as to show Mrs. Smythe-Bellows the drawing room?"

Before Cassie could protest, the woman seized her arm and dragged her off.

Cassie was afraid she knew what Benjamin expected of her. Still, she carefully seated Mrs. Smythe-Bellows in the far corner of the room and attempted to make her escape. Unfortunately, believing herself to have found a kindred spirit, the woman refused to let her go.

She soon realized why her brother had saddled her with Barbara's aunt. The woman was a vicious gossip. She set about prying into every aspect of the Bentbrooke family, obviously unsatisfied by the quick and, for the most part, honest answers Cassie gave her. When the family proved of little interest, she launched into the sordid details of the lives of the guests. By dinner, Cassie had learned that Lord Trolby had seduced a thirteen-year-old schoolgirl, Lady Alice Hensley was in love with her neighbor's gardener, and Myron Crubb liked things Greek. When Mr. Compton kindly offered to lead Cassie and his sister in to dinner, Mrs. Smythe-Bellows scolded him for being inattentive.

After dinner, the party adjourned to the sitting room, where card tables had been erected. Cassie had given up any notion of enjoying herself and did not resist as Mrs. Smythe-Bellows dragged her off to the sofa, which had been pushed into the corner, for more criticism and gossip. Most of the older guests settled themselves for whist. A few of the younger people selected partners to promenade about the room. She saw her brother glide by with a rapt Barbara Compton on his arm and knew that he, at least, would count the night a success.

"My dear girl," Matilda Smythe-Bellows gasped, "how could you!"

Cassie started, glancing hurriedly at her gown in fear she had somehow spilled sauce down her bosom. She could see nothing amiss.

Mrs. Smythe-Bellows leaned forward, rapping her on the wrist with her fan. "You did not tell me you knew the marquis de Renard."

Cassie swallowed, praying her face did not display her guilt. "I . . . I believe we may have met. Why do you ask?"

"Did no one warn you? My dear child, you should not have invited him to your home!"

"Invited him?" Cassie frowned. Mrs. Smythe-Bellows's eyes widened in glee. She swept her fan in the direction of the doorway. Standing framed in the center, immaculate in his evening black, stood the marquis. Cassie gasped.

"You should well show shock, my dear. I take it you did not invite him, then?"

When Cassie could do no more than shake her head, the woman became even more elated. "I knew it!" she cried. "The man is far too encroaching. His family is completely disreputable, yet he walks about as if he were the lord and master of all he surveys. Oh, he can be charming; I will grant you that. If he would put his charms to better use, no lady could resist him. Or perhaps I should not use the word 'lady.'"

Cassie blinked at the sound of the woman's wicked chuckle. The marquis was indeed surveying the scene as if from on high. Tonight he played a consummate gentleman. His dark hair glinted in the candlelight. His double-breasted coat emphasized the lean lines of his body. His glance searched the room. Just for a moment, she imagined what it might be like to be the object of his search. Would his eyes light with pleasure as he caught sight of her? Would his steps quicken as if he could not be kept from her side another moment? As she watched, he nodded to the couple crossing in front of him. The woman stiffened, only to whisper frantically behind her hand after they had passed. The man cast him a glance over his shoulder. Several heads turned in his direction, setting off a fresh chain of whispers.

"Well, what are you going to do?" Matilda Smythe-Bellows demanded. "He clearly has joined us unbidden. He is no gentleman, my dear, despite that title. His mother had some minor connections to a few prominent families, but she married a French aristocrat, and we all know what happened to them."

"What?" Cassie asked, mesmerized. The marquis wandered into the room, pausing to put a hand on this gentleman's shoulder, to nod in greeting to a lady. He was moving nearer. Was he looking for her? What could she say to him here?

"Guillotined!" Matilda brought her fan down with a chop that made Cassie jump. "His entire family, dead. There is no one left to dispute him if he claimed a bloodline to Louis the Fourteenth himself. The only reason he is sometimes received, if you ask me, is that he is related to His Grace, the duke of Devonlee. The duke bought him off with a letter of marque. Privateer, you know. Pirate, if you ask me."

"Pirate?" Cassie frowned. "I thought he was an astronomer."

"An astronomer!" Matilda choked on her laughter. "Is that what he told you? My dear girl, most likely the only heavenly bodies he studies are those with the least amount of clothing on. I have heard no stories about him, mind you, but these naval men are all alike."

Cassie barely noted what the woman was saying. The

marquis had turned and was moving closer to Benjamin. As Cassie watched, her brother glanced up and saw their uninvited guest. Benjamin frowned ever so slightly, then purposely turned his back.

"The cut direct!" Matilda crowed. "That for you, my fine marquis."

The marquis stopped abruptly, turning the motion into a graceful halt beside a small group of people. They spoke pleasantly for a moment; then he strolled back to the door. Cassie knew she should be relieved. She would not have to face him. Benjamin would not confront him directly. Unfortunately, she felt only disappointment.

He reached the door to the room, glanced about one last time, then turned right, going deeper into the house.

Nine

"Excuse me," Cassie murmured, rising. Mrs. Smythe-Bellows rose with her, but Cassie put out a hand to stop her. "If you wouldn't mind? I must find out about our unwanted guest."

The woman collapsed with a sigh onto the sofa. "All right, but promise me you'll tell all when you know!"

Cassie gave her a polite smile that she hoped would satisfy, then hurried from the room, purposely avoiding her brother.

The corridor stood empty except for the footman, who was just returning to his position near the door. A quick conversation revealed that he had seen no one. But his dark eyes narrowed as if in expectation. She had a sudden vision of him attempting to throw the marquis out. She did not want to think of the resulting scandal, for of course the marquis would resist, and probably quite well if he was the pirate Matilda Smythe-Bellows intimated. Small wonder his handsome face was tanned from the sun, and his well-cut coats rippled with muscles. She could more easily picture him at the helm of a ship, fighting the waves, than squinting through the eyepiece of a telescope.

She glanced back down the corridor behind the main stair. Where was he? If he had only gone in search of a servant to fetch his cloak and hat—if he had even brought those—he would surely have returned by now.

"Cassie!" hissed a voice from overhead. Looking up, she

saw Liza sitting by the newel post at the second-story overlook. Her ward was waving for her to come up. With a last look about, Cassie lifted her skirts and climbed to join her.

"Did you see him?" Liza demanded.

"Who?" Cassie asked, almost afraid to know the answer.

"The gorgeous gentleman with the dark hair. He is easily the finest-looking fellow at the party, saving the major of course. Who is he?"

"The marquis de Renard," Cassie replied, thinking it would not hurt to tell her ward as much of the truth as possible. "And he was not invited. He is an interloper. Has he left?"

Liza's eyes widened. "No, indeed. He went down the corridor toward the dining room. What shall we do?"

Cassie thought carefully. She could alert Benjamin, but calling away the host would definitely warn their guests that something was wrong. Benjamin would not thank her for that. Besides, he had an unreasonable dislike of the marquis; she could not quite believe he was so prejudiced against the French. She could alert Pierson, but most likely he would be no more circumspect than the footman. Certainly he couldn't match the marquis in physique. She had a feeling it would be safer if she investigated. She rose from Liza's side.

"Stay here. If you hear me scream, send the footman and Pierson as quickly as you can."

Paling, Liza nodded.

Cassie strolled down the corridor with far more confidence than she felt. He could not have reached the dining room, she reasoned, or a servant in there cleaning would have directed him on his way. That left only one door that was out of sight of Liza's vantage point: the library door. She paused. Why would the marquis be interested in the library? The possible answer sent a chill through her. She put her hand on the newly appointed gilt handle, saw that she was trembling, and tightened her grip. Slowly she eased open the door.

* * *

Hearing the door open, Devon slid into the shadows along the wall, thankful that he had not had time to find a lamp. The room was fairly dark; any fire that had been burning had long since been extinguished. Someone had left the curtains open, and faint rays of moonlight spilled along the floor and glinted off the glass-front bookcases across from the fireplace. Noise from the party flowed through the opening door, to be swallowed in the stillness. Against the light, he saw a tall, slender silhouette. The voice confirmed that it was Cassie.

"Hello? Is anyone here?" She took a few more steps into the room.

Devon shook his head at his bad luck. He had seen her watching him, but her wide eyes told him she found his presence shocking. The fact was regrettable but necessary. He hadn't thought she'd follow. As hostess, she wouldn't be able to leave her guests easily. The party had seemed such a perfect time to find the journals, with the residents, guests, and servants busy. He could make a quick appearance, then slip out to search the house. If he found the books, he could read them or take them with him, returning them after their use to him had ceased. Now he was caught, unless he could make her leave the room. Was it possible to frighten the redoubtable Miss Bentbrooke? He slid along the wall, reached over her head, and snapped the door shut.

She whirled, becoming a shadow like him, although with eyes used to the dark, he could make out her movements. Instead of running, as he had hoped, she straightened.

"Monsieur le Marquis, I know you are in here," she said firmly. "You might as well show yourself."

She was a determined one; he'd give her that. He did not answer her. The silence was heavy. If she thought she was mistaken, perhaps she would leave before he had to take more drastic action. If he could take it. She had a way of putting him off his guard. She took another step forward, the cock of her head telling him that she squinted into the shadows. She wasn't entirely sure he was here. He let her go on guessing, watching her. In the black dress, she was darker than the shadows. Though more fashionable than her other outfits, the dress barely did her justice. She needed lighter colors: pale blues, soft grays, sunny yellows—something to let her delicate skin shine. He shook his head again at the fanciful thought. He was here to steal the journals, not advise the woman on fashion!

"Come out this minute," she demanded, "or I'll get my brother."

She was endlessly honest. He knew it was no bluff. He would have to find another way to get her to leave. He stepped silently into the moonlight. She caught her breath.

"Your servant, madam," he said, inclining his head in a bow. "How gratifying that my presence was missed so soon."

Her tone was prim. "You were not invited, sir. I must ask you to leave."

"Leave?" He drew himself up and squared his shoulders. The movements were meant to intimidate, although he carefully kept his tone friendly. "My dear Miss Bentbrooke, I was under the impression you were hoping I'd stay."

"What?" He could feel her surprise. "Your imagination has gotten the best of you, sir. I only followed you to make sure you caused no trouble."

Did she suspect his plans for the journals? Did it change anything if she did? Once he got the books away from the house, she could prove nothing. For now, he had to be sure that she would remain silent about what she had found, for fear of ruining her reputation, or that before she betrayed him he'd have enough time to check the volumes he could see stacked on the shelves.

"Trouble, Miss Bentbrooke?" he replied. "I assure you, I am quite harmless." Belying the words, he purposely strolled out of his patch of moonlight and became a shadow once more.

Obviously uncomfortable, she retreated toward the door. "Gentlemen who hide in unlit libraries are rarely harmless," she told him, glancing wildly about her.

He moved up beside her and spoke in her ear. She jumped. "Have you so much experience with unlit libraries, then? Or merely the gentlemen who hide in them?" He laid a hand on her shoulder, as light as a caress. Under the lace, was her skin as soft as it looked? She stiffened. He was succeeding. Another few moments, and she would be running from the room.

"I have servants, guests," she warned him. "If I scream, they'll be on you in an instant."

"Would they? What a pity to interrupt our tryst." He toyed with the tendrils along her face, grazing her cheek. Her hair was softer than he had expected, slipping like strands of fine silk through his fingers.

She jerked away and spun to face him. "Stop that immediately. My brother has given you the cut direct. Don't make me follow his lead."

He chuckled. "But, *cherie*, what can I possibly have done to make you so angry? You followed a strange gentleman into a dark room. Surely you expected something like this." Before she could cry out, he pulled her into his embrace.

She was stiff in his arms, but almost the instant his lips claimed hers, she melted. Instead of gasping or pulling away, she trembled, swaying closer to him. He felt her arms steal up his back, caressing him. She pressed her curves into him as if seeking to become one body. Against all his intentions, he warmed, deepening the kiss, drinking her in. She tasted as sweet as brandy from his cousin's private stock, her touch no less heady. The extent of his arousal unnerved him, and he jerked away, stumbling back into the moonlight. His face must have betrayed his shock, for she chuckled.

"Really, Monsieur le Marquis. If you allow yourself to be followed into a darkened room, surely you expected that."

He could do no more than smile and swept her a bow to hide his surprise. He had thought to kiss an alabaster statue and ended up embracing a flame.

"Your point, Miss Bentbrooke," he managed. "I allow myself vanquished. Do with me what you will."

They were playing a game, yet she seemed to be reveling in it. Indeed, she was better at it than he would have dreamed. "Very well," she agreed. "As your captor, I demand you tell me why you came in here. And don't start with that trysting business. You did not know I was following you, and while I admit you are quite kind on the eyes, surely you are not followed by strange women in every house you enter."

"Ah, too true," he allowed, playing along with her. "Encounters such as ours are all too rare in your staid British Empire. I came in to read a book."

She stiffened in obvious disbelief. "A book?"

"This is a library, is it not? I assumed you would have books here."

"Of course we have books here. The question is, why would you want to read one?"

The bantering tone helped him to pull his wits together. Perhaps if he went forward with his original plan while they talked, he could locate the journals before she stopped him. Another kiss might win him his freedom. The singing in his blood informed him that another kiss might also cost him his freedom, but he ignored it. He could feel her gaze following him as he made his way to the desk, cradled among the bookcases. "Your party was quite tedious. I thought to find better amusement."

He cast her a look over his shoulder to let her know that she had provided that and more. She stiffened again, but he did not give her time for the stinging reply she was no doubt considering. Striking a flint, he brought the desk lamp to life. He scanned the upper shelves, seeing only titles of Greek and Latin classics, then crouched to peruse the lower.

She was obviously curious. "You really cannot be looking for a book," she argued, venturing forward a little ways.

He had finished the first shelf and continued to the next. "And why not? Do you think I cannot read?"

"I assume noblemen's sons receive an education in France as they do in England. However, I was warned about you. You are a pirate. You sail around the world preying on other ships. I fail to see how that leaves you much time for literature."

He wondered what else she had heard, and how much she believed. "Books can be welcome friends on long journeys. And some books are prizes in themselves because they are rare. Some are never seen outside highly valued collections."

She gasped. "You *are* after the journals! Thief!"

He barely heard her. The shelf before him held what appeared to be bound journals. He felt his heart speed even as his hands reached for them.

"Please." Though the word was said quietly, it stopped him. "Please don't take them."

He kept his back to her. "They mean so much to you?"

"Yes." Again the word was barely a whisper. "I don't think you could understand. They're all I have of my father."

All she had of her father. He understood better than she could know. The treasure, and the reputation behind it, was all he had of his father. At eleven he could only watch as his uncle left with it. Until twenty-five he had been chained to the duke's demands. For the past five years he had hunted and planned. The journals, the final clue, were within his reach. But if he stole her father's memory in the process of restoring his father's honor, he lost everything he hoped to gain.

His hands fell back to his sides. "Fathers are important.

Forgive my intrusion, Miss Bentbrooke. I will go before I cause you any more pain."

He turned and found her eyeing him incredulously. "You have them in your grasp, and you're leaving, just because I asked?"

"I disappoint you?" He chuckled. "That's a first. If you prefer, I would be happy to steal them."

"That won't be necessary." Her smile was watery.

Perhaps not, but he still needed them. "I will call tomorrow, and we can do this the proper way."

She sighed. "Benjamin wouldn't allow it."

"Even if I was courting his lovely sister?"

She blinked as if he'd shocked her, then shook her head. "Since I have been warned about you, perhaps you should be warned about me. I am plain, penniless, and untitled. I would not be worth your efforts."

He could not have disagreed more and offered her a salute. "Indeed, *cherie*, I appreciate the warning. But you must let me form my own opinions. For now, I shall take my leave."

She stood silently as he swept past her. At the doorway, he paused. It did not seem right to leave such a one standing there alone. There was an intelligence, a fire, and a sweetness he hadn't expected. He offered her his best smile and saw her blush anew. "Another time, *cherie*." And he left before she could refuse.

Ten

Devon walked home from the Bentbrooke town house, deep in thought. The journals had nearly been in his grip, and he had given them up. For what? Because a woman appealed to the memory of his father? A woman who was a self-professed oddity? A woman whose kiss set his blood on fire? When had he become so foolish as to align himself with an English spinster?

A smile lit his lips. A spinster she might be, but only because so many Englishmen lacked vision. Her cool coloring and intelligent conversation no doubt made them think she was icy at heart. He knew better. There was a passion in her. He had meant the kiss to frighten her. It was he who was frightened. A woman such as this might make him forget all he was trying to achieve, if she knew how to wield her potent charms as a weapon. Yet she used them guilelessly, artlessly. Or so it seemed.

However, the more he learned about the proper British Bentbrookes, the more it troubled him. Her explanation of dressing as a maid for propriety's sake made little sense, her brother's sudden wealth even less so. He had inquired about the major but had been unsuccessful in learning the exact extent of the man's inheritance. It was possible that the Bentbrookes were as rich as was rumored. It was also quite possible that they had already found the treasure.

So where did that leave him? Much as he was coming to

admire her, he could not trust her. He certainly couldn't trust the major. Yet he had to find a way to read the journals. The major would clearly not welcome a social call. The sister would have a hard time explaining one. Still, she seemed his most promising chance. His smile deepened. Perhaps he could satisfy both his desires after all. Miss Cassiopeia Bentbrooke was about to get herself a devoted follower.

Cassie waited a long while before she felt composed enough to leave the library. Her brush with the marquis had left her confused and not a little breathless. She had certainly skirted the bounds of propriety tonight. She had always been careful to avoid being labeled wanton. It surprised her more than a little that wanton felt terribly good.

She could not imagine what had possessed her to return his kiss that way. He had clearly been trying to frighten her. At first, she had merely wanted to show him that he would have to do better than that to scare Cassiopeia Bentbrooke, but the feel of his arms around her and the touch of his lips had been surprisingly sweet. She had thought being kissed by a notorious privateer would be daunting, but she had only felt a longing to stay in his arms, warm, loved, safe. Safe! She must be mad!

She gazed for a few moments at the three bound journals, all that she had left of her father's painstaking work. She should do as his colleagues had encouraged her—translate them from the code she and her father used and donate them and the translation to the Royal Society. At the very least she should probably lock them away for safety. She'd look for a place in the morning.

But why had Devon Sebastien wanted them? A privateer was surely a far cry from a petty thief. And if he wanted to steal something, her mother's silver in the dining room or her father's early Shakespeare portfolio would be worth more to most people than the journals. She felt as if she'd been handed a painting with several key pieces cut out of it. She simply could not tell what she was looking at.

She knew she should return to the party, but she had no idea what she could say to cover her absence. She refused to confront Matilda Smythe-Bellows. In the end, she informed Pierson that she was retiring with a pounding headache.

Liza was waiting for her on the second floor landing. "I didn't hear you scream, and I saw him leave. What happened?"

Cassie managed a smile, draping an arm about her ward's shoulders and propelling her upward toward their bedchambers. "Nothing worth telling, love. He was merely misdirected."

"You're teasing me," Liza accused. "You were in there a very long time to simply send him on his way. Was he charming? Oh, please, Cassie, tell me!"

Cassie sighed, trying to think of something she could tell the impressionable girl. She could not risk that the information would get back to Benjamin. "He was charming, very much the gentleman, despite what some would say." She smiled thinking of his shock when she had returned his kiss.

"What else! You have the dreamiest look in your eyes."

"You must leave me some things to myself," Cassie replied with a laugh, hugging her. "Let us just say that he was far more interesting than I had ever dared to hope. And very likely, I will never see him again."

Liza's face fell. "Why not?"

"He has far more important things to do; he is a privateer. Besides, I gave him a set-down, so it is unlikely he will seek me out again. Now, it is late. We will talk more tomorrow."

Her ward flounced off, clearly unsatisfied. Cassie couldn't help her. She was no more satisfied as she made her way to her own room and her observations.

* * *

Late that night, the duke of Devonlee let out a sigh that set Ames to quivering. "I pay you and my agents a handsome salary," his employer said, "and this is the best you can do?"

Ames grimaced. "I only summarize to save time. But the gist of it is that Captain Sebastien has been successful in entering the house, and, by all appearances, you were right that Miss Bentbrooke is taken with him." He giggled nervously.

The duke waved a hand. "I have no desire to hear how he bedded her, only that he succeeded in gaining access to her father's work. Yet *that* you cannot tell me."

"Your agent reports that they were alone in the library for some time tonight. The captain left quietly. Surely he learned something."

"Perhaps," the duke allowed. "I cannot see a woman, even a beautiful woman—and this spinster does not qualify as such—persuading my cousin from a course he has chosen."

"Some women can be most persuading," Ames ventured.

The duke's eyes narrowed. "So I have heard. Unfortunately, neither of my late wives proved to be such. They were not capable of thinking for themselves, which I must admit I had thought would be a benefit. What a pity they were also not able to give me an heir. Ah well, at least I have no one to watch over my shoulder, worrying that I spend his estate."

"A mixed blessing, to be sure," Ames replied. "But a good thing that Captain Sebastien was born on the maternal side. At least he cannot inherit."

"No, but he can still cause me a great deal of trouble. Watch him. If he changes his habits, let me know immediately. No one must stand between me and the Sebastien jewels."

Cassie slept late the following morning. Liza tiptoed in once, but, after a look at the clock told Cassie she had missed the service at St. George's, she waved her ward heartlessly out. Time enough later for the Spanish Inquisition. Maybe by then she would have figured out some better answers.

She didn't awake again until she heard the snap of the shade. As she opened her eyes, Benjamin stepped into her field of vision. His honey-colored brows were drawn together in a thundercloud. She blinked, hastily sitting up.

"So," he snapped, "you deign to awake."

"I cannot imagine why my having a few extra hours' sleep has made you so cross," she complained, tucking the covers around her. "Or have you some odious list I must complete again today?"

He glared at her. "You've ruined us, you addlepated fool!"

She resisted the urge to tell him that there was no such thing as a nonaddlepated fool and tried to remain calm. "If you will tell me what I have done to so displease you, perhaps we can think of some way to assuage your sensibilities."

He ran his hand back through his wavy hair as if to clear his mind. "You really don't understand, do you, Cassie? Everything was going so well, too. The Comptons liked me. The party was a great success. And now, this morning, the scandal."

"What scandal?"

He stared at her intently. "I do believe you're innocent." He brightened. "We can dismiss it as servants' gossip. No one of the ton can get away with such ridiculous tales. We'll make you into a great martyr. This could be just what I need!"

"Benjamin," Cassie snapped, "will you please tell me what's going on?"

"All right, all right. Liza was telling me that she had it from Cook, who had it from the Reynolds's man Henry, who had it from a lady friend of his who knows the Comptons' groom. How did she put it? You were right that she does have the most delightful way of stating things."

Cassie's alarm rose anew, but this time for her ward. "When did you see Liza without me?"

Benjamin frowned at her. "At breakfast, if you must know. If you decide to sleep to all hours you cannot expect the rest of us to wait to eat."

"You may not, but she can," Cassie maintained. "I don't want you spending time with her, Benjamin. She isn't out yet, and I'll thank you not to put ridiculous notions in her head about what society is all about."

Benjamin snorted. "Ha, as if I could! She seems to know more about it than I do, though how she came by that knowledge living with you, I have no idea. Now, do you wish to hear this amusing *on dit,* or not?"

"I suppose I must," she allowed, vowing to have a word with Liza later that morning.

Benjamin took up his most pompous pose. "It would seem that a certain notorious Frenchman has made another conquest. We are not speaking of the battles on the seas but of the war between the sexes in our own fair capital. A certain marquis has been seen for protracted periods of time alone with a certain Miss B. Betting at White's is sure *not* to include marriage."

She gazed up at her brother. "I don't understand. What has this to do with me?"

"Oh, you are priceless, sister. How could I have been so deceived? Ah, well. It means, dear heart, that you are rumored to be the marquis de Renard's mistress."

Whatever she had been expecting, it was hardly that. She stared at him for another moment, then felt a smile spreading. So, the oddity was desirable after all, and by one of the most notorious of gentlemen. It was rather gratifying that London thought her capable of such intrigue.

Her brother's smile faded. "You're not laughing. Cassie, do not tell me there is truth to this."

She glared at him. "Oh, Benjamin, don't be an ass!

You've only to look at me to know it's a lie. Be logical, if you can. Do I look like the sort of woman the marquis would pursue?"

He eyed her carefully, cocking his head as if the story had changed her somehow. "On the whole, no. But lately . . ." He shook his head. "No, it doesn't make sense. One does not offer a *carte blanche* to someone like you. Which is just as well. I nearly had the Comptons hooked. I shouldn't like to lose them over something so ridiculous as your *inamoratas*."

Cassie started to tell him that whatever lovers she had or didn't have was hardly his business, but something in his tone disturbed her. "What do you mean, you nearly had the Comptons hooked? You are courting Barbara, if memory serves."

He avoided her gaze, which only raised her unease. "Certainly I am courting Barbara. But one must impress the family if one wishes to make way with the daughter."

"And are you making way with the daughter?" Cassie probed.

"I'd better be," Benjamin muttered. "For all the blunt I've had to outlay, she had better be worth the effort."

"I am certain she is," Cassie replied, watching him closely. "What did you tell me the first day? She is lovely, accomplished, sought after. How much did you say she was worth?"

Benjamin stared at her for a moment, then shook his head. "I should have known better than to try to lead you on, shouldn't I? You're still the bright one, aren't you, Cassie?"

Knowing he spoke the truth didn't make her feel any better. "You want to marry her for her money."

He did not deny it. "At thirty thousand pounds, Miss Compton's the ripest plum and I intend to pick her. Father left me next to nothing; I would have been through it in a year."

"Then we are truly poor?" The familiar claws of worry

sank into her stomach. "You lied about the inheritance as well?"

"Of course I lied about that! I sold my commission and used the money to pay for our debut. Do you think I want the Comptons to see me as a fortune hunter? I told you, they want a title. I had to offer them something in its place."

"And the marvelous Major Bentbrooke wasn't enough?"

"It never has been," her brother informed her savagely. "You have no idea how difficult life is as a nobody, Cassie."

She raised an eyebrow, but he didn't notice.

"I'm sick and tired of taking orders from dolts with half my intelligence," he ranted. "Father may have left me no money, but he left me the famed Bentbrooke charm, and I intend to get the most I can for it."

Cassie felt physically ill. She curled back into the bed as far as she could and hugged herself.

"And you needn't look so stricken, *dear* sister. You'll be well paid for your part in this. And you'll do it cheerfully, or you and your precious ward will be out on the streets."

She gasped. "You wouldn't dare!"

He grabbed her by the arms and pulled her roughly to her feet. "I would dare. I mean to do this, Cassie, and I need your help. Alone, I look like a fortune hunter. If I have you beside me, I look respectable. What Englishman could refuse a soldier, fresh from the wars, with his invalid sister beside him?"

"Invalid? What do you plan? Am I to be consumptive, or merely a helpless cripple?"

"Neither. I think 'dotty spinster' will be adequate to evoke pity. You seem to manage that well enough."

"How dare you," Cassie cried. "Let go of me this instant." She lashed out with her feet, but Benjamin moved aside with ease. "You can bully me all you like," she declared, scowling at him. "You can't confine me like this when you take me out with Miss Compton. I will tell her all about your plan."

"Then I jolly well won't take you with us," he growled.

"You cannot stop me. You have no hold on me!"

He released her so quickly she fell back onto the bed. She longed to rub her aching arms but refused to give him the satisfaction of knowing how much he had hurt her.

"Oh, dear sister, that is where you are wrong. I have the best of holds on you. You claim to care for dear Liza Kearney. How will you face her when you must tell her she no longer has a home? This is my house. You stay here on my sufferance."

"You are vile," Cassie spat. "We will make our way without you. We have done so before."

"So you said. If you could not live here in any style, how will you manage when you must pay for the housing as well? Oh, I daresay you might be able to turn a hand at being a governess or companion. But what of Liza? She's far too young to be useful to any decent family. I'm terribly afraid she would fall to prostitution. Do you know that word, Cassie? It means . . ."

"Stop!" Cassie shrank from him and covered her ears. Had she wished for Liza's mythical treasure earlier? How much more she wished they had it now. With such wealth she would not need her brother. She could warn the Comptons and Benjamin be damned. As it was, she was well and truly trapped. She wanted to demand that he take his horrid scheme and leave her home, only it was no longer her home. It would be she and Liza who would be forced to leave.

"Well?" he demanded. "What will you have, sister? Are you going to help me, or shall I send you packing?"

She lowered her hands in surrender. "As you said, I have little choice. I will not help you, Benjamin, but neither will I work against you. That is the best offer you will get."

Eleven

A short time later, Cassie sat picking at her toast, listening to Benjamin's tedious instructions, a cup of hot chocolate beside her. He had plans to follow up on his party. Understanding his true goal, she could barely eat. She was only thankful Liza had already gone to lay flowers on her mother's grave as she often did on Sundays. She vowed to swear the girl to silence about the marquis. The less her brother knew about the clandestine meeting in the library, the better.

Benjamin was rising to leave when Pierson appeared with a card on a silver salver.

"Visitors?" Benjamin asked with a smile, winking at Cassie. "So soon? It appears our party was even more successful than I thought. Who is it to see me, Pierson?"

"The marquis de Renard, sir," the butler intoned. "And he asked for Miss Bentbrooke."

Benjamin stared at Cassie accusingly. "No interest in you whatsoever, did you say?"

Cassie knew she had paled at the announcement. Much as she longed to see Devon again, it was the worst possible timing. If he had waited even another quarter hour, he would have missed Benjamin entirely, and she might have had a chance of keeping this visit, too, a secret.

"Oh, Benjamin," she snapped, trying to brazen it out, "don't be ridiculous. Perhaps he forgot his gloves. I assure you, it has nothing to do with this gossip."

Benjamin's eyes narrowed, but he turned to Pierson. "Make Lord Renard comfortable in the withdrawing room. My sister and I will join him shortly."

"Certainly, sir," Pierson intoned. "I'll tell the rest of the staff to go on about their afternoon off."

"Surely you don't have to come with me, Benjamin," she tried as the butler bowed himself out.

"Surely I do," Benjamin corrected her. He seized her arm and drew her to her feet. She winced as his fingers found the bruises from his attack that morning.

"He wasn't supposed to be at the party last night to begin with," Benjamin reminded her, glaring into her eyes. "How did he get there? Did you invite him, Cassie?"

She shook her head. "No, though may I remind you that it would have been my right to do so. I live in this house, too."

"Only because it amuses me," he sneered. "Go carefully, Cassie. You may be the big sister, but I've learned a trick or two in the military."

"Apparently even beating up helpless females."

He released her. "You are hardly helpless. Now, let's go meet your friend. And remember, I'll be watching."

Part of her wanted to pull away, to dash to her room and lock herself in. The other part wanted more than anything to learn why the marquis had come. Was he intent on seeing the journals? Or was he truly here to see her? She shook her head. Did she really hope the mysterious marquis was here because of her? She doubted he'd come to apologize for last night. In fact, she rather hoped he hadn't. The memory of that kiss was going to sustain her for a long while, and she was loathe to have it done away with by an apology. But she was given no chance to decamp, for Benjamin motioned her upstairs to the withdrawing room before she could lodge another protest.

The marquis rose as they entered. In the light of day he looked like any other handsome gentleman, the aura of mystery lessened by the ordinary navy coat and fawn trousers, not unlike what her brother was wearing. His face was impassive; she could not tell his mood.

Benjamin was anything but a good host as he stepped forward. There was a suspicious glint in his azure eyes, and his smile was hard. He offered the marquis the barest of bows. "Lord Renard, how can we be of service?"

Devon's gaze swept over him and alighted on Cassie. She did not think it was her imagination that it warmed as it did so. She felt the color flooding to her cheeks and sank onto the nearest chair. His mouth twitched as if fighting a smile, but his face was hooded when he turned to Benjamin.

"Major Bentbrooke, thank you for receiving me. I came to apologize for my behavior last night."

Cassie caught her breath. Would he ruin all with a confession? Again, his gaze crossed to her, and she steeled herself to return it, shaking her head no. She could do no more than that before Benjamin, too, turned to her, his gaze considerably less warm.

He scowled at her, then returned his gaze to the marquis. They stood toe to toe for a moment, clearly sizing each other up.

"Won't you sit down, Monsieur le Marquis?" Cassie asked hurriedly with pleasantness she hardly felt.

He bowed his head in acknowledgment, then seated himself in the chair nearest hers. If she moved her knee, it would brush his. Cassie's jaw tightened as she held her smile. Was he intent on causing trouble? Surely he knew they were the subject of gossip. She supposed it was possible his servants were not as well informed as theirs apparently were. Having had no servants of her own, she certainly hadn't realized there was such a covert information chain until this morning.

Benjamin had no choice but to sit on the sofa opposite them. "Apologize, did you say?" he prompted. "For what, my lord?"

Cassie swallowed, but Devon answered readily enough. "Why, for joining your party, of course. The marquis of

Hastings assured me that he would ask you to include me. Only later did I realize he had been unable to attend and had forgotten to speak to you. You must find me rag-mannered."

The last statement was directed at Cassie. Something in the way he said it indicated that he was not referring to the party. "No offense has been taken," she murmured. "Surprises can be pleasant."

This time his smile appeared. "I'm glad you think so. I must admit I found it pleasant."

"There you are, then," Benjamin proclaimed, bringing all eyes back to him. He smiled congenially and leaned against the sofa. Cassie was not fooled for an instant. Benjamin pleasant was often Benjamin at his most dangerous. Her instincts proved true as he continued. "I'm sorry, of course, that Lord Hastings could not attend. Is he ill, do you know?"

Devon leaned back as well, crossing one booted leg over the other. "No, he is well. Duty prevented his attendance, I would suspect. He is much in demand at the War Office."

"Yes, of course." Benjamin nodded sagely. "It must have been gossip that he is in poor health. Gossip can be so damaging, don't you find, my lord?"

Devon pursed his lips thoughtfully. "Certainly. Although some gossip can be rather entertaining. It can even further a particular activity, haven't you found?"

They were on difficult ground again, and Cassie could not like it. The words could have been taken as a challenge. It was obvious that her brother took them so.

"I'm sure I don't know what you mean," he replied. "I try not to listen to gossip."

"I generally don't listen, either," the marquis allowed, "unless, of course, the person about whom everyone is gossiping is a particularly interesting person."

"I find some people encourage gossip just by living," Benjamin countered.

"And some people live very narrow lives," the marquis replied.

"True," Benjamin allowed tightly while Cassie bit her lip to keep from laughing out loud. In a battle of wits with the likes of Devon Sebastien, her brother was sadly outclassed. The marquis seemed prepared to make allowances.

"Was there something of particular interest today?" he asked as if providing Benjamin an opening. More likely he was only providing her brother enough rope to hang himself.

"Only for those who enjoy scandal," Benjamin replied with what Cassie knew to be feigned boredom. "Sad what some people consider interesting."

"And are you as fascinated with gossip as your brother is, Miss Bentbrooke?" Devon inquired politely, as if ensuring that she was part of the conversation. Again, she had the feeling that the question was far from harmless.

"Not generally," she replied honestly.

"And do you find today's topics as distressing as your brother does?"

Now she knew he was talking in innuendo. She considered how to answer, feeling her brother wait for her reply.

"I was taught not to believe everything I hear," she told them both. "One must form one's own opinions, Monsieur le Marquis. I'm sure you've heard that said before."

His mouth twitched, but he bowed his head in acknowledgment. "Very wise of you."

Benjamin seemed to relax; Cassie let herself do likewise.

"Of course," Devon continued with an unholy twinkle in his eyes, "I find there is usually a core of truth in every story related by gossips."

Cassie knew her heart was speeding and cursed her telltale cheeks. Benjamin's eyes had narrowed.

"For instance," Devon went on as if nothing had happened, "people are forever talking about the weather here in England. And rather dismal weather it generally is, too. However, I hear they predict lovely weather for later this afternoon. I have a new phaeton I'm longing to try out. Would you care to join me, Miss Bentbrooke?"

She stared at him. His smile was welcoming, his eyes

more green than gray as if the thought of being with her had warmed them. *How very delightful it would be,* she thought, *to ride about London in the company of this intelligent, handsome gentleman. What a shame I am not suicidal.*

"I'm sorry, my lord," she murmured. "I believe I have a previous engagement." She glanced quickly up at him and saw a look of disappointment cross his face.

"Oh, sister," Benjamin interrupted congenially. "I'm sure our aunt would not mind if you miss tea just this once. Cassie is so devoted to our family, my lord. She generally takes tea with our aunt Myrtle every Sunday afternoon, don't you dear?"

Cassie shot him a look of suspicion. They had no living aunt, and he knew she had little to do except observe the stars. Benjamin had made it quite clear that he did not want her to further her acquaintance with the marquis. That he encouraged her now could only mean he had some plot simmering.

"But she grows so petulant in her old age," she protested, glaring at him. "I fear she will never forgive me. I know I could never forgive myself."

"Nonsense," Benjamin replied, undertone strong as stone. "I shall explain it to her. Besides, you would not want the marquis to think we had taken offense after all, would you?"

Cassie clenched her teeth. *Willful child, willful adult,* she thought. Well, she was tired of his assumption that she was going to do his bidding in every little thing. She might have agreed not to hinder him, against her better judgment and for Liza's sake, but she had not agreed to embroil the marquis in some unknown plan of her brother's. Besides, the marquis's innuendoes implied that he had heard the gossip. Surely he would not want to fan the fires of scandal, particularly with so unlikely a tool as the ever logical Cassiopeia Bentbrooke. And she did not want to spend any more time fighting with him about her father's journals.

"Please, Miss Bentbrooke," Devon put in with an eagerness that cut through all her arguments. "I would like the opportunity to show you I can behave like a gentleman."

Cassie glanced at each of them. Neither was in his right mind, she was sure. The drive would only serve to further the scandal. It would do her reputation no good. It would make the marquis a laughingstock. It could very well endanger Benjamin's plan.

It would give her over an hour alone with the most dashing gentleman it had ever been her privilege to know.

She smiled at them both. "Thank you, Monsieur le Marquis. I would be delighted to join you. Say, four this afternoon?"

Twelve

Both Benjamin and Liza lectured her on her behavior before the drive. The speech by her brother was much as she had expected. He started by bullying her, pacing about the sewing room, where she had retreated for some much-needed time to think. She finally got him to admit he had a reason to allow her to go.

"I know you are not at your best in society," he said, "but try just this once to show your charm. Get him to talk about himself. I want to know why he is in London and why he is interested in us."

Cassie raised an eyebrow. "Us? I thought you were sure he was after my virtue."

"You couldn't possibly interest him," Benjamin replied with an airy wave of his hand that sent her spirits crashing. "And I see no reason for him to want to pursue my acquaintance. My guess is that he asked you on this drive to learn more about us. Tell him nothing. Learn all you can."

"If you're so intent on investigating his affairs," she challenged, stung by his assessment, "you go driving with him."

"I have to pay a call on Miss Compton. But I expect a report from you when you return."

"You may expect what you like," Cassie replied with a toss of her head. "I never agreed to be your spy. You will have to be content with me going."

Benjamin scowled and opened his mouth for what she

was sure would be a stinging rejoinder. At that moment, Liza entered.

Seeing Benjamin, she dropped a deep curtsy. "Oh, Major Bentbrooke, I didn't know you were here."

"My brother was just leaving," Cassie told her, although the determination in Benjamin's eyes let her know the conversation was far from over.

"Please don't go on my account," Liza protested. "I was just bringing up some messages." She held out a pile of envelopes and cards eagerly. "Cassie, did you see how many invitations we received? The party was clearly a success!"

Benjamin leaned over to view the collection in her hands. "We *have* developed a following. Did you look at them?"

"Only a little," Liza confessed, eyes shining. "See, here's one from the Trolbys. They asked after me, you will notice. May I go too? It's only a tea. And one from Lord and Lady Hensley—it's a garden party. And one from Mr. Crubb, although that is only for the major. There must be dozens!"

Cassie rose and took them from her ward. In reality, there were only ten, although Cassie still marveled at the number. The people at the party last night must have rushed home, penned the invitations, and had them hand-delivered. All, with the exception of the one from the eccentric Mr. Crubb, invited Benjamin and his sister to some sort of gathering within the next fortnight. The positive response to her brother was irrefutable. She wasn't sure whether to be pleased or depressed.

Benjamin smiled at Liza indulgently, patently ignoring the dark looks Cassie cast him and strolling to seat himself on the window bench she had vacated. He engaged Liza in a spirited debate over which invitations he should accept. Cassie gritted her teeth at his high-handedness.

"And there are several others here that would help you meet Miss Compton more often," Liza concluded. She paused, face almost wistful. "That is your intent, isn't it, Major?"

He rose, looking bored. "Of course. She is my delight, and I will not rest until I have won her fair hand. Thank you for the advice, my dear. I promise you I will consider it closely before making a decision." He nodded to Cassie. "And I hope you will heed my advice as well, dear sister."

"I always heed *good* advice, dear brother," Cassie assured him with a bright smile. He nodded again and quit the room.

"He only has your best interests at heart," Liza assured her. "I heard the servants talking, before they left for their afternoon off, that the marquis was to take you driving. I told you he wasn't only misdirected! Perhaps we will have two Bentbrookes courting." She sighed suddenly. "Though I cannot understand why Miss Compton should take so long. Is she heartless?"

If she isn't, she'll soon wish she were, Cassie thought. "Miss Compton seems very nice. You must give her time. Benjamin has been courting her less than a week."

"If someone like the major were courting me," Liza declared, "I wouldn't make him wait so much as a day!"

"Things are seldom as simple as that, Liza," Cassie replied with a sigh. "Deciding to spend your life with a man is too important to leave to a whim."

"Love is hardly a whim!" Liza cried. "Love is like being offered a rare and beautiful treasure! Turning it down is unthinkable!"

"Then I hope you are never in the position to turn it down," Cassie said with a smile. "For now, do not hold out too many hopes for this drive."

Liza returned her smile. "Well, of course not. It is only a drive, after all."

Cassie found herself repeating those words as she chose another of her black dresses and a black satin pelisse and waited for the marquis to return. She kept repeating them silently as he led her out to where a high-perch phaeton stood ready. The tall, elegant carriage was lacquered a shiny black, with red stripes outlining the brass-bound wheels and ornaments. A lanky groom in black-and-red livery lowered a step for her to mount, his straw-colored hair blowing in the breeze. She glanced to where the perfectly matched pair of blacks muttered in their red leather harness. Even the marquis was dressed in a coat of black, with black trousers disappearing into boots as shiny as his carriage. Catching his gaze on her, she raised an eyebrow.

"Do you always travel in such style, my lord?"

To her surprise, he lowered his gaze sheepishly. "The English thrive on scandals. It would not do to disappoint."

At least she was dressed appropriately, she thought as she accepted his arm to climb up into the black leather seats. The muscles under the fine black wool could have thrown her for yards, she was sure, or held her through the night. As her face flamed at the thought, he jumped up beside her. The groomsman waited at the curb, and they set off at a sharp pace toward Hyde Park.

They had not gone a block before Cassie noticed that people were staring. Groomsmen standing by waiting horses turned their heads as they passed. Ladies trailed by footmen began talking behind gloved hands. Gentlemen on horseback reined in their mounts. She tried to convince herself that it was the elegant carriage and horses, but she felt her cheeks heating.

"It appears the gossips were right," Devon murmured beside her. When she smothered a gasp, he grinned. "The weather, Miss Bentbrooke, is lovely today. Is it not?"

"Lovely," Cassie managed with a tight smile.

Clucking to the horses and chuckling to himself, the marquis de Renard drove them into the park.

"Did I understand you are new to London, Miss Bentbrooke?" he inquired politely as he slowed the horses to a leisurely trot. "I received the impression that this is the first time you've seen the park." His long-fingered hands held the reins lightly, but she had a feeling it would take little effort to handle his team. She saw him again standing behind a ship's wheel, gripping it, turning it to his will. She could imagine those same hands caressing her shoulders. She swallowed.

"What did you say?" she managed.

"The park, Miss Bentbrooke. Is this your first time?"

"No," Cassie replied, thankful to return to safer topics. "But I come here infrequently even though I was born and raised in London."

"Ah, then you haven't seen much of England?"

Cassie made a face. "I have never been farther away than Brighton. We had a summer cottage there for many years, until my father died."

"So your father did all his work in London."

The question was polite, but it led them closer to the subject of the journals. She veered away. "And your work? I thought you were interested in the stars as well."

"Oh, the stars and I are old friends. They have seen me safely through many a voyage."

She could not help being disappointed. So, he *had* lied about being an astronomer. "You navigate by them, I suppose."

"But of course. I believe you knew I am a sea captain."

She frowned. "A privateer, you mean? Then why pursue an interest in astronomy?"

"Must we speak of that?" he asked, gazing out over the heads of his horses. "The park is lovely, and a lovelier woman is at my side. Surely we can find something better to discuss."

He was probably right, if she had been a socially astute woman like her mother. If Cassie could not talk about astronomy, she wasn't sure what to say. She refused to spy for Benjamin, but perhaps getting the marquis to do most of the talking wasn't such a bad idea. "Very well," she said. "What would you like to discuss? Your naval career? Is that how you made your fortune?"

"My cousin's fortune," he corrected her. "My family fortune was lost during the Terror."

She eyed his well-cut coat. "You don't seem to be doing too badly. If you have enough to eat and can still afford a carriage and horses such as these, you are wealthy indeed."

He raised a brow. "And what would a Bentbrooke know of starvation?"

She smiled grimly, gazing at the trees they passed. "Far more than you would think, Monsieur le Marquis."

"English customs frequently amaze me. Is it not customary for a brother to support an orphaned sister until she weds?"

"Most assuredly." She was surprised that she could say the words with only a trace of bitterness.

"Then why," he asked with exaggerated innocence, "should you starve? Are you not wealthy?"

The trap had been sprung. She cursed her social ineptitude for not seeing it being laid. Her mind whirled through possible explanations. She could not tell him she was suddenly rich—she knew that for a lie. Could she admit she had no money of her own and was forced to accept Benjamin's sordid handouts? Her pride forbade it. She could hardly confess the burden she carried in Benjamin's wicked plan. Yet she hated not being able to be truthful with him. It was almost as if a bond was forming between them, a bond she could not further without risking that she and Liza would be thrust back into poverty or worse.

She could feel him watching her. "Well," she said, "wealth is a relative concept. I seem to have developed a headache. Would you take me home?"

He obligingly urged the horses toward the nearest gate. "Of course. But why do I have the feeling you are running away?"

Cassie raised her head. "Will you badger me?"

"Must I badger you? It is unlike you to dance around my questions."

"It is unlike anyone to doubt my answers," she countered.

"Have I done something that would make you think me a liar?"

"Come, Miss Bentbrooke," he replied with a smile. "After last night you cannot expect to be treated like an innocent."

She choked on her building frustration. "Last night? Are you so arrogant that you think one kiss in the dark makes me your slave? Let me depress your notions of godhood, my lord. Your kiss is not that remarkable."

"Ah, and I had so hoped to shine above your other beaux."

"I have no other beaux," she informed him.

"Then the English are as blind as I have always thought. Only your servants seem blessed with any intelligence."

He was playing with words again; even in her anger she recognized it. "Do you refer to that story about us? Are you mad? Do I look even remotely capable of intrigue?"

He grinned at her, green flecks dancing in his eyes. "Somehow, telling you no seems more dangerous than telling you yes. Let us simply agree that your behavior so far has piqued my interest."

Cassie sighed, suddenly defeated. "Lord Renard, please believe me when I say that attracting your interest has been the most amazing thing in all my staid little life. But I cannot keep that interest under false pretenses. I am no adventuress. I am simply an English gentlewoman who has had to rely on her own wits for too long. If you are searching for intrigue, you must look elsewhere."

"Once again, you seek to warn me away, my dear." His regretful sigh sounded insincere. "I am not so easily pulled from my course. What I set my sights on, I generally reach."

"Of that I have no doubt. I merely wish to point out that you are not seeing what you thought. You may have set your sights on a wildcat, my lord, but if you persist on your course you will find you have bagged an English tabby."

He chuckled as he drew up beside the Bentbrooke town

house and his waiting groomsman. "Then at least allow me to escort you in, my lovely kitten."

She blushed as he jumped from the seat and came around to hand her down. His grip on her was firm and confident, but she felt a shiver of pleasure run through her when his other arm encircled her waist. For just a moment, she stood in his embrace. For just a moment, she contemplated staying there. Then, arm warmly tucked in his, she let him lead her up the steps. What had she accomplished with this drive? She hadn't become the spy Benjamin wanted, for which she was thankful, but the handsome man beside her was still an enigma. Would he ask to call again? Her heart beat faster in hope.

To her surprise, Pierson did not whisk open the door as they drew close, forcing her to knock at her own house. Even as she did so, she remembered the butler mentioning that the servants had Sunday afternoon off. With an embarrassed smile, she explained the situation to Devon and pressed on the latch. The door refused to open.

"Allow me," he said with a chuckle, only to frown as the door did not budge. Cheeks heating, Cassie rapped the brass ring harder. The sound echoed inside. No one came. Neighbors returning from a walk in the park eyed her as they strolled past. Devon tipped his hat. They whispered to each other. From the curb, the groomsman frowned.

This would not do. He would think her a ninnyhammer! She fumbled in her reticule for a key and tried it in the lock. It no longer fit. The lock had been changed.

Unease curled around her, threatening to tighten into panic. "Excuse me," she murmured to Devon before raising her voice. "Liza! Open the door!"

Somewhere off the entry a door slammed.

Devon caught her arm. "Something's wrong."

The hairs at the back of her neck stood up. "I have a key to the back door as well. It may still work. Follow me."

Thirteen

Alert for trouble, Devon followed her down the steps. He paused only a moment with Thomas, who had been playing groom.

"What is it, Captain?" his second mate murmured, blue eyes bright. "I watched the square like you asked. Nothing's happened."

"Watch the door," Devon commanded. "If anyone comes out, delay them."

Thomas nodded. Devon could only hope that Bertrand, at the back, knew what was happening inside. The locked door and noise might mean nothing, or they might mean someone else looked for the clue to the treasure. He hurried after Cassie.

The English habit of building in terraces only prolonged their walk, giving his tension too much time to grow. He could feel it growing in the woman beside him as well. Cassie's steps were hurried and her slender shoulders tense under the black pelisse. It took them minutes to reach the back of the house. He glanced about the alley that led to the rear yards and mews but caught no sign of Bertrand. Frustrated, he followed Cassie to the kitchen door. It swung open at her touch.

The easy entry when the house was supposedly empty only confirmed his fears. He pulled her back. "Stay close to me. We don't know what we'll find." He expected her to argue, but she bit her lip, nodding, and scurried behind him. She followed so closely, in fact, that as he moved into the kitchen he could feel her skirts brushing his legs.

The room was unoccupied. Crockery stood ready on the oak table in the center of the room, as if awaiting the return of the kitchen staff. Most likely he and Cassie were alone in the house, any intruders having had ample time to escape, but he couldn't take that chance.

Three doors stood at intervals along the wall to his left. "Where do they lead?" he asked, pointing.

"Two lead to the butler's room and the pantry," she murmured. "The second one from the window is the servants' stair to the upper floors. Shall I check the others while you go up?"

Tempting, but he didn't like having her out of his sight. He was never sure of her reactions—the English tabby one moment and the wildcat the next. "Better that we stay together," he replied. Deciding that any intruder would prefer to be on the main floor, where there was more avenue for escape, he moved around the table and eased open the door to the stairs. Steps led upward, dimly lit from the floor above. He climbed carefully, hugging the wall, where there was less likely to be squeaky boards. She followed his lead—by instinct or practice, he wasn't sure. At the next landing, he paused at the door to listen. He could feel her tense behind him. He turned the handle slowly and peered out. The passage before him yawned empty as well. The next door, he knew, led to the library.

He felt her tremble as he approached the open door. Peering inside, he caught his breath. She saw the devastation at the same time, shoving past him even as he tried to hold her back.

The cozy room from the night before was in shambles. Not a book remained on the shelves; they lay spine-up in haphazard piles about the room, as if flung away in disgust. Satin that had been hung on the single wall without bookcases had been torn down, showing discolored plaster underneath. A painting that had hung over the mantel lay twisted on the floor.

"Oh, no!" she cried, throwing herself to her knees beside it. The painting had been flung over the brass andirons, the point piercing the canvas. Carefully, she lifted it free, turning it over. The auburn-haired woman in the painting sat with back straight, gloved hands folded calmly in her lap, almond-shaped eyes staring off as if nothing in the world could possibly be significant enough to ruffle her poise. The metal had cut through the woman's heart. Cassie swallowed, running her fingers over the painted cheek. "This is my mother."

Would he have been that calm, Devon wondered, had he seen what they had done to the Renard estate during the Terror? "Steel yourself," he murmured gently. "It is worse."

"What could be worse than this?" she challenged, turning. He nodded toward the space behind her. Glass glittered on the floor from the broken fronts of the empty bookcases.

She rose, paling, and he reached out to catch her. She swept his arm aside, stumbling to the shelves. "My father's journals!" She glanced wildly about the room, scrambling from pile to pile, tossing books about. The empty shelves mocked her. He could feel her pain. Anger rose inside him at the injustice.

She stopped, letting her hands fall to her sides. "Why?" she breathed, blinking away tears. "Why would anyone want old scientific journals?"

"Perhaps they thought they could sell the books to a collector," he answered, knowing even as he did so that he was lying. Someone else knew about the treasure, and they had found the clue first. All that remained was to see whether he could still somehow wrest back the jewels. He needed time to think. "Would you like to stay here while I check the other rooms?"

Cassie gazed at him dazedly. "I . . . I don't know. Give me

a moment." She glanced again at the empty shelves. The loss of the journals hurt her as much as it did him, if for another reason. He had to stop himself from taking her in his arms. Now was not the time for comfort. Now was the time to act.

She seemed to sense it as well. She closed her eyes and took a deep breath. "We should check the other rooms. They may have stolen something else."

He could tell she hardly cared. He held out a hand as she opened her eyes and crunched gingerly through the glass, helping her the last distance. She didn't even look at him.

Furniture had been tossed about in the sitting room, as if the thieves were searching for hidden valuables. *Did they think the treasure was hidden in the house itself, then?* he wondered as they continued on to the dining room. Had the Bentbrookes a greater involvement with his uncle than he had thought? Had his uncle perhaps lived here at one time?

The dining room appeared to be untouched, though the door to the sideboard stood open, showing the glint of bone china, ghostly in the half-light from the door. Devon followed her in as she peered into the open drawers. "The spoons are missing from Mother's silver."

"The thieves got this far and were interrupted," he guessed.

From the hall, a voice echoed. "Pierson? Cassie? Liza? Where is everyone? Bloody hell!"

"Benjamin," Cassie confirmed. She hurried out the door, nearly colliding with her brother. Devon silently closed the drawers on the sideboard, listening to their conversation. How would the fine major deal with being robbed?

"Cassie, what is the meaning of this?" Benjamin demanded. "The sitting room is a shambles."

"The library is worse," she explained with a presence of mind that Devon could only admire. "We have yet to check the upstairs or the kitchen. And I don't know where Liza is."

"I sent her to look at materials in the shop windows. The clothes she wears are atrocious. What is he doing here?"

Devon stepped to Cassie's side, offering Bentbrooke the shortest of bows. "If I may be of service, Major. I was returning your sister home when we found this. She would not listen to me to remain outdoors while I surveyed the damage. Perhaps if you stayed with her, I can continue the search."

He did not expect the man to agree. He was right. "Very kind of you," Benjamin all but sneered. "Unfortunately, there seems little point. Surely the miscreants have fled with whatever they could carry."

"Father's journals," Cassie said quietly.

"Don't be ridiculous," Benjamin snapped. "Who'd want a pile of moldy old books? More likely they've cotched Mother's pearls and the silver."

"I don't know about the pearls, of course," Devon replied, watching him, "but all that was taken from the silver was a few spoons."

Benjamin frowned. "You mean they really *did* steal Father's journals?"

Cassie started suddenly, turning to face Devon, wide eyed. The silver of her eyes glinted with cold fire. "You!"

Devon did not allow himself to flinch. "Miss Bentbrooke, are you all right?" he asked with a frown. Benjamin eyed him.

"I told you how important those journals are to me," she stormed. "You didn't have the courage to steal them while I watched, so you concocted that ridiculous story about wanting to take me for a drive to steal them!"

"I assure you, Miss Bentbrooke, I had no part in this," he replied gravely, stung that she would think him a coward, and a vandal at that. "I deplore senseless acts of violence. My father died that way. Whoever did this was no better than an animal."

"An animal who reads," Benjamin quipped.

Cassie shook her head. "Whether they read or not is immaterial. My father and I wrote in our own code. The journals are useless to anyone but me. Once the thieves learn that, they will destroy the books. All my father's work, everything he and Mr. Kearney hoped to achieve, lost!"

Devon started. "Mr. Kearney?" he asked casually.

"My father's assistant," Benjamin supplied.

Devon did not trust the man to volunteer information. By the way Cassie glanced at him, she had the same suspicions. "Perhaps this Mr. Kearney might help you to re-create the information," Devon suggested, waiting for the response.

It came shortly and disappointed him. "He is dead," she replied. "Killed in a carriage accident years ago. And while I could re-create the most general of conclusions, I could never remember all their day-to-day observations that prove those conclusions valid. No, without the journals, my father's life and all my own work have come to naught."

Benjamin shook his head. "Well, the stars are still there. I daresay some enterprising chap will eventually rediscover what Father and Kearney learned. So all is not lost. I'm just thankful nothing more important was taken."

"Benjamin," Cassie said quietly, "you are an idiot."

"Now, now, sister," Benjamin replied calmly. "You are obviously overwrought. Lord Renard, thank you for seeing my sister safely home and through this unpleasantness. I beg your pardon for cutting short your visit, but you must see that she is done in."

Devon knew he was being dismissed. It did not disturb him. He had learned a great deal. And he might be able to learn more. "Of course," he said with a bow. "I quite understand. If you need more servants to help clean, I would be happy to send mine."

"Very kind, but not necessary," Benjamin replied, ushering him toward the door. "With the afternoon off, our servants should be well rested. Thank you again for your help."

"Would you like me to inform Bow Street?" Devon offered as he stepped out the door.

"No, no. No need to summon the magistrates. I will make a full report once I know for certain that the books and the silver were the only things stolen. Good day, my lord."

Cassie eyed her brother as he shut the door soundly. Her nerves were raw from the loss of the journals, but her reasoning had not gone begging. Before she could voice her growing suspicions, Benjamin turned to her, face stern.

"Out with it. You suspect the marquis had a hand in this. Why?"

Cassie crossed her arms over her chest. "Let me get my facts straight first, Benjamin. You changed the locks on the door without telling me, you decided which day the servants would have off, you insisted I drive with the marquis, and you sent Liza shopping when all the stores are closed on Sunday. In short, it was your idea to leave the house empty. And you refused to send for the Bow Street Runners just now. What game are you playing?"

"You are aware of all my plans. I would hardly seek to damage what cost me a pretty penny to begin with."

"Oh!" Cassie cried, realizing just how much of a setback the damage had done to her brother's attempt to refurbish the house. He had spent his commission money and his real inheritance on those rooms. It did seem unlikely that he had been involved in the robbery. Yet she could not shake the feeling that he knew more than he admitted.

"Oh, indeed," he continued. "I can hardly afford to refurbish the rooms again. We will set up the sitting room with the furniture that wasn't damaged and keep guests from the library. As this event will no doubt be spread as rumor, you will be seen shopping in the finest stores for replacements."

"Can you afford that?" Cassie asked with a frown.

"I said shopping, not buying. You will claim that nothing suits your fancy. Once I have won Barbara's hand, you may choose whatever you like."

"I will live quietly," Cassie insisted. "I want no part of your blood money, Benjamin."

"Hardly blood money," Benjamin countered. "I'm the one giving away a chance at a better future. Miss Compton should count herself lucky to catch the esteemed Major Bentbrooke."

"You are the most arrogant—" Cassie began heatedly, but Benjamin held up his hand.

"Can we forgo the tirade? Tell me what you learned about the marquis. Do you suspect him of staging this robbery?"

"No, Benjamin." She stalked past him for the stair. "I no longer suspect Lord Renard. If you must know, I suspect you. And if I ever prove my suspicions true, you had better watch your back, dear brother."

Fourteen

"What happened?" Thomas asked as his master stepped slowly down to the curb. "You were in there long enough. No one came this way until that cocky nob showed up."

Devon's jaw was tight, his eyes unseeing on the street. "Take the carriage to the house. I must find Bertrand."

Thomas frowned. "Aye, aye, Captain. But what is it? You look as if you've taken a ball across the bow."

"Assemble as many of the crew as you can find quickly. We have at least a dozen in London, don't we?"

"Aye. Is this it, then? You know where the treasure is?"

Devon shook his head. "Just be ready." He strode past the carriage and down the block.

The walk seemed even longer this time. Why hadn't he thought someone else might seek the treasure? Three families had joined with the Renards, trusting his family to convert their wealth to gemstones to escape the Terror. His uncle was to carry the jewels to England and appeal to Devon's English relatives for assistance. But even a brief acquaintance with the duke of Devonlee, then newly appointed to his position, had convinced Jean-Luc Sebastien the jewels were safer with him. He had left for London before the duke could discover him. Or so Devon had thought.

Could the duke know of the treasure? The man was cold and cunning, but he had never given Devon any reason to believe he knew that a fortune in jewels was missing. That only left the families and their descendants. As far as he had been able to learn, the Debusses had been martyred to Madame Guillotine. Bertrand was all that remained of the Travalliers. Henri had had an older brother, but no one knew his fate. Surely he could not have learned more than Devon. And Devon was all that remained of the House of Renard.

Unless his uncle still lived. But if he lived, he'd know what had happened to the treasure. He'd have no need to steal the journals. So was their theft mere coincidence?

He had reached no answer when he came up the narrow alley a second time. Bertrand was still not in evidence. He checked to make sure the Bentbrooke groomsman and coachman were busy in the carriage house, then sidled along the wall to where it ended in the little gated garden. Seeing no sign of Bertrand, he dared a sharp whistle. The whinny of horses in the stables was his only answer. He was about to move on when he saw the lithe figure of his purser dashing toward him. A slight Frenchman with dark-brown hair and moustache, and a mincing walk that tended to earn him the jeers of his fellow sailors, he could climb the rigging and be back to the deck in the time it took the others to reach the first rung.

"Two of them," he panted as he drew abreast of Devon. "Clumsy fools with no more brains than a seagull. I do not know what they took, but they carried it away in a cloth bag that jingled, and they headed toward the wharves. They spoke of wine and tavern women."

Devon let out a breath. Grinning, he clapped Bertrand on the shoulder. "Good work. I seem to have developed a powerful thirst. Let us go visit some taverns."

"But can we find them?" Bertrand asked with a frown.

"If we cannot," Devon replied, "I may have to ask my cousin for yet another favor."

* * *

"What do you mean, they were robbed?" the duke asked quietly. "Are you saying my agent was doing his job for once, or are you saying someone else beat us to the treasure?"

Ames choked to keep the nervous giggle from escaping. "Neither, actually, Your Grace. Your agent was attempting to keep Captain Sebastien under watch. In the meantime, the house was robbed."

The duke narrowed his eyes. "And you are certain my cousin was not behind it?"

"Reasonably so," Ames allowed. When the duke frowned, he hurried on. "That is, I'm fairly certain. Your agent was watching from the park, and he relays that Captain Sebastien looked quite shaken when he left the house."

"Where is he now?"

Before Ames could answer, a footman appeared at the door. Ames hurried to intercept him, keeping his conversation hushed. He snatched the note from the man's hand and scurried back to the duke. Swallowing, he held out the sealed note with a trembling hand.

"From Captain Sebastien," he managed.

"Well," the duke snapped, "read it!"

Ames jumped, then fumbled to break the seal. Scanning the words, he slumped in relief. "He has not found the treasure. In fact, he asks for your assistance."

"In catching the thieves?" the duke guessed.

"No," Ames replied with a frown. "In placing an ad to appear in the morning paper."

Cassie had time the rest of the afternoon and evening to ponder her suspicions as she and Liza helped the returning servants to put the house to rights and Cassie paid the servants for their first week of work. As the marquis had foretold, nothing else proved missing. She almost wished something had been stolen. She could then perhaps convince herself that her brother had arranged the theft to gain additional funds. Unfortunately, try as she might, she could see no way for her brother to profit from the robbery.

But no more could she convince herself that the thief was connected to Devon Sebastien. Even though she had been out with him, and Benjamin had lied about an appointment with a fictitious aunt, the marquis could not have known the servants would be out. She was not sure what he knew about Liza, either. In her anger, she had wronged him. But where did that leave her father's journals?

She still had her latest journal in her room, but she could not bring herself to study the stars that night, knowing the larger work might be lost to her. She slept fitfully and awoke early the next morning to wander to the breakfast table. Her brother was just finishing, and Liza wasn't up yet. Cassie had glanced in her mirror long enough to know that there were dark circles around her eyes and her color was wanting. Benjamin, on the other hand, was his usual dapper self. He patted her head as he passed, causing a few more tendrils to escape from her coil of hair, and pointed at the *Morning Post* still on the damask tablecloth.

"I ride with Barbara Compton," he announced. "Check for rumors in the society portion of the paper, will you? I shall be back later."

Cassie grimaced as he exited. The chocolate Pierson handed her tasted bitter, but somehow she didn't think it was the brew. Reluctantly she pulled the paper to her and began a slow perusal of its contents. Her spirits lifted when she found no obvious mention of either the marquis de Renard or the robbery. She was about to put the paper down in relief when she noticed an advertisement, prominently displayed on the front page.

WANTED, old journals, papers, and diaries, the more obscure the better. Gold paid for the right artifacts. Inquire at 2312 St. Martin's Lane, Marylebone.

She frowned, letting the paper fall to the table. How long had this ad been running? She didn't remember seeing it before, but then she had never really looked. What if it had been running in the past and the thieves had stolen her father's journals in response? Surely the collector who lived on St. Martin's Lane would not want the journals if they were stolen. Or perhaps he could be persuaded to part with them so long as he earned a profit. Even a collector would balk at journals he could never read. Perhaps she had a chance to regain them if she acted quickly.

Snatching a muffin from the sideboard, she scurried past a startled Pierson. Liza met her in the corridor and followed her back to her room. "Where are you going now?" her ward complained. "You said we would spend the day together. You never told me how your drive went."

"It was lovely," Cassie replied, rummaging through her wardrobe. "And we will spend time together, love, only not this morning. I may know how to retrieve our father's journals."

Liza clapped her hands. "Oh, Cassie, how marvelous!"

With a cry of triumph, Cassie pulled her old black bombazine from the back of the closet, together with a rumpled cap. Liza's eyes widened.

"The servant game?" she whispered, as if realizing how Benjamin might react. She tiptoed closer. "Surely we have a footman who can escort us now. Why must you go in disguise?"

Cassie hesitated. She had tried so hard to shield Liza from her brother's degenerate side that she could hardly confide her concerns that her brother was somehow involved in the theft of the journals.

"We do not know who has the journals," she said truthfully. "I am loath to reveal my identity until I know it is safe to do so. If the thieves know who they robbed and they were to catch sight of me or Benjamin, I don't know what they might do. I cannot chance that they will destroy the journals. Do you understand?"

Liza nodded. "Only let me come with you."

Cassie shook her head. "It might be dangerous. As we did when I checked on the marquis, you must send for aid if you suspect I'm in danger. If I haven't returned by dinner, give Benjamin this." She wrote the address on a piece of paper on her writing table.

"What am I to do if he asks for you in the meantime?" her ward asked, eyes wide.

"Tell him I am out shopping for furnishings, as he requested. Oh, and tell him there was nothing of interest in the paper." She silently prayed he would not notice the advertisement or, if he did, connect it with their father's journals.

The plan decided, Liza helped her into the maid's costume. Then they slipped down the back stairs and through the house, knowing the front rooms had less staff than the kitchen. Liza lured the footman from the front door, and Cassie found herself on the street.

She loosened the strings on her reticule enough to pull out fare to hire a hack. At least the money Benjamin had given her for clothes shopping would go to a good cause in this instance. Head respectfully bowed, she hurried around the corner and out of the square. A short walk led her to a waiting carriage for hire.

"Yer mistress need a coach, luvie?" The hackman grinned down at her, showing wide-spaced brown teeth. He appeared to be only a little older than she was, but his face was weathered in wrinkles.

"Her ladyship asked me to go on an errand that's too far to walk. I have a quid for you to take me to 2312 St. Martin's Lane, wait while I run my errand, and return me to this spot. Are you interested?"

His grin widened. "I'm always interested, luvie. And you can keep part of that money for some friendly company." He winked at her.

Cassie felt herself blushing and ducked her head to keep him from seeing it. "My mistress would beat me if she knew. Another time, perhaps." She clambered into the coach before he could say more.

She wasn't sure what she expected of St. Martin's Lane but was nonetheless relieved to find it just outside the edges of Mayfair, on a street as shabbily genteel as her own. In fact, it was so close that she indeed could have walked had she but known the direction. The house was from an earlier time, before terraces. It stood a little back from the street, with an overgrown garden in front. The white shutters on the multipaned windows needed painting, and the gate on the fence hung crooked. A dapper little man with a bottle-green coat was just taking down a "For Rent" sign from the wrought-iron fence as she alighted.

Seizing her chance, she hurried forward and dropped a deep curtsy. "Pardon me, sir, but my mistress would be most grateful if you could tell me who took this house."

The little man turned, revealing pudgy cheeks and a button nose. He looked her up and down, and she nervously curtsied again.

"Now, now, my girl," he boomed. "No need to quiver. I won't eat you, not unless you ask very prettily." His laughter echoed across the square, and the hackman joined in. Cassie kept her eyes demurely lowered. To her dismay, the solicitor chucked her under the chin with a pudgy finger.

"Here now, girl, cat got your tongue? Give us a kiss and we'll soon find out."

Not another one, Cassie thought. She had never had problems before—now two in one day! What, were all the men of London suddenly desperate for females? She managed what she hoped was a convincing sniff. "Lord bless you, sir, but please don't delay me. My mistress can be awful cruel."

"Beats her, she does," the hackman put in helpfully.

"Well, we can't have that," the solicitor replied goodnaturedly. "Tell your mistress that she need have no worries as to who is joining her fair neighborhood. The gentleman is a nob, for all he's a Frenchie."

Cassie raised her head to stare at him. "A Frenchie?"

"Oh, and half-English too, if what the gossips say is true. Yes, my girl, this house has been taken by none other than the marquis de Renard."

Fifteen

Cassie peered around an overgrown mulberry to eye the front walk of 2312 St. Martin's Lane. She could have sworn she had heard footsteps. With a sigh, she realized it was only a girl-of-all-work across the street, returning from some errand. She sank back behind the shrubbery screen.

She wasn't sure how long she had stood there, body pressed against the cold brick of the house. It must have been at least two hours since she had dismissed the hack with the excuse that her errand would take longer than she had thought. It was only the truth. Once she had learned that it was the marquis who had advertised for journals, she knew she had no choice but to stay as long as she dared in hopes of learning more. She had therefore slipped through the small front garden and slid between the house and the mulberry, dislodging a family of pill bugs and several large spiders in the process.

She wasn't sure what she would learn. If he had rented the house only recently, perhaps the ad had been placed by the previous owner. The coincidence of the theft and the ad seemed to make that unlikely. If only he were innocent! Perhaps he was attempting to find the journals as a favor to the Bentbrookes, but she did not see why he wouldn't tell them if that were so. Try as she might, however, she could think of no other logical reason for him to want to retrieve the journals. Her mind conjured up theories as far-fetched as his being some sort of library militiaman, rescuing antiques from the hands of vandals and punishing the perpetrators. Or perhaps her father's astronomy texts held some hidden meaning for Napoleon. Wasn't it said he used the stars to tell his fortune? She shook her head—she sounded as fanciful as Liza! All she could do was watch and wait. Much as she hated to admit it, she was becoming the spy her brother had commanded.

A shuffling heralded the arrival of two heavy men in burlap coats. Both men had battered noses and missing teeth. Neither was very clean; their coats were dusty and their trousers caked with grime. The shorter of the two hugged a canvas bag to his side. Muttering to themselves and glancing about, they shambled up the walk to knock at the door. She ducked behind the bush to prevent being seen.

She couldn't understand what the men mumbled, but she heard a light voice with a heavy French accent respond. "*Mais oui*, gentlemen, you have come to the correct address. Follow me." The door snapped shut.

She eyed the house, looking for some way she could enter unseen. All the windows on the first floor were above her head. Those on the ground floor were barred and curtained. She could neither get in nor see in. And she could hardly knock at the front door and expect to be admitted. She considered going to the back door and talking to the servants but could think of no plausible excuse for them to let in a strange maid. Shaking her head in frustration, she settled back to wait once more.

Some time later the door opened to let the two men out. Their steps seemed lighter than when they had entered, and when the taller of the two glanced at the shorter, there was a pleased grin on his homely face. Drat the marquis! Their pleasure could only mean that he had paid them, which meant he might even now be in possession of her father's journals.

She debated following the two men and trying for confirmation, but they seemed such hard types that she didn't like to think how they might treat a young lady in a maid's costume. She briefly considered returning home and enlisting Benjamin's aid, but somehow she didn't think he'd be too pleased with how she had gotten the information in the first place. Before she could decide on a course of action, she was seized from behind and jerked around.

"Who are you?" Devon demanded. Then he started in obvious recognition. A grin spread on his handsome face. "My lady maid, has anyone ever told you, you bear a striking resemblance to Miss Cassiopeia Bentbrooke?"

"Oh, stop it," Cassie snapped, pulling out of his grip. She started to demand that he return the journals, but he held a finger to his lips and nodded toward the street, where her thieves were quickly disappearing from sight.

"Wait a moment," he whispered, "and I promise we will talk." He darted past her, but she caught his arm, determined not to let him escape. He spun back far more quickly than her touch warranted, and before she knew it, he had pulled her against the hard line of his body and kissed her. Emotions surged through her at the touch of his lips—elation, annoyance, longing, embarrassment. Before she could think clearly, he broke away, face drawn in a half smile. He saluted her, then turned to slip out of the garden in pursuit of the thieves.

She stared after him, absently rubbing her lips with the back of her hand. Whatever had made him do that? Was it possible he felt some sort of attraction to her after all? She shook herself. He had probably only kissed her to prevent her outcry. There was no reason for her heart to be beating so unreasonably fast. The real question was, why was he following the thieves if he already had the journals?

Before she could settle on an answer, he was back. "My man continues the chase," he said by way of explanation. "With any luck, we will learn who hired them."

"They didn't take the journals by accident, then?"

He shook his head, not bothering to deny that they had indeed taken the books. "Not if I understood their comments. I suspected as much from the way they vandalized your home. Thieves smart enough to recognize the value of the journals would be too smart to waste time in unproductive damage."

"But who would know about my father's journals?" she asked, thinking that she was probably speaking with the most likely suspect. Still, if he had hired them, he would have no need to follow them. He could hardly be doing it for show, as he obviously had had no idea she was watching. Besides, if he had hired them, there would have been no need to place the ad in the *Morning Post*.

He shook his head. "I have no idea. Have you had any interest in them lately?"

Cassie raised an eyebrow. "Aside from you, do you mean?"

"Yes," he said with a smile, "aside from me."

"The duke of Devonlee called the same day you did. But he hardly seems the type to steal."

"Oh, he might steal," Devon replied. Cassie looked him askance, and he shrugged. "He is my cousin. I suspect he came to help me." He cocked his dark head. "Did he ask for the journals specifically?"

"No. Only my father's effects. Of course, I refused."

He smiled. "I'd have liked to see that—the duke facing refusal. Any other interest?"

"Only an old colleague of my father's, but he has spoken of them many times before. He knows I would explain the conclusions if he were truly interested, so I cannot believe he would stoop to hiring thugs. Over the years, there have been other scientists who showed interest, but again, they had only to ask."

"A scientist does seem an unlikely thief. Perhaps my man will return with an answer. Until then, would you care to join me inside?"

"Inside?" Cassie gazed at the dark brick house. The

overgrown shrubbery and barred windows suddenly looked ominous. "I don't think that's necessary. If you would just return the journals to me."

He chuckled. "Miss Bentbrooke, you continue to try to play the English tabby. I am not fooled. A proper English tabby would never be caught spying."

"Well, if that isn't the pot calling the kettle black," Cassie exclaimed, but she felt a tug of a smile at the absurdity of the situation. "Surely you understand, Monsieur le Marquis, that lurking outside your house and venturing inside are two very different things."

He crossed his arms over his chest, half smile in evidence. "Do you tell me, Miss Bentbrooke, that the English would forgive you for dressing as a maid and crawling about in my bushes but hold you in contempt if you stepped inside to retrieve your own belongings?"

"But of course," Cassie answered with a grin. "The first makes me odd. I shall not comment on what the second makes me. I have made a life of being a *proper* oddity, Monsieur le Marquis. You must believe me in this area."

He shook his head. "Very well, then. Wait here. I will bring the journals to you."

He did just that a few minutes later. Cassie eagerly seized them, holding them so that she might thumb through the pages of the first.

"It is undamaged?" he asked, watching her.

"Yes," she replied, handing him the volume so she might check the second. Casually he opened the book and scanned the page. He frowned, looking closer.

"This is gibberish. It does not even appear to be English."

"It is notation," Cassie explained, confirming that the second volume was intact as well. "My father developed it to speed his documentation process. I know how to read it." She leaned over the page he had opened, and pointed to the first paragraph. "There, you see those numbers? They are the time and date of the observation.

Those that follow are the coordinates of the part of the sky my father was studying. They are keyed to a painted celestial map."

"Is it lost as well?" he queried, turning the pages.

"No," Cassie replied, bending to check the third volume. "It's hanging in my bedchamber."

"An interesting place for a map," Devon observed, face bland.

Cassie eyed him and decided to ignore the comment. "The rest is what he observed. Here, for example, it says 'Jupiter is arising six minutes sooner than predicted, confirming my theory that Copernicus' time keeping was slow.'"

"Or your father's watch was fast," he quipped.

"Perish the thought." Cassie laughed, closing the book and pulling it back into her arms. "Father left nothing to chance. Every clock in the house was set by the time of the Greenwich Observatory and checked on a weekly basis. He was very precise."

"A good trait for a scientist, I would imagine. Have you read all the journals, then?"

The question was casual, but she sensed an intensity behind it. She wasn't sure she wanted to let him know the extent of her knowledge regarding her father's work. He certainly didn't laugh at her as often as others did, but her astronomical work was too close to her heart. "I haven't thanked you for getting these back," she said instead. "It was very kind of you. What did you have to pay those men? I will have Benjamin reimburse you."

He laid his hand on the books. "There is no need. It was my pleasure to be of service. Besides, I do not think your brother would appreciate my assistance." His hand moved to caress her cheek. "Nor do I think you would care to admit how you came to retrieve them."

Cassie swallowed, telling herself her nervousness was from concern over Benjamin's reaction and not from Devon's touch. The butterflies dancing in her stomach had no doubt been awakened by the heat that spread from his caress. She could see the green deepening in his eyes as he watched her. She swallowed again. "But the cost, your time . . ."

"Let us say," he murmured, closing the distance between their lips, "that I expect to be richly rewarded for my troubles."

Cassie closed her eyes, willing him to kiss her again. When he did not, she snapped her eyes open. He was regarding her with a gentle smile.

"I ask only that you read them to me."

She stared at him. "Why? What possible interest could you have in astronomy?"

"I told you the stars and I are old friends. It amuses me to learn more about them. I am a student of science."

She peered closer. The green-gray eyes mirrored his innocent smile, but they were far from warm. A determination had settled there that chilled her.

"You could learn about the stars from any astronomy text," she told him, holding the books a little closer to her chest. "I doubt my father's sometimes cryptic remarks would be very helpful. Most of his observations are very boring."

The smile changed to a frown; his eyes became as cold as a winter sea. She backed away from him.

"Thank you again for rescuing the journals," she offered, moving around the shrub to the garden. "I would be happy to recommend a useful text to learn more about the stars."

"You refuse me, then?" he murmured, following her.

Somehow, the very act sounded heretical. He shared that with his cousin: most likely few people refused the marquis.

"I don't mean to offend," she replied as cheerily as she could. The gate bumped her backside and she fumbled behind her for the latch, balancing the ungainly volumes in her arms. "You have been very kind and gone to a great deal of trouble. But these books are very precious to me, and I don't feel comfortable passing them about with laymen. Unless you can give me a better reason, I fear I must insist on taking them home. Now."

Sixteen

Devon glared at her, frustrated on all sides. His forays into the taverns along the wharves had allowed him to identify the thieves but not capture them. As Bertrand had diagnosed, they were a pair of ex-fighters who would do anything for a pitifully small amount of money. When they did not appear in the evening as everyone predicted, he feared they had already met with whoever had hired them. He could only hope the ad his cousin had commissioned earlier would bear fruit. Unfortunately, the plan depended on one of the pair actually reading or having told someone who could read of their catch.

He had had several responses that morning, but none of the industrious thieves or desperate noblemen had the Bentbrooke journals. He had been sure he was too late when the two thugs had appeared. As important as getting the journals had been, it was just as important to learn who their sponsor was. With any luck, Bertrand would bring him news before the day was out.

But perhaps he had already found a spy. He watched the woman before him tremble, for all she smiled with determination. Innocent or cunning temptress, she baffled him. The quick kiss he had stolen was the least she should pay for being caught. Yet once again the surprise and sweetness of her face had been his undoing, and before he had thought better of it, he was handing over the hard-won journals.

And what was his reward? She clutched the books to her more closely than a maiden clings to her virtue. The location of the treasure could be revealed in that illegible notation. She was the only one who could decipher it for him.

He spread his hands and smiled amiably. She had enjoyed his kiss, or she would not have invited another. Perhaps he could use that to his advantage.

"My dear Miss Bentbrooke," he murmured soothingly, "I mean no harm. Perhaps you are right—other astronomy texts would be easier to read. But I would be forced to read them alone. These we could read together. Would that not be more enjoyable?"

She peered at him as if she thought him drunk or mad. "Enjoyable for whom?"

"Why, for us both." She was a slippery one. The moment he thought he understood her, she made some statement that changed his picture entirely. He took another step toward her. It was obviously too close. She succeeded in opening the gate, bolted through it, and slammed it shut, staring at him over the black bars.

"Why can't you just tell me the truth?" she demanded, and he was surprised to see what appeared to be tears behind her eyes. "My brother assures me that you cannot be interested in me. There is nothing enjoyable about being read incomprehensible text by someone you don't even like."

He shook his head. She was far too agitated for this to be some game. Much as he was annoyed with her at the moment, much as he wanted to get his hands back on those books, he wanted more to slap the fools who had put such nonsense in her head. Was everyone around her an idiot? Could they truly not see how attractive she was? He felt himself smile grimly as he considered that perhaps they had not seen her as he was seeing—head high, pale hair floating about her face like gossamer, silver eyes flashing brighter than lightning in the night sky.

"I am not lying when I profess to enjoy your company, *cherie*," he replied. "Will you not accept that?"

He could see the struggle in her. Her mouth twitched, and her fair brows drew together as she considered his request. "I'm sorry to doubt you, my lord," she said at last. "You will never know how sorry. My brother does not trust you, and while I frequently find myself in opposition to his opinions, I must agree with him in this case. You are not what you seem. I fear I must ask you not to call on us again. Good-bye."

"Wait!" He did not need to touch her. Years of training kept the authority in his voice. She stiffened as if against her will. Even as she resisted, he fought one last battle and lost.

"I must know what is in those journals," he confessed. "They may be the only clue as to what happened to my family."

She hesitated. "I was told your family was murdered during the Terror."

He nodded, swallowing the pain that always arose when he thought of his father and French grandmother. "Most were. My mother died much earlier. One escaped—an uncle. His name was Jean-Luc Sebastien."

"I have never heard of him," she replied quickly. "Why do you think my father's journals will help you find him?"

"He brought me to England when I was a boy, to be with my cousin the duke. Then, as now, England was at war with France. My uncle preferred the company of his countrymen. He left my cousin's estate for London, where he hoped to join other émigrés. I located a few elderly Frenchmen who claim he arrived. But of my uncle, I can find little other trace."

"But the journals," she prompted when he hesitated. "How do they come in?"

"At home, my uncle was an amateur astronomer. All the Sebastiens are sailors; he was a navigator who grew to want to know more of the stars. He even took his telescope when he left. I thought perhaps he had continued his studies in England. I appealed to your Mr. Pond, who found a mention of my uncle. It seems he coauthored a scientific paper with a noted British astronomer. Your father."

"What!" she cried, staggering back. "That's impossible! My father was very careful in his choice of collaborators. I knew every one of them—well. None went by that name."

"But that proves nothing," Devon pressed, sensing that his tale had weakened her resistance. "My uncle might have only met your father at night, and then rarely. It was a rather obscure paper. I believe Mr. Pond had to go to several gentlemen in the Royal Society before he could find one with a copy. One, Mr. Herbert Montague, refused to part with it."

She smiled knowingly. "He wouldn't. An avid historian is Mr. Montague. He is the one who urged me to safeguard Father's journals. What is it?"

He knew she had seen his frown. "I only find it strange that this man is so possessive of another's work."

"You would not find it strange if you knew Mr. Montague. He was never a very good scientist, according to my father. Small wonder he prides himself on knowing what others are doing. I imagine he thinks it hides his own lack of endeavor."

"Perhaps," he allowed. Two men rode by on horseback; one of them gazed at Cassie curiously. She must have noticed as well, for she looked after them, biting her lip.

"Please, Miss Bentbrooke," he urged, daring to touch her shoulder. It was surprisingly frail for one so strong in will. Her head whipped to face him. "Please, won't you read the journals to me?" he begged as humbly as he could. "There may be some mention of my uncle or at least the topic the paper discussed that would give me some clue to continue my search."

She stared at him, unblinking, for several seconds, and he wondered what he would do if she bolted. She took a deep breath and straightened. "Very well, I will read the journals to you."

He seized her hand and kissed it fervently, only to have to catch the journals before she dropped them. "Thank you, Miss Bentbrooke," he murmured, handing them back with a bow to cover his smile at her discomposure. "You have made me a happy man."

"But," she amended, accepting the books back from him with a blush, "you must promise not to tell my brother. As I said, he does not trust you. I doubt your story would help. It is a shame, really, that you did not explain from the beginning."

He grimaced. If she knew how little he had told her, she would no doubt rescind her offer. "Your brother met me with hostility from the first. Do not forget that England is still at war. I may fight for the British, but there are many who would gladly turn me over to the French. Some of my countrymen would delight in seeing me fed to Madame Guillotine."

She shivered and glanced over her shoulder as if the mob from the Bastille approached even then. He could not help but grin, turning the smile quickly into a concerned look as she glanced back at him.

"Be that as it may," she said firmly, "I would find it easier if you did not meet my brother too often. He generally goes riding each day at half past two. If you were to call then, we could go through the journals together."

He bowed. "I am your servant, Miss Bentbrooke. Tomorrow at two-thirty it is. Would you like me to escort you home?"

She hefted the books closer once more. "No, indeed, thank you all the same. It is not far." She cast him a look then that told him she found his choice of houses more than coincidental. He could only bow again as she hurried down the street with her precious burden. As he straightened, he smiled. By this time tomorrow, he would be back on the trail of the treasure.

* * *

In truth, Cassie did not know what to make of Devon's story. It certainly explained his interest in Benjamin and the journals. It might even explain why he had come calling on her first, since either Mr. Montague or another of her father's colleagues from the Royal Society could have pointed her out. What it did not fully explain, however, was why he had to wait so long to explain, or why he had to sneak his way into their home. There was something else going on, she was sure, but she was also sure that the only way to determine what it might be was to share the journals with him. Perhaps if she saw which portions were of most interest, she would find out what he was really after. In the meantime, she could ensure there were no more attempts to steal the books.

With this in mind, she bundled the journals and her cap in a fold in her skirt and went boldly through the front door. The footman did not so much as look curious as she awkwardly climbed the stair. She was congratulating herself in her room within minutes.

With the journals safely in her closet, and one of her new dresses on her back, she went in search of her ward. It was still over an hour before dinner, but she wanted to make sure that Liza knew she was home, so that she did not give the game away to Benjamin. To her surprise, she found Liza taking tea with Benjamin in the sitting room.

She had to admit they had done well in moving about the furniture to cover the damage. While the grouping of sofa and chairs was not as elegantly matched as before, still they appeared stylish. The rosewood sofa was positioned to hide a rent in the ruby Aubusson carpet. The painting of her mother had been patched and brought in to cover a hole in the plaster. Liza was sitting by the gold fan fire screen, blushing as she poured for Benjamin. It was the look of proprietary pleasure on her brother's face that shook Cassie.

"Good afternoon," she called and had the satisfaction of seeing her brother start.

Liza's blush deepened, and she set the teapot hurriedly down. "Good afternoon, Cassie. You are back from shopping? Were you successful?"

"I achieved my objectives for today," Cassie replied, strolling into the room and taking the seat beside her brother on the sofa. "You two look cozy."

Her concerns only deepened when Liza's eyes widened and the girl looked away. Benjamin took a sip of his tea, then smiled graciously at Cassie.

"And why shouldn't we? Haven't you always said Liza is like a younger sister to you? If one sister is out, I must make do with another."

Liza only looked more miserable.

"How good of you to care for your family," Cassie quipped. "And how do you do with Miss Compton?"

He set the teacup down and rose. "I cannot determine whether I have engaged her affections. If she has not come around by next week, I plan an all-out assault at her ball."

"Assault?" Liza gasped, head up at last.

He reached to chuck her under the chin, which only sent the color back to her cheeks. "Military cant, my dear. Love is as much a campaign as a war. A romantic ball, a dance or two, a moonlit stroll. What better way to offer for a woman?"

"What better way, indeed," Liza said with a wistful sigh.

As he left the room, Cassie silently hoped he was right. If he won Miss Compton's hand in the next week, she would be free to learn what the marquis wanted.

And she would not have to fear for Liza's virtue.

Seventeen

Bertrand was livid when he returned that night. The thieves had done nothing but spend Devon's money and brag about how brave they were to trash the house of a great war hero. The only clue to the one who had hired them was their insistence that he was a mouse. Devon ordered his man to keep watching them. If their quarry had found them once to hire them, he might seek them out again when they did not return with his prize. He also kept a man on duty at the house, just in case. Without knowing who hired the thieves, all he had to go on were those accursed journals. He could only hope to learn more from Cassie tomorrow.

Cassie had a difficult time getting her brother out of the house the next day in time for her rendezvous with Devon. Benjamin had, for no obvious reason, engaged Liza in a game of ninepins, and their heads were close together over the polished wood board. She had to remind him twice over the fall of the pins that it was time for his daily ride, and he had confessed that Miss Compton was to join him in the park.

"Promise me a rematch, infant," he chuckled with a wag of his finger at Liza, whose eyes sparkled at his teasing.

"Whenever you like, Major," she replied demurely. "But the outcome, I fear, will be the same."

He laughed. "Minx. You should know better than to issue me a challenge like that."

"Benjamin," Cassie snapped, "you're late."

Still chuckling, he quit the room.

"What do you think you're doing?" Cassie demanded of Liza.

She blanched. "Is it so very wrong to enjoy his company?"

"Yes!" Cassie cried. When her ward jumped, she tried to soften her tone. "He is as good as betrothed to another, Liza. And he is almost related to you."

Liza hung her head, busying herself with putting away the game pieces. "I know. It's just that I admire him so."

"Do not!" Cassie urged, praying she would not have to tell the girl the truth. "It is best if you stay away from my brother. When you have your season next year, love, you will have dozens of beaux, more handsome and admirable than Benjamin."

"Never!" Liza declared, jumping to her feet. Cassie recoiled in surprise. "There will never be a man as fine as the major; I know it!" She burst into tears and fled the room, passing a startled Pierson in the doorway.

"The marquis de Renard is here, madam," he managed.

Devon strode into the room moments later, bowing over her hand before taking a seat beside her. His gray eyes danced with green flecks; his smile was warm. He was dressed in a navy coat and tan trousers, again very similar to the dress her brother affected, but there the resemblance ended. Benjamin wore the clothes of a London Corinthian and looked dapper. Devon wore the clothes of a London Corinthian and looked commanding. But then, she had a feeling he could wear nothing at all and look that way. Just the thought made her duck her head in embarrassment.

"You were successful in getting your brother out of the house, I see," he noted, making her wonder whether he had been watching. She thought suddenly that he could have been the man Liza had seen, then realized that he had been standing on the doorstep when Liza had been frightened.

"Yes, Benjamin has left," she replied, rising. He jumped to his feet as well. "But I did not wish to bring down the journals until I knew he was gone. I shall return shortly."

He bowed, and she hurried to retrieve the books. When she returned, she found him standing before the Lawrence painting of her mother. Liza had done a good job of mending the rent. The woman in the picture looked as if she were in command of the world, just as Cassie remembered her.

"Your mother was a beautiful woman," he commented.

Cassie nodded, setting the first volume of the journals on the sofa beside her and spreading the skirts of her black silk day dress. "I look nothing like her, I'm told."

Moving to sit beside her, he took her hand and raised it to his lips. "Your beauty is all the more precious because it is rare."

The warmth of his caress sent heat to her center. "Don't." She snatched her hand away. "You don't have to be nice to me. I understand why you're interested in the Bentbrookes."

He paused, eyeing her. "Oh?"

"You want to find your uncle. You think my father's journals hold the key. I understand about wanting a family, my lord. I agreed to help you. There is no reason for you to continue this flirtation."

He drew himself up, hand on his heart. "Miss Bentbrooke, you wound me. You expect me to be in the presence of a lovely woman for the days it will take to learn your father's secrets and not flirt? As well ask me to go without food—no, without air to breathe!"

She laughed despite herself. "You are doing it entirely too brown, Lord Renard. I think we shall both get on quite well if you keep your exaggerated compliments to yourself."

"The task you set is great." He sighed with martyr-like resignation. "But I shall try."

She nodded, opening the first volume.

"I will not exaggerate any compliments I give you," he concluded.

She shook her head and found her place.

She had decided that the easiest way for him to search the books was for her to preview them and flag possible sections. Accordingly, she had reviewed approximately a quarter of the first volume the night before. Now she explained her process to him and set about reading the observations she had indicated with bookmarks.

"This section seemed different to me," she pointed out to him. He bent closer, and the scent of him washed over her—salt air, warm leather, and temptation. She felt herself leaning toward him and shifted her seat farther to the left instead.

"Up until now," she continued doggedly, "my father uses first-person singular—'I saw this,' 'I checked that.' Now here, on page eighty-two, he starts saying 'we.' This was before he was willing to credit my work, so he cannot refer to me."

She could feel his frown and wondered if her observation warranted it. "Could he refer to this Kearney fellow?" he asked.

"Possibly. I think Stephen Kearney joined us when I was eight or nine."

"What do you remember about him?"

She glanced at him. The intensity in his returned gaze heated the room. "A great deal, I suppose," she allowed. "He lived here with us, after all. Why? How could he be connected with your uncle?"

He shrugged, dropping his gaze and the temperature. "My uncle did not trust the English. It is possible he decided to take a false name."

"But the paper was published under his own name."

"Vanity," he explained. "What was Stephen Kearney like?"

The explanation made little sense, but she decided to withhold judgment until she had heard more. "A kind man, friendly. Shortly after he became Father's assistant, he fell in love with Yvette, my governess, and they married."

"Yvette," he mused. "A Frenchwoman, or one of you English pretending the part for higher pay?"

"Oh, she was French. At least, I think she was. My mother spoke the language fluently, but when Yvette spoke it, you knew you were talking to a Parisian."

He nodded. "An émigré, then. And Kearney, could he speak French?"

"I believe so, but that's no indication. Every gentleman of any worth learns to speak French. He did not have an accent as Yvette did, and he rarely spoke anything other than English and Latin, so I really couldn't tell you whether he was French."

"And he was a gentleman, even though he served your father?"

She cocked her head, thinking back. "I assumed so. He seemed to know as much as Father in many ways—perhaps not in astronomy but in philosophy and literature. I got the impression from the way he talked that he was well educated."

"My uncle was educated at the Sorbonne, one of the finest universities in France. He would have been your father's equal."

She sensed he wanted to say her father's better. She could not hold it against him. His pride in his French ancestry was a shield he held against those who would persecute him. In this sense, it was not unlike her study of astronomy. But could Stephen Kearney have been so accomplished an actor? "I don't remember where Mr. Kearney claimed to have been educated. The second son of a country parson, I believe Father called him. I cannot see how he could be your uncle."

"What did he look like?" he asked, obviously unwilling to give up on the idea.

"Tall, though not as tall as you. Dark hair, shot with

gray. I think his eyes were gray or blue, a lighter color. He really wasn't very unusual-looking that I recall."

He sighed, shaking his head. "You could have described my uncle or half of Britain. You said your father indicated he had company in his observations. When was this?"

"April 1793."

He frowned. "My uncle and I left France in the fall of 1792. He had intended to stay there with me, but as I mentioned, he felt more comfortable in London. I never heard from him again. My cousin arranged for my school and upbringing. I could not leave him until I reached my majority, as you English call it. By then I owed him a great deal of money."

"He bought your letter of marque," she confirmed.

He eyed her. "You are well informed. Actually, he paid the bond and security all privateers must have. It is supposed to keep us from taking the goods of friendly nations, including our own. As soon as I had paid him off, I determined to locate my uncle. I have since found men who claim to have shared lodging with him in the winter of 1792. So, he arrived in London and could have contacted your father in time to be the April companion. You said your father did not credit your work. Surely you were too young to be an astronomer then. You would have been no more than ten."

"I was eight," she said softly, remembering. "I started helping him when I was seven. He said I had a fine hand. And I loved being with him, up there under the stars." She realized he was frowning at her again and smiled self-consciously.

"Did you eventually work with this Kearney fellow?"

She shook her head. "I became Father's official assistant because of Stephen Kearney, in a way. When Mr. Kearney was hit by a passing carriage and killed, I was eighteen. That would have been 1803. Mother had already given up on my marrying; it was obvious even her connections would not be enough to get an offer for me. But

Father was unable to find an assistant he trusted, and I had shown not only interest but some aptitude in the field. Only a few years earlier, Caroline Herschel had been granted a salary from the king for her services as an astronomer, so why not Bentbrooke's daughter? Everyone was rather pleased with the arrangement."

"And you, you were satisfied by this as well?"

She turned the page in the journal. "I find the stars fascinating, Lord Renard. Why shouldn't I be happy that I was allowed to do nothing but study them? Shall we continue?"

She was glad he did not press her. She did feel grateful she had a calling. Only when he was near did she start to wonder about what it would be like to be loved, to love in return.

"I'm sorry I interrupted your reading," he murmured, and she had a feeling he was apologizing for more than that. "What else did you find? Was there any mention of a comet?"

Cassie smiled fondly. "Oh, the comet. Is that what the paper was about? My father's favorite theory. After studying a number of historical accounts, he was convinced that the comet which visited the earth in the Egyptian period was the same one that had appeared in the Middle Ages and was destined to reappear in 1785. When it did not, he became obsessed with timekeeping, certain that it was to blame for the difference in his calculations."

"But the paper indicated they had found the comet."

"He and Kearney spotted it in 1801. A paper by a German astronomer a few years earlier provided an easier way to calculate the elliptical orbit of a comet than the method my father was using. As it predicted, the comet appeared in the skies over England that winter. I remember how my father's whoops rang through the house. A very quiet man, my father. When he shouted, you knew something tremendous had happened. Mr. Kearney was so pleased, he even engraved a locket for Liza to commemorate the occasion."

"Where is the locket now?" He could not hide the eagerness in his voice. Sure as she was that Kearney could not be his uncle, she did not see how the locket could possibly help him.

"Liza, my ward, wears it always. It is one of the few things she has from her father."

"Would she let me see it?"

Cassie shrugged, wishing she could help him. His face had grown almost boyish in his desire, eyes wide and shining. If he wanted to see the comet so badly, she knew another way to show him. "It doesn't matter. I can show you the same design. It's on my father's celestial map."

He leaned back with elaborate casualness. "The map in your bedchamber?"

"It was once mounted on the roof, where my father could refer to it during his studies, but I feared the wind and rain would harm it. I have an equatorial mount on my instrument that makes the map obsolete, anyway. Would you like to see the map?"

He stared at her, a half smile slowly forming. "Very much. However, I feel I must remind you of your claim to be a proper oddity. Does hosting a man in your bedchamber come under the same category as crawling about in his bushes?"

"It does if it's in the name of science." She stilled the voice inside her that argued the point. "Besides, someone might have seen me go into your house. No one will see you enter my bedchamber. Come, now. My brother won't be out all afternoon."

Eighteen

Devon could not believe she would actually take him into her bedchamber. He wanted more than anything to see this map and the symbol of the comet. Surely it would tell him where to start looking for the treasure. Yet something in him felt drawn to protect her from her own folly.

For all his teasing, she had to know that she was the subject of gossip. He had been seen bringing her home Sunday. And his visits over the next few days, all carefully timed to occur while her brother was out, were sure to attract notice. Perhaps she had lived alone too long and didn't realize that the silent servants could be quite loud in their opinions when away from their masters. If they had gossiped about his rendezvous with Cassie in the library, how much more would they talk when it became known he had been above the first floor?

Bemused, he followed her from the room. She crossed the entry to the stair, her steps calm, her back straight. Thinking of the woman in the painting, he realized she had indeed inherited something from her mother: her remarkable poise in situations that would unnerve another. She had only reached the second step, however, when she froze. Turning slowly back, she peered around him, brow creased thoughtfully in a frown. He felt the hairs prickle at the back of his neck, but when he turned to find what concerned her, he saw only a tall, burly footman on duty beside the front door. The fellow stared straight ahead, eyes trained on a spot approximately in the center of the stairway, arms at his side. He was as impassive, impressive, and invisible a servant as his cousin had ever hired.

Cassie, however, seemed to find something troubling in his demeanor. "Who pays your salary, Jacobs?" she demanded. Her tone was as strict as a schoolmaster's at Eton.

To Devon's surprise, the fellow hesitated. His gaze flickered down to Devon then rapidly up again. "Major Bentbrooke, of course," he murmured.

"Wrong!" Cassie proclaimed, and he flinched. Devon watched with interest as the man's hand reached back as if to grab the door handle and flee the house.

"We pay you weekly, Jacobs," she continued determinedly. "Who hands out the coins?"

He blinked. "You do, mum."

"Correct. If gossip were to spread about me, what do you think would happen to those coins?"

Devon hid a smile. So, she had learned after all. He could only hope this tactic would work.

The footman swallowed. "They might be less?"

"Possibly. Or they might fail to appear at all. On the other hand, silence can be rewarded. Do you understand?"

His hand fell back at his side. "Yes, mum."

Nodding, she turned to continue up the stairs. Her gaze caught Devon's, and his grin sent color to her cheeks. He knew it was not his imagination that her steps became more hurried as they climbed. That only made him grin all the more.

At the top of the second flight of stairs, she turned left and crossed the short hall to one of the bedchambers. Before she could open the door, one on the opposite side of the stairs opened, and the dark-haired girl wandered into the corridor.

Cassie saw her immediately and blanched. The girl saw them immediately and stared. Devon considered letting them ogle each other, but he wanted more to see the map.

He bowed low. "You must be Miss Bentbrooke's ward?"

The girl stared a moment more, then slowly curtsied. "My lord."

Cassie cleared her throat. "Yes, my lord. May I introduce Elise Kearney? Liza, this is Devon Sebastien, Marquis de Renard."

Devon started, peering closer. Intent on the clue to the treasure, he had not made the connection between Cassie's ward and Stephen Kearney. "Was your father Stephen Kearney?"

She nodded, biting her lip. Clearly not used to social occasions as strange as this, she cast Cassie a look of appeal.

"Yes," Cassie replied, filling in the gap made by her silence. "Her mother was Yvette, as I've mentioned to you. When they died and my parents died, I became her guardian. Liza, Lord Renard believes he may have known your father."

He offered the girl a smile, searching her face and form for anything familiar. She was certainly dark enough to be a Renard, and the eyes were greener than his, but in the piquant face and curving form he could see no strong family resemblance. She stared back at him.

"Do you know why you're named Elise?" he asked gently.

She nodded. "My father said it was my grandmother's name."

Devon caught his breath.

"What is it?" Cassie asked beside him.

He did not take his eyes off the girl in the doorway. "My ship is called the *Lady Elise*, after my paternal grandmother. She would have been Elise Sebastien, Dowager Contessa de Renard."

Liza gasped, hand going to her breast. "I'm in the aristocracy!"

Cassie stepped between them. "The marquis *thinks* your father and his uncle might be the same person, Liza, but we don't know that for certain. Do not start building faerie stories."

"I never build faerie stories," Liza assured her, although in truth a strange light glowed in her dark eyes. "Won't you stay to tea, my lord?"

"Regrettably, I must be on my way shortly. Another time, perhaps." He looked askance at Cassie, who took the cue.

"Yes, Liza, his lordship and I have been studying Father's journals. I wanted him to see the star map, but I think it best if we do so without interference, if you take my meaning."

The girl started to look petulant; then her brow cleared suddenly. "Oh, of course, the major!"

Cassie smiled. "Yes, dear. My brother should be home shortly. I'm sure it would be all right if you watched for him."

Their amateur code was amusing to watch. The girl actually winked at Cassie, as if he would not notice. "Yes, certainly I shall do that." She dropped a hurried curtsy. "Good day to you, my lord. I hope we can talk more another time."

He swept her an elegant bow that set her giggling nervously. She clattered down the stairs to the first floor.

He grinned, rising. "What a charming young lady."

Cassie beamed at him. "Yes, she is. I vow she will break every heart in London when she is presented next year."

Devon eyed her. "I have a difficult time imagining you as the society matron, launching your young charge into the world."

She stiffened. "That is how it is done in England, my lord. If Liza is to have any chance at happiness, she must have a season. I intend to see her well settled."

"With your brother's influence, that should not be hard."

He had meant it as a compliment, one of the few he was willing to grant the major, but she paled again. "You wanted to see the map," she said and threw open the door.

It was a long, narrow room with an oak-framed fireplace at one end and a single window at the other. Between the two and opposite the door stood a simple black-walnut four-poster bed with an overhanging top that nearly touched the opening door. The counterpane was a faded blue; it covered a single rather thin pillow. Remembering the satin quilts and lace-edged bolsters that had littered his grandmother's bed, he found it difficult to believe it was a woman's room.

She flashed him a nervous smile as she scurried to the window, which was partially obscured by the books and papers spread on the writing table below it. "Let me fix this. You can see it much better by candlelight."

Taking her cue, he crossed to the fireplace and struck a flint to light the brace of candles that stood on the mantel. Drawing the drapes darkened her side of the room even as the candles brightened his. He carried the brass holder to meet her at the foot of the bed. Her eyes glowed silver in the light. She stared at him as if she had forgotten why they had come up here, and a soft rose blossomed in her cheeks. He would have liked to know what she was thinking, but he knew they did not have much time.

"The map?" he felt compelled to ask, much as he admired the look of her upturned face.

She raised her gaze to the ceiling. Looking up, Devon beheld the stars.

What he had taken to be the top of the bed was a reproduction of the night sky. Slats of wood, stained and bowed, arched over them. The constellations and stars had been painted in place in gold and silver. As he raised the candles higher, the points sparkled.

"Amazing," he breathed.

Beside him she smiled. "Yes, it is. Come here." She took the candles from him and led him deeper under the canopy. Pushing on his shoulders, she forced him to sit on the edge of the bed. Then she crossed to the other side of the bed, set the candles on the nightstand there, and sat down as well. Before he could question her, she stretched out on her back beside him, gazing upward.

He tried not to think about how he generally reacted when an attractive woman lay next to him. The candlelight framed her face in lines and shadows and drew his eyes first to her parted lips, moist and pink, then down her graceful neck to the rise and fall of her bosom. That way lay temptation. Leaning back beside her, he trained his eyes and thoughts upward.

"This is what you would see," she murmured as if she had not seen his hesitation or the hunger he was sure must have lingered in his eyes, "if you were to lie on a hillside just south of London on midsummer's eve at midnight." She raised a hand to point at the constellations. "Ursa Major, Ursa Minor, Hercules, Libra, Sagittarius . . ."

"Cassiopeia," he added, watching for her blush.

She did not disappoint him. "Cassiopeia," she agreed, cheeks reddening. "And there, that streak to the north, that's my father's comet."

He straightened, leaning on his elbows to get a better look at the design. It was a painted ball of white with a slight taper at one end as if it were traveling through space at great speed. A faint ellipse encircled it, with numbers scratched along the side—longitude and latitude, his navigational experience told him, yet the numbers did not make sense. He did not think they were any coordinates he had sailed to. So it wasn't a clear map to the treasure. He tried to think of any way it could be a clue. He saw only white paint on a black board.

"What is it?" she asked, and he knew she must have been watching him.

He shook his head. "Nothing. I don't recognize the symbol. I had hoped it might mean something to me."

Her hand reached out for his, squeezing softly. "I'm sorry. I know what it's like to lose a family."

He pulled his hand away and rose, feeling suddenly buried under the weight of the dark map overhead. "I should go. Your brother will be home soon."

"Yes," she replied with a sigh, sitting up. He offered her

his hand. As he pulled her to her feet, he also pulled her into his arms. With her lips only inches away, it seemed a shame not to close the distance.

It was a quick kiss, no longer than any of the others he had stolen from her. But this one was different. She was softer in his arms, warmer, sweeter, as if she wanted to be there as much as he suddenly wanted her there. The hesitation he had felt in her in the past had vanished. His kiss was no longer a curiosity; it was desired. She wanted him as much as he wanted her. The knowledge was heady, and for a brief moment he considered granting both of their desires. But as he drew back, she sighed and opened her eyes.

"You promised not to flirt," she murmured sadly.

"I promised not to flirt insincerely," he corrected her, cupping her chin in his hand. "If you think that was insincere, *cherie,* perhaps I had better kiss you again to prove my intent."

Her eyes widened, but she did not gainsay him as he lowered his mouth to hers.

"Cassie!" hissed a voice from the hall. "Cassie, hurry! He's home!"

Nineteen

Cassie jerked away from him at Liza's call. For once in her life, she was glad of her brother's abysmal sense of timing. One more kiss and she would have lost her virtue. Lost it? She would have begged Devon to take it. Seizing his hand, she pulled him toward the door.

"Hurry, you must go!" She knew her urgency had more to do with the potency of that last kiss than the nearness of her brother. By the amused smile on Devon's face, he knew it, too.

Liza was already greeting Benjamin at the door. "Major Bentbrooke," she clarioned so loudly that he must have wondered if she'd gone deaf. "Home so soon?"

Cassie drew Devon to the servants' stair, scrambling down the steps. She paused only long enough to listen at the door to the kitchen.

"Your brother has spies everywhere, I take it," Devon whispered in her ear. His breath was light, and before she could answer, she felt the brush of his lips against her hair.

She waved him away, heart pounding faster than it should. "Be serious. If you want to hear my father's journals, you must stay away from my brother."

"Does he dislike me so much then?" The whisper was almost a purr. In the dark of the stair, it seemed more dangerous.

She decided not to answer. Steeling herself, she swung open the door and set off across the kitchen as fast as was remotely proper. The new cook paused with ladle in midair, and his assistant froze in the act of stoking the fire. Brazening it out, she stalked to the back door, bringing Devon with her, pointing out features of the house as if she were giving a tour to a perspective buyer. As she steered him into the backyard, she felt eyes peering out the kitchen window. She led him across the little yard only to stop short when she realized there were a groomsman and coachman fussing about the mews. Oh, for her own house again!

He cocked his head. "Thank you for safeguarding my reputation," he said with a smile. "And may I call again tomorrow, at the same time?"

Despite the subterfuge, she would have liked nothing better. He was far more intelligent than her brother and far more interested in her work than Liza. And with that last kiss, she had concluded that he had some feeling for her after all, even if it wasn't as decidedly proper as her family would have once expected. But duty called.

"I'm sorry," she said with a sigh. "I expect my brother to be home most of tomorrow. We shall be preparing for a ball."

"Another party so soon?" He raised a brow.

"Not here, I am glad to say. The Comptons are throwing a ball, and we have been invited." Her tone must have betrayed her lack of eagerness, for he frowned. "I know how much you want to hear about my father's work. But after an affair such as this ball, my brother will likely spend most of the day recuperating. Best try for Friday."

He did not look pleased, but he bowed over her hand, proper, detached. "Very well," he clipped. "Good day, Miss Bentbrooke." She watched him let himself out of the gate and stride down the alley. She had disappointed him. But it galled her that he was more disappointed to be kept from her father's books than he had been when their tryst was interrupted. She stalked back to the house to intercept Benjamin.

That her brother was also in a foul mood was evident the moment she saw him. He was bent over one of the trunks in the sewing room, the contents clattering fearfully with his efforts. She could hear him muttering from the doorway.

"What's happened?" she demanded.

He raised his head to glare at her. "She turned me down."

Cassie did not have to ask who he meant. Relief flooded her. "Then we can stop this charade."

"It is *not* over," her brother snapped, hurling a silver sipping cup back into the trunk.

She flinched. "But if she turned you down . . ."

He leaped to his feet. "I still have permission to call, and call I shall, for all that she appears to have fixed on another fellow." He strode to the window seat and threw it open, sending the cushions flying in all directions.

"Someone's beat you out," she summed up. "Imagine a mere mortal being preferred to the great Major Bentbrooke."

His head snapped up. "Don't start, Cassie. I'm in no mood for your sarcasm. Especially since it's your precious marquis who seems to have ousted me."

"What?" she gasped. Her hands flew to her lips, which still tingled from his kiss. Her annoyance at his attitude changed to fear. Was this some game after all? "Benjamin," she said, "you must be mistaken. Why would he be interested in Miss Compton?"

Benjamin laughed derisively. "She's beautiful, charming, and wealthy."

"That proves nothing," she argued defensively. "I have never once heard that they were seen together. Certainly she did not so much as look at him when he appeared at the party here. Besides, Mr. and Mrs. Compton invited you to their ball, not him. Surely that shows you have their approval."

"I thought so. I was so sure, in fact, that I encouraged her to let her father announce our engagement at the ball."

"And she refused."

"Quite charmingly. Miss Compton is tenderly regretful that she does not return my sentiments at this time. As if I could not see through all her questions about you and the marquis."

"M-me and the marquis?" she stammered as he slammed the seat shut. "Why were you discussing me and the marquis?"

"I wasn't discussing you and the marquis. She was. That was my point."

Cassie shook herself. He was too angry to notice her stammer. She should be grateful—and silent. "I still don't see why you are so worried. If you have her parents' approval, however misplaced it may be, she will have to accept you."

He looked thoughtful for a moment, then shook his head. "I've seen her wind her parents around her finger. No, I must renew the attack. Where have you put it?"

She frowned. "What are you looking for?"

"Father's telescope. I assume you kept it. By rights, it's mine."

"By everything that's decent, it's mine!" she proclaimed, hands on hips. "I know how to use it; I studied the stars alongside him; I helped advance his theories. You are not to lay a finger on it without my permission, do you hear me?"

He paused to eye her. "Everyone within a mile's distance of the house hears you. I'm not planning on selling it or damaging it. I just want to use it."

"Why?" she demanded.

"If you must know, I thought I'd show Barbara the stars. It seemed like an excellent gambit to get her alone in the dark."

"You are disgusting," Cassie spat. "I won't let you use Father's equipment to compromise some poor girl."

"She isn't a 'poor girl.' That's entirely the point. And I'm not planning on compromising her—at least, not yet." He offered her a sunny smile. "Come on, Cassie. Just let me borrow it for a bit, please?"

She scowled at him for a few moments. She wasn't sure she should cooperate with him any more than she already had. But all of her longed for his plan to end so that she and Liza could regain their lives. She threw up her hands. "Oh, very well, but not Father's telescope. I use that in my studies. Liza won't mind if you borrow Mr. Kearney's."

Benjamin pouted as he followed her from the sewing room, but when she pulled the case from under her bed, he nodded with satisfaction.

"Yes," he murmured, running his hands up and down the sleek mahogany case. "This should do nicely."

Cassie rolled her eyes. "You haven't even seen the instrument yet." As she worked the brass catches to open the case, her gaze fell on a discoloration on the wood. The lid snapped open, and Benjamin reached for the three-foot-long metal tube that lay in the faded red velvet lining.

Cassie stared at the diamond-shaped mark, lighter than the rest of the wood. A ragged pinpoint hole pierced each of the horizontal points of the diamond, as if some sort of name plate had once been nailed in place.

"How does it work?" her brother demanded, putting his eye to the wide end.

Cassie shook her head, reaching to take it from his grip. "You see the small piece extending here on the side? That's where your eye goes. You move it in and out to focus it, like this." She bent her head and tried to focus the piece, but her view was hazy and tinted green. She raised her head. "The speculum is tarnished. I should have expected as much with it sitting about all this time. If you leave it with me tonight, I'll have it ready in time for the ball tomorrow."

Benjamin rose, nodding. "Excellent. And you'll have to tell me something to point it at. How about Father's comet?"

"Father's comet," she replied with a sigh, "won't be passing the earth for well over a thousand years."

He shrugged, striding to the door. "Someone else's comet, then. She won't know the difference."

"Neither will you," she muttered, but he was already out the door.

She returned the telescope to its case and rocked back on her heels. Until today she had never thought to compare her father's telescope to Stephen Kearney's. She was not a little surprised to learn that the second son of a country parson, who had to work for a living, could afford a scope easily twice as good as her father's. And for all the grandeur of the scope and the case, he had seen fit to destroy the one piece of information that might have indicated to whom it belonged.

Devon found Bertrand waiting for him when he returned to the rented house. The little man scrambled to his feet from where he was playing cards with Henri on a packing crate and proceeded to relate that the journal thieves had been captured attempting to rob another home. Devon shook his head. First the delay with Cassie and now this. He looked to Henri to take a message to Ames. Not only did he want a chance to question the thieves, but he needed to see what the duke's connections could learn about Stephen Kearney. However, he found his first mate already holding out a note that had come earlier. Devon took it from him, broke the seal, and read the contents. What an end to a frustrating day. Shaking his head, he crumpled the note.

"Is it bad?" Henri asked, frowning.

"My cousin presumes to find me a bride." He thought of Cassie and suddenly grinned. "I wager you a quid he heard those rumors. A Devonlee wed to a bluestocking! Never!" His smile faded. "Only he will never remember that I'm not a Devonlee."

He was about to throw the note into the fire when something in it tugged at a memory. Reopening the paper, he peered closer, and his grin returned. "The devil! He does me a service after all. It appears I have been invited to a ball. How do you think the brave major will take it when he learns that Miss Compton prefers her men dark and dangerous?"

"Two favors?" The duke of Devonlee raised a finely chiseled brow. "The puppy grows presumptuous."

Ames spread his hands. "You did wish him to find the treasure for you, Your Grace. He asks only for assistance to question the thieves and to learn more about this Stephen Kearney fellow."

"The thieves are immaterial to me," His Grace replied dryly. "I cannot imagine they were hired by anyone of refinement. They obviously knew nothing about the treasure, or they would never have let the books out of their hands. Encourage the magistrates to execute judgment quickly. Do we have a robbery or two with which we could connect them?"

Ames nodded thoughtfully. "Yes, I believe we could make it look as if they stole the diary of Lady Frances. That should cover the blackmail your agents have been conducting."

"Blackmail," the duke pronounced with a tisk. "Shall we try for a more congenial term?"

Ames made a note on the paper before him. "Certainly, Your Grace. Encouragement? Inducement?"

The duke smiled. "Better. Too bad Lady Frances's payments couldn't save the Rembrandt. I trust you found a buyer?"

"Lord Brentfield was most accommodating," Ames assured him. "I used the money to pay your tailor."

"Good. And this Kearney fellow, what is so important about him?"

"Your cousin does not say," Ames replied, reading over the note again. "I will let you know what I learn."

"Excellent. And did my cousin take our bait?"

Ames nodded so vigorously, he felt his nose twitch. "Yes, most assuredly, Your Grace. Mr. Compton informed me that Captain Sebastien accepted the invitation within an hour of receiving it. He will be at the ball tomorrow night."

"And both the Bentbrookes will be in attendance?"

"Oh, yes," Ames warbled gleefully.

"Excellent," the duke purred. "That leaves only the girl and the servants. They should be no trouble. At last we will end this. We finally know what Alfred Bentbrooke's works look like, and we know that they will be unguarded tomorrow night. Tell my agent to proceed."

Ames made another note on his paper. Then he looked up with a frown. "And Captain Sebastien's first request? About the two thieves in Newgate? How shall I answer him?"

"No answer required," the duke replied with a smile that sent a chill up Ames's spine. "If I read the Comptons' interest correctly, by the day after tomorrow my cousin will have too much on his hands to worry about those fellows."

Twenty

Cassie perched on the scroll-backed chair on the far edge of the Comptons' cavernous ballroom. Across the floor, people laughed, sipped champagne from fluted crystal goblets, and discussed topics with scintillating wit. She smiled politely at Matilda Smythe-Bellows, who held court in the dowagers' circle, that corner of the ballroom where the elderly spinsters and widows were wont to congregate. There wasn't a woman around Cassie who wasn't old enough to be her mother. For once her black evening dress did not stand out, for the dowagers dressed as somberly as crows. But somehow, their topics of conversation were not what she had expected.

"Scandalous," Matilda intoned, nodding to where a young lady was giggling behind her fan while a fellow in regimentals attempted to peer down her décolletage.

"Scandalous," chorused the other women around her, applying their own fans studiously.

"Impudent," she determined, training her gaze on a young man who was caressing the arm of a woman easily twice his age.

"Impudent," the women agreed, nodding.

"Disgraceful," she decreed, turning up her nose at an elderly couple who had chosen to dance, hopping about the set with delighted smiles on their wrinkled faces.

"Disgraceful," the women declared.

Cassie gritted her teeth.

"And how would you assess the ball, Miss Bentbrooke?" Barbara's aunt demanded.

A dozen pairs of inquisitive eyes swiveled in her direction. Cassie's cheeks ached from keeping her smile in place.

"A decided bore?" she offered.

The chorus gasped, and Matilda Smythe-Bellows glared.

"My brother's events," she proclaimed, "are never boring."

Cassie stood and shook out the skirts of the black satin ball gown. "Ah, well, then it must be the company." Knowing the resulting muttering was entirely her own fault, and feeling rather pleased about it, she strolled away from them.

The glorious feeling of independence was short-lived, however. Away from the herd she felt immediately vulnerable. Beautiful ladies capered about the dance floor on the arms of handsome gentlemen. Others strolled along the dance floor or gathered in groups. Laughter floated in the air along with the music from the string quartet. The night outside may have been dark and chill with an October wind, but the ballroom was light and warm and full of joy. Cassie felt like a colly bird among a flock of peacocks.

She looked about for a potted palm behind which she could hide, but before she could make good her escape, her brother stepped to her side. In the bright red of his regimentals, with medals hung from his broad chest, he was easily the most presentable gentleman at the ball. She had seen him dancing every dance, but only one with Miss Compton. He nodded to Cassie, rocking back and forth on his heels and rubbing his hands gleefully, and she knew she was about to hear of his latest triumph. Resigning herself, she reflected that it could be no worse than what she had been enduring in the dowagers' circle.

She was wrong.

"I've convinced Barbara to join me in the garden," he confessed with a chuckle. "She will slip away right after this dance." He nodded to where the accomplished Miss Compton minced her way through a country dance with her beaming father. "Keep the gossips busy."

Thinking of how she had done just that, Cassie cringed. "If you are both discreet," she suggested hopefully, "you will hardly need me to cover for you."

Benjamin eyed her. "Do not spoil this for me, Cassie. The marquis has not arrived as planned. Barbara is miffed. I can use that to my advantage, if you help me."

Glancing back, she met Matilda Smythe-Bellows's unforgiving stare. Then her brother's words penetrated her fog of frustration. "They invited the marquis de Renard?"

"Amazing, isn't it? Must be handy having a cousin who's a duke. Rumor has it His Grace put in a good word for the fellow. Renard even accepted the invitation. Barbara was in alt, I can tell you. But for all that, Renard did not take the bait. I will not be so slow."

The dance was ending. Couples separated, applauded politely, turned to find the next persons to whom they were promised. Her brother patted her shoulder, ready to stroll around the room to where a set of double doors led out onto a wide terrace overlooking an ornamental garden. Cassie had been given a tour earlier by the Comptons and knew her brother could probably find a way to get lost in the winding paths through the well-manicured beds. And she would have to keep Matilda Smythe-Bellows occupied while he did so.

She shivered as the sets formed for the next dance and the music began. Benjamin nudged her toward the dowagers' circle. She turned to go, then felt her brother stiffen. Looking over her shoulder, she saw that another gentleman had joined the dance. Barbara Compton was curtsying warmly to her new dance partner, a tall, well-built gentleman with dark hair and the unmistakable air of command.

"Renard," Benjamin growled.

Cassie stared at the couple as the dance began. As always, Devon looked tall and elegant in his evening black.

But tonight he somehow looked even more splendid. There was a diamond stickpin in his silky white cravat, and the cut of his coat emphasized his lean grace. He exuded charm. More than that, he exuded temptation. The hint of danger and promised excitement seemed to hang about him like a rare perfume. Certainly Miss Compton had been affected by it. He murmured something, and she dimpled. As they circled their group, his hand lingered at her waist, drawing her closer than was warranted by any dance Cassie had ever seen, and she leaned into the embrace. Cassie wanted to think the attraction was the product of her fevered imagination, but her brother sucked in a breath and she knew he had seen it as well. As the couple moved to the end of the set and were forced to stand idle for a moment, Devon bent to whisper into the woman's ear, and Miss Compton blushed with a gossamer giggle.

The ballroom was suddenly suffocatingly hot. Cassie brushed past her rigid brother and stumbled across the room. Fumbling with the gilt handle on the door, she shoved through. Lanterns led along the terrace to the stairs at the far end. She ducked into the shadows beside the door and huddled in the chill night air.

"What did you expect?" she demanded aloud, rubbing her hands up and down the black lace of her sleeves. "He told you he's an incorrigible flirt. Did you really think he meant anything by it?" She gave a shaky laugh. "Be logical about this, my girl. Did you actually think you were special?"

Tears threatened, and she blinked them back. She had to stay angry. She focused on the picture of Miss Compton smiling up into his handsome face. Had she looked so foolishly adoring when he had come to visit? Had her eyes glowed with such longing when he'd kissed her? Had she made such an utter fool of herself? She started shaking. Before she could stop herself, the tears overspilled and she buried her face in her hands.

How long she stood there sobbing, she had no idea. She barely heard the door open and the quick footsteps to her side.

"Tell me who made you cry," Devon murmured, "and I'll cut out his heart for you."

Cassie gulped back her tears, wiping her eyes hurriedly with a damp finger. "I'm fine. It's nothing. Please go back to the dance. You looked as if you were enjoying it."

He stiffened, then leaned against the wall beside her, becoming as dark a shadow as he had on the night of their first tryst in the library. "I am with the woman I came to see. Why should I want to leave?"

"Stop it!" Cassie cried. "This is all a game to you, but it isn't to me. I thought I could play it. But I can't just pretend I like someone or let them pretend they like me. It hurts me, here." She thumped the breast of her black gown. "I don't want you to pretend anymore, do you understand? I don't want to be cozened or flattered. I am an ugly, unwanted, penniless spinster with too much intelligence and not enough charm. I'm tired of pretending that anyone thinks otherwise."

He did not move from the shadows, but she thought he sighed. "Who tells you such filth? It is nonsense. Is that really how you see yourself?"

She dashed the fresh tears away. "I am a realist, Monsieur le Marquis. And I own a mirror."

"It must be aged and warped," he quipped. He reached to take her hand, and she snatched it away. He reached again and held it firmly. She glared at him.

"*Ecoutez,* listen to me. There are some things in life whose beauty is not apparent at the surface. A fine white china plate must be tapped to hear the ring of truth. A painting by a master must be studied to see all the detail. *Allez,* come here. Let me show you."

Feet dragging, she reluctantly allowed him to lead her down the terrace to the steps to the garden. She wanted his words to be true; oh, how she wanted them to be true. But she'd heard his pretty words before and could not believe there was substance behind them.

Across from the garden steps, another set of doors led back into the house. Whatever room it was, it was not in use for the party, for there was only darkness inside.

"I give you a better mirror," he proclaimed, pointing to their wavering reflections in the glass panes of the doors. "*Voilá!* You see the woman there, with hair as soft as moonlight and eyes that rival the stars? This is your ugly spinster? Oh, no, *cherie,* this is Titania, queen of the faerie world."

Cassie stared at the elegant creature in the glass. Even dressed in darkness, she held herself tall and graceful. Moonlight and torchlight glinted off the pale hair, as if she wore a halo. The man beside her was as dark and dangerous as Lord Oberon himself, and just as desirable. The elegant woman made him a worthy mate. She let out her breath. "If only I always looked like that."

"Carry that image in your mind, *cherie,* and you will always look like that. Now, dry those tears so we can return to the ball. I have always wanted to dance with a faerie queen."

She managed a watery smile, patting her cheeks with the back of her gloves, which seemed to be the only thing dry. She had just accepted his offered arm when he hesitated, head coming up as if listening. Then, finger to his lips, he drew her back out of the light of the torch.

Someone else had come onto the terrace. Cassie was grateful that Devon's senses were better than her own, for she had heard nothing. She could not make out who it was, slipping from shadow to shadow, but the brief glimpses told her that the short stature and slender build could only be a woman. The swish of skirts as the intruder drew closer confirmed her guess.

"Lord Renard?" came a tentative whisper she recognized as Barbara Compton's. "My lord, are you here?"

Cassie pulled away from Devon and glared up at him. He shook his head, raising his finger to his lips again.

The woman had drawn into the torchlight at the top of the steps to the garden and stood on tiptoe, peering over the shrubs into the night beyond. "Lord Renard?"

Cassie frowned. What was the woman trying to do? Devon clearly had no interest in meeting her, or surely he would have found an excuse to send Cassie inside. Or was she still being misled? The rules of his game grew more complex each time she thought she had come to understand them.

As she watched, Miss Compton sank onto her feet. Her face as she turned was a study of annoyance and frustration. Farther along the terrace, the door from the ballroom was thrown open and slammed shut. Miss Compton stiffened even as Cassie slunk back against Devon. His arms encircled her protectively, and she was glad for them even in her confusion.

Miss Compton had obviously heard the door as well, and the footsteps that approached. She glanced furtively about. Then, to Cassie's astonishment, she seized the cap sleeve of her pink silk ball gown and ripped it at the seam.

"Benjamin," she cried, stumbling forward and falling into his arms as he moved along the terrace. "Oh, Major Bentbrooke, save me!"

Twenty-One

Cassie started forward, but Devon drew her back against him before she could interrupt them. It was clear to him what the chit in front of them was going to try. He thought it best to keep them both clear of it.

"Barbara, what's happened?" Benjamin demanded, holding her at arm's length and peering into her face.

"Oh, Benjamin," she said with a shudder. "I thought he cared, but you were right." She let out a sob and pasted herself against him once again. "All he wanted was my virtue!"

Cassie struggled in Devon's grip, and he had no choice but to tighten his hold on her. Normally, cradling her against him would have pleased him no end. Now he was keenly aware that any movement could mean exposure.

Benjamin had a similar hold on Miss Compton. "Have no fear, love," he murmured. "The marquis de Renard won't touch you again. I promise."

Cassie scowled up at Devon. He shook his head at her. He half expected her to stomp on his instep, but luckily the couple was retreating to the doorway. As they slipped into the darkness, Cassie wrenched herself out of his arms.

"Why did you hold me back?" she demanded. "She accused you of attacking her!"

He shrugged, enjoying the fire in her eye and the color in her cheek. This was his wild cat, his tigress. He wondered if she knew how magnificent she looked when her emotions were engaged. "And this should disturb me?" he asked calmly.

"Of course it should disturb you! She's blackening your good name."

"Most Englishmen think very little of my name to begin with," he reminded her. "I doubt this will make matters worse."

"You don't understand." Moving closer, she peered up at him. "If her father believes her, you will be forced to marry her."

"You assume that I care a fig for her reputation or my own. I assure you, I will not be marrying anytime soon, especially not to a cunning debutante like Miss Compton. Unfortunately, I can hardly return to the ball." He bowed. "May I have the honor of escorting you home, my dear Titania?"

"Benjamin would be furious," she replied. Then she giggled. "I would be delighted, Monsieur le Marquis. But how are we to escape with so many enemies between us and the front door?"

"Quite easily," he said, offering his arm. "We will use the garden gate."

She accepted his arm and walked with him down the steps into the torch-lit gardens.

As if it were a lovely spring day, they strolled through the night. The paths of the garden wandered past plants trimmed and banked for winter. Indeed, now that Devon was away from the house, he could feel the chill in the air. She rubbed a hand up the lace sleeve of her gown, as if she felt the cold, too. Unbuttoning his coat, he slipped it over her shoulders.

"I'm all right," she protested, stopping as if to remove it.

He caught her hands on the jacket. "Even the faerie queen can take a chill. Please, leave it on. When I take it back, it will have your scent."

She swallowed, eyes huge. "If that is your desire."

He smiled at her. "If you grant me my desire, *cherie*, you will not go home tonight."

She immediately started peeling off his coat again. He pulled her into his arms.

"None of that. I promise to behave properly. Haven't I been the perfect gentleman so far?"

She gazed up at him with narrowed eyes. "You kiss me at the least excuse, Monsieur le Marquis. That is not the mark of a perfect gentleman. Perhaps I should return to the house."

He should let her do just that. He recognized the warning signs in his own body. She played on emotions he had kept too long buried. When he was in her company, he forgot his goal. Indeed, he found his goal becoming her pleasure. She gazed up at him with those liquid silver eyes, waiting for his answer. He turned away with difficulty, only to find his gaze alighting on one of the nearby bushes. Even in the late season, a few deep-crimson flowers still bloomed, brittle amid the olive-colored leaves. He reached out to snap off a flower, then handed it to her with a bow.

"You will be safe going home with me," he murmured. "I give you my word."

Some of his fellow Frenchmen would have laughed at his gesture, seeing the word of a Renard as worth nothing. Yet she accepted the flower in all seriousness, burying her nose in the thick petals. Her gaze, when she raised her eyes, was dreamy.

"Very well," she replied. "If you can find this mythical garden gate, I would let you escort me home."

He rather hoped he never found the gate, but he offered her his arm, and they set off down the path once more.

He found his mind wandering as much as the path. Henri had suggested he seduce Cassie to find the clue to the treasure. He had initially resisted the idea because he had thought he felt more attraction to the Bentbrooke maid than the spinster, never dreaming they were one and the same. Watching her out of the corner of his eye, her alabaster face bending every so often to bring the flower within inches of her delicate lips, he rolled the idea around in his mind again. He had little doubt she'd make a magnificent mistress. The fire in her had attracted him from the first. He felt it still, flashing in her eyes when he flirted with her, heating him when they kissed. Still, unmarried young ladies were generally not fair game. He wondered if he could even broach the subject without scaring her off again.

Down the path to their right he spotted an ivy-draped doorway. Before she could raise her head from the flower, he turned her carefully to the left.

"What will you do when your brother marries?" he asked casually.

She started. "What makes you think my brother is thinking of marrying?"

"Is it a secret he courts Miss Compton? He is rather blatant about it."

She grimaced. "Yes, I suppose he is."

"So," he pressed, "when they marry, what becomes of the dutiful sister?"

"I shall see that Liza has a season, as I told you."

That could take some time. But then, the girl was pretty. If Bentbrooke popped for a dowry, she might be snatched up quickly. "And then?" he asked.

She shrugged. "I suppose I will continue my studies." She paused to look up, as if remembering that there might be stars overhead. He glanced up as well, only to see a dark-brown sky, smoky from the chimneys of London and ready to rain. He reached out to touch her cheek. "It seems like a lonely existence, *cherie*."

"Most scientific pursuits are," she replied calmly, but she stepped away from his touch. "And when do you return to your ship? Or have you given up being a privateer?"

"My ship is being repaired," he told her truthfully. She waited patiently for the rest. When he was silent, she shook her head and sighed.

"We passed the garden gate. Are you ready to go home yet?"

Now Devon shook his head. He should have known better than to try anything with this one. No matter what he did, she was already two steps ahead of him. He offered her his arm once more and led her out of the garden.

It was only a matter of minutes before they found his carriage among the many thronging the square. He sent Thomas back for his and Cassie's belongings. Handing her into the carriage, he jumped in behind her. Before she could protest, he bundled the lap robes about her.

"Do I look as if I were made of ice?" she asked.

He didn't dare answer the question. "I am only trying to redeem my reputation as a gentleman."

"You did not care a fig for your reputation when Miss Compton slandered it. Why should my opinion matter?"

He met her gaze straight on. "It matters far more to me than anything Miss Compton could say. But if you are intent on being a martyr, I'll take one of those back. It's cold."

She swallowed, hurriedly peeling off one of the thick velvet robes. He accepted it and draped it about his shoulders. A moment more and Thomas was back. He jerked his head to indicate he wanted a word alone with Devon.

"A moment while I put on my cloak," Devon said to excuse himself.

Out of the coach, Thomas shook his head. "I don't know what you did, Captain, but the house is fair buzzing. Miss Compton hasn't returned to the ball, and her papa is making excuses. The servants say she's gotten herself in trouble, and they were asking a lot of questions about you."

Devon shrugged. "Let them ask. Tell them nothing. It will blow over."

Thomas nodded toward the waiting coach. "Are we going home?"

For a moment Devon considered attempting it, but

somehow he thought Cassie would protest. And he had given his word.

"No," he replied. "Let's get Miss Bentbrooke home. And I'll leave you that bottle of brandy from last night if you can get us there before her brother."

Cassie wrapped the robes more closely about her as Devon reentered the coach. She wished she had six more of them to cover her trembling. She wasn't cold; in fact, she felt severely overheated. And it had everything to do with the gentleman sitting so calmly across from her.

Did he have any idea what he did to her each time his hand brushed her cheek? Did he know how her traitorous body reacted when their lips touched? His dark-eyed gaze met hers, and she had a feeling he knew exactly how potent he was. She was playing with fire. She shivered.

He started to remove the black velvet robe he had thrown over his cloak.

"Don't," she yelped. She had seen the muscles rippling beneath his white silk shirt even in the garden's torchlight. She could imagine them now. She didn't need a further viewing to set her nerves tingling. He frowned, and she clarified. "Don't bother taking that off. I'm fine."

He settled against the cushions on his side of the coach. "You're not very good at accepting assistance, are you?"

His man hit a bump, and her knee touched his. She jerked away, feeling her face flaming.

"I haven't had anyone to help," she managed. "My brother was away for years. I took care of myself and Liza for much of that time. And I never learned how to obey orders."

"Or like receiving them," he guessed. "Will you take a suggestion, then? I think you were right in keeping our friendship a secret. After tonight I would not be surprised if your brother called me out."

A finger of fear traced down her spine, but she shook

her head. "Not Benjamin. What Miss Compton described as your cavalier treatment only served to further his cause. He will be far too busy ingratiating himself with her to bother about you. Still in all, I think it best if you wait for a note from me before coming over Friday."

"You found nothing else in the journals, then?" he asked, and she could sense his frustration.

Suddenly she remembered what she had found. "I nearly forgot with all the commotion at the ball. I was looking at Stephen Kearney's telescope yesterday. It is a beautiful instrument in an elaborate case, much finer than you would expect the second son of a minister to possess. Would you recognize your uncle's instrument if you saw it?"

"It is possible." She heard the eagerness in his voice.

"We'll look at it as soon as my brother goes out," she promised. "I want you to see the end of the case especially. Someone's pried off the name plate. Perhaps to hide his identity?" His face lighted, and she reached across the space to squeeze his hand. "Oh, I do so hope I'm right!"

Like conspirators, they grinned across the carriage at each other. Something in his eyes made her stomach knot. She pulled back her hands and folded them primly in her lap, turning her eyes away so that she wouldn't see whether he was annoyed or relieved by her gesture.

Moments later they drew up to the house. He threw off the robe and leaped out to hand her down. "Could I come in with you and see it now?" he ventured.

She shook her head. "I'm afraid my brother took the case with him tonight."

He hesitated, frowning at her. "Why would your brother want the telescope?"

"It's a long story. I promise you, he won't damage it. Will you see me to the door?"

He nodded absently, and her spirits plummeted. Reminding herself that it was his family he sought, not her hand, she allowed him to lead her to the door. Once again, no one opened it for her. Sighing, she reached for the handle. His hand caught hers.

"It's too quiet." She felt him stiffen. "Are your servants out again?"

A chill ran up her spine. She shook her head. "No. Jacobs should be on duty."

"Let me," he said. He stepped in front of her, shielding her from the entry. Carefully he eased open the door and peered inside. "Stay close," he murmured.

"I wouldn't dream of doing otherwise," she assured him.

He edged down the corridor toward the dining room. He shot a glance toward the sitting room, but she could see that it was dark, the fire unlit. She was almost afraid of what he would find in the library. He seemed to sense her fear, for he reached back to take her hand and give it a squeeze of encouragement.

The door of the dining room swung open, and Pierson moved calmly into the corridor. Devon froze. The butler paused. It was a mark of his professionalism that he did not so much as blink to find the mistress of the house sneaking about with a man at one in the morning.

"Might I be of assistance, madam?" he asked politely.

Cassie shook her head and came out from behind Devon, feeling decidedly foolish. She could sense the tension going out of Devon as well. "No, thank you, Pierson. It was so quiet when the marquis brought me home that I thought perhaps we'd been robbed again."

"It is late, madam," he explained. "Miss Kearney has retired. I had the rest of the staff go to bed—except Jacobs, of course." He glanced around them and frowned. "Who should be on duty at the front door."

Cassie felt a chill run up her spine again. She met Devon's gaze.

"The journals," they chorused.

"Madam?" Pierson asked.

"No time," Cassie snapped, hurrying for the stairs. "Check the library, Devon. He'd try there first. I'll check upstairs." She did not wait to see whether he obeyed, but lifted her skirts and clambered up the stairs. Throwing open the door of her room, she ran to the wardrobe and yanked open the doors. Dropping to her knees, she snatched up the apron on the bottom of the closet. Her father's journals were there. She rocked back onto her heels, closing her eyes in a prayer of thanks. Rising, she glanced around the room again. Everything else appeared to be in order. Pierson had left a candle burning for her return. She went to the writing table by the window. Her papers lay as she had left them.

Her own journal was gone.

She gasped, rifling the papers, heart pounding once more. "Not again."

There was a movement below her in the garden, a darker shadow in the darkness. She stifled a cry and turned to run to the door. She nearly collided with Devon on the stair.

"My father's journals are safe," she told him. "But the thief is making off with mine through the mews."

"He won't get far," Devon promised. He leaped down the stairs and dashed for the servants' stair to the ground floor. Pierson jumped out of his way, then stared after him.

Cassie came down the stairs more slowly. What a night! What a week! She had been proposed to and proclaimed an heiress. She had been robbed and ridiculed. She had had to protect her belongings, her family name, and her virtue.

She was more than a little afraid to find out what would happen next.

Twenty-Two

Devon moved silently through the garden, dagger in his grip. Why hadn't he considered the footman? He had wondered at the tension in the man the day Cassie had confronted him with keeping their visits a secret. She had asked the footman who paid his salary, and the fellow had looked ready to bolt. Small wonder when the man had obviously been in someone else's pay all along. Was he the spy of the fellow who had hired the first thieves, or had someone else entered the game?

He had not reached the mews before a hiss brought him up short. Bertrand materialized out of the shadows by the carriage house. A quick conversation revealed he had seen no one.

Devon frowned. What had made Cassie so sure the footman had come this way? She must have seen someone from her bedroom window. Could it have been Bertrand? Where was the footman? He advised his man to remain alert and returned to the house.

Cassie was waiting for him, along with her impressive butler, who stood sentinel behind her. The hard set to his mouth was the only sign that he was displeased that a robbery had taken place in his well-run establishment.

"Well?" Cassie asked; then, as her gaze fell to his empty hands, she bit her lip.

"I didn't see him," he admitted. He could feel her disappointment. After reading her father's journals with her, he was beginning to realize how much this stargazing meant to her. She was truly starstruck. He took her hand and brought it to his lips. "Do not worry, *petite*. He will not get far."

She swallowed and retrieved her hand. "You are being kind and far too optimistic. He has succeeded in stealing my work. I will have to face that. Right now, I want to know why. Why are my father's journals—and mine—suddenly so popular?"

Devon raised a brow. She had reason enough to ask, but he doubted he could come up with an explanation that would satisfy her. Before he could decide, the front door slammed.

"Benjamin," she gasped. She pushed Devon toward the back door. "You must go. He'll be furious if he finds you here."

"Promise me you will meet me tomorrow," Devon ordered, backing toward the kitchen door. "With the telescope."

"Yes, yes, fine," she chattered. The color was high in her sculptured cheeks, her eyes bright. He would have liked nothing better than to steal another kiss, but she was frantic to get him out of the house, and the butler loomed behind her.

"Hyde Park," he said. "Three o'clock."

"Four," she countered. Then she shut the door in his face.

"Where is he?" Benjamin demanded, striding into the kitchen.

"Who?" Cassie asked, making a show of studying the pots hanging from a rack near the door. "These seem to be fine, Pierson," she said to her butler. "You may tell the staff I approve of the job they're doing." She glanced pointedly at the man, but he simply remained his usual impassive self. The only indication that he was considering her words was a slight frown.

"*Who?*" Benjamin bellowed. "The marquis de Renard. Don't bother denying he's here. I saw his carriage out front."

Of course his carriage would be in front of the house. How long would it take him to circle the terrace? Five minutes? Six? Somehow she had to keep her brother busy that long.

"How very odd," she trilled. "He was kind enough to see me home when I developed the most dreadful headache. We got back some time ago. I was certain he must have left by now."

"Not before we have words," he growled, turning away.

"Wait!" she commanded, hurrying to intercept him. "There's something you should know."

He eyed her with a frown. "Quickly, then. And it had better be important."

"It is," she assured him. "We had another robbery tonight."

"What!" her brother yelped. "When? How? What was stolen?"

"I assume it happened while we were gone. Even Mr. Pierson was oblivious. You see, it was one of the staff."

He puffed out a sigh. "This is ridiculous. I'll deal with you later." He started forward again, and she blocked his way.

"But Benjamin," she persisted, "he stole my journal."

He blinked. "Your journal? Do you mean a diary?" His eyes widened, and he seized her arms. "What did you write, Cassie? For God's sake, tell me you didn't write about Barbara and me!"

She had him now. Oh, how she ached to make him squirm. But she couldn't lie so blatantly, not even to her blackguard brother.

"It wasn't a diary, Benjamin," she explained. "It was my journal, where I write down my scientific observations. I left it in my room, in plain view. It's gone."

He let go of her. "Maybe Liza borrowed it. Or the maid

moved it. Get out of my way, Cassie. You can't shield him forever."

No, she thought, *just for a few more minutes.*

"But Benjamin," she said aloud, "don't you understand? The footman stole my journal, just like those thieves stole Father's journals. What is it about the work Father and I did that makes it valuable enough to steal, not once but twice?"

Benjamin frowned. "I don't know. You tell me."

"I wish I could. But my mind doesn't seem devious enough. Think, Benjamin. Why would anyone want old scientific notation?"

She obviously had him intrigued. With narrowed eyes he studied her, and she could swear she saw the ideas churning in his mind. But after a moment he shook his head.

"I can't understand it, Cassie. The books can't be any good to anyone but you and Father. No one else can even read the blasted things. Now, let me pass."

She heard the clock in the sitting room chime half past one and stepped aside. Benjamin barreled down the hall and out the front door. A thought burst into her mind in his wake, and she stood mesmerized.

Stephen Kearney could have read the journals. Stephen Kearney had written some of the entries. Stephen Kearney was supposedly the long-lost uncle of the marquis de Renard. Why did all the mysteries in her life keep pointing back to Devon?

As he circled the terrace, Devon's mind raced. He had a possibility and another mystery. The former was Stephen Kearney's telescope. He had never thought to look for his uncle's instrument. Could it have hidden the jewels? If so, had Cassie's father or brother found them first? Then there was the mystery of the footman who had disappeared into the night. It was a shame he had mistaken Cassie's journal for her father's, but he could not be sorry that the books were safe. Still, he would have liked to get her book back for her. His only hope was that Henri might have seen something.

When he reached the front of the house, Thomas stopped him.

"Henri has a present for you, Captain," he murmured with a grin, nodding toward the park. "Seems a little bird attempted to fly the coop, carrying someone else's belongings."

Devon felt his own grin forming. He glanced up at the clouds, which had parted to show a waning moon.

"It's a lovely evening," he said aloud for the benefit of anyone who might be watching. "I think I'll walk through the park. Meet me on the other side."

It took every ounce of his British discipline to stroll casually across the road to where a streetlamp illuminated the entrance to the small park. The shadows of the night closed around him, and he hurried his step.

"*Ici,*" Henri called.

Devon darted into a copse of trees. As his eyes grew used to the dark, he made out his first mate standing over a huddled figure. Henri shoved a heavy volume at Devon.

"*Voilá,*" he proclaimed triumphantly. "He tries to steal the clue, *oui*?"

Devon tucked Cassie's journal under his arm. "You have redeemed yourself, Henri." He nudged the man at Henri's feet with his toe. "And you, what do you have to say for yourself?"

"I didn't mean nothing," the man sniveled. Henri reached down and hauled the fellow to his feet. His dark-brown hair was as rumpled as his brown livery. By the faint light filtering through the trees, Devon could make out a darker streak under the footman's nose—the result, no doubt, of blood. Before he could comment, the man jerked himself out of Henri's grip.

"I'm an honest man, I tell you," he declared. "Major Bentbrooke told me to bring that to him. I just did my job."

Devon frowned. "And why would Benjamin Bentbrooke want his sister's journal? If he wished to see it, he had only to ask."

The fellow started, then turned the move into a shrug. Devon wasn't fooled. As he had suspected, the fellow had mistaken Cassie's journal for her father's. He must have watched her read the book to Devon. The journal in his hand was the same size and color as the older books. If it had been lying out while the others were safely hidden, it was small wonder the fellow had been fooled.

"How should I know why the major wanted it?" he was blustering. "Nobs have strange ways. He told me before he left to get the book from her room and bring it to him at the ball."

"You lie," Henri growled. "I should beat the truth from you."

The footman cringed, and Devon eyed him thoughtfully. Though Henri outweighed him by at least fifty pounds, the man was almost as tall and looked to be nimble. The livery jacket did nothing to hide the play of muscles. A match between them would have been like pitting a bear against a lion: the result would have been in question. Even if Henri had had the element of surprise the first time, it would not explain the fellow's submission now. He wanted them to believe he was afraid.

"Who paid you to steal the journals?" Devon asked softly.

The footman wiped his nose across his sleeve. The act was telling to Devon. No servant willfully damaged a uniform; the repair would come out of his meager salary. The fellow was a spy. Someone else was after the jewels.

Anger long kept buried welled up from inside him. He dropped the journal and grabbed the fellow himself. French poured from his mouth, loud, guttural, furious. Henri growled in agreement.

"You're crazy," the footman declared.

Henri stepped menacingly up behind him. The footman stiffened.

Devon took a deep breath. He had to regain control. Much as his French half yearned to do as Henri suggested and beat the truth out of the fellow, his British half was appalled by the idea. The mob had beaten his father before having him beheaded, with no more proof of treachery than Devon had right now. He would not perpetuate that mistake. He released his grip and stepped back, taking another breath to calm his surging anger.

The footman watched him. Even as Devon took another step back, the man slammed his boot up behind him, ramming the heel into Henri's groin. The big Frenchman gasped, stumbling back and curling in on himself. The footman bolted.

The anger obliterated any reason.

"*Merde*," Devon swore, starting forward. He glanced at Henri, trying to see how badly his man had been hurt.

"*Allez*," his first mate groaned, waving the hand that was not clutching himself. "After him!" Devon ran.

The footman had started down the path away from the Bentbrooke house. Devon followed, hurtling through the darkness. He had to catch the fellow if he was to learn who his enemy was. A branch whipped his face, but he did not let it deter him. He caught the corner of a bench with his knee but kept going. It was only when he stumbled over a fallen tree that his British half cried halt.

He paused, panting, gazing around him. The path wound through the dark park. Occasional stretches were littered with patches of moonlight, but most of it was in shadow. The uneven light and the overgrown foliage made dozens of hiding places possible. The footman could have run ahead, doubled back, or could even be waiting next to Devon, and he would never had known it. By the time he reached Thomas for help, the footman would have disappeared. He was outwitted.

He swore again. He had lost. Denied an outlet for his

frustration, he could only stalk back to attend to his first mate. He had recovered Cassie's journal, but he still had no clue who else sought the work.

Or how close they were to cheating him out of his treasure.

Twenty-Three

Cassie was thankful that when Benjamin went out the front door, Devon and his carriage were gone. She was less pleased by the stinging lecture her brother delivered. When she refused to listen, he shook his head. "Just do as I tell you. Stay away from Renard."

She had no intention of doing so, and less intention of informing her brother of the fact. "What about the telescope?" she asked. "You were going to take it with you tonight. May I have it back now?"

Muttering under his breath, he went to retrieve it from the hall table. Returning to where she waited on the stair, he handed over the instrument with ill grace.

She retreated to the safety of her room. She considered continuing her observations, but only for a moment. It was too late to spot the comet, and her journal would need to be replaced before she could make any meaningful progress. Besides, she had too much on her mind to focus.

Why would a beautiful, wealthy, sought-after young lady like Miss Compton resort to a lie to trap a man into marriage? Cassie could not deny Devon's attractiveness; she had certainly been tempted to do things out of the ordinary to catch his attention. But claiming him to be a brute would hardly endear the fellow to Barbara's parents. Or was her pretense designed to rouse some display of manliness from Benjamin? But he had already proposed, so why would she need him to prove his love? It made no sense.

Neither did the theft of her journal make sense, at least on the surface, though she was sure it had been mistaken for her father's. But why was everyone so interested in the blasted journals? Devon wanted to find his uncle. The duke wanted to help him. Herbert Montague wanted to find a comet of his own. What did the two thieves and her footman hope to gain from them?

She posed the same questions to Liza when she met her ward in the breakfast room shortly after noon the next day. The girl relayed that the servants were certain the footman had been a spy for Napoleon, who was said to be obsessed with the stars. Cassie dismissed that out of hand. The tyrant didn't need to terrorize one insignificant English amateur astronomer.

She found Liza's other news less easy to dismiss. It seemed Benjamin had been short with Liza and the staff, and Mr. Baxter, the new cook, was sure it was because the marquis de Renard had beaten him out of Miss Compton's hand.

"He said the marquis had tried to force himself upon her," Liza admitted. "Miss Compton has been horribly compromised."

"Drivel!" Cassie declared, setting down her cup of chocolate with a clink. "You've seen the marquis, Liza. Does he look as if he'd have to force a woman to do anything?"

Liza swallowed. "Well, no. But I'm beginning to learn that not everyone is as he seems."

"Who do you mean?" Cassie asked, suspicious.

She shrugged. "Our footman, for one. And then there is Mr. Montague, declaring undying devotion when there are moments I think he cannot abide us. Are all men so deceitful?"

Cassie sighed. "Oh, Liza, I wish I knew. I believe the marquis is innocent, at least as far as his involvement with Miss Compton. In other matters, I don't know what to think."

"We should learn more about him," Liza said sagely.

"What does he do when he is not with us? With whom does he associate?"

Cassie eyed her. "I suppose the servants think he's horrid."

"They are divided," Liza replied. She went on to summarize what she had gleaned from her various sources belowstairs. It matched what Cassie had been told. His mother, a cousin of the duke of Devonlee, had married into the French aristocracy, only to die shortly after Devon was born. Not much was known of his early childhood, but it was supposed that he had had the usual pampered experiences of the only son of a powerful French lord. When his father had been taken hostage in Paris, Devon and an uncle had escaped to England. But instead of being greeted warmly by his English relatives, Devon had been raised as a poor relation. In later life, he had distinguished himself as a privateer. Indeed, he was said to have amassed a fortune in prize money, yet he never seemed to have sufficient funds. Most of what he currently owned, it was rumored, had been bought on credit with use of the duke's name.

"Mr. Baxter thought perhaps he gambles," Liza concluded. "But he has seldom been seen to play at the gentlemen's clubs, so I don't think that's likely. The Patters' groom says he spends it on French women."

"The Patters' groom is an idiot," Cassie replied. But, though she didn't like the idea, it wasn't that far-fetched. Devon likely had no trouble finding accommodating ladies, of any nationality.

"The Patters' groom may be wrong, but the marquis is a mystery," Liza proclaimed. "I do not see how we could possibly be related. My father wasn't even French. I revise my original opinion. We should stay away from him."

Cassie shook her head. "I promised him I'd meet him today."

"Why?" Liza frowned with obvious worry. "Cassie, please tell me you are not taken with this fellow."

"Don't be silly," Cassie snapped. "I am only helping him

read the journals. Benjamin has expressed such overt dislike of him that I have no choice but to meet him in Hyde Park. If you are concerned, you can come with me."

She was sure Liza would agree, for the novelty and the excuse to get out of the house. To her surprise, her ward demurred.

"No, thank you. Mr. Montague will be here for tea. I shall cover for you."

Cassie frowned. "You will forego an outing, for Mr. Montague? Are you feeling well?"

"I'm fine," Liza assured her. "Please go without me and enjoy yourself. But be careful."

Cassie was just that. She had her coachman keep the carriage about ten yards behind her as she strolled along the paths edging the drive. Even though the October day was brisk, with a biting wind, a number of people braved the cold to stroll about. She stopped to stare in envy at the thick ermine muff one young lady carried, wrapping her own gloved hands more deeply into her black wool cloak.

"Shall I offer you my coat again?" Devon murmured in her ear.

Cassie blushed and stepped away to look back at him. His white silk shirt and buff pantaloons did not look as if they would warm him without the brown wool jacket he wore on top. "No, thank you," she told him.

"Ever the brave one," he commented. "I insist we finish our business quickly, then. Your lips are turning blue."

She compressed her mouth self-consciously. "So will yours if you take off your coat."

"And if my lips chill," he murmured, bending closer, "will you warm them?"

His smile was seductive, his very warm lips only a foot from her own. She would not be so brazen as to close the distance.

"You are impossible," she snapped. "Did you wish to see Stephen Kearney's telescope?"

"Very much," he acknowledged, straightening.

"It's in the carriage." She hurried to retrieve it, thankful for an excuse to get away from his distracting presence. She could scarcely think when he was near. She hefted the case in her arms and brought it back to him. When she held out the box, he seized it eagerly.

"Is it your uncle's?" she asked as he ran his hands over the case as lovingly as Benjamin had done. In fact, watching the way his fingers stroked the mahogany set her cheeks blazing anew.

"I don't know," he admitted. "But it could be."

She pointed to the empty spot on the end of the case. "Surely that held a name plate once."

He regarded the spot. "Yes, most likely. It would not surprise me if my uncle had an engraved plate on the case identifying it as his. He was very particular about his instrument. I remember him having an argument with a helpful servant at my cousin's. The servant wanted to carry the case; my uncle refused, in no uncertain terms. He took it with him when he left for London." His hands stroked the case once more. "Would you mind if I kept this for a day or so, to examine it more closely?"

The request seemed excessive, and her suspicions rose. Yet what could he do with it? Even if he sold it, she still had her father's. But the instrument wasn't actually hers.

"We should ask Liza. It belongs to her. Can you tell enough just by looking at it?"

"Perhaps," he replied. "Give me a moment." He squatted to set the case on the ground. Snapping it open, he lifted out the instrument and tipped it end to end like a level.

"Does it work?" he asked, glancing up.

She nodded. "I polished the speculum two days ago for Benjamin."

He eyed her. "The speculum?"

"The instrument is a Cassegrain reflector, one of the finest I've seen. It reflects the light from the stars off two pieces of metal made from a mixture of copper and tin—the speculum. The metal tarnishes easily."

"So you opened the tube to clean the metal. Was that the first time you'd done so?"

She frowned at him. Why would he care whether she polished it once a decade or once a day? Was he accusing her of being lax in caring for the instrument? "Frankly, I hadn't opened the case since Stephen Kearney died," she informed him.

He nodded absently. "There was nothing else inside it, I take it."

"No, nothing I would not have expected. Shall I open it for you now?"

"No," he replied. He did not even bother to put the instrument to his eye. "And why did your brother have this in his possession? He is not an astronomer."

He made it sound as if she had committed heresy. She felt compelled to defend herself. "He wanted to show Miss Compton the stars. I could hardly let him use Father's."

"He had it with him at the ball, then?" he asked sharply.

"Yes." Her frown deepened. "Why? Is it damaged?"

"We shall see," he murmured. She thought he would look through it at last, but he handed the instrument to her. She carefully lifted it to her eye. The Hyde Park corner hove into view in perfect detail. She lowered the telescope in time to see him feeling along the inside of the case. His eyes were closed as if in concentration. Suddenly he stopped, and his eyes snapped open. His fingers, against the far end of the case, stiffened. To her surprise, the bottom of the case slid into itself to reveal a hidden compartment. She bent to peer with him inside it.

It was empty.

He said something in French under his breath, and though she had never been taught the word, she was sure it was foul.

"What did you expect to find?" she asked.

"A note," he replied. "A journal, a letter, something to tie this to my uncle. Where is your brother?"

Cassie blinked at the non sequitor. "He left before I got up this morning. Why? What's wrong?"

"Nothing," he said, and she knew he lied. "It is simply disappointing to find the case empty. The answer must be in your father's journals."

"Well," she sighed, "at least we have those."

"We have yours as well," he told her, though she thought his mind was far away. "I found it in the park across from your house. Give me a moment and I'll return it to you."

Cassie stared at him. "You found my journal?"

He shook himself, then offered her a wry smile. "I should have told you sooner, but I was preoccupied. Stay here. I'll get it." He glanced at the case again as if wishing it would miraculously give up its secrets, then turned on his heel to stride to where his carriage waited behind some trees.

Cassie shook her head as she laid the telescope back into its case. Something was going on, and now her brother was involved as well. She didn't think Devon was going to explain it to her, if indeed he knew the truth.

It very much looked as though she was going to have to find it on her own.

Twenty-Four

"*Rien*," Devon muttered under his breath as Thomas drove him home. "Nothing. Again."

He had been certain when he'd seen the case that he had found the treasure. It was possible he had been right that the jewels had once been hidden there. He could think of no other reason for his uncle to build a secret compartment—if the case had belonged to his uncle to begin with.

But if it had, where were the jewels? Could Benjamin Bentbrooke have found them? Or had he found a clue to their whereabouts? Was that why he had ordered the footman to bring him the journals, to decipher the clue? Or had the footman lied about that? The only way he could be sure was to set one of his men to shadow the major.

And what if the case truly had belonged to Stephen Kearney? Where did that leave his search? No further along, he feared, than when he had first begun. He would have to keep reading the journals with Cassie. She had agreed to allow him to visit again the next afternoon.

He had one other chance. Ames might have been able to learn something about Stephen Kearney. Determined, he rode out to his cousin's estate outside London, a little over an hour away. As usual, Ames had to be convinced to help him right then. His Grace's affairs took precedence. However, after receiving Devon's previous note, Ames had evidently searched his files and now produced a list of every clergyman currently in practice in the Church of England.

Devon could not imagine why the fellow would need such a list, but Ames seemed to be a magnet for esoteric bits of information. He forgave him everything when he had found an elderly rector in York by the name of Kearney.

Ames had already dispatched a letter asking the fellow whether he had had sons and what had become of them. Devon rode home, but before he retired for the night, a groom brought word that Ames had also been able to locate a death record for Stephen Kearney. The date of death corresponded to when Cassie had implied the man had died. That it had been an accident, with the man being run down by an unknown carriage, made Devon wonder. If Stephen Kearney had been his uncle, could the accident mask murder? Had someone killed to gain the treasure? But if that were the case, surely the jewels would have surfaced by now. The Sebastien diamonds would be hard to mistake. Yet, if the treasure had been found, why were so many people interested in the Bentbrooke journals?

He hoped they might learn the answer the next day, but he did not gain any clues. Cassie read and interpreted portions of the journals as she had promised, but he heard nothing that shed any more light on the mystery of Stephen Kearney, his uncle, or the treasure. In fact, he spent much of the time admiring how her pale hair reflected the autumn sunlight. It was perhaps his close study that made her more skittish than usual. In fact, she had excused herself as he said good-bye, leaving her ward to walk him to the door.

He took a moment to study the girl again. She kept her head respectfully bowed as she escorted him down the stairs from the withdrawing room, where he had been reading with Cassie. "What do you remember about your father?" he asked.

She smiled. "Quite a bit. I was nine when he died."

"Did he ever tell you anything about his family?"

Her smile faded. "Very little. He was a missionary before he joined Lord Bentbrooke. He came to London to save the French émigrés from hellfire. I'm sure he would have converted my mother if he could. The pope is an evil man; did you know that?"

"I was raised Catholic," he replied. "I don't remember thinking the pope such a demon."

They reached the bottom of the stairs; the butler waited by the door. The time for questioning was over, at least for now. She curtsied. "So good of you to visit, my lord. Do come again."

He had to smile as he bowed. Cassie had not given him a date to return, but her ward had just provided an excuse to call. "Your servant, Miss Kearney. Perhaps I can see you tomorrow."

She dimpled, and he was out the door before the major could return.

He made his way about his other tasks for the day, his mind once more sifting through possibilities. If Stephen Kearney really was the son of an English rector who had come to London to save the French, why had he taken a position as an assistant astronomer? Or had the girl taken bits of conversation and woven them into a fanciful story, as children often did? If he was Jean-Luc Sebastien, the tale held a kernel of truth, for his uncle had indeed come to London on a mission: to distribute the jewels to their rightful owners. He had thought only death would stop his uncle, but the more he learned, the more he saw that Jean-Luc had wanted to keep the jewels for himself. Madam Fortune had frowned, and his uncle had simply become someone else.

He headed toward White's to see how Bertrand fared with the major, who was likely there. But he hadn't gone half the distance when he realized he was being followed.

It started with a general uneasiness, as if he had forgotten something. Then, as he turned onto St. James, a movement seen out of the corner of his eye made him look back. Busy Londoners hurried in both directions. Well-dressed ladies walked side by side. Burly footmen or hatchet-faced abigails followed, arms laden with packages. Gentlemen strode toward White's or Brooks'. He saw nothing that should give him pause. Shaking his head, he continued.

Bertrand, loitering on the street across from the club, reported that Bentbrooke was indeed inside but that Compton was with him. Having no interest in facing the man with the rumors flying about his daughter, Devon decided to head for the French quarter to check on a few of his crew who had been injured in the last sea battle. He paused to rub the back of his neck as the uneasiness returned.

Bertrand stiffened. "What is it?"

"I feel as if I'm being followed," Devon murmured. "Move back and watch. If you see anything, whistle."

His man nodded again, walking back the way Devon had come. Devon continued on the street. He had not reached the corner before a sharp whistle pulled him up. He whirled in time to see a maid in black dart into a shop. So, his instincts hadn't failed him. Nothing like a good chase to while away the afternoon. Grinning, he set off down Pall Mall at a brisk pace.

He played with her at first, walking faster, then suddenly slowing so that she was forced to avoid him. But after a half hour, the game began to cloy. He had calls to make, and evening would be coming shortly. Time to find out who his shadow was.

But try as he might, he could not seem to catch her. He detoured around corners, dashed down alleys, and doubled back on himself. Just when he was sure he could catch her, she disappeared. He'd spend minutes wandering about the area, and when he'd give up and start out for the north again, a figure in black would appear at the edge of his sight. She seemed to sense his tricks before he tried them.

Finally, he slipped into a shop doorway, determined to wait until she appeared. He stood for some time and was about to give up again when she hurried past. He fell into step behind her. He only caught a glimpse of her, for she seemed to sense his presence and ducked into a store that sold women's undergarments.

The glimpse was enough. The maid was tall and elegant, dressed in a worn black gown with a shabby cloak on top. He had little doubt that if he pulled off that silly cap, white-gold hair would spill out. Cassie was playing the maid again. Why?

He doubled back and strolled in front of the shop with deliberate calm. A few moments later, she fell into place behind him. Mademoiselle Bentbrooke wanted adventure, it seemed. It would not do to disappoint.

Cassie swallowed, hoping somehow that would force her heart out of her throat and back down into her chest where it belonged. She doubted it would stop the wild beating. He had almost caught her! She had to be more careful if she hoped to learn what he was up to.

She still wondered at her own audacity. Traipsing about London as a maid was not going to help her reputation. It certainly wouldn't help Benjamin's plan. Perhaps both those facts had encouraged her to try it—those and her own curiosity to learn more about the marquis. But she had to be more subtle.

She thought perhaps she had succeeded, for he stopped taking precautions and strolled down the street as if he no longer felt in any danger. She was so busy following him, however, that she did not notice right away that they had moved out of the fashionable west end and headed north into less hospitable territory. The houses and shops grew more crowded, less expensive. Dirty children hopped between rivulets of sewage, and horses were few. While in Mayfair she had blended in among the other servants scurrying about their masters' business; now she stood out like a crow among sparrows. More than one child paused to stare at her as she hurried along, and when she darted into an arched entry to avoid detection, she collided with a washerwoman who shouted at her in French.

As she backed hurriedly out into the street, muttering apologies, she realized she had lost sight of him. For a moment she panicked. She nearly ran the next block, scanning about her. There was no sign of him. Worse, she was deep within the slum area, and she had no idea where she was.

Men lounging on doorsteps seemed to leer at her. The dark windows of the houses stared like eyes. Hugging her cloak to herself, she hurried to the next corner and glanced in all directions. The slum stretched as far as she could see.

Then she caught her breath. To the left rose a church steeple. It was St. Pancras, where Liza's parents were buried. She might have lost the marquis, but surely she could find her way home from there. She set off at a brisk trot, never noticing that a man stepped out of the shadows to follow her.

"Nothing?" The duke of Devonlee eyed both his men with raised brows. Ames cringed. Jacobs stood straighter.

"Sorry, Your Grace," the ex-footman informed his employer respectfully. "I barely escaped with my life. But I can go back. I know the household routine now. Sunday the servants will have the afternoon off. I still have a key to the house."

The duke shook his head. "From what you tell me, the journals will be useless to me. If we are to read them, we will need the spinster as well."

Jacobs cracked a grin. "That should be no trouble."

Ames shivered.

The duke eyed him. "Mr. Ames would appear to disagree with you. Do you still find this woman so formidable?"

Ames nodded. "Most assuredly, Your Grace. This very afternoon she chased your cousin all about London."

"I beg your pardon?" His Grace drawled.

"Miss Bentbrooke dressed as a maid and followed Captain Sebastien about the city. The last I saw before bringing Jacobs here, they were heading toward St. Pancras."

The duke shook his head. "Another time this would be amusing. Now I tire of the game. I do not need to see what that rector in York will write back to us. From what you've already learned, Ames, I am certain Stephen Kearney was Jean-Luc Sebastien. I am equally certain he left some clue as to the whereabouts of the treasure, most likely in those accursed journals. And I would wager that Miss Bentbrooke can tell me what that is. Jacobs?"

The burly fellow stepped forward sharply. "Your Grace?"

"Return to London and pick her up. It is time I had another discussion with this formidable spinster."

Twenty-Five

Devon shadowed Cassie through the streets. Once in a while an émigré, catching sight of him, would nod in greeting. Others turned away. The son of Francois Sebastien was a familiar sight here. They accepted with ill grace the food and money he provided. Few could pass up the opportunity to tell him again how his family had betrayed the Debusses, Travalliers, and Richards. They had entrusted their wealth to the former marquis de Renard, trusted the mighty Sebastiens to bring the jewels to England. The proceeds from the treasure were to pay for the families' upkeep in exile, until they could return to France and reclaim their estates. Henri had seen his father die in poverty, next to others who should have slept on silk sheets and drunk fine wine from gold goblets. Bertrand, who should have been educated at the Sorbonne, had been forced to become a purser.

He shook his head to clear the dark thoughts that always assailed him here. He would find the treasure; he would right the wrongs. Dwelling on the matter didn't help anyone.

He gazed up the street and spotted the dark figure disappearing in the direction of St. Pancras church. Surely she wouldn't go there. It was an older church, the only place in London where the French Catholics could be buried. Many of the French still in the city lived in the apartments and houses around it. He knew that few of them would talk to her, but their gossip was not what he feared. He could not let her see what was in the churchyard. He hurried after her.

Cassie peered into the church, hoping for a glimpse of Mr. Baker, the rector who had the living. She and Liza had spoken to him several times when they had come to decorate the Kearneys' graves. An older man with deep-set, owlish eyes, he was always calm and helpful, as quiet as the shadows that filled the empty church. At the moment, she could have used some of that calm.

When she didn't see him, she started around for the side, where the churchyard lay. At the very least, she would know her way home once she stood beside the graves. Although Liza's father could have been buried elsewhere, Cassie's parents had been certain he would want to be near his wife, who had had to be buried in the Catholic cemetery. Stephen himself had mentioned the matter as he lay dying, she remembered, making Liza promise to take care of her mother's grave. It was a sad fact, she knew, that sometimes people of the lower classes were turned out of their graves for others. Thankfully, Liza's constant care had prevented anyone from attempting to remove her parents.

The churchyard was as quiet as it always was. Huge sycamores, their leaves curling brown and just beginning to fall, shadowed the carefully tended grass. White stones with darker lintels and moss-encrusted vaults stood silent. The faintest of breezes moved among the stones, like whispers from the sleeping souls. Cassie glanced to the left, where the Kearneys were buried. Even from here she could see the twin stones, side by side. She could not read the inscriptions, but she knew them by heart. Stephen's stone neatly cataloged dates of birth and death and finished with an inscription about his work as an astronomer. No one had known what year Yvette had been born; her stone bore only the date of her death, November 15, 1793. She had died after knowing her daughter for only a few days. Stephen had chosen the inscription: *She should have had better.* If he was indeed Jean-Luc Sebastien, the words were even more appropriate than she had always thought.

Beyond the stones the sun was setting, and the air was growing chillier. Cassie wrapped her arms about herself. As she turned for the gate she and Liza used to leave the yard, she spotted the minister on his knees pulling weeds from around one of the many stones near the edge of the yard.

"Good afternoon, Miss Bentbrooke," he greeted her, rising to dust off his worn trousers. "Here to see to the Kearneys again?"

She could hardly tell the gentleman that she'd been playing chase with a privateer all afternoon. "And you are taking care of your charges, I see," she replied instead.

He smiled. "Of course. I hate to see anyone neglected." He waved down the line of stones, many with inscriptions in French. "So few have family here anymore, although at least this one gets a visitor from time to time."

He waved down at the stone beside him. Cassie stared.

The stone had been cheaply cut, and even now the inscription was fading. She bent closer. Then she sucked in a breath.

"Jean-Luc Sebastien," she read aloud. "Born 1755, died 1792." There was more below it, but she couldn't make it out. She bent even closer.

"It says," Devon murmured behind them, "look to the heavens for your reward."

Cassie jerked upright. The rector smiled at him. "Good afternoon, my lord. Helping the poor again? Do you know Miss Bentbrooke?"

"She is with me," he said, taking her elbow proprietarily. "And it is late. We should return to your brother now, my dear."

The day darkening along with her thoughts, she managed a tight smile for Mr. Baker's benefit and let the marquis lead her toward the gate. When she saw that a large vault hid them from the rector's view, she turned on Devon.

"How dare you! You knew all along he was dead!"

He shrugged, and she had to tighten her fists at her sides to keep from striking him. He took a step forward, and she took a step back, fetching her hip sharply against a stone. She stumbled, and he reached out to steady her. She scurried out of his hands.

"Don't touch me. You lied to me. You said you wanted to see the journals because you wanted to find your uncle. But you knew he was dead. According to that date, he died before Stephen Kearney ever met my father!"

"According to that date, he died before he ever penned that article with your father."

She stiffened, realizing he was right. "How could that be?" she demanded, unwilling to let go of her anger. It was her only shield against his very potent charm.

"I don't know. That's why I must see your father's journals. They may give me some clue as to what happened."

"And you expect me to believe that?"

He sighed. "My dear Cassiopeia, use that marvelous mind of yours. What do I have to gain? You said yourself, your father's journals are only good for scientific study. How could reading them serve any other purpose?"

How indeed? That was the question she could not answer. "I don't trust you," she said aloud. "There's something you aren't telling me."

"And what would that be?" he asked, leaning against the stone. That put his face within a few feet of her own, close enough that she could see the green deepening in the gray. She took another step away from him.

"I don't know. But you do. Please just tell me."

"What, exactly, do you think I know?" He offered her a half smile, looking up from under his brows.

She sighed. "A very great deal more than I do. On any

number of subjects. Now, stop this circular logic. I'm tired of innuendo and secrets. I want the truth."

His smile faded. "Mademoiselle Bentbrooke, I cannot offer you any more information than you already have. I am no angel, *cherie*. But I have tried not to play the devil with you."

She could not argue that. Even now he was discussing the issue with her rather than demanding why she had followed him. Perhaps he really didn't know anything more. Perhaps she had been around her brother so long that she saw conspiracies where none existed. Perhaps the marquis was merely an extremely handsome, virile gentleman who wanted to find his family. Perhaps she should retire while she had the chance.

"You've played as fairly as I believe you know how," she said. "But you must remember: I am a scientist by training. I need evidence, facts to examine. The information I have so far is woefully inadequate to form any substantial theories."

"Is that why you followed me around this afternoon—in search of more information?"

She grimaced. "I should apologize for that. Yes, I thought perhaps I'd learn something more about you."

"And did you learn anything?" he purred.

She felt her lips curling in a smile. "You live in the world of innuendo, don't you? I suppose it has stood you in good stead, if everything they say about your cousin is true."

"What do they say about the duke?" The light in his eyes told her the answer interested him more than his tone indicated.

"That he raised you as a poor relation. I imagine he is a hard man, perhaps a ruthless one. But you indicated he helped you in your search for your uncle."

"My cousin is endlessly helpful," he quipped. "What else did you learn about me?"

"You've been subsidizing the émigrés," she replied and

was rewarded by his reaction. He stiffened away from the stone and frowned. "Admit it, my lord. The rector said as much. I'd wager you hire their men for your ship and pay them more than you would otherwise. You don't need to make atonement, you know."

He took a step toward her again, and this time she stood her ground. "What do you mean? For what am I making atonement?"

"For the way the French aristocrats abused their servants, of course. I very much doubt you ever abused anyone. I also doubt these people expect you to apologize for an entire generation."

He shook his head. "I see what you mean about the danger of formulating theories on little information. Rest assured, *cherie*. I do not apologize for those who have already paid the price, in blood. Next time you decide to spy on me, perhaps I can point you in a more informative direction."

What had she gotten wrong? She sorted through the facts she knew again: his childhood with the duke, his privateering, his wealth that seemed to disappear too quickly. Suddenly another theory presented itself, a far more personal theory. Perhaps he did indeed subsidize the émigrés, but it was their women he paid, not their men. She colored.

"I should not have resorted to spying on you," she told him. "Please accept my apology."

"The tabby apologizes for the wildcat," he answered with a chuckle. "Come, let me see you home."

"That isn't necessary," she replied, thoroughly embarrassed that she had followed him on an assignation. "I can find my way back to Mayfair. I'm sure you have others to ... visit."

He chuckled again. "I came to check on some of my men. If I were searching for a mistress, *cherie,* I would look closer to Mayfair."

Surely her cheeks were flaming. "I'm sure that is none of my business."

He succeeded in capturing her arm and drew her toward the gate. "You complain when I do not offer enough information, and you complain when I do. What do you want from me, mademoiselle?"

She gazed up into the depths of his gray-green eyes, feeling the strength of his arm against hers. What did she want from him? Honesty? What if he told her he cared nothing about her? Undying devotion? Not if she had to share it with every woman in London. His love? Not if it meant living a lie.

"Your escort home will be sufficient, Monsieur le Marquis," she replied. "For now."

Twenty-Six

The walk home in the deepening twilight was uneventful. Cassie said little as she walked beside Devon, and he found himself hesitant to breach the silence, for fear her conversation would be as fierce as the scowl on her face. He had thought for a moment in the graveyard that she knew everything. Thank God she still lacked a few pieces of the puzzle. Knowing her as he was coming to do, he wondered how she would react if she knew he was really after the treasure. If she knew the whole story of his family's failure, would she scorn his company? She would never demand a cut of the money, but her censure would bring enough pain.

He bowed over her hand when they reached the house on St. Mary's Circle. "I will call tomorrow, as I promised your ward."

She nodded absently, pulling the cap off her hair and stuffing the piece of linen into her pocket. "That will be fine."

"Half past two?" he pressed, watching her. The lamp beside the door had been lit, and it set her hair to glowing.

She nodded again. "That will be fine."

What was going on behind those silver eyes? He wanted to know, and he feared to know. "Are you all right?"

"Yes, I'm fine." She glanced up at him then quickly back down. There was speculation in those eyes, of a kind he had seen before, but generally not from a proper English lady.

It surprised him, and it flattered him. Reaching out, he brought her hand to his lips, brushing a kiss against the skin of her wrist.

"*Cherie*," he murmured, "if you wish to see me sooner, you have only to send me a note."

The wildcat flared to life. She snatched back her hand as if he had burned her. "I'm sure I can contain myself."

Devon smiled as she turned toward the opening door. He had been wrong earlier. She wouldn't make a magnificent mistress. She would put every other woman in London to shame. He would almost have given up the treasure for a note calling him to her side. Almost. He turned to descend the stair. A hand on his arm pulled him up short.

"Not so fast, you French bastard," Benjamin snarled. "I demand to know where you've been with my sister."

Devon turned back, eyes narrowed. Better men than this one had called him such a name and worse, and he had kept his temper. He might have kept it this time as well, if his eyes had not been drawn to where Bentbrooke's hand gripped Cassie's arm so tightly that his knuckles whitened. Devon's blood heated.

"Let her go," he ordered. "Your quarrel is with me."

The major only pulled her closer. She grimaced. "That's what I'm trying to determine," Bentbrooke growled.

"Benjamin, stop it," she demanded, struggling in his grip. "You have nothing to complain about. The marquis did me a service by escorting me home from shopping."

"Before or after he bedded you?" her brother challenged.

She blanched.

"Your sister," Devon said quietly, "is a lady, Major Bentbrooke. If you would like her to remain so to others, I suggest we take this conversation somewhere private."

It was obvious to Devon that Bentbrooke could care less about his sister's reputation. "Oh, no, you don't," the major declared. "I've had enough of your skulking about in dark corners. That may be the way you do things in France, but it's not how we do things in England."

"No," Devon replied. "Here you enjoy tormenting defenseless creatures in public."

"I am not defenseless," she informed him. She stomped the heel of her half boot neatly down on her brother's instep. When he flinched back, she bumped him hard with her hip and toppled him into the entryway. Then she slammed the door shut in his open-mouthed face.

"Run," she advised Devon.

Devon didn't know whether to laugh or shout in anger. His wildcat was in full force and had never looked more magnificent. Still, he had no doubt her brother would make her pay for what she had done. "And leave you to deal with his wrath? Never."

She shook her head, grabbed his arm, and pulled him toward the park. "Run, I tell you. I am perfectly capable—"

"Traitor!" Benjamin shouted, diving out of the doorway and running to them. "Jezebel! How dare you side with this coward? Can't you tell he's trying to ruin you?"

Devon smashed his fist into the underside of Bentbrooke's jaw. Cassie's brother went down in a lump on the pavement.

"Come with me," he said to Cassie, shaking out his hand. "He is a madman."

"He is an idiot," she corrected him. "And if I come with you, it will only substantiate his ridiculous claims. You knew people were already speculating about you and Miss Compton?"

"Yes, but as she was the one to start the rumors, the only distress she feels must stem from the fact that I have not tried to defend myself. Nor will I. I have done no wrong."

At his feet, Benjamin moaned.

Devon considered his options. He could leave the fellow in the middle of the pavement and run off with his sister, but Cassie did not appear to be willing to cooperate. In fact, she would no doubt serve him as neatly as she had her brother. He could attempt to mollify the fellow, but he was in no mood to be conciliatory.

Cassie put her hands on his shoulders. "Leave. Now. I can handle Benjamin."

"So can I," he assured her.

Her brother struggled to his feet. He rubbed his jaw and glared at Devon. Devon eyed him with no less annoyance.

"You'll pay for that," he promised. "I demand satisfaction."

Devon rolled his eyes. A duel was the last thing he needed.

"What you ought to demand is the truth," Cassie told her brother. "The marquis has done nothing wrong."

"Why do you women persist in defending him?" Benjamin complained. "I spent half the afternoon with Barbara Compton. She didn't want me to call him out, either."

"Then perhaps you should have listened," Cassie replied heatedly.

"If you are both quite finished," Devon put in, "I'd like to go home."

"You are going nowhere," Benjamin informed him, "until we've settled this."

"There is nothing to settle!" Cassie cried. "The marquis has been nothing but a gentleman to me, and he has been no less to Miss Compton."

"You're blind," Benjamin sneered. "He tried to rape her at the ball."

"He did no such thing," she scolded. "He danced with her in full view of an entire ballroom of people, and the rest of the time he was with me."

Devon shook his head. She was trying to defend him, but her brother had put him in a hole, and she was only digging it deeper.

"Oh?" Benjamin said quietly. "And where, exactly, were you alone with him?"

She did not see the trap. She raised her head higher. "We took a walk in the garden, and he took me home."

Any other brother would have demanded his intentions. Though he was sure the major did not care, he did not miss the cue. Benjamin returned his hostile gaze to Devon, who met it straight on. "And do you intend to offer for my sister?" the major demanded.

Devon opened his mouth, but Cassie answered for him.

"He does not," she snapped. "No offer is necessary, and none is expected."

None might be expected, but suddenly he wondered about the advisability of making one. Certainly she attracted him as few women had ever done. It would be an excellent way to annoy his cousin, who had already tried to prevent an alliance. But did he love her? He shook his head. The question was moot. Miss Bentbrooke obviously had other ideas.

"If I might make a suggestion—" he tried.

"I disagree," Benjamin snarled as if he had said nothing. "He's ruined my sister's reputation, and by God, he's going to pay for it."

"You are determined to call him out," Cassie accused. "He is twice the man you are, Benjamin. I would apologize now while you have the chance."

Devon wondered how they would react if he simply took Cassie's hand and walked away with her. He couldn't seem to get their attention any other way. Perhaps he could signal Henri, who should be on duty in the park, to make some kind of diversion. But glancing around, he noticed that they had succeeded in attracting the attention of others. The lamplighter had moved his way to the street lamp nearby and had been standing for several minutes, watching. Another couple, dressed to go out for a dinner party, paused before their carriage to stare and whisper. Pierson was standing in the doorway, mouth tight, and he could see Liza's pale face peering out of the second-story window.

"Apologize?" Benjamin shouted. "I have no reason to apologize. My family name has been damaged. He's turned you into a lightskirt. I tell you, I will have satisfaction."

"Enough," Devon declared. "I care nothing for my reputation, but I will not have you damage your sister's. I shall be happy to give you satisfaction, any time or place you name, so long as you agree to leave Miss Bentbrooke out of it."

"Done," Benjamin agreed while Cassie cried a protest. "My second will call on yours. You will send me the names of the mourners."

"*Avec plesir*," Devon drawled. "Who are your closest friends besides mademoiselle?"

"You're actually going to let him force you into this?" Cassie demanded. When Devon frowned at her, she threw up her hands. "Very well. I wash my hands of the pair of you. Just don't expect me to crown the victor, unless it's with the sharp end of a fireplace poker!"

Twenty-Seven

"What was the meaning of that ridiculous tirade?" Cassie demanded when she and her brother returned at last to the house. "And do not tell me it had anything to do with your brotherly feelings for me. You pinched me, bruised me, and called me disgusting names. You have no feelings for anyone but yourself."

"So sorry to offend," he snarled sarcastically. "You might look at your own behavior."

"My behavior!"

"Your behavior. You are supposed to be helping me, Cassie. Instead, you go out of your way to consort with the enemy."

"The marquis de Renard is hardly the enemy," she informed him, stalking for the stairs. She knew she was not thinking clearly, but she was certain her brother wasn't thinking at all. A duel, for God's sake. One of them would likely be killed, the other jailed for murder. Any way she looked at it, she would lose a man who was part of her life.

Benjamin followed her to the door of her room. "He may not be the enemy, but neither is he an ally. He's French, for heaven's sake! He doesn't have a penny he didn't wheedle out of his cousin the duke, and he doesn't have a single plausible reason for hanging around us."

"I thought you had determined that he was after my virtue after all," she challenged.

"Most likely he is. But I can't believe that's the only reason. I don't trust him, and I don't like him."

"And that's sufficient reason to challenge him to a duel?" She eyed him incredulously.

"Sufficient enough when you add in the fact that he dallied with Barbara Compton as well."

She shook her head. "You will not give up harping on that one note, will you? I tell you for the last time, he is innocent. I think you want to fight him because he threatens your plans for Miss Compton."

He did not bother to deny it. "He is a thorn in my side, and I intend to excise him."

"But this duel is a stupid idea, Benjamin. He is a seasoned fighter. He'll kill you."

"Don't pretend that fact saddens you," he jeered.

"I shan't. But whether you believe it or not, I do not wish you dead. Nor do I wish to see the marquis incarcerated for murder."

"Ha!" Benjamin declared. "I should have known you'd be worrying for him. And well you should. He may be a seasoned fighter, but so am I, Cassie. I'm a retired major of His Majesty's forces. I've seen my own share of fighting and lived to tell the tale. I'm pretty handy with all the weapons of war. Let's see—should it be swords or pistols?"

Her blood ran cold just thinking about it. "Stop it! You cannot win. Do you think Miss Compton will thank you? She fully intends to marry him, or she wouldn't have tried to trap him."

"So you claim. Her distress seems very real to me."

Cassie snorted. "It was designed for that purpose. You are a man, and she is an expert at playing on your male need to protect what you fancy is yours. But I promise you, Benjamin, you will not win her this way. If you kill the marquis, you will never see her dowry. Send him a note, Benjamin. Call it off. For everyone's sake."

He shook his head. "You are an innocent, Cassie. The

duel will go on, the day after tomorrow. And don't get in the way, or you'll live to regret it."

He stomped back down the stairs and slammed out of the house. Cassie shook her head. He was an idiot, as she had told Devon—an idiot for proposing this duel and an idiot for thinking she would sit idly by. She turned to go into her room when a movement caught her eye. Liza's door was slowly opening. Her ward peered out at her, pale and wide-eyed.

"I heard everything," she murmured, a tear tracking down one cheek. "Major Bentbrooke is a cruel, unconscionable dastard."

Cassie nodded sadly. "Yes, Liza, he is."

"Why did you let me make a fool out of myself?"

Her pain was so evident, Cassie wanted to hug her close. "Why don't you come into my room and we can talk?" she suggested.

A few moments later, her ward was curled up on the bed, Cassie seated beside her, a damp handkerchief in one hand.

"And so he really intends to marry Miss Compton for her money?" Liza asked, hiccoughing back a last sob.

Cassie nodded. "Yes. His story of undying devotion only extended to her dowry."

"Why didn't you tell her? She must be warned!"

"I agree. I reacted the same way when he told me. But my brother has a rather good hold on us. He threatened to throw us out on the streets if I refused to go along with his plan."

"He wouldn't be so cruel," Liza protested.

"Oh, yes," Cassie said with full assurance, "he would."

Liza rose to pace the room, lavender skirts swishing with her agitation. "I cannot understand it, Cassie. He seems so nice, most of the time. Surely there is some goodness in him. He bought me new gowns. He didn't have to do that. He spent time with me as if he enjoyed it. There would have been no reason for him to pretend. I don't understand how he can be so charming one minute and so evil the next!"

Cassie sighed. "Neither do I, love. You probably don't remember how Mother used to give in to him. He seems to think it perfectly all right to do anything he wants as long as he gets his own way. What we must do is find a means to keep him from hurting anyone else."

"But how?" Liza exclaimed.

"First we must stop this duel," Cassie replied. "If I write a note to the marquis, will you take it for me first thing in the morning? I don't know whom to trust among the servants."

"Surely Mr. Pierson would help us," Liza protested.

"Possibly," Cassie allowed. "But I can't take any chances. Lives hang in the balance."

Liza swallowed. "I'll take it, then. What will you tell him?"

"I'll ask him to meet me at the park tomorrow," Cassie replied. "And there I will beg him to back out of the duel."

"Shouldn't we do the same with the major?"

Cassie shook her head. "I've tried. My brother is not in the mood to listen. We will start with the marquis and see where that leads."

Liza nodded, though she did not look convinced. Cassie did not belabor the issue. In fact, she was glad when Liza said she would prefer to take supper in her room. She had a great deal to think about.

She had enough time that night to search for the comet, but the sky was overcast, and she could not see the stars. She couldn't see much of anything else, either—why Benjamin was so very pigheaded, why Devon had agreed to meet him, why people wanted to steal her father's journals. As she went to bed that night, she could only pray that she would somehow get through to Devon the following day. Surely a night's rest would help him see reason.

***

She was less sanguine about the matter when she met Devon in Hyde Park the next afternoon. Given her brother's challenge, having Devon keep his appointment with her to read the journals had been impossible. She wasn't even sure he would accept her request to meet. She had John Coachman stop the carriage near the Hyde Park corner and requested him to return for her in an hour. Then she strolled through the park, ignoring the frigid autumn breeze, trying to be inconspicuous. Few people followed her example, and none of those ventured to engage her in conversation. She felt the chill through her black wool cloak all the way to her bones when she thought what would happen if he didn't come. She had to make him see reason. She had to stop the duel. She refused to see him hurt.

It was silly, really, she scolded herself as she wandered through the walking paths. The marquis was a grown man. He had captained a ship during war; he led men. He was perfectly capable of taking care of himself. Yet she felt compelled to protect him. Why?

The answer did not bear scrutiny. She would be a fool to fall in love with him. The best she was willing to admit was that she was in love with the idea of him—the idea of a small French boy growing up alone and finally finding what had happened to the last of his family. She did not want him to lose—his goal or his life. She had to convince him this duel was a mistake, if it took everything she had.

She was nearly breathless by the time she reached the riding track called Rotten Row, but she found him waiting in a many-caped greatcoat near where the track ran by the Serpentine, just as she had asked.

He pressed her hand to his lips, and she did not pull away as she had done so many times before. She might as well enjoy his touch while she could. If she had to play her trump card, she would not be seeing him much longer, anyway. And if she didn't stop the duel, she might never see him again. She shivered as his kiss burned her skin, but she let him linger, relishing the connection with him. As he raised his head, he turned it slightly as if trying to see beyond her breathless smile. She feared he had noticed her gesture, but he merely tucked her hand in the crook of his elbow as they turned to walk along the path between the riding track and the water.

"And so you could not contain yourself after all," he teased.

She stiffened, then realized he meant her note. Or did he? She glanced at him out of the corner of her eye and saw he was smiling. She shook her head.

"Let us speak plainly, my lord," she said. "My brother has challenged you to a duel, supposedly in my honor. We both know there is nothing to fight about."

"I disagree," he replied. "He treats you abominably. I would be delighted to teach him a lesson."

"What lesson can he learn if he's dead?" Cassie countered.

He kept his eyes forward. "If you called me here to beg for his life, save your breath. I have no intentions of killing your brother."

"So much the worse," Cassie snapped. His head jerked around, and she knew she had shocked him. "Have you never heard the saying that you do not slap a king; you kill him?" she tried explaining. "You do not want to leave a wounded Benjamin behind you. You will have to watch your back the rest of your life."

He frowned in obvious confusion. "Are you asking me to kill your brother, then?"

"Heavens no!" Cassie gasped. "It will be just my luck you'd be caught and sent to Newgate for murder. Dueling is against the law in England, my lord."

"Then you are worried for me?"

She could feel herself blushing. "I do not want to see anyone hurt, Monsieur le Marquis. Is there no way you can back out?"

"*Non*," he barked, and she could hear the French accent

thickening. "He blackens my name; he threatens you; he interferes with my goals. I will be silent no longer."

"I do not feel threatened, and he will not interfere for long with our plans to read the journals," she told him. "You were perfectly willing to be silent when Miss Compton blackened your name. What difference does it make if it's Benjamin?"

"Your brother is a boil," he replied, "and I will lance it before it festers."

"Why are you both so stubborn?" she cried, pulling him to a stop. "Can't you see someone is going to get hurt?"

"What I see," he replied coldly, "is that you are set on defending him. You waste my time, mademoiselle."

She shook her head. "If this is an exhibition of male consequence, I am heartily glad I had so few suitors. Is there nothing I can say to dissuade you?"

"Nothing," he said, and the set of his jaw reminded her of her brother. It was time to play her trump card.

"What if I offered you a bargain?"

He blinked. "A bargain?" His smile formed slowly, and he leaned closer. "What kind of bargain?"

She swallowed. She could see by the green deepening in his eyes that he had a very particular bargain in mind. And it was not the one she had planned. "You want my father's journals. I'll give them to you."

He stiffened. "But you have refused to do so many times. This means so much to you?"

How could she tell him how much? Every time she thought about how he might be hurt, she felt physically ill. If he were killed, part of her would die with him. "Yes," she said. "This means that much to me."

She thought he might take a moment to consider the magnitude of her offer, but his answer was immediate. "*Bon*, I accept, on two conditions."

She cocked her head, uneasiness coiling around her heart. "What conditions?"

"One, you will bring them to me tonight at my house, alone."

She thought for a moment. The request was a bit unreasonable. If she were seen coming or going, her reputation would suffer. But she had managed to visit the nearby house once already without anyone noticing. She should be able to slip out and return again without Benjamin being any the wiser.

"All right," she agreed. "And the second?"

"You will stay with me until we have read them all."

Twenty-Eight

He thought for a moment he had gone too far. She stiffened, eyes widening, and took a step back. Color blazed across her face as if he had struck her. For all the liberties he'd taken, she'd never slapped him, but he wouldn't have been surprised if she did so now. That didn't matter. She had offered him an opening, and he would have been a fool not to take it. It was possible he would gain his treasure, and his mistress, tonight.

"*Vous comprenez, cherie?*" he murmured, watching her. "I want you to stay until we read every notation in those journals."

"I understand," she replied, lowering her eyes. He could see no more than the hood of her cloak and could only guess what she must be thinking.

"It may not be possible to read them in one night, my lord," she replied calmly. "If my brother wishes to call you out for one walk in a moonlit garden, I hesitate to think what he would do if I spent the night at your house."

She was being her usual logical self. For once he wished she'd leave that part of herself and bring only her passion.

"Surely you can handle the major," he told her.

Though she kept her eyes downcast, he heard the hesitancy in her voice. "Sometimes. But you ask a great deal, my lord."

He crossed his arms over his chest, ready to argue. "And

you ask a great deal from me. Apologizing to your brother will make me appear a coward in the eyes of the ton and my crew."

She flinched, darting a glance at him. "I didn't think of that."

"Then think of it. At sea, the captain's ability to command is based on respect and fear. Do you think I will inspire either when it is known I refused your brother's challenge? Worse, that I cringed before him?"

She stood for a moment as if she were thinking about it. He let her ponder, watching closely. The dark cloak hid her face and form effectively, but he did not need to see them to be reminded of the effect they had on him. He felt as if he were holding his breath. She must have been as well, for she suddenly inhaled deeply.

"Very well," she said. "I can see the trade is even—my reputation for yours. I will come, but I cannot stay past three. Benjamin would know, otherwise."

One night. It was less than he wanted but more than he had a right to expect. "Very well," he agreed. "How do we proceed?"

"When I see a note from you to my brother calling off this duel," she replied, "I will know you kept your part of the bargain."

"And how will I know you will keep yours?" he pointed out.

She raised her head and met his suspicious gaze boldly. "You will have to trust me, Monsieur le Marquis."

Trust her. So simple and so impossible. His father had trusted his wealth and position to shield him; his father lay in an unknown grave. After years of hiding, his uncle had trusted her father with his true name and, less than a year after penning that article, had been run over by a carriage. There had been a boy once, alone, afraid, who had tried to trust the duke of Devonlee and only met cool disdain. Trust was not a gift he bestowed lightly.

She must have thought his silence was agreement, for

she took another step back. "I must go. I'll await your note this afternoon, my lord."

"And I will see you tonight," Devon replied.

She nodded, then turned to hurry out of the park. And that nod was all he had to ensure her cooperation. It was pitifully small but it would have to do.

Cassie nearly ran back to the carriage. She didn't dare look over her shoulder, for fear he was watching.

"It's the journals," she scolded herself aloud. "This isn't an assignation. He's teasing you again. He just wants to learn what happened to his uncle. This is no different from having him to the house or meeting him in the park."

Yet it was different. The curl of excitement in her stomach assured her it was different. The drum of anticipation that beat in time with her heart told her it was different. She was going into a man's house in the dead of night. If she wasn't very, very careful, she would come out a fallen woman.

She pulled up short at the realization, nearly colliding with another couple out for a stroll. Behind her came a grunt of surprise. She whirled, fear chilling her. She was just in time to see a man turn and hurry back the way she had come. He was tall and broad-shouldered, but the beaver hat he wore covered his hair. He seemed familiar, but she did not recognize him. She swallowed, willing her heart to slow its frantic beating.

"You are a sad spy," she murmured, turning toward the Hyde Park corner once more. "If you can't even make it home without scaring yourself, how do you think you will manage tonight?"

She thought about it on the ride back to the town house. She should have been clever enough to think of another option. Yet part of her wanted to meet him alone. Part of her wanted to spend intimate time with him, even if that time consisted of no more than sitting side by side, reading her father's notations. More, she wanted to feel him next to her, wondering whether he'd be tempted to kiss her again, wondering whether there was anything she could do to tempt him to do that and more.

As soon as she entered the town house, she hurried for the stairs, planning on reviewing the journals in her room. She did not reach the first step before Pierson intercepted her.

"Madam? Mr. Montague is waiting in the sitting room."

Cassie shook her head. She had no time for this nonsense. "It isn't even Thursday," she told her butler. "I don't suppose he'd consent to go home and call again another day?"

Pierson's impassive demeanor cracked in a brief smile of understanding. "Most likely not, madam. Miss Kearney has already ordered tea."

Cassie sighed as she handed him her cloak. "Very well, then. I'll join them." She forced her mouth into what she hoped was a pleasant smile and went into the sitting room, determined to get Herbert Montague to leave as quickly as possible.

The little scientist rose hastily at the sight of her. He was dressed in his usual brown suit. She was glad to see that someone had taken his beaver hat away. At least she would not have to watch him wring it to death. Across from him, Liza caught Cassie's gaze and raised her eyebrows in question. Cassie gave her a quick nod, and she brightened in obvious relief.

"Good afternoon, Mr. Montague," Cassie greeted him. She sat before he could move to take her hand, if he would have done so. He blinked at her behind his glasses for a moment, then plopped himself back down on the sofa.

"Is everything all right, Miss Bentbrooke?" he asked. "Miss Kearney has not been able to tell me anything of import. There have been any number of comings and goings of late. I believe I even heard rumors of a robbery?"

"I assured him we were fine," Liza put in, smoothing down the skirt of her green-sprigged muslin gown.

"Rumors will fly," Cassie said blithely. "Yes, Mr. Montague, we had a robbery. Luckily, anything that was of value has been recovered."

He blinked again, leaning forward, nose twitching, as if to contradict her. "Are your father's works safe?"

Cassie smiled tightly. "Certainly. Why wouldn't they be?"

She waited for his usual bluster about leaving science in the hands of a woman, but to her surprise, he paled and swallowed visibly before answering. Liza frowned at his reaction.

"The time has come, Miss Bentbrooke," he said with considerable care, "to give your father's works to someone who can appreciate them. I will not leave today without them."

Cassie shook her head even as Liza rolled her eyes. "I am getting sick and tired of hearing about those wretched journals," Cassie told him. "Believe me, Mr. Montague, I am quite ready to give them to the next person who asks." She held up her hand as Herbert leaned forward again, this time eagerly, and Liza cried out in protest. "However, I will not. The journals are mine, and I will do with them what I think is most appropriate."

Herbert hopped up again. "He's offered you money, hasn't he? I'll double his offer!"

Cassie recoiled from his vehemence. "Really, Mr. Montague. If you cannot control yourself, I must ask you to stop these visits. I would not accept money for the journals."

His eyes narrowed craftily, and he sank into his seat to lean toward her conspiratorially. "But I can offer you three thousand pounds."

Liza gasped, and Cassie stared at him.

His eyes widened in alarm. "Four thousand, then? Five?"

"Mr. Montague," Cassie managed, mind whirling, "please. Whatever would make you think my father's work would be worth so much money?"

"He found something; I'm sure of it!" The little man was so agitated that he rose to pace, hands waving in the air. "I don't know what he found, but it was important, earth-shattering, precedent-setting. Why else would the duke of Devonlee be interested? I may not know too many in society, but Reginald Ames is well known as His Grace's man. Graduated with me with honors from Princeton, you know. He came to see me personally about your father's article on the comet."

Cassie's brow cleared, and she shook her head again. "Is that what started all this? Mr. Montague, Mr. Ames was helping the marquis de Renard. He believes the man who coauthored the article was his uncle, Jean-Luc Sebastien."

"Immaterial," he replied with a wave. "That is only a story to play on your emotions, Miss Bentbrooke. Your father found something of vital importance, and they seek to claim it."

"The treasure!" Liza cried, leaping to her feet as well. "That's it, Cassie! That's why everyone wants the journals. There must be a clue in them to my father's treasure!"

They both started jabbering at once, but Cassie could only sit, stunned. The treasure? She had thought it merely a figment of a dying man's imagination. But even if it were real, why would it have anything to do with her father's journals? Their jabbering turned to bickering; she could not concentrate. She held up her hands, then rose to her feet. "That is enough, both of you!"

They sputtered to a stop and glared at each other.

"I don't know what this girl is talking about," Montague said with a sniff. "The duke of Devonlee is a wealthy man. He has no need for some whimsical treasure. He is seeking to steal your father's fame."

"So you decided to steal it first," Cassie countered.

He paled, but his chin came up defiantly. "I will do what I must to protect science from the abuses of amateurs."

Cassie eyed him. She had never known him to be so passionate. Just how far had he gone to protect the journals from infidels? Had he hired the thugs? Bribed the footman? Or was Liza right? Did the marquis de Renard and the duke of Devonlee suspect the journals held the key to some treasure? But what? And where was it now?

Before she could ask any more questions, Pierson appeared in the doorway.

"A letter for you, madam," he intoned, crossing to bring her a sealed note. "From the marquis de Renard. The groom is waiting for a reply."

Cassie accepted the note and broke the seal, feeling all eyes on her.

"I have done as you asked," Devon had written in a bold hand. "I have sent a note to your brother calling off the duel. My carriage will be at the edge of the square tonight at ten. Do not disappoint me. Renard."

She must have paled, for Pierson asked, "Is everything all right, madam?"

Cassie tucked the note in her sleeve. "Yes, Pierson. Thank you. Make sure my brother gets the other note the moment he arrives, will you?"

"Of course, madam," the man assured her gravely. "And what shall I tell the groomsman?"

They were staring at her, and even though she knew they could not understand what the marquis was asking of her, she felt herself blushing. She raised her head proudly and met their stares in turn. Herbert lowered his gaze. Liza bit her lip. Pierson stood imperceptibly taller.

"You may tell the groomsman," Cassie said, "that I agree."

Twenty-Nine

"Would you care to explain why you continue to fail?" the duke purred.

Ames flinched. "I am not failing, Your Grace. It is your other agents. They are rude—utterly lacking in finesse. I will not deny their usefulness in other situations," he hurried on when the duke raised a finely chiseled brow at his bravura in questioning his employer's choice. "But as I said, Miss Bentbrooke is . . ."

"Formidable," the duke finished. "Yes, I know. Still, Jacobs has never failed me before. He was able to infiltrate the household staff at the Bentbrookes', and he brought us a description of the journal. A shame my cousin stopped him before he could deliver it to us."

"A great shame," Ames commented.

"And you say he nearly had the spinster this afternoon?"

"Yes, Your Grace. But there were too many people about, and he was concerned that if he attempted to capture her it would attract attention."

The duke steepled his fingers, flexing the joints ever so slightly as if weighing his options. He gazed across his private study, thoughts apparently as focused as his sharp eyes. "So, we cannot steal the journals, nor can we abduct Miss Bentbrooke. I fear there is only one solution."

"We give up," Ames agreed with a martyred sigh.

"Not in the slightest," the duke replied. "We simply convince the young lady to bring the journals to us."

Ames frowned. "Why would she do that?"

The duke smiled. "Leave the plotting to me, Ames. I shall give you detailed instructions. For now, maintain surveillance on my cousin and the spinster. I want to know everywhere they go and everyone they see. It appears I will have to wait a little longer, but I intend to have my treasure shortly."

"And if Miss Bentbrooke refuses to cooperate?" Ames asked.

The duke's smile deepened. "Her usefulness to me ends when I know the location of the treasure. It is only fitting that her life end then as well. We can dispose of her and the journal at the same time."

Cassie managed to get Herbert Montague out of the house without giving up the journals.

"I understand your concern," she assured him. "I promise you no one will study the journals for their scientific value before you do. I simply need a few more days to decode my father's notation."

He had peered at her through his glasses, and she thought surely he would argue with her. But he only nodded. "Very well. Send word when you are ready."

She had no sooner gotten rid of him than Liza set upon her.

"I tell you, it's the treasure," she bubbled. "It explains everything!"

"I grant you it would explain a great deal," Cassie replied. Conscious of the servants now, she motioned her ward toward the stairs. She led the girl to her room and closed the door behind them. "Truly, Liza, I don't know what to make of it. Someone chasing a treasure makes no more sense than the duke of Devonlee wanting to prove a scientific theory."

"But someone thinks the journals have value!"

"So it would appear. I'd give my brother's inheritance to know what."

"Oh!" Liza cried, bouncing up from her place on the bed. "I nearly forgot. You met with the marquis to stop the duel. What did he say? Why did he send you a note?"

Cassie eyed her ward for a moment, wondering how much to tell her. She didn't want Liza to worry, but on the other hand, she would need help to slip out of the house. With reluctance, she explained the situation. The girl's eyes widened.

"But Cassie, you can't go! What if someone saw you? You'll be ruined."

Cassie shrugged, although the same thought had chilled her only an hour ago. "Why would anyone see me? And what do I care if they do? I'm past my last prayers, Liza. No one will want to marry me, anyway."

"But your reputation?" Liza protested. "How will you hold your head up in public?"

"Because I shall know the truth," Cassie countered. "The marquis doesn't have designs on my virtue; Liza, he has designs on my father's journals."

"And Mr. Pond?" Liza pressed. "Will he understand that you are honorable? Will your reputation affect your ability to be an astronomer?"

Cassie opened her mouth to protest, then snapped it shut with a frown. She had never considered that. It was difficult enough to get the Royal Society to take her seriously, even after the noted success of Caroline Herschel. A woman had yet to be admitted to the select group. Her father had only been offered a place after his accurate prediction of the comet's return. Would she ever be admitted to their ranks if they thought her a harlot?

She took a deep breath, and Liza eyed her anxiously.

"It doesn't matter," she said quietly, letting her dream slip through her fingers and feeling as if a part of her went with it. "Most likely they would never have admitted me, anyway. I haven't exactly been diligent in watching for the Great Comet."

"You've been under a great deal of strain," Liza protested loyally.

"I doubt other scientists would understand. Still, the choice must be made. I cannot sit by and watch Benjamin or the marquis be killed. And I do not see any other solution."

Liza sighed dramatically. "You are so brave, Cassie. I hope I have such strength of character when I reach your age."

Cassie snorted. "Don't praise me. I'm giving up a doubtful future as an astronomer for a few moments of certain excitement with the marquis. That doesn't make me heroic. It makes me pathetic. Now, enough philosophy. Let's discuss more important matters. What shall I wear?"

Liza grinned. "Something black, what else?"

That did not present a problem. In fact, Cassie was a little surprised at how easy it all was. Benjamin did not return from his club for dinner, and Liza maintained a strict silence on the matter in front of the staff while she dined with Cassie.

Somehow, Cassie had thought sneaking out of her home late in the evening would be harder than in daylight, when the servants were busy at their daily tasks. The lack of a footman helped, of course. Liza was able to keep Pierson busy in the library. Cassie slipped out with no one to stop her.

Once on the street, however, she balked. The lamp across from the house cast a feeble glow that didn't reach the middle of the pavement. She glanced up for her stars, only to see clouds scudding past a waning moon. The night seemed dark, cold, all too quiet. It was as if every house in the square held its breath. Windows stared at her like accusing eyes.

"It's for the best," she said aloud.

Her voice echoed back to her off the stone walls. She lifted her head, hugged the journals to her chest, and swept down the walk for the corner.

Her courage almost failed her again when she saw the black lacquered coach waiting for her. The four black horses who drew it stamped their feet, sparking hooves against stone. The steam that puffed from their nostrils could easily have been the smoke from the fires of hell. She swallowed, steps faltering. The driver hopped down to swing open the door for her. He was dressed in a black cloak with a hood so deep she could not make out a face. She glanced between him and the dark cavern of the coach.

"This is the marquis de Renard's carriage, isn't it?" she asked, voice squeaking in a throat gone suddenly tight.

The coachman pulled off his hood to reveal straw-colored hair as wild as hay in a loft. With relief, she recognized his very British grin from earlier rides with the marquis.

"Yes, mum," he said, sweeping her a bow. "Don't worry. The captain's waiting for you. I'll get you there right and tight. My name's Thomas, and you just whistle if you need anything."

Cassie nodded, managing a smile. She stepped forward and felt his hand on her elbow, helping her up into the carriage. The seats were of black velvet with red piping on the edges. Black shades trimmed with fringe shuttered the windows. There was a voluminous black velvet cloak lying folded on the seat.

"The captain thought you might like that," Thomas told her when she reached for it. "It's cold out tonight."

She wasn't in the least cold, but she recognized the value of additional covering. She slipped it about her shoulders and settled against the squabs. Thomas gave her another grin before shutting the door on everything she had known.

Her nerves tightened with each turn of the wheels. Her reasoning had seemed so logical in the bright light of day. In the dark it seemed faulty, if not silly. She was no match for the marquis when it came to matters of intrigue. Just wearing his cloak set her mind turning into forbidden channels. She fingered the soft, thick velvet and fancied she could smell his scent. The salt air and warm leather were there, but the temptation was stronger. The cloak was suddenly hot beneath her fingers. She would never make it through tonight with her virtue intact.

Surely they could find someplace else to meet, some place proper. A church, perhaps. Or a crowded restaurant, where she could bring half a dozen friends for protection. Of course, that was part of the problem. She didn't have half a dozen friends. Mr. Pond was in Greenwich, Mr. Herschel at Slough, and Mr. Montague, while close and passionate about the journals, was hardly likely to protect her against the marquis de Renard. Neither was Liza. And she could not tell Benjamin. Cassie was alone, going to a rented house to meet a notorious privateer. She was an idiot to think she could handle this.

The carriage stopped, and she felt it rock as Thomas hopped down. A moment later he opened the door for her. He offered her his arm, and she swallowed. It was now or never. Her virtue or Devon's life. She took a deep breath and forced herself to accept his arm.

He stepped back as soon as she was on the ground.

"Aren't you coming?" she asked as he turned away.

He turned back to knuckle his forehead in deference. "Sorry, mum. I should see to the horses. It will be a while before you'll need them."

"Not so very long," she squeaked. Then she cleared her throat. "That is, I won't be staying any longer than needed."

He nodded as if in understanding. "Still, the horses will want their beds. Don't you worry. The captain will take care of you."

She felt her face flame at his implication. "Do you all speak in innuendo?" she demanded. "How can you run a ship that way?"

"Sorry, mum," he repeated with a rueful grin. "I meant no disrespect." He sobered suddenly. "You won't tell the captain I treated you badly, will you? I could cut out my own tongue, and you can be sure he'll do it for me."

As quickly as her blood had heated, it chilled. "He treats his men so badly?"

"No, no, you misunderstand me." He shook his head in obvious frustration. "The captain's a gentleman through and through, whether you count it from the French side or the English. Every man on his crew is handpicked and proud to be there. When he has to discipline one of us, he's fair. We know that." He rubbed a gloved hand against a stubbled jaw. "But I don't like to think how he'd discipline someone who was brash with his lady."

Cassie stared at him. "His lady?"

He quirked a smile. "Lord love you, miss, but you are a cool one. You're well matched. Now, please, go in before someone sees you."

Cassie nodded, more than a little dazed by the man's words. She moved through the wrought-iron gate and tangled yard for the door. The captain's lady. Was that how his men saw her? Was that how he saw her? He'd called her a wildcat and he'd called her a faerie queen. Somehow, being called his lady was the best of all. Any other time she would have been completely delighted with the idea, but at the moment all she could think about was one question.

How did the captain greet his lady when she arrived at his door in the middle of the night?

Thirty

"What is taking so long?" Devon growled, clenching his fists to keep from reaching for the drapes in the sitting room. "I heard the carriage a full ten minutes ago."

Henri pulled at the unaccustomed cravat at his throat, squirming in the black knee breeches and coat Devon had forced him to wear. "You would like me to go see, *non?*"

Devon sighed. "*Non*, Henri. We will wait, like gentlemen."

"But tonight you like waiting even less than I do," Henri guessed with a grin. "Do not worry, *Capitaine*. Everything is ready."

Devon glanced around the room. Everything did seem to be ready. He had dressed with extra care, choosing the black coat and knee breeches of the London elite. His cravat was whiter than Henri's and tied even more elegantly. Even the house was well dressed. The place had not come furnished; they had been making do with whatever they could carry from the ship. In anticipation of this meeting, he had had the sitting room furnished with an upholstered sofa of soft blue velvet, a walnut side table, and a lamp with a stained-glass shade of sapphire. An oriental carpet graced the floor that Henri had grumblingly polished. It was a cozy, inviting, intimate arrangement. He should be pleased.

"Are you sure you would not like some of the champagne we took off the last prize?" Henri asked him.

Devon shook his head. "We will need our wits if we are to solve this mystery."

"But after the mystery is solved, you will celebrate, *non*?" Henri persisted.

Devon didn't answer him. In truth, he rather hoped that would be the case. He could think of a number of ways to celebrate their success, all of which had to do with taking her upstairs to the walnut bed he had also ordered on impulse. Just the thought of her, willing in his arms, set his pulse pounding. Perhaps he should take the champagne. He felt as tightly wound as the anchor chain of a ship. And he had no idea why. By morning he would know the location of the treasure, and, with any luck, he would have had more than a taste of Cassiopeia Bentbrooke.

There was a tentative knock at the door. Devon stiffened, and Henri grinned as he went to answer it. The hesitancy in the knock told him the English tabby was in charge. For some reason, that did not ease his tension. In fact, as he heard her murmured greeting to Henri, just as hesitant as her knock, his hands began to sweat.

She stepped into the sitting room, the journals like a warrior's shield in her arms. Henri must have taken the cloak he had sent her, for she wore only a black silk gown. The dress hung from her figure in graceful folds, the color bringing out the shadows under her cheekbones and making her hair appear nearly white. Silver eyes wary, she moved into the room.

He swept her a bow. "Mademoiselle Bentbrooke, you honor me." As he straightened, he saw that her eyes had narrowed.

"I told you I'd come," she chided. "I do not break my word, my lord."

He inclined his head in agreement, then motioned her to the sofa. If she noticed the lack of other furnishings in the otherwise spacious room, she did not comment. She seated herself and balanced the journals on her black skirts.

Devon sat gingerly beside her, but she pressed herself

back to put as much distance between them as possible. He shook his head.

"I will not bite you, my dear," he assured her. "Tonight there is one thing of most interest to me." He laid his hand over both of hers where they lay clenched atop the books. He caressed the stiff fingers, willing them to open to him. Her gaze flew from her lap to his face, and she paled.

"The journals," he told her with a smile.

She swallowed, looking away again. "Yes, of course. The journals."

She did not sound relieved. In fact, she sounded just the slightest bit disappointed. Could she want him to seduce her? She had played the game with him, but she had drawn a firm line. How far was she willing to go beyond it?

He reached out with a finger and traced the line of her jaw. She closed her eyes at his touch. Desire pulsed through his veins.

"*Cherie*," he murmured, "I told you before. If you want something from me, you have only to ask."

She opened her eyes and met his gaze. The longing pierced what was left of his resolve. Yet he was not sure of the English tabby. He leaned toward her, watching for signs of fear, and slid his arm around her. She pressed back away from him, against the arm of the sofa, but that only brought her up against his hand. It was but a flick of his fingers to push her forward to meet his lips.

He kissed her cautiously, but only for a moment. As before, she melted into it. She tasted as sweet as the promise in her eyes. As he deepened the kiss, drinking her in, she sighed softly. The books slid to the floor with a thud that he barely registered. The tabby was gone, wiped away by the touch of their lips. The wildcat leaned into his embrace, returned his kiss, encouraged him to take more. The fire racing through him did not need any fuel. He gathered her against him with one hand and took everything she gave. She ran her hands up around his neck, caressing him. The movement dislodged his hand from her lap and brought it up to her breast. Before he could sense more than the soft roundness, she jerked away, scrambling to her feet.

"I can't—we can't." Her silver eyes were wild, and her breast heaved. She wiped the back of her hand over her swollen lips as if to wipe away his touch. "I'm sorry, my lord. I'm afraid I was never meant for intrigue."

He shook his head, willing his pulse to slow. He could not imagine forcing a woman, particularly not this woman. She would be worth having only if she came willingly. But his body didn't seem to want to listen to his ethics. He bent to retrieve the books, hoping the movement would help dissipate the desire that burned through him.

"You are magnificent, *cherie*," he told her, "whatever you choose to do. For now, sit. I will be a gentleman. You will read. *Vous comprenez?*"

She caught her lip between her teeth as if fighting tears, but she nodded in agreement. Then she settled herself on the edge of the sofa, as far from him as she could get. He handed her the books solemnly, and she accepted them just as gravely. Swallowing, she opened the first journal to the spot where they had stopped the last time.

And she was magnificent, he thought as he leaned back against the opposite arm of the sofa to listen. How many women could have sat so calmly after nearly surrendering their virtue and read dry scientific notation with nary a tremor in their voices? Yet she did just that, telling of her father's work and explaining discrepancies. As she read, her eyes took on a glow of passion anew, and he found himself jealous of the stars. She had given up her life for them. All he asked was one night. The next time he saw that look, he wanted it directed at him.

He was not surprised when he caught the far-off notes of a church bell chiming midnight. She flexed her shoulders and shifted the books on her lap.

"You have been reading for nearly two hours, *cherie*," he murmured. "Would you like something to drink? To eat?"

"No, thank you," she replied, raising her gaze long enough to offer him a smile.

He returned the smile. "This isn't the underworld, my dear. You won't be damned to spend eternity here if you let a pomegranate seed pass your lips."

Her smile deepened. "True, but I cannot afford any more distractions. The longer I stay, the more likely someone is to notice."

"Your brother?" he surmised, and had to quell the revulsion that rose at the mention of the fellow.

"Let's not start that again," she chided, turning a page. "For some reason the two of you have taken each other in dislike. There is no need to belabor the issue. Nor is there a reason to encourage it. Let us continue."

He would have liked to argue but closed his mouth and nodded. Her brother treated her worse than sailors did a wharf cat. For that alone he would have liked to take the fellow on. But the treasure had to come first.

She continued reading, but he couldn't help noticing that she kept hunching her shoulders as if to ease a crick in her neck. Her voice was beginning to crack as well.

"Sorry," she said at one point after clearing her throat. "I'm not used to talking so much. At night the stars are my company, and Liza can usually be counted upon to keep the conversation going during the day."

"Perhaps we should stop for a while," he suggested. His mind immediately conjured up any number of interesting ways to pass the time. She eyed him, and he could see by her dubious expression that she suspected what he was thinking.

"But we have an understanding, Monsieur le Marquis," she reminded him. "I do not go back on my word."

"No," he replied with a smile, "I can see that you do not. But I can also see that we are getting nowhere."

Cassie sighed. "I can find nothing that I have not found a thousand times before," she admitted. "There is no mention of Jean-Luc Sebastien."

"*S'il vous plait*," Devon replied, reaching for the books. When she hesitated, he repeated in English. "If you please? May I see them?"

She paused a moment longer, then shifted the heavy volumes into his lap.

He thumbed through the stiff pages, feeling her gaze on him. The strange notations were becoming almost familiar now. He could make out a phrase here and there. His eyes were drawn to the numbers. "What do these mean?"

She leaned over to peer at where he pointed. "Those? They are telescope settings."

Devon traced the number with his finger. "Coordinates?"

"If you like. They are directions for the observation of heavenly bodies."

"Can you tell which heavenly body corresponds to which set of numbers?" he pressed, sure he was onto something.

She frowned. "The object will be the one described in the observation below. That is the entire point of the journal."

"And if there was a mistake? If the coordinates actually pointed elsewhere, could you tell the mistake by looking at the numbers?"

She leaned back and eyed him narrowly. "What are you getting at, my lord? My father would never make such a mistake, and even if Stephen Kearney was your uncle, he appears to have been a good astronomer. I doubt he would make such a mistake, either."

She was being logical again. His uncle would not have been so logical. That's what had gotten them into this fix to begin with.

"But if he did," he asked, "how would you know?"

She shrugged. "Easily enough. I would match the time of year and time of night as closely as I could and set my telescope to the same coordinates. If the object described was a fixed object and it was not visible, I would suspect a mistake."

"The sky is so predictable, then?"

"Certain parts of it. The planets and certain stars have rather fixed courses. How do you think sailors have been able to navigate for hundreds of years?"

He nodded. "I understand. Look at these numbers again. Do you see any that vary?"

She cocked her head, studying the numbers. Then she raised her gaze to his.

"I do not see how these coordinates could possibly tell you anything about Stephen Kearney," she told him. "However, it is possible they could lead you to his treasure."

Thirty-One

Cassie had the satisfaction of watching his pupils dilate in shock. Then he surged to his feet, toppling the books to the floor with a crash.

"You knew?" he roared. "You *knew*?"

He grabbed Cassie by the arms and hauled her to her feet. Astonished by the change in him, she could do no more than blink. Here was the dangerous Frenchman Benjamin had warned her about. This was the passionate side she had only sensed in his kisses. His chest heaved, and a muscle twitched in his cheek. His eyes burned into her. Before she could even answer him, French poured from his lips, swift, condemning. She had learned the language but not the words he used. Somehow, she didn't think the polite world used them very often. She supposed she ought to be frightened, but she was far too surprised by his reaction to feel anything but fascination. As he held her, the sitting room door slammed open, and the large fellow who had met her in front barreled into the room.

"*Qu'est-ce que c'est, Capitaine?*" he barked.

Devon snapped his mouth shut and glared down at her. She could see the anger in his eyes, and more. It was as if he had been betrayed by someone he held most dear. Yet why would that be, when he was the one who had lied?

"Mademoiselle apparently knows about the treasure," he growled to his man. Turning her head, she saw Thomas coming up behind the big Frenchman, eyes wide.

The French giant sucked in a breath. Then, eyes narrowed, he moved to tower over her. "Should I make her confess?"

"Confess what?" Cassie snapped, forcing herself to meet the malevolent black gaze nearly a foot above her own. "Stephen Kearney told his daughter about a treasure on his deathbed. We looked for it, often. It was my mother's favorite parlor game. We found nothing."

"Why didn't you tell me?" Devon demanded.

"Why didn't you ask?" she countered. "You claimed to want to find your family. I had no idea you were really looking for a treasure I never believed existed."

He stared down at her for another moment. "You play a dangerous game, mademoiselle," he muttered. "Henri, Thomas, leave us. I will resolve this."

Henri backed away, frowning, but Thomas offered her a wink of encouragement before disappearing into the dark corridor.

Cassie faced Devon squarely. The anger simmered in him like a pot about to boil over. Something told her she ought to feel betrayed as well. After all, he had lied to her. But all she felt was a keen disappointment in him.

"So," she said, hands on hips, "was any of it true? Do you even have an uncle named Jean-Luc Sebastien? Did he know my father? Could he be Stephen Kearney?"

"Yes," he spit out, but she got the feeling he didn't wish to be in the same room with her, much less carry on a conversation. "Yes, he is my uncle, and he knew your father, and I believe he took the identity of the real Stephen Kearney, who is probably buried in the grave with my uncle's name on it. And yes, it was important to me to learn my uncle's fate."

"But it was more important to learn the whereabouts of his treasure," she concluded.

Fire flashed in his dark eyes. "Not more important, but just as important. You cannot know what the treasure means to me."

She glanced pointedly around the barely furnished room. "Oh, I can imagine. Being the marquis de Renard must come with a high price. What did you tell me—you had an image to maintain? I'm sure a few thousand pounds wouldn't hurt."

He shook his head, jaw hard. "You know nothing about me."

"You're quite right," she snapped. "Despite my best efforts, I know less than nothing about you. And what I thought I knew is apparently a lie. Herbert Montague was right—you did concoct a story guaranteed to play on my emotions. How very disappointing."

He flinched. "The story was for the most part true. I told you I wanted to find my family. The treasure is a legacy from my father, just as those blasted journals are a legacy from yours." He waved a hand contemptuously at the carpet, and she realized that the journals lay in a jumble at his feet.

"Oh!" she cried, kneeling to set them to rights. One of the books had landed shut. The others had landed askew, and she smoothed out the bent pages before carefully closing them again.

"Are they damaged?" he asked, begrudgingly, she thought.

"Nothing permanent," she replied, sliding them onto the sofa before rising. "Now, would you care to explain what you really meant with all those questions about the coordinates?"

He met her gaze with all the belligerence of a child denied a favored treat.

"Stop that this instant," Cassie demanded. "No one has harmed you or cheated you out of anything. You cannot expect people to volunteer information about something you haven't confessed an interest in. Do you want my help or not?"

She could see the struggle in him and marveled at it. Emotions chased across his eyes like clouds crossing the moon. Chief among them was fear. He was afraid—of her. How did he think she could possibly hurt him? The answer was too wonderful and far-fetched to be believed. Had she really managed to reach his heart? It would certainly explain his violent reaction to her supposed betrayal. She felt a sudden longing to hold him close and promise him she would never hurt him. But she sensed he had heard similar promises too many times, with disastrous results. And there was every chance that she was seeing in his reaction exactly what her heart wanted to see. All she could do was stand tall and hold his gaze until it cleared.

"Very well," he replied. "Like it or not, I cannot do this without you. But before we continue, I must know. What price do you put on your help?"

She frowned. "Price? What do you mean?"

"Oh, no," he warned. "Do not play the tabby now. There was a price for you to come here tonight—your brother's life. I expect you have a greater one to help me find the treasure."

Cassie stared at him. "Sometimes, my lord, your arrogance is beyond endurance. We have already established that this evening was a fair bargain—your reputation for mine. Besides, I cannot imagine you are bereft that you did not get to kill my brother. I doubt you prefer facing a murder charge or having to flee the country. It would have been a little hard to trace your uncle and the treasure from Naples, *n'est-ce pas?*"

He frowned, most likely at the sarcasm that dripped from her French. "Do not claim you came here tonight for my sake."

She threw up her hands. "Oh, no, of course not. No one in her right mind would do anything to help Devon Sebastien. I came here tonight because I like the chance that someone may call me a whore. It's delightful when people cross the street to avoid being seen near a fallen woman like me. You never struck me as an idiot, my lord. Pray don't start now."

He ran his hand back through his hair. "I don't know what you want of me."

Cassie felt his pain and confusion. She clenched her fists to keep from reaching out to him. "Is it possible," she asked, gentling her tone, "that I want nothing? I like being with you, my lord, and I thought you enjoyed my company as well. Or was that an act?"

"No." The word was said quietly, but she could hear the force behind it and knew it for the truth. She smiled.

"Then let me help you."

When he did not answer, she opened her hand and set it on his arm, feeling the muscles tense beneath her fingers. She gazed up into his stormy eyes. "Please, Devon? You said if I wanted something I had only to ask. I'm asking. Won't you let me help you?"

He reached out and ran a hand down her cheek, leaving a trail of heat she felt to her stomach. The icy gray was fading from his gaze, the green deepening as it always did when she was close. "Do you know how long it's been since anyone was willing to help me without a price?" he murmured.

"A bit longer than since anyone has been willing to help me," she countered gently.

Understanding sprang to life in his eyes. He took her hand and pressed a kiss into the palm and another at the pulse that had started to pound in her wrist at his touch. "We are alike, you and I," he told her. "People of two minds: logic and passion. One cannot rule the other, or all is lost."

"True," she replied, watching the way the lamplight brought red highlights to his dark hair. "And neither of us is willing to let the passion win."

He slid his arm about her waist and pulled her to him. "For you, *cherie*," he murmured as his lips neared hers, "I could make an exception."

She tensed for his kiss, but it was gentle this time, as if he pledged her his heart. The promise of it was nearly her undoing. She found it so easy to surrender to this man. Yet she knew he would go no further than she gave him permission to go. And even for him she was not willing to make an exception.

She pulled away from him with a sigh. "Thank you, my lord."

He did not pursue her, raising an eyebrow instead. "My lord? I swore I heard my name from your lips a moment ago."

She could feel herself blushing. "Forgive me. You did not give me leave."

"Then I give it now, Cassiopeia."

She grimaced. "Cassie, please. Only my father ever used the full name, and it felt uncomfortable even then."

"But are you not Cassiopeia?" he teased. "Queen of the Heavens?"

She opened her mouth to deny it, but the words seemed to echo a memory. She gasped. "The Heavens! Of course!"

"What?" He frowned. "This means more to you?"

"Yes, of course." She giggled thinking of it, and his frown deepened. "Your uncle's gravestone, remember? 'Look to the heavens for your reward.' Don't you see? He was giving us a clue. You were right. The location of the treasure has something to do with the stars."

The way he smiled at her, like a teacher at a prize pupil, made her realize something else as well. "Liza was right. Everyone wants the journals for the treasure."

His smile faded, and he nodded. "Someone besides us knows their worth."

So he was not behind the thefts. That did not surprise her. She suspected Herbert Montague after their conversation that day. But he would not be after the treasure; he cared only for science.

"Could it be your brother?" Devon asked. "How much does he know?"

"Less than nothing," Cassie quipped. "I doubt he even remembers the old game of looking for the treasure. He certainly hasn't mentioned it since he came home. He is as mystified as to why anyone would want to steal the journals as I was. And the only reason he was interested in the stars was to have an excuse to get Miss Compton alone in the dark."

That wrung a chuckle from him. "For that, I could almost like him."

"Well, I couldn't," she replied with a sniff. "But at least it proves he has no interest in the journals."

He eyed her for a moment, then shrugged as if deciding she knew too much already. "I did not just happen to find your journal in the park that night. Henri and I caught your footman. Unfortunately, he escaped before we could learn much. However, he confessed your brother asked him to steal the journal."

"What?" Cassie cried. "That's impossible. Benjamin would have no use for the journal. He can't even read it."

"Are you sure?" he countered. "Can he be fooling you?"

Cassie considered the idea. Had their father ever taught Benjamin? Perhaps when he was younger? Lord Bentbrooke had never been overly fond of his son. And she was just as sure that Stephen Kearney had never taught him. She shook her head.

"No, Devon, I'm certain. Benjamin would have no use for the journals. The footman must have lied. What else did he say?"

"Nothing of import," he replied. "This speculation is getting us nowhere. I suggest we focus on the coordinates. What I was trying to learn by my questions was whether my uncle might have pointed the telescope in a particular direction."

"As a clue to the whereabouts of the treasure." Cassie nodded in understanding. "Of course. A logical assumption. The only way to check would be to try the locations ourselves."

"I have the glass from my ship," he immediately offered.

Cassie shook her head. "We need the proper mount as

well. Stephen Kearney would have been using an equatorial mount, like my father's. What we really need is to use that instrument, which is on the roof of my house. Unfortunately, I can hardly invite you to visit, particularly at night."

He grinned at her. "I would not be concerned, *cherie*. The night, and your roof, will not present a problem."

Thirty-Two

He was the most determined man. Cassie had, of course, demanded an explanation, but he had merely kissed her on the end of her nose and called in Thomas to take her home. His delighted grin had let both of his men know that she was an ally, and Henri actually bowed to her on her way out. Devon had promised to see her after nightfall, which would be at about six o'clock the following evening. Not sure whether to be amused or annoyed by his renewed enthusiasm, she had allowed Thomas to drive her home.

Slipping into the house proved to be as easy as slipping out, for Liza was watching.

"The major has yet to return home," she whispered after following Cassie to her room. "What if he goes straight for the site of the duel?"

"The marquis won't be there. It will serve my brother right to cool his heels for a bit."

Unfortunately, Benjamin did not agree with her. She felt as if she had barely gotten to sleep before he banged through her door the next morning, furious that she had intervened.

He shook Devon's note under her nose. She glanced at the politely worded message and gasped. "He apologizes—to you and to me. And he asks your permission to court me! What joke is this?"

"A poor one," her brother assured her. "As if I'd let him

near you. You are to have nothing to do with him from this moment out, do you hear me?"

"Certainly I hear you," she replied, swinging her legs out from the covers so swiftly he was forced to take a step back. "I will do what is best, Benjamin, for all of us. You should be pleased. If he is seen as a coward, that should help your case with Miss Compton."

He snorted. "I wouldn't count on it. She is determined to have the marquis. Why, I shall never know. I begin to think I should try elsewhere."

Cassie brightened. "Then you will stop this charade? We can live normally?"

"Normally? Sister, you defy the definition of the word. No, the Bentbrookes are never normal, worse luck. I'll have to give it some thought." He started for the door, then turned to eye her. "By the by, do you know of any reason for the infant to take me in dislike?"

"Liza?" She knew exactly why her ward's reaction to her brother had cooled, but she wasn't sure Benjamin would like the idea of Liza's knowing the truth. "Why do you ask?"

He shrugged. "She's too quiet. I thought perhaps she might be ill—there are dark circles under those emerald eyes of hers, and her skin is even more creamy than usual."

"I'll check on her," Cassie promised.

He nodded. "If I have offended her, let me know, will you? I should like to make amends."

Cassie nodded in turn, wondering, but he left before she could question him further. That did not stop her from locating and questioning her ward. Liza admitted to finding it hard to be in the same room with him. The longing in her voice, however, told Cassie she had not given up on Benjamin. Cassie told her about their discussion that morning, and both agreed to encourage him to end his scheme.

She had thought perhaps she would hear from Devon during the day. Indeed, it was difficult to sit through service at St. George's, wondering whether she would find a note when she returned. However, by the time dinner came, there was still no word. Perhaps he had changed his mind. Yet she had never known him to veer from a course he had chosen, unless it was at her request. She wondered if he knew how much harder it was to ask him to stop each time he kissed her. He was right—it was a dangerous game they played. One of these times, she would not be able to tell him no.

By nightfall, with no word from him, she donned her black wool cloak, climbed the stair to the roof, and set up as she usually did for her observations. Glancing up, she saw the first stars shimmering in the deepening night. Cassie took a deep breath. As if God were blessing her work, tonight there were no clouds, and the moon was nearly a sliver as it rose. It was a perfect night for viewing.

She slid the leather cover off the telescope, wiping away the accumulation of grime and coal dust that had still managed to find its way through the protective shield. Then she carefully adjusted the instrument until she could see most of the northern horizon. She focused in on the North Star, tantalizingly bright above her.

During the day, she had gone through the journals and noted those coordinates penned in Stephen Kearney's hand. She had copied the observations on a single sheet of paper, hoping that might simplify her work tonight. Now she adjusted the instrument for the first reading. It took her a moment to crank the handle that rotated the scope horizontally, then another moment to angle it vertically. She had just bent her head to the eyepiece when she heard a noise behind her. As she glanced up, Devon materialized out of the darkness by the chimney cap, his clothes as smoky brown as the night around them.

Cassie stiffened. "How did you get up here?" she demanded.

He grinned, teeth white in the soft gleam of the hooded lantern at her feet. "I told you I have my ways. Any luck?"

She shook her head. "I've only just started. You didn't climb up the side of the house?"

"And if I did?" He sauntered to her side and cocked his head, eyeing the telescope.

"My brother will have fits," she predicted. "Do you mean you can simply walk up the side of our house, and no one notices?"

"It is a bit more difficult than that," he assured her. "And your brother had taken the coach, leaving no one in the mews. So go ahead. I'll watch."

She started to bend her head again, but all she could think about were his eyes, staring at her the way he had been eyeing the telescope. The idea unnerved her. She raised her head again. "This should be a partnership," she told him. "It will go faster if you help." She pointed to the columns on the carefully written sheet at his feet. "I divided the entries made by your uncle. They were taken at various times and dates, as you can see. We can check those made between July and February. I've already compensated for the time differences."

"The North Star is visible all the year." He frowned at her calculations.

"Yes, but in general the various constellations appear to move about throughout a calendar year as the earth rotates." She realized she sounded as if she were lecturing and smiled in apology. "It really isn't as dry as it sounds. Whatever Jean-Luc was looking at in the spring could be hidden from us as we approach winter. Likewise, what appears on the horizon at nightfall will move higher in the sky as the night progresses. We will follow his readings by each time period. I have the scope set for the first entry."

He perched calmly on the edge of the dais near her feet, but she could feel the tension in him. He expected her to find the clue immediately. She was certain that if his uncle had been so helpful as to spell out the clue, she would have found it already. The work was going to take a while. She took a deep breath and focused through the eyepiece.

"And?" he asked.

A church steeple stood squarely in her way. She raised

her head and gazed at him sympathetically. "No good. I was afraid of this. All I can see are rooftops."

"Why would one point a telescope so low?" he asked.

"The observation probably wasn't made from this location. Father and Mr. Kearney took trips outside the city from time to time, just so they could see more of the horizon. I believe I told you we had a house in Brighton. The setup I have here is particularly poor for comet sighting."

"But is that not your specialty?" he probed.

"Yes, but there wasn't a great deal I could do about the situation. I couldn't justify spending money to raise the dais or move to another house."

"Or to give yourself a dowry? You never married."

His tone was without judgment, but she felt herself bridling. "The lack of money had nothing to do with it. I had no interest in marrying." *Until you came along*, her heart added. She told it to be quiet. "Which reminds me, you told Benjamin you wanted to court me. Why the lie?"

He shrugged, looking very French, but he avoided her gaze. "Is it not the customary thing to say to a brother? 'I assure you, sir, my intentions are honorable'? Would you prefer I say, 'Frankly, Major, I'd like your sister in my bed and naked, not necessarily in that order?'"

She stared at him, too surprised to be shocked. "Is that how you really feel?"

He met her gaze at last, eyes heated with an emotion she was afraid to name. "Yes."

"Oh." Her throat was suddenly tight again, and despite herself she took a step back. He rose to his feet as if to prevent her flight. She had no idea how she was supposed to respond to a blatant admission of forbidden passion, but running didn't seem appropriate. Always before, he had teased her, resorted to innuendo. Even last night he had made it a game. She had told him she preferred plain speaking. It would be silly to deny it now. It would also be silly to deny that a part of her was thrilled at the idea of lying in his arms. She was not certain what men and women did together in bed, but she was certain Devon would be very good at it.

She swallowed, hoping to find her voice. "I am flattered, Monsieur le Marquis. But to think I might stir your passions is amazing to me."

"But not unwelcome?" He cocked his head, waiting.

"No," she admitted, "not unwelcome."

He took a step toward her, and she held up a hand to stop him. The hand trembled, and she took another step back. He hesitated.

"You must understand," she said as firmly as she could over the hammering of her heart, "much as I am flattered by your regard, I cannot accept anything further. I may not understand what you want from a mistress, but I understand enough to know that I should not be one."

"I think you underestimate yourself," he replied. "And as for not understanding, it would be my pleasure to teach you everything you need to know."

She could not help but smile at the eagerness that had crept into the otherwise conversational tone. "Of that I am certain. However, I'm not sure it would be pleasure I'd feel when you returned to your ship. I fear we are at an impasse, my lord."

He shook his head. "Not an impasse. I know I have lost when you start using 'my lord' again. But I only admit to losing the battle, not the war."

She moved back to the telescope to prove to him the topic was closed. "Why don't you read me the next set of coordinates, and we'll see if we can't find that clue. That is, after all, why we're up here."

He smiled as if he wanted to argue with her, but he read off the numbers. She ordered her mind to focus, adjusted the instrument, and tried again. The star was easy to find this time. Her resolve was another thing entirely. Part of her felt noble for refusing him; the other part called her nobility nothing but foolishness. She had been offered a chance at pleasure. She wasn't likely to get another opportunity. Would it be so wrong to accept?

"Cygnus," she pronounced, straightening, determined to return to the task. "He was probably looking at Deneb—it's that brilliant white star." She pointed directly to the north, and he rose to peer into the darkness.

"My men call it the Northern Cross," he told her. "Does it have some other significance?"

She shook her head. "No. Cygnus means *swan*. I can't think of anything that would connect it to Stephen Kearney, or the treasure. This sounds like a normal observation. Try the next."

He bent to eye the chart in the light of the lantern and read her the next set of numbers.

She shook her head. "Ursa Major. I know that one by heart. I don't see how the Great Bear helps us any. Next?"

"Is there no faster way to do this?" he asked.

"None that I could determine," she apologized.

He sighed and read her the next set of coordinates.

They continued for some time, with no luck. Generally she managed to keep her focus, and when she caught him eyeing her with speculation from time to time, she did not let that deter her. Some of the settings he read pointed her to various rooftops, others to well-known star clusters. A few were more intriguing locations in the heavens, but none seemed to have any special significance. Everything seemed to have a logical reason for her father to have studied it.

By midnight Devon was making senseless shapes along the edges of her calculations. The stars were blurring out of focus, and she knew it wasn't the telescope.

"Let it go," he murmured when she asked for yet another entry. "It was a valiant try."

Cassie frowned. "I cannot believe we were so far off course. Everyone wants those journals. Why else unless they hold some clue?"

He shrugged, then winced as his muscles obviously

protested. He rose and stretched, rolling his shoulders to work out the stiffness. She watched, fascinated by the ripple of muscle under his close-fitting coat. The weathered tan of his face matched the brown of his jacket and trousers. He could have been carved of mahogany save that he was so marvelously fluid. He caught her staring and grinned. She felt herself blushing.

Lowering her gaze, she forced herself to focus on the dates and entries below her.

"We were all bewitched by the promise of the journals," he said softly. "So much information must contain the words we wanted to hear. We were wrong, *cherie*. It is only science."

She shook her head, determined to prove her theory correct. "There must be something more here." She stared at the neat rows of numbers, then frowned, bending closer.

"What do you see?" he asked, bending beside her. His shoulder brushed against hers, and she knew that if she had turned her face, it would have taken little for their lips to meet. Her mouth went dry, and she had to swallow before telling him.

"When you read me the entries, I didn't see a pattern," she explained. "The sightings were uneven, too many days apart. But here, on paper, it is obvious. I don't know why I didn't see it sooner. Those entries I can't see, the ones on the rooftops: they all occur on the fifteenth."

Devon frowned. "The fifteenth?"

"The fifteenth of each month." She pointed to the dates on the page. "See? Month after month, year after year. His first reading is always the same location on the horizon. It is as if the date and place are significant to him."

He raised his head and met her gaze. "My father was taken to prison on July 14, 1791. My Uncle Jean-Luc and I left for England the next night."

Cassie felt a chill run up her. "Then it is important!"

"It may well be that you have solved the mystery," he agreed, although the caution in his voice told her he was afraid to hope. "But we still do not know where to start the search."

"The reading must point to a planet, constellation, or star that would give us some clue," she mused. "As I can't see it, I can't tell you what it would be. Oh, what I wouldn't give for a clear horizon!"

"You said your father and my uncle used to go out of the city to observe," he said. "Could we do so as well?"

"Certainly, if we had some place to set up. Unfortunately, Father sold the Brighton house years ago. And I hesitate to set up in some unknown field without permission."

His eyes had narrowed. "How much space do you need?"

"About the size of this dais. Level ground. No trees or other obstructions near. A hilltop is perfect. Why? Do you know someone who has such a space near London?"

"I do, although I'm not sure what I'll have to do to get him to grant me another favor."

Thirty-Three

The next morning, Devon strode down the marble-tiled corridor from the kitchen of his cousin's estate on the outskirts of London. Servants cried out in alarm behind him, and he was certain at least one zealous footman was hastening to follow. They could follow all they liked. The important thing was that he reach the duke first, before anyone could warn him.

The duke looked up as he entered the private study. Ames gasped and huddled over the desk as if he could bodily protect his employer from Devon. His cousin raised an eyebrow.

"Are your manners completely lacking?" he asked coldly. "Or isn't it customary in France to knock before entering?"

"I have no idea what customs the Corsican monster has created," Devon replied. "I knew what would happen if I knocked. I'd be having a polite conversation with Mr. Ames. I want to talk to you."

"I see," his cousin said. "And to what do I owe this dubious honor?"

"I need a favor."

He watched as the faintest of smiles curved the duke's mouth. His cousin leaned back in the desk chair and steepled his fingers. The morning sunlight glinted off the ruby ring.

"Reason with the servants, Ames," he said. "My cousin and I will come to terms."

Ames hurried from the room with obvious gratitude.

The duke nodded toward a chair. Devon refused to accept; in a battle for control with his cousin, he took whatever opportunities he could. Now he stood taller and looked down his nose at the man. The duke eyed him in return.

"You may spare me the theatrical captain's stance," his cousin drawled. "You wanted a favor. Let's hear it."

Devon relaxed his stance but remained standing. "I am considering marriage. I would like to bring her family here for your approval."

He hid his satisfaction as his cousin actually paused, fingers stilling. Then, his eyes narrowed, he asked, "The Comptons? I've heard some nonsense about you and the daughter. Her dowry might be considered adequate."

"No," Devon replied. "Not Miss Compton. I wish to marry Miss Cassiopeia Bentbrooke."

Again his cousin paused, and Devon had to fight a smile. Twice in one conversation—his skill was obviously improving.

"Out of the question," the duke said. "She brings no advantages to the family."

"You have been misinformed," Devon told him coolly. Even though he knew it was a game, something in him rose fiercely to her defense. "She comes from a respected family, her brother inherited a sizable portion and plans to be generous in her dowry, and she is intelligent and lovely. She is also content to stay at home while I attend to more pressing matters." Only the last was a significant stretch of the truth, but he knew his cousin would appreciate the sentiment. Nor did the duke disappoint him.

"A rare find, to be sure," he mused. He tapped his chin with his fingers. "Perhaps I should snatch up this paragon myself."

Devon grinned. "She wouldn't have you. She has a besetting sin—she thinks for herself."

"Ah, well," the duke sighed, "every apple has its worm.

Very well, if you want me to meet the creature, I suppose it is my familial duty to comply. Where and when?"

"Here, the day after tomorrow."

The duke frowned. "Is there some reason for such haste?"

Devon spread his hands. "I am eager to embark on the sea of matrimony."

"Meaning she won't allow you familiarities until she has the ring on her finger," his cousin replied. "She does indeed think. Singular creature. I'll have Ames send the invitations immediately. Be here the day after tomorrow. I'm certain it will be amusing for all involved."

The smile he added did nothing to assure Devon of the truth of that statement.

Cassie was amazed to find she had slept to her usual time of one in the afternoon. She had been certain the events of the past few days would keep her awake. She now knew why the journals were so popular, but not who else sought them so vigorously. She had assumed Devon wanted money, for it certainly seemed he spent it freely, but by his words and reaction she felt something deeper was at play. She also had no idea how her brother fit into the picture. Was he, too, out for the treasure? Was that why Miss Compton's dowry had suddenly lost its luster? Above all, how was she going to keep Devon at bay when her heart begged her to give in? She was sure all the questions would keep her up, but she slept soundly and went to the breakfast table ready to find answers.

Liza, however, did not look so well rested. As Benjamin had commented the day before, her eyes were swollen and her cheeks blotchy. She had dressed in one of her old black dresses, which only made her look more worn.

As Cassie was seated, Liza sighed; the sound held no melodrama, just a deep sadness.

"Liza," Cassie called softly, "you cannot be in love with Benjamin."

Her ward met her gaze dejectedly. "Can't I?"

"No!" Cassie declared. Her determination only made her ward look more disturbed. She reached out and squeezed the girl's hand. "I'm sorry. Of course you cannot control feelings like love. But you are very young, Liza. I'm sure what you're feeling is merely infatuation."

Liza nodded, but she looked far from convinced.

Before Cassie could say more, Pierson appeared, to hand her a sealed envelope. "This just arrived by courier, madam. The fellow is waiting for a reply."

Liza shook her head. "I must say the marquis is impatient."

Cassie picked up the heavy linen square. "That's not the marquis's handwriting," she mused, eyeing the precise lettering. Turning it over, she found a crest sealed in the scarlet wax—a rampaging lion. As Liza frowned, Cassie broke the seal and opened the envelope. The message made her raise her brows.

Liza sprang from her seat to read over her shoulder. Her dismal mood vanished as if a candle had flared in the darkness.

"The duke of Devonlee?" she cried. "A house party? And I'm invited as well? How marvelous!"

"How strange," Cassie corrected her. Was this Devon's way of getting her to an open place with her telescope? He had refused to tell her more before taking his leave last night. When she scolded him for even thinking about climbing down the side of the house, he had only pulled her into his arms.

"Give me a kiss, *cherie*," he had teased, "and I'll float down."

If she thought too long about the kiss they had exchanged, her cheeks would be blazing again. She focused on the letter before her. He had obviously convinced his cousin to issue this invitation. If the duke had been persuaded to help, he must know about the treasure as well. Perhaps he was not as cold as she had thought, if he would help Devon recover his family fortune. Inviting her brother and Liza certainly made a good story to keep her ward safe and her brother oblivious. But wouldn't everyone think the marquis was serious in his intentions? Benjamin certainly thought so. At the sight of the invitation, he let out a low whistle.

"It looks as if I don't need to chase Barbara Compton after all. If the marquis is serious, we can negotiate a tidy wedding settlement. The Devonlees should be good for it."

"You forget," Cassie replied, "the marquis is the poor relation. I doubt the duke will wish to buy him a bride."

"You leave this to me," her brother ordered. "We have a chance here, and I intend to see you make the most of it."

Nothing she could say could dissuade him. In the end, she decided that if the duke of Devonlee was as clever as everyone said he was, he'd be more than a match for Benjamin. She knew there would be no marriage. Devon was after the treasure, and possibly her virtue.

She was convinced until the boxes arrived late that afternoon.

"What are these?" she asked Pierson as he brought them to her room.

"Packages, madam," Pierson replied, as if she were blind. "I believe they are from the seamstress."

Liza had followed him into the room. "More dresses?" she accused. "When did you go shopping without me?"

"I didn't," Cassie assured her. Pierson hesitated, but she waved him out. She stood over the boxes, mind racing. Benjamin could not have had time to order her dresses for this house party, and he wouldn't have wanted to spend the money. She hadn't left anything under the seamstress's care. Who else would be so presumptuous as to order dresses for her?

"Cassie?" Liza ventured. "Aren't you going to open them?"

"There must be some mistake," Cassie said. "They're probably for someone else on the square." She eyed the boxes with as much enthusiasm as she might have accorded a poisonous snake. If the dresses were for her, they could only be black. She had no interest in seeing them. And she certainly had no interest in seeing the lovely dresses someone else would wear.

Liza rummaged through the boxes, scanning the names. "They are all addressed to you. Oh, please open them. If they are hideous, we can send them back. But what if they're lovely?"

Cassie eyed them again, then glanced at her ward's pleading face. She took a deep breath and threw off the first lid.

Liza gasped, crowding closer.

Lying in the box was a silk walking dress striped in lavender and gray. Clever tucks molded the bodice, and soft ivory lace edged the graceful neck and long sleeves. Cassie's hands shook as she picked it up and smoothed down the full skirt. The silk slid through her hands in gentle folds. "There must be some mistake," she murmured, feeling tears choking her.

"Then let's not tell anyone," Liza replied greedily. With eager hands, she began opening the other boxes as well. There were two day dresses of bright sprigged muslin and three evening dresses in soft blues and rose satin. At the bottom of the last box was a card. It read,

If you hurry, cherie, you can have these fitted. Madam Tulane has promised to work nights. Then others will have the pleasure of seeing the faerie queen. Devon.

She bit her lip to keep the tears from falling. She told herself again that he was not serious. He was being kind, tremendously kind, impossibly kind. He was only thanking her for helping him find the treasure. Or worse, bribing her to be his mistress.

But she couldn't seem to convince her heart.

Thirty-Four

The coachman arrived right on time two days later. Cassie watched from the doorway as an amazing number of trunks and bandboxes were loaded, but she kept the case containing her father's telescope in her arms. The instrument had not been moved any farther from the roof than her bedchamber since her father's death. She had had to work part of the night to disassemble it for packing. She was not about to surrender it to an unknown footman now.

Liza stood beside her, trembling with anticipation. Her black curls framed her face inside the straw bonnet, and her complexion looked clearer than it had in days. Her attitude was infectious, and even though Cassie knew the expedition was not what it seemed, she felt her own excitement rising.

Benjamin also looked pleased by the event, until Cassie handed him the telescope so she could climb into the carriage.

"You cannot want this thing with you," he complained. "I assure you, His Grace will not be impressed."

"I'm not bringing it to impress His Grace," Cassie countered, seating herself and holding out her arms for the instrument. "I told you, I have obligations to Mr. Pond."

"Surely your comet can wait."

"Comets are visible for only a matter of weeks, Major," Liza told him before Cassie could explain herself. She accepted the groom's arm to climb into the carriage as well.

Grumbling, Benjamin had no choice but to hand in the instrument case so that he could get in. With the telescope on Cassie's lap, he was forced to sit beside Liza. Cassie was the only one who looked less than pleased by the arrangement.

It took nearly an hour to reach the duke's estate. Liza exclaimed over every bit of scenery from the west end of London out Kensington Road, and Benjamin entertained her with stories from his days in the military. Cassie's mind continued to wander to the upcoming party. She had her father's journals safely tucked under the now fitted dresses at the bottom of her largest trunk. But watching her brother tease Liza until she blushed, she wondered whether she would get a chance to use them. Benjamin and Liza thought they were going to a house party, perhaps even a betrothal party. How was she supposed to study the stars for clues when she would be the center of attention?

They had been clear of the city and were rolling through gentle country when the coach slowed for a gated drive. Running along fallow fields, the road curved up to the front of a gray stone manor. As the carriage drew to a stop, liveried servants ran to secure the horses. Others hurried to lower the step and open the door. Benjamin alighted first and turned to help a wide-eyed Liza. Cassie coughed to remind him to help her as well. With a resigned sigh, he accepted the telescope. Moving to the door, she found herself facing Devon.

"Allow me, Miss Bentbrooke," he said with a smile as he held out his hands to her. She put her hands in his, leaning as she stepped from the coach. She knew she did not weigh much for her height, but she could not detect so much as a tightening of his muscles. In a moment she was standing next to him on the graveled drive.

"Welcome, welcome!" a small man warbled at Devon's elbow. Cassie recognized Ames. Devon introduced the duke's secretary to Benjamin, and they all walked up to the house.

From the outside the manor had appeared large, with a central block three stories tall and recessed wings disappearing back in either direction. Inside, Devon escorted them up the sweeping grand staircase and down a long corridor to a series of guest rooms. Liza and Cassie had bedchambers on either side of a sitting room, and Benjamin had a suite on the other side of the corridor.

In fact, everything inside the house was on as grand a scale as the outside. She was certain four people could have slept in the massive walnut bed in her room, and the matching wardrobe still looked empty when a helpful maid had hung her few dresses and cloak.

Mr. Ames had insisted they join him for a late nuncheon, and she changed from her traveling dress into one of the sprigged muslin dresses. On the way back down the corridor, they were escorted by a pair of footmen. Liza bubbled with questions about social customs, which Cassie was grateful her brother could answer. She could only hope he was telling the real truth and not his unique version of it.

Mr. Ames was a congenial host, asking questions about Benjamin's military career, which kept her brother talking. Cassie wondered whether the stories he told were accurate. If even half of them bore some resemblance to his life, his time in the military could not have been as dismal as he had tried to paint it. Perhaps Liza was right—there was some hope for her brother after all. Liza certainly thought so—her eyes seldom strayed from Benjamin the entire meal.

With the three of them pleasantly occupied, Devon found a way to speak to Cassie.

"I see you were able to bring your father's telescope," he murmured from his place at her right. "I have a spot beyond the gardens where we can set it up. How much time will it take?"

"An hour, perhaps two. We should start when we've finished here if you want to observe tonight."

"Tomorrow will be soon enough." He smiled. "You wore the dress. I wasn't sure you would."

She fingered the soft folds of the green-sprigged muslin gown. "They are all beautiful. I couldn't resist. I know I shouldn't accept them."

"But you will," he insisted with a smile. "It is the least I can do to thank you."

She smiled in return but knew it was forced. His gratitude was the least he could do, and the last thing she wanted him to feel. Somehow, the dress did not seem as lovely after that.

As they finished the final course, a servant came and murmured something to Mr. Ames, who rose hurriedly.

"If you will excuse me for a moment," he said with a bow. "The other guests have arrived, and I must see to their comfort."

Cassie frowned even as Devon rose as well.

"Other guests, Mr. Ames?" he asked, and she could hear the suspicion in his voice. "What other guests?"

"The Comptons, of course," the secretary replied pleasantly. "His Grace was certain you'd want them here as well."

Devon stared at the man, fists balling at his sides in impotency. What had made him think he could get the better of his cousin, even for a moment? Devonlee had done it again—thwarted him so neatly that Devon hadn't even seen it coming. No doubt the duke would find the antics of the title-mad debutante and her affronted father endlessly amusing. But avoiding them would keep Devon too busy to devote time to Cassie and the treasure. He couldn't even protest. It was his cousin's home, and what the duke wanted, he got.

"Do you have a death wish?" Bentbrooke asked when Ames left the room. "You have to know Compton wants your head, Renard."

"No, Compton wants my title," Devon corrected him. "And he will not get it. Your sister has already stolen my heart."

If he thought to lighten the frown on Cassie's face, he failed. She looked even more miserable after his statement. She would give them away if she wasn't careful.

"And if you wouldn't mind," he continued, putting a proprietary hand on Cassie's arm, "I would like a few minutes alone with Miss Bentbrooke. Now."

She stiffened, but her brother was diplomacy itself. "Certainly," he agreed, waving her from the table. "Take as long as you like. I'm sure I can trust you with my sister's virtue."

Cassie shot him a dark look, but she rose and followed Devon out the side door onto the terrace.

"I swear I knew nothing about the Comptons," he told her immediately.

She shivered, but he didn't think it had so much to do with the crisp fall air as the potential problems. Nevertheless, he shrugged out of his coat and draped it about her shoulders.

"What can your cousin be thinking to invite them?" she asked, fingering the fine wool absently. "Is he so far removed from society that he is deaf to the rumors?"

"Hardly," Devon replied. "More likely, he thought it entertaining."

She wrinkled her nose. "Entertaining?"

"He considers himself of greater importance than others," Devon tried to explain. "He is like a little boy watching a colony of ants struggle along. If you can add a twig to stir up the anthill, you have more to watch."

"Is that why you pretended to my brother that you are in love with me?"

He stiffened, then immediately scolded himself. She could not know the insult she dealt him by comparing him to his cousin. "We needed a story to cover our real reason for being here. I had already asked your brother for permission to court you, in my apology to halt the duel. It made sense to follow that course. For now, we must deal with this issue of the Comptons. Dare we enlist your brother's aid to keep the fair Miss Compton away from your work?"

"Possibly." She gazed out over the formal gardens, nearly bare now with the coming of winter. "But I wouldn't advise telling him about the treasure."

So she didn't trust her brother, either. "That was never my intention," he assured her. He pointed to where the gardens gave way to a grassy knoll. "I thought we'd set up the scope there."

She nodded. "An excellent choice. You can see for miles." She slanted him a glance that made him suddenly aware of how close she stood to him. It would be nothing to reach out and pull her to him. "Perhaps you'd like to change your mind and set up the instrument this afternoon," she murmured. "That ought to keep you away from the Comptons."

He smiled. At the moment, he could not imagine anything finer than spending the afternoon with her, although he could think of several activities more pleasant than erecting a telescope. Something of what he was thinking must have shown in his eyes, for her cheeks darkened in a blush. He reached out to trace the edge of her cheekbone with his finger, and the color deepened.

"You could make this visit a great deal easier on me," she murmured with a sigh, "if you'd behave yourself."

He raised an eyebrow. "My dear Cassie, I try to behave myself in your presence, but do not expect miracles."

She frowned. "I understand you must make a pretense in front of Benjamin and Liza, but surely when we are alone you could be yourself."

His grin widened. "Myself? You mean, you wish me to act as I normally would when we are alone?"

"Precisely," she declared.

"*Bon*," he agreed, and pulled her into his arms to be kissed.

She did not struggle, but the fire he usually felt did not kindle. Surprised, he drew back. Her silver eyes were dark with emotion, but it was not passion.

"I offered to help you, Monsieur le Marquis," she said. "Don't make me regret that."

As he frowned, she pulled off his coat and shoved it at him. "Here. We should return to the others. Let me know when you're ready to set up the telescope."

She slid back through the terrace door, leaving him standing, perplexed, in the cool fall air.

Thirty-Five

Cassie never spent such a difficult afternoon. As everyone had suspected, the Comptons were equally surprised and annoyed to find the Bentbrookes in residence. Mrs. Compton promptly retired to her room with a headache, Mr. Compton cornered Ames with demands to see the duke, and Miss Compton altered between casting soulful glances at Devon and glaring at Benjamin. As they waited for the duke to appear, Devon stood by the door as if he wanted to escape. Her brother, obviously certain that Cassie had a fortune in the marquis, did nothing to placate the Comptons, and Liza sat on the window seat overlooking the gardens and brooded. Cassie finally joined her in self-defense.

"If this is bad, imagine what dinner will be like," she told her ward.

Liza shuddered. "At least I know the major was never truly serious about courting her. She acts like a spoiled child."

Cassie glanced to where Miss Compton was attempting to get her father's attention away from Ames. The set of her jaw was a bit mulish. Cassie shook her head.

Devon chose that moment to stroll up to them. "You win," he told Cassie. "I cannot stand waiting for my cousin to make his grand entrance. Let's set up the telescope."

"I'll go get it," Cassie replied, pleased at the excuse to escape.

"May I help?" Liza begged. Cassie nodded, and the three of them moved to the door.

Miss Compton's face was puckered as they passed.

"She looks as if she's lost her last friend," Liza commented, glancing back.

"She looks as if she's lost a title," Devon countered. "I understand from gossip at White's that the Comptons have had some financial setbacks. My title and my cousin's fortune are all that motivates her. She will find someone else."

Cassie exchanged looks with Liza and knew she was thinking the same thing. Benjamin had gotten away just in time.

They retrieved the telescope and took it to the garden. Her father's equipment included a tripod, making it easy to erect initially on the spot Devon had chosen. The ground was not as even as Cassie would have liked, however, necessitating finding props for the three legs. Then the instrument had to be checked for damage from its shaking in the carriage as well as from its disassembly and reassembly.

While she worked, Liza chattered away helpfully. Devon joined in, but after a time Cassie noticed he was directing the conversation toward the girl's family.

"I understand you have a locket from your father," he asked at one point.

Liza beamed, fishing in her bodice with girlish innocence. "Yes, would you like to see it?"

"Very much."

Cassie watched as her ward held out the necklace and Devon bent over it. He touched it gingerly, turning it over and back. Liza worked the catch to swing open the center.

"This is a miniature of my mother," she told him.

Devon held the locket up closer. "She was lovely. Like her daughter."

Liza blushed, obviously pleased. He let go of the locket, and Cassie saw a shadow cross his face. Remembering how he had lost his father, she felt for him. She wanted to reach out and smooth the frown from his face, but she knew it would only cause more difficulties. She returned her gaze to the telescope and busied herself with it.

Liza lost interest in the work after a while, wandering back to the house with the promise to stay safely in her room, reading until dinner. Devon, however, stayed by Cassie's side, watching with apparent interest while she did her work. She wanted to be pleased by his attention, but she was certain he was only doing it to hide from the Comptons. Besides, it still stung that he had blithely admitted that his declaration of devotion was a patent lie.

The sun was setting when she finished the last adjustment.

"There," she proclaimed, straightening. "We are ready to begin, and just in time."

Devon glanced at the horizon, which glowed a warm gold. "Shouldn't we wait until later?"

"The observations start at half past five," she reminded him. "We should do so as well if we hope to see what he saw."

He sighed, kicking a rock away from the base of the telescope. "We will need another excuse, then. Surely my cousin will expect us to join him for dinner."

"Must we?" Cassie complained, making a face.

He eyed her. "I agree the situation is difficult. Perhaps if we made it worse, the Comptons would leave."

"How could we make it any worse?" she demanded.

"We could announce our engagement."

She stiffened. Was he intent on ripping out her heart? No, it was all just a game to him. "No, absolutely not," she told him. "I won't lie about that."

"Why not?" He looked genuinely puzzled. "You know the duke expects me to make an offer. That is why you are here. Why not oblige him?"

"You didn't tell your cousin the truth?" She stared at him, aghast.

He frowned. "Of course not. My cousin knows nothing about the treasure, nor will he until it is safely in my hands."

She knew she had paled. "Then he must think I'm your mistress as well. No wonder he's refused to join us this afternoon. He thinks he's invited a whore to visit."

"You are not a whore," he spat. "And a few stolen kisses do not a mistress make. You don't seem to have it in you to be wanton, worse luck."

"Is that supposed to be a compliment or a complaint?" she demanded, stung. "I'm sorry if my kisses were not sufficiently inspiring. I'll try to do better the next time you accost me."

"Stop it," he ordered. "Believe me or don't. I will make your excuses at dinner. Begin your observations." He turned and started for the house.

She stared after him, blinking away hot tears. How dare he speak to her that way, as if she were a recalcitrant servant! She had half a mind to take the telescope and return to London. What had she been thinking to offer to help someone so arrogant and pleasure-seeking?

The sky was darkening, but now a brighter light flared on the western horizon. Cassie cried out as the Great Comet in all its glory blazed into view. Wiping the tears from her eyes, she fumbled with the telescope, trying to turn it.

"What is it? Are you all right?" He was again beside her, concern in his voice, as if their quarrel had never been. "I heard you cry out. Are you hurt?"

"The comet," she gasped, cranking the scope to the west. "This is my chance! Oh, Devon, help me!"

He wrapped an arm about the telescope and dragged it around. Cassie adjusted the vertical angle with hands that shook.

"Would you write for me?" she asked, afraid to take her eyes away from the instrument as she focused on the ball of fire.

"You would trust me?" he murmured, and even in her excitement, she heard the surprise in his voice.

"Of course," she replied. Then she focused on the comet. "Come on, my beauty. Show me what I want to see. Aha!"

"What?" he asked.

"The tail," she breathed. "I can see the tail."

"I take it this is good?"

She smiled, adjusting the telescope ever so slightly to bring the comet into better focus. "This is very good. This is what I've been waiting for. This will prove I'm as good a scientist as my father. Are you ready?"

"I have the quill and your journal. I will write as you showed me. Proceed."

She fired off the coordinates and the time of day, as well as the location of the observation. "The head of the Great Comet is approximately three arc minutes across," she told him. "The tail is perhaps sixteen degrees long, with a slight curvature. It is definitely distinguishable into two branches. The comet head resembles a bright nebula. That part of the head pointing toward the sun is a little brighter and broader than that towards the tail. The planetary disk is a little eccentric." She paused to catch her breath. In the silence, she could hear the quill scratching on the paper. When it stopped, she raised her head. That ought to show Mr. Pond that she knew her work. She glanced at Devon's bent head, his tight grip on the quill.

"Would you like to look?" she asked softly.

He raised his head to meet her gaze. "Very much," he said with the same longing in his voice as when he had asked to see Liza's locket. He set aside the journal and rose.

She moved to make room for him. "The eyepiece is here, on the side."

"An odd place," he remarked, bending to fit his eye to it. She reached around him to adjust the instrument for him. It was like holding him in her arms, her body leaning into his. She could feel the warmth of him through the cloak; she felt it to the center of her being.

She swallowed. "Can you see it?" she managed.

"Not quite, I . . . oh!" She felt him stiffen and smiled, remembering the first time her father had lifted her up to the scope and let her look. The wonders of the universe had opened up to her. She had never been the same. He raised his head slowly, as if reluctantly, and met her gaze in wonder.

"It is beautiful."

Her smile deepened. "Yes, it is."

"I feel as if I have intruded," he told her quietly. "You had a goal, a dream, work that pleased you, and I have interrupted it, haven't I?"

"A bit," she admitted. "But when I send this information to Mr. Pond, it will make up for the observations I've missed. Besides, you brought excitement to my life."

He waved to where the comet's glory was slowly fading into the darkness. "What could be more exciting than that?"

"This," she replied, moving into the circle of his arm. She put her hands on his shoulder and pressed her lips to his. He did not move; perhaps he was afraid to move after her comments earlier, but she felt his lips warm under hers. Withdrawing, she offered him a smile. "Whatever happens, Devon, thank you. I'm sorry I was rude earlier. It has been a beastly day, until now."

He did not let her pull completely away, cupping her hips under the cloak with his hands. The intimate touch seemed right, and her hands slid over his, relishing the feel of him.

"I should be more patient," he murmured, catching and holding her gaze. "You have heard too many insults. It is ridiculous to think a few compliments could erase them all. Let me make excuses for both of us, and I will rejoin you. We will watch the stars together."

She nodded, and he released her at last. Touching his fingers to her lips in promise, he strode for the house.

Cassie watched him go, then turned to watch the comet fade into nothing. As the night darkened, she moved mechanically into her work, readying the telescope to copy Stephen Kearney's observations. As she did so, she could not help thinking about her words to Devon. He deserved her thanks. What a change he had wrought in her life! She had not been willing to share her work with even another scientist, yet now she let Devon help her with the most important observation of her career. She glanced down at where a breeze ruffled the pages of the journal. His bold handwriting stood out next to her precise notation. A tender smile curved her mouth. Yes, she wanted him to share the stars with her, just as she wanted to help him find the treasure. She wanted to share everything with him. She had tumbled from fascination to friendship to something far more. It was time enough that she acknowledged that she was in love.

The telescope reset, she sat heavily at its base. In love. Cassiopeia Bentbrooke, spinster, recluse, scientist, oddity—in love. It was more beautiful than the rings of Saturn, more splendid than her comet's tail. It was warmer than the sun and fuller than the moon. She was too logical to think that it was any more within reach. Devon was a flirt, and though he seemed fond of her and had admitted he desired her, she had no reason to think his feelings went any deeper. Even if they did, he was slow to trust. She could not be certain of ever winning his love.

But, at the moment, with the comet gone and the rest of the heavens open above her, she found that hope was enough. Time would only tell whether Devon's attraction to her would outlast her usefulness in finding the treasure. She would take what was offered her and rejoice that she had been given an opportunity to love.

That, after all, was the greatest adventure.

Thirty-Six

Devon watched as the woman beside him bent her fine-boned face to the telescope once more. They had been at it for two hours. At first he had enjoyed having her point out the stars and planets to him, sharing her pleasure. Her glow rivaled the marvels of the universe she explained. But before long, his mind and senses began to wander. First it had been the moonlight shining on her pale hair. Then it had been the way her slender fingers slid along the barrel of the telescope. When she pursed her lips in thought, he had to stop himself from pulling her into his arms. He had promised himself not to attempt seduction until she finished her work. At this rate, he would not be able to keep that promise another fifteen minutes.

"I thought you had finished your studies and were only going to recheck the readings on the fifteenth," he ventured.

She kept her eye to the tube, but he heard the frown in her voice. "So did I, but I'm not getting the results I expected."

Now he frowned as well. "Something wrong?"

"Not yet." She raised her head and stretched, arching her back. Her breasts were silhouetted against the lantern light, high and firm. Devon threw down the quill and rose.

"What is it?" she asked.

"You," he replied. When she paled, he added, "and me." He ran a hand back through his hair, trying to clear the spell of her from his mind.

She took a step toward him. "I don't understand, Devon. Are you giving up on me?"

He started laughing at the irony and choked off the sound as she recoiled. "*Non, non. Ecoutez, cherie. Tu est magnifique.*"

"I speak French," she replied warily. "But I don't like it when you do. You usually end up yelling at me or kissing me senseless."

The latter was exactly what he had in mind. "Then let me say it in English," he returned, pulling her to him. "You are more lovely than any comet, *cherie,* and far more rare. Forget the treasure for tonight. Stay with me."

She caught her breath, and he waited for the refusal she must give, determined to use every argument against it.

"Very well," she replied. "Let me secure the telescope for the night."

Devon dropped his hold, stunned. She moved calmly back to the instrument, shuttering the lens, pulling the cover from the base to drape it about the telescope, opening the lantern so they could see to return to the house.

"Did you just agree with me?" he demanded.

"Yes," she replied, gathering up the journal and her calculations. "If you would be so good as to bring the quill and ink?"

He frowned. His French half told him to accept his good fortune, but his English half was suspicious at the sudden capitulation. "Do you understand what you just agreed to?"

"Somewhat," she replied calmly. "You can't expect me to know everything. I am a spinster and a virgin, after all. But I believe you promised to teach me."

He found himself staring, incredulous. "You agree to be my mistress?"

She paused. "You didn't ask me to be your mistress, if I recall. You asked me to stay the night with you. I would imagine there is a difference."

"Not in my mind." He watched her frown in confusion,

but he knew there was a difference. And he knew what he had suggested was wrong. He went to her and took the journal and paper from her arms, bending to lay them carefully at the base of the telescope. Then he faced her squarely.

"Forgive me. You should not be my mistress, Cassie."

She hung her head. "I see. I suppose I should have agreed before you had time to reconsider. I thought you desired me."

"I do, Cassie, I promise you." He marveled that she couldn't tell how much.

She smiled tightly. "But not enough, it would appear."

"Are you trying to test my resolve? Don't, *cherie*. My principles are not so deep. Offer yourself to me again, and I may yet say yes."

She stepped into his arms as she had done earlier, meeting his gaze. "Please?" she whispered as she had done when she begged him not to steal the journals. "Please, Devon? Show me what it feels like to be loved."

With a groan he pulled her into his embrace, his mouth seeking hers. She came willingly, gladly, wrapping her arms about his waist under the cloak and pressing herself against him. He could feel the curves of her body, the eagerness of her hands on his frame. Her breath was soft and swift against his mouth, her lips demanding. It would have taken little for him to give her all she asked.

Devon forced himself to break the kiss, keeping her close to him.

"*Non*," he swore. "Not this way. Not here. You should be loved, *cherie*, well and truly." He dropped kisses on her cheek, across her forehead, and down her nose before taking her lips again. She was sweet as always, but now salt mingled with the honey. Devon pulled back again.

"Do you cry?" he asked, surprised.

"No." She hiccoughed. "Yes. I'm sorry. It's just so wonderful to hear you speak such words, to feel that you want me. I never expected it."

He kissed the tears from her cheeks, and she laughed and sobbed at the same time. "You should be told often and passionately how magnificent you are," he assured her. "You deserve better than to be anyone's mistress, Cassie. You should be a duchess, a queen."

"But not a marchioness?"

The words were wistful, tentative. The tabby was once more overtaking the wildcat. He had lost his opportunity, but somehow he didn't mind. He traced her jaw with one finger. "You would be a marvelous marchioness, *cherie*. A marchioness of a respected family. I cannot offer you that. The name of Renard is nothing but a curse to those who once revered it."

"How can that be?" she asked, and he watched as her pale brows drew into a frown. He pressed a kiss on first one, then the other. She squirmed away.

"You're avoiding the issue," she accused.

He sighed. "And you are pressing your advantage."

Her frown deepened, and he knew she would not give up until he had told her everything. It surprised him that he did not seem to fear it. He let go of her to sit before the telescope, motioning her to join him. She did so, but he was pleased to find she cuddled against him. The touch of her body made the story less difficult to tell. He wondered whether she knew that.

"The treasure we seek is not entirely mine," he explained, draping an arm about her. "When the Terror began, the local aristocrats feared for their lives. But they equally feared the journey to England. Stories abounded of how the first émigrés had been robbed or murdered. The Renards were respected. We also had ties to England. Surely we could help get their wealth out of France so that if they were forced to live in exile, at least they would not live in poverty."

She laid her head against his shoulder. "So your uncle brought the money to England."

"Not money," he replied. "Jewels."

"Jewels?"

He nodded. "My father had everyone convert what they could into gemstones. The stones were easy to carry, easy to hide. He had it all planned."

"But he didn't come with you?"

"He was to go with us, but he was caught and taken to Paris to die." Even twenty years later, the memory hurt. "I didn't know until later. My uncle brought me to the Devonlees."

Again a memory intruded: the duke, younger then, standing on the grand stairway of the house behind them, looking down the stairs and down his nose at his cousin. Devon felt his back straightening now, even as it had then. Cassie put a hand against his chest. The memory receded, and with it the hurt.

"I should have realized something was wrong when my uncle did not continue on immediately," Devon went on. "He was to meet the other families in London. Yet he stayed at Devonlee for several weeks."

Her hand pressed on his chest as if to capture the pain. "Perhaps he was just being cautious."

"That's what I thought at the time. But when I was finally free of my cousin, I traced my uncle, as I told you. He was clearly having second thoughts. He did go eventually to London and spoke with Henri's father, who was near death from his ordeals. Henri was only a child at the time, even as I was, but he remembers overhearing his father tell my uncle about the deaths of the Debusses, one of the families who had paid him, and the dire needs of the others' children. My uncle must have decided that with so many of the original members of the pact dead or dying, he could safely keep the jewels for himself."

She sucked in a breath, and he tensed, but she merely cuddled closer.

"I do not use the title of the marquis de Renard when I deal with my countrymen," he continued. "They do not believe my family is worthy of any title, save perhaps that of thief." He waited for the heaviness of the shame to cover him, as it always did when he remembered, but for the first time he felt lighter. It was as if in sharing the burden, it had lifted from his shoulders. His arm tightened around her. "You do not judge me?"

"You are not your uncle," she said simply. "I am not my father. We make our own choices."

He felt himself smiling and marveled again. "*Mais oui.* But of course."

"Your choice," she continued, "has obviously been to return the jewels to their rightful owners. But if your uncle kept them for himself, how do you know he didn't use them?"

"I wondered. But when I saw that paper he wrote, and traced it to your father, I realized he must have kept them. Why else work as a servant?"

"Why else tell his daughter there was a treasure?"

"Precisely. He may have hoped to return to France with the jewels, recapture his lost life."

"How ironic," she murmured. "I remember Napoleon pardoned the émigrés just a few months after Mr. Kearney was killed. He almost made it."

"I'm sorry he had to die, but I'm glad he didn't make it. There are those who still need the jewels. We must follow the trail." He rested his cheek against the satin of her hair, content for the moment just to hold her. But, to his surprise, he felt her stiffen.

"Perhaps not," she said quietly. "I can't see anything, Devon. That spot on the horizon, the one we thought was the clue? I can't find it."

He raised his head, frowning. "What do you mean?"

"There should be something there—a star, a planet, a nebula. I've tried recalculating the angle, taking the season and time of night into account. I've tried adjusting for the slight variation in latitude between London and your cousin's estate. I've focused the telescope on both near and far targets, to no avail. I don't know what else to do. I've failed you."

He ought to feel a crashing disappointment, but his heart was too light to grieve again. "No, *cherie,* you haven't failed. You wanted to help me, and you have succeeded. I set out tonight hoping for a seduction, and it was I who was seduced. You are a potent force, Mademoiselle Bentbrooke. Come, let me walk you to your room."

"Not *your* room?" she asked with a tremor in her voice.

"Not tonight," he replied, and even though his heart told him it was the right thing to say, he also knew it was going to be a long, lonely night.

But somehow, he thought, he'd sleep well for the first time in years.

Thirty-Seven

For Cassie, sleep was a long time coming. One moment she soared. She had touched his heart and, in doing so, opened her own so fully that she knew she would never be the same. The next moment she crashed. She had failed him. The journals held nothing but dry scientific notation. Yet he hadn't abandoned her, even when she had admitted her failure. Surely there was hope for them.

When at last she slept, she did so fitfully, plagued by dreams in which towers and rooftops obscured her vision. No matter which way she turned her telescope, something else blocked her view of the skies. She awoke frustrated and was relieved when a maid brought her a breakfast tray. At least she wouldn't have to face the Comptons or Benjamin. And she wasn't sure she was ready to face Devon until she could control her own thoughts.

She was trying to decide how long she could avoid them when there was a knock at her door. The helpful maid answered it to report that Mr. Ames wanted a moment of her time. Cassie agreed, and the secretary bustled in to bow to her. He was dressed in a neat brown coat and breeches, and she found herself pleased that she had decided to wear the lavender-and-gray striped walking dress, for she fancied for once that she looked just as neat.

"His Grace was most interested in your work last night," he said after they had exchanged greetings. "He wondered if you would be willing to explain the matter to him. Perhaps demonstrate the use of your instrument?"

"Certainly," Cassie replied, thinking that she could safely share the comet's discovery with him. "At his convenience."

"If you could bring the journals, now might be a good time," he ventured.

Cassie smiled. Here was the perfect excuse to avoid the unpleasantries of an afternoon with the Comptons. Surely later she would be ready to talk to Devon about their next steps. "I would be delighted."

She was less delighted when Ames ushered her into the duke's private study on the first floor. The room was much like the man: austere and forbidding. Dark paneling covered three walls, and the fourth was set with a huge window that overlooked the grounds. Against the backdrop of the brown autumn fields sat a huge black walnut desk. Any other man, she was certain, would appear tiny behind the massive piece of furniture, but the duke somehow made it his throne. Now that she knew him for Devon's cousin, she looked for some resemblance and saw only a thin-faced man with black hair and deep-set blue eyes, dressed in a black coat of superfine wool.

"Miss Bentbrooke, a pleasure," he said, though she did not think he looked pleased.

She dropped a curtsy. "Your Grace."

He waved to a chair before his desk. "Won't you sit down?"

She took the chair with a nod. When he sat, she spoke again. "I understand from Mr. Ames that you are interested in my work."

"Very interested. It was entertaining watching you with my cousin last night."

She felt her face burning. How much had he seen?

"Do not distress yourself, Miss Bentbrooke," he said pleasantly. "I know you are no doxy. I also know my cousin can have no interest in you. He would be a fool to marry so far beneath himself, and he is no fool. I know exactly why he brought you here. So tell me, where is the treasure?"

Ames watched as the woman blanched. His hands gripped the leather-bound volumes they had sought for so long. He could scarcely believe he finally held them. So much bother for so little! He'd had to follow women around the city, interview thugs in prison, plead with men who hadn't risen to half his rank in college. He'd even had a courier rush to York to meet that rector. The fellow had written back a voluminous note detailing how his son Stephen had gone to London to minister to the French émigrés, but had disappeared in the spring of 1792. The old man had heard his son had died of pneumonia serving in the French slums near St. Pancras. He had no idea that one of the Frenchmen his son was trying to convert had taken his son's name and personal belongings and gone to work for the Bentbrookes. No doubt the real Stephen Kearney was buried in Jean-Luc Sebastien's grave.

Any way Ames looked at it, he had had to do far more work than was required for so simple an investigation, and it was all Miss Bentbrooke's fault. He rather hoped His Grace would make the creature pay. Nor was he disappointed. In his usual manner, the duke enjoyed playing with his food before consuming it.

"Come now, Miss Bentbrooke," he chided. "You didn't honestly think I was ignorant of the treasure, did you?"

She raised her head and met the duke's gaze straight on. Ames was appalled by her arrogance. "Exactly what treasure are we discussing?" she asked coolly.

"Do not play games with me," the duke snapped.

Ames was certain such a tone would put her in her place, but to his surprise she actually frowned in annoyance.

"I do not play games, although I begin to think it is an inherited trait in your family. I simply asked because I feel it is important to make sure we are discussing the same thing."

"Very well," he allowed with an indulgent half smile that sent a chill down Ames's already weak spine. "I am referring to the Sebastien treasure, a fortune in gems, smuggled out of the south of France for several French families nearly twenty years ago by Jean-Luc Sebastien, who had the misfortune to die before I could learn its whereabouts."

"An inconvenience, to be sure," she commiserated, though Ames heard her sarcasm. The woman was still pale, but she wore her righteousness like a royal robe. He glanced at his employer to see how he was taking the reaction, but if anything he looked amused.

"Decidedly inconvenient," he assured her. "But I hope to rectify matters. Where is the treasure, Miss Bentbrooke?"

"I have no idea," she replied.

Ames glared at her, and His Grace's eyes narrowed dangerously. "You tell me you spent nearly the entire night with my cousin and you learned nothing?" he asked suspiciously.

"Less than nothing," she admitted with an annoyance Ames did not think was directed at His Grace. "I was certain I knew the answer, but I was wrong."

"I see," the duke replied, steepling his fingers. "And what do you intend to do now?"

She shrugged. "I have no idea," she repeated. "We were certain the clue to the treasure was in my father's journals, but I've studied the information from every angle. I . . ." She stopped suddenly, staring off into space, brow furrowed. The duke leaned forward, nostrils flaring like those of a hound who's caught the scent.

"Yes?" he urged. "What?"

She shook her head. Ames had the impression she was far away, working out a scientific solution in her head. The very idea that a woman could do so unnerved him.

"The angle," she mused. "I calculated any number of angles except the obvious one. If Jean-Luc Sebastien really was Stephen Kearney, and he shot the same location every month, year round, he couldn't have been looking at a star.

It had to be a physical location, on the horizon, at that angle from my father's roof."

The duke nodded. "Excellent. Then you know where to find the treasure after all."

She blinked, and her gaze fell on the duke's desk, focusing at last. "Not entirely. To be certain, I shall have to check the observation from my father's mount on my roof."

"Very well." The duke sat back in his chair, and Ames straightened as his master's steely gaze swept to him. "Ames, make the arrangements. I want the calculation made tonight."

Ames bowed. "Of course, Your Grace. But if I may point out, I foresee a few difficulties. What shall I tell Captain Sebastien?"

The woman was staring at him again as he straightened, and he found it hard to focus on the duke's response.

"Excellent point, Ames. We do have a few things to tidy up. Leave my cousin to me. I suggest you ask Jacobs to keep an eye on Miss Bentbrooke."

"It was you all along," she said quietly. Something about the tone made Ames flinch. "You knew about the journals."

His Grace merely chuckled. "Ames and my cousin always said you were clever. Yes, Miss Bentbrooke, I have been behind some of the attempts to steal those journals. Some, but not all. Your friend Herbert Montague nearly outfoxed us several times."

She shook her head. "I thought so. He hired those thugs."

He nodded, eyes kindling. "Very good. Yes, he did. I thought perhaps he would succeed in convincing you to marry him, as well, but you were helpful in that regard. He was an annoyance, to be sure, but I knew I would triumph in the end. Now, seeing as you are such a clever woman, I'm sure you can understand why it is in your best interest to cooperate."

She crossed her arms over her chest. "Not entirely. You

must know I care nothing for social standing, and your cousin has already done a thorough job of destroying what reputation I had. I agreed to help the marquis because I admire him. I fear I cannot say the same for you."

Ames's mouth dropped open. As the duke's mouth tightened, Ames shook himself. "Now see here," he blustered. "Do you have any understanding whom you address?"

"Of course she does," the duke said quietly, and Ames paled. "She simply doesn't care. And that, Miss Bentbrooke, is your mistake. You Bentbrookes have consistently underestimated me. Your father made the mistake of allowing Jean-Luc Sebastien to use his real name on that insignificant paper, which led me to him after years of false trails. You were foolish enough to let Mr. Montague know of the journals, which took me another step. Then you blithely confess your knowledge of the location. Do not be so foolish as to think you can thwart me now. Your sole reason to remain alive is to be of use to me. When you cease to be of use, Miss Bentbrooke, you will cease to be. I trust I have made myself clear."

Devon had awakened much earlier. He had hesitated to come downstairs, but glancing out his window, he had seen the Comptons loaded into their carriage for London. Barbara had been animated in her conversation with her mother, and any qualms he had felt about rejecting her vanished. She would no doubt find another fellow who would be willing to part with a fortune for the glory of wedding her. He had more important matters to tend to.

He needed to talk to Cassie. He had felt her frustration last night when she had failed. It was a bitter pill for him to swallow, yet it seemed all the more difficult for her. Her science had failed, therefore she doubted her use. He was the one who should despair, yet all he wanted to do was comfort her.

The journals were clearly not a clue after all. He was left

with nothing. For all he knew, Stephen Kearney had been who he claimed, the son of an obscure Yorkshire minister, and Liza was no relation to him at all. He was once more without family or honor. Yet there was a strange sense of rightness about the entire affair. He could not understand his attitude. But he had a feeling it had something to do with Cassie.

He took a chance and tried her room but found it empty. He took a greater chance and cornered Liza, but the girl denied having seen her guardian that day.

"I would not worry, my lord," she told him. "Cassie often remains abed until after one. Surely she will be down shortly."

Unwilling to concern her, he had thanked her and gone in search of Ames. Like a spider in its web, his cousin's secretary always knew what was happening in every aspect of the estate. He found the man easily enough, not far from the center of the web, outside his cousin's study.

"Ah, Captain Sebastien," Ames greeted him. "I was about to go looking for you. His Grace would like a moment of your time."

"In a minute," Devon replied. "First tell me what you know about Miss Bentbrooke."

Devon's concerns increased as the man blanched.

"Mr. Ames," he threatened, taking a step closer.

Ames cringed. "Really, Captain, I don't know what you want of me. The duke perhaps knows more about the situation."

Devon chilled. "He'd better," he clipped, turning on his heel and striding for the study. "And if he doesn't, I'll be back to find you, Mr. Ames."

He did not wait to see the secretary's reaction. Nor did he wait to announce himself. His cousin sighed as Devon stormed through the door of the study.

"Where is she?" he demanded.

For once his cousin did not make a game of the matter. "I see you've noticed Miss Bentbrooke's absence. I feared as much. But she was adamant, and I felt it the gentlemanly thing to do to assist her."

"What are you talking about?" Devon asked with a frown.

"She came to me this morning," the duke replied. "Quite early, actually." He shook his head. "The poor thing was in tears. Kept saying she had failed you. I assumed she was helping you with your search for your uncle."

Devon waved the issue aside. "Yes, go on."

"She was most upset. Insisted on leaving, on spending some time to herself. She asked for a carriage and driver. I believe she wanted to go to Brighton."

Devon listened to the dispassionate recital, but he could see the glitter in his cousin's eyes. "You were happy to oblige," he accused, "knowing that took her away from me."

The duke spread his hands. "I did what any gentleman would do to assist a lady. For what it's worth, I was rather taken with the chit. If you still wish to marry her, you have my permission."

Marry her? At the moment he wanted nothing so much as to strangle her. Had nothing he said penetrated that clever brain of hers? Why did she persist in seeing herself as beneath his notice? She had no reason to blame herself—she had done everything, come up with ideas, tested them, ruled them out. He might not be any closer to his family or the treasure, but he had eliminated one entire path.

Marry her?

Of course he wanted to marry her! He was in love with her. She was hardheaded and warmhearted, cool-tempered and hot-blooded. She was clever and kind and consistently, ruthlessly honest. She was a clean, crisp breeze filling the sails of his soul and sending him flying toward his dreams.

Marry her?

The moment she said yes.

"Brighton, you say?" he asked his cousin. "Why Brighton?"

"I believe the family had a summer cottage in the area," the duke replied. "Perhaps she still has friends there. She has a several-hour lead on you, but if you take one of my lighter carriages, you may overtake her."

"Thank you." Devon bowed and quit the room, mind whirling. There was so much he wanted to say to her. So much he wanted to do. He had only reached the grand stairwell when the truth hit him.

She would never have left without making sure her ward was well cared for.

The chill he felt before engulfed him anew, and he stopped with one foot on the stair. She would never have applied to her family for help, let alone the duke. She would never have run away without facing him. Not his honest Cassiopeia, his Titania, his queen of the heavens, his wildcat. His cousin was lying. And the reason made his heart start racing.

The duke knew about the treasure.

And he thought Cassie held the key.

Thirty-Eight

Several hours later Cassie sat stiffly in the duke's closed carriage. Her hands were folded in the lap of her lavender-striped walking dress; her half boots rested squarely on the paneled floor. Though the afternoon was chill, she refused to shiver. Even her eyes remained trained on a single spot in the black silk lining, approximately six inches from the duke's right ear.

Only her mind raced.

They meant to kill her. She had no doubts on that score. The duke had made it plain her life depended on how useful she could be to him. Once she confirmed the location of the treasure, he would do away with her.

And she knew the location. She was certain of it. Too many times when she had tried to follow Stephen Kearney's directions, she had wound up staring at a church steeple—the steeple of St. Pancras. She had suggested the date had meaning. Now she was sure. It wasn't the day Devon had left France. It was the day Yvette Kearney died. Cassie had no doubt that the jewels were buried with her.

But the villain across from her must never know that. She refused to betray Devon, and nothing could have induced her to support the duke's monstrous self-consequence. She had no idea why a man who could afford estates from one end of England to the other would pursue an obsession with additional wealth that didn't belong to him, and she had no interest in finding out. She might have led a sheltered life, but she recognized evil when she saw it. She could not let him win.

But how to stop him? She had considered screaming when he had had Jacobs escort her from the manor to the waiting carriage. But the ex-footman had kept a determined hand over her mouth. Her attempts to squirm loose had only gained her several painful yanks to her hair and a wrenched arm. And their travel along the back of a little-used wing had virtually eliminated any chance that someone might see and wonder about her.

"Are you always so quiet?" the duke drawled, giving the shade on the window the slightest of tugs as if to ensure that no one could see inside.

"I generally prefer to converse with people I like," she replied. "You know the type—those with character, moral fiber, intelligence?"

"Surely you don't think I lack intelligence," he chided.

"No," she told him. "Only the strength to use it."

He shook his head. "I cannot imagine what my cousin sees in you. Are you this outspoken with him?"

"I am this outspoken with everyone. Your cousin simply has the manners and assuredness to appreciate it."

He barked out a laugh. "The puppy with manners. How amusing. If he behaves for you, it must be love. What a pity neither of you recognized it sooner."

"On that we quite agree," she said. Then she clamped her mouth shut as he chuckled again. This time the sound had an ugly edge that made her stomach knot. She had to think of something!

"You won't win," she warned him. "You can't drag me into a London town house in broad daylight. Someone will surely raise the hue and cry."

"That is why we will go through the mews," he explained patiently. "Your brother let the servants off when you came to visit me, did he not?"

She did not answer, though she knew he was right. He clucked sympathetically.

"Poor bluestocking. How very distressing it must be to find that someone else can outthink you after all."

"What about the telescope?" she demanded. "And the journals? I cannot continue the observations without them."

"I had my servants dismantle your tripod and store it with the instrument in the boot. Ames follows with the journals. He seems inordinately pleased to have them in his possession at last. Never fear, my dear. I have thought of everything."

His words sent a chill through her, a chill that only deepened as she realized he was right. When they alighted at the house, the mews stood empty, none of her neighbors was about, and Jacobs triumphantly brandished a key that gave them access to the town house. He also led them unerringly through the house and up to the roof, where one of the duke's grooms brought the case holding her father's telescope.

"You see, Miss Bentbrooke," the duke proclaimed, "you have everything you need. Now, set up and be quick about it."

She glared at him, and he only smiled at her frustration. Was she truly helpless? It could not be. She had managed every crisis alone. There had to be something she could do, someone who could help her. She glanced up to where her stars were just beginning to show through the twilight. She floated a fervent prayer upward.

Inspiration struck.

She had to fight to keep the smile from her face. Instead, she knelt carefully and unlatched the instrument case. Opening the lid, she lifted the telescope from the velvet bed. She made a show of pulling out the eyepiece, polishing the lens, tightening the fittings on the polished brass case. Jacobs stalked about the roof like a hungry lion, Ames fluttered about like a startled sparrow, and the duke watched them all like a vulture waiting for the kill. She carefully lifted the tube to her eye and gasped. With satisfaction, she saw the duke stiffen.

"A problem, Miss Bentbrooke?"

"A decided problem." She lowered the tube. "Your servants are ham-handed. The instrument is damaged. It will take me weeks to regrind and realign the lenses."

The duke pursed his lips. "I would encourage you to find a quicker solution."

Cassie climbed to her feet even as Jacobs took a step toward her, one fist raised in warning. "You may encourage all you like. My father's telescope is useless."

His brow darkened, and Ames scuttled out of reach.

"There's another tube in the house," Jacobs put in. "I saw it with the major."

"Find it," the duke barked.

Jacobs moved to comply. Cassie wanted to scream in vexation. All she had done was buy herself some time.

"I suggest, Miss Bentbrooke," the duke said quietly, "that you find a way to make the next instrument work. Remember our discussion about usefulness. I'm sure you wouldn't want to be retired from service prematurely."

A few blocks away from the Bentbrooke town house, Devon leaped from the carriage. Thomas, Henri, and Bertrand were hot on his heels, jumping from their places on the roof like stones thrown from a sling. Barking orders, he sent them flying for weapons. Benjamin Bentbrooke stuck his head out of the carriage window.

"You'd better be right about this kidnapping business, Renard," he warned. "I wouldn't want to be on the wrong side of your cousin."

"Don't worry, Major," Devon assured him, tightening his hands at his sides. "I know what the duke is doing. I should have seen this sooner. Henri, *allez*!" This last to his first mate, who lumbered behind the others. "Stay here and protect Miss Kearney," he ordered.

Henri halted, scowling, but his look quickly changed to deference as Liza alighted from the carriage.

"Be careful, my lord," she pleaded with Devon, her youthful face tight with worry.

He squeezed her hand. "I will bring her safely back to you. I promise."

She smiled bravely and went with Henri.

Devon turned to meet Benjamin's frown. "Will she be all right with him?" he asked.

"He will protect her with his life," Devon assured him. "And as he can be considered a servant, her reputation should be safe."

Benjamin nodded. Bertrand and Thomas streamed past the carriage. Thomas tossed Devon his sheathed cutlass, which Devon caught with one hand. Buckling it on, he jerked his head to Benjamin. "Coming, Major?"

"We're walking?" he asked, but Devon moved to join his men, leaving Benjamin no choice but to clamber down and scurry after them.

He caught up with them before they reached the corner. Devon put a finger to his lips. "Stealth and silence, Major. Can you handle that?"

Benjamin nodded, wiping the back of his hand across his lips. Devon jerked his head to the north, and Bertrand and Thomas loped off through the alleyways for the park. Devon headed for the mews with Benjamin beside him.

As they moved through the gathering dusk, Devon glanced at the man beside him. It had been a gamble turning to Cassie's brother for help. Yet once he had explained the situation and offered the man ten percent of the treasure, Bentbrooke hadn't hesitated. It was he who had suggested, when Devon had gone back to confront his cousin only to find the man gone, that Cassie's most useful location would be the town house.

By the time they reached the mews, it was already dark. No lights gleamed from the house, and Devon couldn't see anyone on the roof, although he thought he heard a snatch of voices from above. Down the ill-lighted alley he saw the duke's groomsmen, walking the team of horses. They would be even with the gate in perhaps ten minutes.

"Open the door and let Bertrand and Thomas in the front," he instructed Benjamin in a terse whisper.

"What are you going to do?" Benjamin demanded with narrowed eyes.

Devon pointed up. "I have my own way to your roof."

Shaking his head, Benjamin moved to obey him.

The climb was more difficult than it had been the first two times. Then he had gone carefully, to keep from awakening a sleeping household. Now he went swiftly, to avoid detection by the grooms. The sword hanging from his waist hampered his movements, and his fears for Cassie dulled his mind. She could not be harmed. A part of him would die. He had to keep his wits about him, for her sake. At the moment, he would gladly have given his cousin the treasure, if it meant Cassie were safely back in his arms.

Despite his concerns, he didn't slip once. Long before the groomsmen reached the carriage house, he was ready to heave himself onto the roof. There he paused, however, inching his eyes over the parapet to survey the expanse. Someone had lit a lantern, and by its glow he could see Cassie bent over a telescope. The size and position of the eyepiece told him it was not her father's. Relief surged through him. He wasn't certain his cousin was capable of murder, but he refused to take chances with Cassie's life. He looked for the duke and spotted him behind her and to one side, standing warm in his many-caped greatcoat while Cassie shivered in the rapidly cooling night. Beside him Ames shivered in his own coat. He couldn't see anyone else, but somehow he doubted Ames and his cousin had been able to get Cassie here by themselves.

"Well?" the duke drawled as Devon slowly raised himself higher. "What do you see, Miss Bentbrooke?"

"A moment," Cassie clipped. Her slender hands moved tirelessly up and down the tube, turning this, rotating that.

"This instrument hasn't been used for near-field viewing for some time. It will take a while to calibrate it."

"She's stalling!" Ames whined, and Devon dropped onto the roof under cover of the complaint. He darted behind the chimney and peered around it to glance toward the stairwell. It yawned empty. Where were Bentbrooke and his men?

"The instrument is ready," Cassie announced. "If I may have my father's books?"

Ames glanced again at the duke, but a curt nod sent him scurrying to her side. Taking the journals from his hands, Cassie opened one to scan the page, then made some adjustment to the telescope. Devon could feel the duke and Ames holding their breath as she lowered her gaze to the tube. He was holding his as well. After a moment, she straightened.

"Nothing," she told them.

"Nothing!" Ames exploded even as Devon let out his breath. "How can there be nothing? All that work and . . ."

"This is not an exact science," she replied coldly. "As we do not know which observation correlates with the location of the treasure, we must try each one. You saw the process your cousin and I went through last night."

Ames snatched the journal from her arms and scanned the page. "All those numbers? That could take hours, days."

"Years, actually," Cassie told him. Devon could hear the triumph in her voice.

"We do not have years, Miss Bentbrooke," the duke said. "To pay my ever-increasing bills, I have mortgaged every property, sold any furnishing, jewel, or art treasure that would not be noticed. I need that treasure now."

So that was what brought his cousin to such treachery. Devon tightened his grip on the hilt of his sword, finding it more difficult to wait every second. Then, from down in the stairwell, came a muffled thump, and Thomas's face hove into view, grinning. Bertrand and Benjamin were right behind him. Devon drew his sword and stepped into the light.

"Sorry to disappoint you, Your Grace," he said. "But you aren't going to get it. The treasure is mine, and so is the lady."

Thirty-Nine

Cassie's heart leaped at the sight of him. He stood with power and purpose, sword gripped in one bare hand, defiant before the enemy. Catching her gaze on him, he smiled slightly, as if in encouragement. Her heart soared. Nearby, Benjamin, Thomas, and another man climbed from the stairwell onto the roof.

"You are outnumbered," Devon informed the duke.

"Your man in the house is out cold," Thomas put in. "We locked out the others."

Cassie breathed a sigh of relief. It was over. She was a little surprised that the duke did not seem to agree. He merely raised a brow, as if amazed at their audacity in confronting him. "It's about time you arrived," he said to Devon. "Perhaps you can get this woman to cooperate."

She gasped. Devon could not be part of this. He must have been too tense to chuckle at the absurdity, but his smile widened. "I never have before," he said to the duke. "I doubt I could now. I suggest that you move away from the telescope."

She started toward him willingly, but the duke's arm shot out, surprisingly strong. "I suggest you rethink the situation," he replied to Devon. "After the trouble you and your uncle put me through, the least you can do is share the treasure with me."

Cassie struggled against the offending arm, but the duke

didn't waver. Her relief dissipated along with Devon's smile.

"I think I begin to understand," he said to his cousin. "It was you all along. You are better at pretending you are someone else than my uncle and I could ever be. *Que je suis fâché, mon cousin.* I am sorry, but the treasure will be returned to its true owners."

"The French?" the duke sneered, holding her in place despite her efforts. "What of your family?"

"They are my family."

She could hear the pride in Devon's voice. He would not bow to this creature of evil. The duke seemed to realize it at last.

"Major Bentbrooke," he said, "I understand you are an enterprising young fellow. I'll give you a quarter of the treasure to switch sides."

With Benjamin behind them, pistol in his grip, Thomas and the other man exchanged worried glances. Cassie caught Devon's gaze again and swallowed. What a temptation to offer her brother. She was afraid to find out how little her life was worth.

"Benjamin," she started.

"I am tempted," her brother replied to the duke. "Unfortunately, I draw the line at fratricide."

Cassie sagged with relief. The duke shook his head. "Pity. It will have to be the girl, then. Ames?"

The little secretary fumbled to produce a deadly looking dagger. Cassie blinked as the duke released her and Ames took his place. He pasted himself against her, pressing the dagger to her side. With their height differences, he only managed to poke her in the ribs. Surely he wouldn't have the strength to shove the thing through her boned corset, let alone the layers of fabric before and beneath it. Not if she moved fast enough. None of the men seemed to realize that, for they all tensed anew.

"Put down your weapons," Ames demanded in a voice that squeaked. "Or the woman dies."

Cassie's tension snapped. "Oh, for pity's sake, that is quite enough." Before he could know what she intended, she wrenched from his grip. She felt the knife grate across her corset. The cool air pierced her torn dress more effectively than the knife had. She stared down at the rent, too shocked to move.

"Cassie!" Devon darted forward. Ames stared at the dagger, obviously perplexed that it had not done more damage, then held it up before him defensively. Ignoring him, Devon gathered her close, pulling her farther away from the danger. She could feel his heart hammering, see the lines of worry about his eyes.

"I'm all right," she said, although she felt herself begin to tremble at what she had just risked. He looked no less shaken as he pushed her protectively behind him and held up the sword. "Drop the knife, Mr. Ames," he ordered. "You're no match for us."

Cassie heard Ames clear his throat, as if nervously awaiting instructions.

"Why do you persist, cousin?" she heard the duke say. "You cannot win. You have always been the one to be outmatched." She couldn't stand not knowing what was happening. Peering around Devon, she saw his cousin bend to pick up one of her father's journals. She caught her breath. Flicking open the lantern, the duke held the volume by the spine and fanned the pages over the flame. Cassie's eyes widened in horror. "Drop your weapons," the duke insisted, "or I will destroy the clue to the treasure."

Her heart plummeted. How many times must she watch her father's work threatened? In front of her, Devon stiffened. She could sense the struggle in him. His back was tensed, his hand tight on the sword. He could not let his cousin win, but he could not let the clue be destroyed. And he knew how much the journals meant to her. His sword wavered, as if it were as undecided as his heart. His men stared at him. Benjamin's eyes were huge. Would Devon bow for the treasure, or for her? Did he not know that the duke would kill them all given the chance?

"Destroy the journals," she called. "They are only so many words on paper. I won't put them before our lives."

"Does she speak for you, Frenchman?" the duke taunted. The edges of the pages curled from the heat. Cassie felt as if it were her heart he burned, but her resolve did not waver.

Keeping his eyes on the duke, Devon reached back his free hand and clutched hers, palm sweaty. "Are you sure, *petite?* Those are all you have of your father."

"Everything I need from my father I carry inside me," she murmured, faith strengthening with his touch. "Love isn't confined to the pages of a book, *mon amour*. You taught me that."

His shoulders lifted as if she had removed a burden. His hand caressed hers in a promise. "Burn the books, for all I care," he told the duke. "We will not bow to you."

The duke sighed. "I can take no more of this. Come and get me if you want me so badly."

He kicked over the lantern, plunging the roof into darkness.

Devon left her side with a rush of air, and she heard the other men dash after him. She blinked her eyes rapidly, but before she could get used to the dark, there was a flash and thunder as a pistol roared. Her breath caught in her throat. Shouts and grunts echoed on either side.

She blinked again and saw a figure a few feet from her, one arm raised as if to strike. She recoiled. The next moment, a heavy body collided with hers, flinging her to the roof. She struck out with her feet and listened with satisfaction to the grunt of surprise. Rolling over on top of the fellow, she tried to scramble to her feet, only to be pulled back down against a formidable male shape.

"Stop struggling," Devon hissed. "Do you wish to die?"

She went limp in his arms. "Oh, Devon, I'm sorry!" Now that she was still, she could see his face in the darkness, scant inches from her own. Sweat dampened his brow and upper lip. A flint sparked, and the lantern flared. Cassie flinched away from the light and felt Devon's arms tighten protectively. Glancing about, she saw her brother unbending from where he had lit the lamp, and the other man with one hand on the back of Ames's neck.

"Would you care to move, *mon coeur*?" Devon asked her with a chuckle. Glancing down, she found she lay full on top of him, her skirts wrapped about his long legs. Her cheeks heated in a blush, and she managed to clamber to her feet.

Devon rose beside her. "Where's Thomas?" he asked. "And my traitorous cousin?"

"Here," Thomas called from the stairwell. Benjamin bent to raise the lantern. Thomas nodded toward the house below. "I think he's gotten away from us."

As if in confirmation, Cassie heard the sound of a carriage in the alley. Devon swore. Dashing past his men, he disappeared into the house.

"His Grace will never stand for this outrage," Ames blustered. "The duke will see you hang for this."

"The duke is very likely fleeing the country," Benjamin informed him.

"Aye, matey," Thomas agreed, moving to poke at the secretary. "How well can you sing, little bird? It may be the only way you'll see freedom."

Ames bristled, but the man who held him tightened his grip, and the secretary subsided. The men started for the door.

"Coming, Cassie?" Benjamin asked.

She moved to the dais, where the journals lay tumbled. The one the duke had threatened was browned but not destroyed. She rather thought her life was the same. "A moment. Let me collect the journals."

He sighed. "Haven't they caused us enough trouble? They didn't even lead us to the treasure."

"Not true," Cassie replied, hefting them into her arms.

"I believe them to be quite accurate. I know where the treasure is, and when Devon is ready, I shall take you to it."

She did not get to take them there until late the following morning. First they had had to summon the Bow Street Runners to take Ames away for attempted murder and kidnapping, among other sundry crimes Cassie was certain would come to light now that the duke could no longer shield him. Devon then sent one of his men for Liza and Henri, and the explanations started anew.

She thought perhaps that might be the end of it, but the ruckus had at last alerted her neighbors, and she was not entirely surprised to find Herbert Montague at her door.

"What are you doing, Miss Bentbrooke?" he demanded, shoving past Benjamin, who had made the mistake of opening the door to his frantic knock. "Why were the Bow Street Runners here?"

"Afraid your ugly little thieves turned you in, old fellow?" Benjamin taunted. Cassie had told him and Devon everything the duke had confessed, and her brother was not in charity with the little scientist.

Montague blanched. "I'm sure I don't know what you're talking about."

"It doesn't matter," Cassie told her brother; then, turning to the man, she continued. "Mr. Montague, I rescind my offer. I had promised you first right to the journals. That will not be possible. I intend to donate them to the Royal Society. I suggest you contact them if you are still interested. Now, good-bye, sir."

"You can't do this!" he protested, but Henri loomed up behind Benjamin.

"Would you like to argue, little man?" he growled.

Montague swallowed apoplectically and quit the house. That was the last Cassie saw of him.

"Do you truly know where the treasure is, mademoiselle?" Bertrand asked when they were at last alone. "Do you understand what this treasure means to me and mine?"

"I think so," Cassie replied. "Jean-Luc Sebastien was to bring a fortune in jewels, gathered from all your families, to London to help you here. Only he never arrived. And you all have been blaming the Sebastiens ever since."

Bertrand and Henri immediately began to protest, but Cassie held up her hands. "Do I lie?" she challenged Devon.

He shrugged. "Whether they blame me is immaterial. I know my family is at fault."

"Your uncle is at fault," Bertrand replied, setting Henri to nodding. "We know better."

"Good," Cassie said as Devon stared at them in amazement. "Now, let me show you your treasure."

It took two carriages—Devon's and Benjamin's—to make the trip to St. Pancras, for everyone wanted to go. She had hoped the explanations were over at last, but Mr. Baker took additional convincing. However, as he had seen Cassie and Liza caring for the dead and Devon caring for the living, he at last gave them permission to probe the grave of Yvette Kearney.

He needn't have worried that they'd have to dig far; after several thrusts of the spade near the stone, the tool rang against metal. Devon dropped to his knees and pulled away the sod to reveal a tarnished brass box two feet long and six inches wide. He yanked it free from its cradle of earth and rocked back on his heels to lay it before the stone. Brushing off the dirt, he worked the clasp. Cassie wondered whether she was the only one to notice how his hands trembled. She could tell that Henri and Bertrand were holding their breath.

The lid protested with a screech, but at last it gave way. The sunlight glinted off a rainbow of hues. Eyes wide in wonder, Devon scooped his hand down and let the stones slide over his fingers. The reflecting light lit his face with a pattern as bright as a stained-glass window at sunset. He pulled out a diamond as large as his fist. Looking up, he met Cassie's gaze.

"We did it," he murmured. Then he surged to his feet, taking her with him. "We did it!"

She laughed as he swung her around in a circle. Bertrand and Thomas hugged each other, and Henri wept. Liza jumped up and down in delight. While the rector looked on in astonishment, Benjamin sank to his knees to stare at the jewels.

Devon set Cassie down only to kiss her soundly. The feel of his lips on hers only made her dizzier.

"Marry me," he ordered.

Cassie gasped. "What? You don't mean that."

"But I do," he insisted. He put his arm about her waist and pulled her to him, as if he were afraid she would try to get away. "If I have learned anything from this treasure, it is that wealth is fleeting. Love is the true treasure."

"Easy to say, my lord," she replied, afraid to take him seriously, "especially now that you have your fortune."

"Agreed," he allowed. "But only a quarter of these are mine. Less, now that I must give your brother a share. However, if you prefer to wed a pauper, I will give it all away this minute."

"Don't you dare," she cried even as her brother's eyes narrowed thoughtfully. "We have all worked too hard for this."

"Then tell me you will marry me," he urged. Cassie gazed up into his eyes and saw hope there, and fear. He had risked much to find the jewels, but in asking for her hand, he risked the one thing she craved, his heart.

"Yes," she said simply.

He blinked, unable to comprehend the answer for a moment; then his face broke into a grin. He pulled her into his arms to be kissed. Of all the times their lips had met, this was the sweetest. His embrace held the promise of love and a lifetime of happiness. Perhaps they were both a little starstruck. When at last he let her go, the rector was beaming, and everyone else in the graveyard was smiling fondly at her.

Benjamin rose. "Congratulations, Cassie. You've got everything you ever wanted."

"More," Cassie replied, glancing at Devon.

"And so do I," Devon insisted. "And so do you, Major. Your share should come to a large enough amount to allow you to live well the rest of your life."

"Ah, but I have expensive tastes. I fear I shall still need that rich wife."

"Benjamin," Cassie scolded even as Liza's face fell.

Her brother winked at her. "Tell me, Renard," he asked Devon, "how soon will you let me pay my respects to your cousin, Miss Sebastien?"

Liza squealed and threw her arms about his neck. "Not soon enough for me," she declared before she kissed him. Cassie bit her lip to keep from stopping her. Time would only tell whether her brother was truly reformed. Liza might have other ideas, but Cassie would make sure the courtship lasted long enough for everyone to be satisfied of the happy ending. As her brother's look of astonishment melted into something more, she rested her head against Devon's shoulder.

"And now what?" she murmured.

"Now," he chuckled, "we will write up your discovery of the comet's tail and send it to Mr. Pond. And after that you will need to retire from your work for a time."

Cassie frowned, leaning back to look up into his dear face. "You would make me give up my studies? Why?"

"I expect you to keep studying, *cherie*," he said with a tender smile. "I would never take my queen of the heavens from the work she loves so much. But after we are married, I plan to give you a far better excuse to stay up nights than to look at the stars."

And that, she found, was a quite satisfactory answer.

AUTHOR'S NOTE

Cassiopeia Bentbrooke was not the only one fascinated by the Great Comet. Otherwise known as Comet Flaugergues, for the Frenchman who discovered it, it blazed in all its glory across the night sky of the world for nearly sixteen months in the early nineteenth century. Only Comet Hale-Bopp, in 1997, was visible longer in recorded history. And it was not as large.

Honore Flaugergues first sighted the glowing ball on March 25, 1811, in Viviers, France. He tracked it until April 1, when the waxing moon interfered with his observations. Scientists continued to track it from August 30, 1811, to late July 1812.

The comet was visible to the naked eye from September 1811 to January 1812 and was viewed as an omen by people around the world. While Napoleon Bonaparte never joined the ranks of those trying to steal the Bentbrooke journals, he, too, saw the comet as a sign—of his divine right to conquer. He chose that winter to invade Russia, where the weather and valiant Russian people offered him his first major defeat.

In September 1811, the comet regularly appeared at dusk and sometimes dawn. By October, it was visible throughout the night, blazing below the handle of the Big Dipper (in the northern latitudes). It must have been a magnificent sight, for its diameter was roughly the same as that of the sun. The tail, which Cassie was trying so valiantly to locate, was 110 million miles long and split into two branches, like a crescent, with the head at the center. In contrast, the tail of Comet Hale-Bopp was only 30 million miles long.

Heinrich Wilhelm Matthäus Olbers of Bremen, Germany, is credited with being the first to observe the comet's tail, in late August 1811. It is doubtful whether John Pond, the Astronomer Royal, knew of his observations by the time Cassie was searching for the tail in September. William Herschel, her fellow astronomer, spotted the tail from his observatory in Slough on September 9 and noted a curvature. However, it was not until September 18, the same night Cassie saw the tail, that he noted the two branches.

Cassie could well have received credit from the Astronomer Royal for her work. However, she could not have joined the prestigious Royal Society. Her idol, Caroline Herschel, along with mathematician Mary Somerville, were the first women to be awarded membership, and then "honorary" only, in 1835. While respected, both were viewed as oddities in their time.

Learn more about the Great Comet and Regina Scott at www.reginascott.com

BOOK YOUR PLACE ON OUR WEBSITE AND MAKE THE READING CONNECTION!

We've created a customized website just for our very special readers, where you can get the inside scoop on everything that's going on with Zebra, Pinnacle and Kensington books.

When you come online, you'll have the exciting opportunity to:

- View covers of upcoming books
- Read sample chapters
- Learn about our future publishing schedule (listed by publication month *and author*)
- Find out when your favorite authors will be visiting a city near you
- Search for and order backlist books from our online catalog
- Check out author bios and background information
- Send e-mail to your favorite authors
- Meet the Kensington staff online
- Join us in weekly chats with authors, readers and other guests
- Get writing guidelines
- AND MUCH MORE!

**Visit our website at
http://www.kensingtonbooks.com**

Thrilling Romance from Lisa Jackson

__Twice Kissed	0-8217-6038-6	$5.99US/$7.99CAN
__Wishes	0-8217-6309-1	$5.99US/$7.99CAN
__Whispers	0-8217-6377-6	$5.99US/$7.99CAN
__Unspoken	0-8217-6402-0	$6.50US/$8.50CAN
__If She Only Knew	0-8217-6708-9	$6.50US/$8.50CAN
__Intimacies	0-8217-7054-3	$5.99US/$7.99CAN
__Hot Blooded	0-8217-6841-7	$6.99US/$8.99CAN

Call toll free **1-888-345-BOOK** to order by phone or use this coupon to order by mail.
Name_____
Address_____
City_____ State _____ Zip _____
Please send me the books I have checked above.
I am enclosing $_____
Plus postage and handling* $_____
Sales tax (in New York and Tennessee) $_____
Total amount enclosed $_____
*Add $2.50 for the first book and $.50 for each additional book.
Send check or money order (no cash or CODs) to:
Kensington Publishing Corp., 850 Third Avenue, New York, NY 10022
Prices and Numbers subject to change without notice. All orders subject to availability.
Check out our website at www.kensingtonbooks.com.

Discover the Romances of
Hannah Howell

__**My Valiant Knight** 0-8217-5186-7	**$5.50US/$7.00CAN**
__**Only for You** 0-8217-5943-4	**$5.99US/$7.99CAN**
__**Unconquered** 0-8217-5417-3	**$5.99US/$7.50CAN**
__**Wild Roses** 0-8217-5677-X	**$5.99US/$7.50CAN**
__**Highland Destiny** 0-8217-5921-3	**$5.99US/$7.50CAN**
__**Highland Honor** 0-8217-6095-5	**$5.99US/$7.50CAN**
__**Highland Promise** 0-8217-6254-0	**$5.99US/$7.50CAN**
__**Highland Vow** 0-8217-6614-7	**$5.99US/$7.99CAN**
__**A Taste of Fire** 0-8217-7133-7	**$5.99US/$7.99CAN**

Call toll free **1-888-345-BOOK** to order by phone or use this coupon to order by mail.
Name_____
Address_____
City_____ State _____ Zip _____
Please send me the books that I have checked above.
I am enclosing $_____
Plus postage and handling* $_____
Sales tax (in New York and Tennessee) $_____
Total amount enclosed $_____
*Add $2.50 for the first book and $.50 for each additional book. Send check or money order (no cash or CODs) to:
Kensington Publishing Corp., 850 Third Avenue, New York, NY 10022
Prices and numbers subject to change without notice.
All orders subject to availability.
Check out our website at **www.kensingtonbooks.com**.